THE PATRON SAINT OF UGLY

BOOKS BY MARIE MANILLA

Still Life with Plums: Short Stories

Shrapnel

The Patron Saint of Ugly

THE PATRON SAINT of UGLY

Marie Manilla

A Mariner Original
MARINER BOOKS
Houghton Mifflin Harcourt
Boston • New York
2014

For information about permission to reproduce selections from this book,
write to Permissions, Houghton Mifflin Harcourt Publishing Company,
215 Park Avenue South, New York, New York 10003.

www.hmhco.com

Library of Congress Cataloging-in-Publication Data
Manilla, Marie.
The Patron Saint of ugly / Marie Manilla.
pages cm
ISBN 978-0-544-14624-2 (pbk.)
1. Catholic Church—Fiction. 2. Mental healing—Fiction.
3. Psychic ability 4. West Virginia. 5. Psychological fiction. I. Title.
PS3613.A5456P38 2014
813'.6—dc23
2013045658

Book design by Chrissy Kurpeski
Typeset in Dante MT Std

Printed in the United States of America
DOC 10 9 8 7 6 5 4 3 2 1

The photo of Mount Etna is used by permission of the photographer,
Paul Gunning. Original line art of trinacria by the author.

For Concetta Ferrari Lapelle Manilla, my Sicilian grandmother,
who has haunted me my entire life

HOTEL SICILIA

SWEETWATER, WEST VIRGINIA

September 9, 1975

    I've just ordered room service, and though I am exhausted I must commit to paper a sketch of my initial encounter with Garnet Ferrari, the subject of the committee's current investigation.

    I was greeted at Garnet's door by her aunt Betty, a flustered soul, all chatter and tics, who genuflected deeply and kissed my hand before I could stop her. She deposited me in the library, where Garnet was standing before the lit fireplace, fists clenched as if she were a pugilist in the ring. She was dressed in track shorts and an orange tank top just a shade off from the color of her hair—a voluminous mane that roams at will. Most of her skin was exposed for my benefit, I believe, as if to say: Take a good look!

    I did.

    The background tone of her flesh is pale, but the birthmarks decorating her skin are varying shades of purple: deep mulberry, magenta, the faintest mauve. It looks as if someone took a map of the world, cut out continents and islands, provinces and cantons, and glued them willy-nilly on Garnet's body. I distinctly identified Alaska on her right cheek, the Aleutians trailing over her nose; Mongolia on one shoulder; Zaire on the other; Crete on her knee;

Chile on her ankle; and many others. There is a kind of beauty in her birthmarks, God's holy design imprinted on her skin.

Garnet directed me to sit as her Sicilian grandmother pushed in a teacart loaded with cookies and a samovar of coffee. Nonna Diamante is quintessentially Old World with her white bun and orthopedic shoes. When she saw me she began to kneel and reach for my hand, but I forestalled the gesture. Nonna backed out of the room mumbling, "Garney, watch-a you mouth and behave."

Once we were alone Garnet broadened her shoulders, thrust forward her chest, and jutted out her chin. The display reminded me of that toad in my sister's garden that doubles its size by inflating with air to deter predators.

Finally Garnet sat, draped her legs over her chair arm, and said, "You know I don't believe any of this bullshit."

Given the resistance—and mockery—the committee has been met with thus far, I was prepared. "Perhaps you don't, but people all over the world do." I pulled from my briefcase a sampling of the many letters the Vatican has received from people claiming to have been healed by Garnet.

"Don't these people have anything better to do?" She sat upright, grabbed the letters, and unceremoniously flung them into the fireplace.

I stifled my impulse to rescue them, fearing that any sudden movement might send Garnet running.

I then pulled out a stack of before-and-after pictures of various healed skin disorders. I fanned them out for her perusal, careful to hold on tight. "Are you saying these are fabricated?"

Garnet looked at the photos and sighed. "I'm not denying that people are being healed. I'm just saying that I'm not responsible."

A sudden roar erupted from the pilgrims keeping vigil outside Garnet's home. Garnet's head bowed under the magnitude of their pleas. When she looked up, her eyes betrayed weariness. "How do I put an end to this crap so I can get on with my life?"

It felt as if we were in a confessional, and I wished I had an inspired answer. All I could do was hand over the standard questionnaire and a tape recorder for her use during our inquiry. "Start here."

Garnet flipped through the onerous document. "Are you kidding me?"

"The Vatican has a duty to investigate, I'm afraid. And we are very thorough."

For a moment it looked as if the girl might cry, an astonishing notion that made me want to scoop her into my arms and hug her, as a father might. But that would have been inappropriate, and perhaps misconstrued. "The sooner you begin, the sooner it will be over with."

Garnet nodded, stood, and led me to the front door, the weight of the world heavy upon her neck.

After meeting Garnet I find myself of two minds. Half of me wants to prove that Garnet is the source of the miracles whether she claims responsibility or not. The other half wants to refute the pilgrims' assertions so that she can live in peace. It is up to God to reveal the truth.

Ah! My veal scaloppine has arrived.

The Legend of Saint Garnet del Vulcano

To the Congregation for the Causes of Saints, Archbishop Gormley in particular:

Before we begin, Archie, I want to reiterate that the only reason I've granted this intrusion is that the sooner you dispel this sainted nonsense the sooner I can reclaim my life, or perhaps claim it for the first time. Then you and the boys can direct your energies to more urgent matters: rescuing victims of the Banqiao Dam breach, for example, or polishing the papal jewels.

Wait. There's Nonna at the door.

(Tank-a him for the vis.)

Archie, Nonna wants me to thank you for the visit; a preemptive nicety, since I can hear her spitting even from here with the *ptt-ptt-ptt* and *tocca ferro,* touching iron, jangling the five pounds of skeleton keys she routinely hauls around—as do I. She's using them to ward off the evil-eye germs she's certain you left in the upholstery. According to Nonna, anyone with eyes as dark as yours surely harbors the *malocchio,* as they call it in Italy, or the *maloicky,* as they say in Baaston, your holy turf. Nonna wondered about that, sending a Black Irish potato eater instead of a *paesano* to do the pope's bidding.

(I never said-a that.)

(Most certainly did.)

I apologize for her ethnic fussiness, but she's mistrustful of murky eyes even if they're ordained, since everyone knows Pius IX was a bad-karma-flinging *jettatura*, even if it was inadvertent. Tell that to the poor schmucks who fell out of windows or tumbled off scaffolding in his papal wake. After you left, Nonna was a whirling dervish of incantations and phallic hand gestures—*manus obscenus: mano fica, mano cornuta*—though I insisted she stop at sprinkling urine, that holiest of all holy waters, particularly mine, which is why I lock the bathroom door behind me even after I flush.

If it will speed your inquiry I will confess that there is magic here, and I don't mean just the practical jokes playing out on my body. Someone or something is responsible for the mysteries I've witnessed in Sweetwater, but it's not me. In addition to environmental factors, in my opinion, the true source is Nonna—

(*It's-a no true! You* are *the descendant of Saint Garnet! You!*)

—It was *Nonna* who packed anti-*malocchio* talismans in her valise when she sailed to America, along with her belief in folk magic—the Old Religion—a faith system, however irrational, that I have been unable to banish from my psyche the way I have the Vatican-sanctioned one.

Admittedly, if it is Nonna, her powers are spotty, so perhaps there's a third alternative neither of us has considered. Hopefully your investigation will discover who the real conjurer is and thus pull the limelight away from me.

(*Garney, you play for the Padre.*)

(*What? Why did you bring my saw in here?*)

(*Why you face-a so mad? He will like-a you playing. She plays-a the most beautiful saw, Padre! It make-a you weep!*)

(*Give me that. This isn't a talent show. And besides, that's private.* Private!)

(*Okay, okay. Don't getta so flust'. Here, have a cannoli.*)

Nonna just made two hundred cannolis for the Saint Brigid bake sale. She's still recovering from carting tray after tray up from the basement kitchen, though at her age she shouldn't be baking for anyone, not even me. Apparently hiring a chef is out of the question. *Such a waste,* she says. And besides, no one can match her culinary skills.

(*That's-a true.*)

Still, her poor knees—creaking as I speak. I've tried valiantly to get her to use the main-floor kitchen, but all those whirring, grinding, icemaking contraptions confound her, especially the Radarange—a complete bafflement. If you really want to unlock a mystery, figure out how *that* thing works. The added truth is she doesn't want to muss anything up.

A *santa* no live in a-squal, she always says.

(*No, I don't.*)

(*Yes, you do.*)

What about Mother Teresa? I always rebut.

That's a-diff. She's from Macedonia. You are Sicilian.

Impossible to argue with that, and I certainly no live in a-squal. At times I still can't believe I'm ensconced up here in our town's founding father's estate, but even you had to force yourself through the throng pressed against my fence. I'm a prisoner behind these walls, afraid to ripple the drapes in case I start a maelstrom of seizures. The power of suggestion, I suppose. Or the power of hope. All those appeals speared onto the tips of my fence, taped to my gate. *Saint Garnet: Heal my daughter's bunion. My son's cauliflower ear. Grandma's varicose veins. Auntie's white forelock.* Charms of arms and legs, ears and eyes, strung on ribbons and tossed into my yard—which makes for dangerous mowing, those medallions flying up like shrapnel. Laughable stuff if I weren't afraid the pilgrims' desperation will have them catapulting over my fence to pluck my eyelashes or yank out my fingernails. They know the power of holy relics, but how I long for the day when they realize that my hair is just hair.

I want to thank you for not grimacing when you first saw me, Padre. I apologize for not being as restrained, but that's one impressive mole on your cheek. The size of a MoonPie and the color of squid ink. Sun Myung Moon could create a whole new religion around you.

(Garney! Clamp-a you lips.)

Sorry. One might think I would be more sensitive about dermatological oddities. Is that why the Vatican sent you? Were they hoping for some mole-zapping proof of my abilities? Or did you volunteer for the gig because it hits close to home?

(No forget-a the gifties.)

Mille grazie for the package that arrived yesterday, especially the forty-two-pack of tapes to use with the recorder, but I'll hurl my*self* into Aceldama if it takes that many tapes to work through your questionnaire. Nonna loves the rosary, which she'll treasure because it has Pope Paul VI's blessing, though she's still pining after Pius XII, her holy heartthrob.

(That's-a no true!)

(It positively is!)

I also appreciate the box of Italian candies. Nonna tittered over the Golia Nera, Rossana, Galatine, Pastiglie Leone. You should know that I have an aversion to penny candy; makes me gag whenever I see it, and with good reason. I am, however, intrigued by *The Newly Revised and Illustrated Encyclopedia of Saints*. When I was a child, before the fish scales fell from my eyes, I used to fawn over the much older *Lives of the Saints* Nonna kept on her bedside table with the red Pergusa blossom pressed inside. Her book was in Italian, so mostly I shivered over the four-color paintings of Saint Bernadette shrouded in hair and of Saint Lucy holding that tray of eyeballs. Often I imagined what my painting would look like when it finally graced those pages: a benevolent prodigy holding a palm full of shriveled skin tags and warts.

When I'm finished with your book I'll catalog it in the library with Nicky's reference sets. Perhaps you noticed my brother's original collection, his passion that I adopted and expanded.

You want the legend of Saint Garnet del Vulcano—my supposed predecessor—so I'll oblige. I was weaned on that baloney even before my umbilical nub withered, and for many years I believed it. In all my phone calls and letters to Catholic saint societies and Sicilian-lore collectors, no one has been able to verify or disprove Saint Garnet's existence. I would think one of your Roman padres could hobble down the boot, pole-vault over to Sicily, and find out once and for all. Though yesterday I got a letter from a lady in Palermo who claims to be a descendant of the original Garnet and thus a long-lost cousin of mine. She wanted five thousand bucks for a down payment on a Rolls-Royce. I did not oblige.

So this is the story Nonna first shared and that my mother told me every night of my childhood. The legend evolved and expanded over the years, the details more explicit depending on my age and how much Marsala Nonna had been drinking.

(I no drink-a too much.)

I don't begrudge Nonna her Marsala. *(I don't, Nonna.)* I would overimbibe too if I had to sleep with Grandpa Ferrari — *riposi in pace,* as Nonna would say, and is mumbling even now, though I don't know why he deserves restful peace, or her loyalty, the mean-fisted tyrant.

Last summer I wrote the fable down with a calligraphy pen, even illuminated it using the Book of Kildare as my guide. It's quite beautiful, Archie — those elaborate Os and gilded Gs. I'll send it to you along with this tape as exhibit A.

Now, picture me sitting in that leather chair by the back window in the library, the one you sat in, with the worn armrests and dragon-claw feet. A regular Alistair Cooke ready to introduce *Masterpiece Theatre.*

O*nce upon a time there was a village named Sughero tucked in a high crag in the Nebrodi Mountains on the eastern side of Sicily. On June twenty-fourth, 1550, at three thirty-eight p.m., a red-haired girl was born to goat-herding peasants.* (Coincidentally, that's my birthday and birth time — exactly four hundred years later. The added weirdness is that Nonna was born on June twenty-fourth too.) *The mother christened her daughter Garnet because of her hair. With pale skin and blue eyes, Garnet was the sprung seed planted centuries earlier by a Viking who swept across the island wearing his antlered helmet and furry leggings. Garnet was an only child, as it turned out, who* not only helped her mother make goat cheese but harvested chestnuts and sheared cork bark with her father.

Garnet's mother fed her daughter enough figs for ten sons — the exact number she dreamed of birthing, when she dreamed of such things. The girl budded into a maiden so alluring that morally deficient boys hid behind bushes hoping to rob her of her virtue. Fortunately, Mother never let her daughter out of her sight, and she kept her apron pocket filled with obsidian shards to fling at the rogues.

The noble village boys were smitten too, but they tried to impress Garnet with feats of strength and endurance.

"I can stand on one leg for three days."

"That's nothing. I can ride a hewn log down the mountain and into the sea."

"Yeah? Well, I can throw rocks into Mount Etna from here."

They would all gaze at the volcano in the distance belching a gray plume and wonder when it would erupt again and clog their fountains with ash, spew lava balls onto their roofs and goats.

But Garnet was not interested in boys. She was in love with God. Every morning when the church bells pealed, Garnet raced to the church, scooted into the front pew, and knelt with her head bent as she hummed an E note that accompanied her prayers. Garnet claimed she was only mimicking the hum she perpetually heard, but though dozens of villagers tipped their ears, no one else could hear it.

When Garnet was thirteen, the family sauntered down the mountain to the shore of the Strait of Messina to trade goods with the Calabrian merchants who had made the three-kilometer voyage.

Mother and Father spread out a blanket to exhibit their wares. Garnet meandered from merchant to merchant eyeing baskets of lemons and olives, sheepskins and coiled rope, and exotic spices: juniper berries, coriander, and sea salt, a tightly controlled government commodity that Calabrian women secretly harvested from salt flats and smuggled out under their skirts to sell to bootleggers.

That day the islanders were edgy because they were expecting a visit from the local duke, or prince, or marquis (the title changing depending on the extent of Nonna's slur; as it increased, so did her propensity to scramble history).

(I no drink-a too much!)

(I really don't care, Nonna.)

Whatever his title, Marquis demanded the villagers' obedience plus their choicest harvest of fruit, grain, and women.

A trumpet sounded as Marquis approached, the village women wiping their children's noses and then stuffing kerchiefs into their décolletage. Suddenly, the rumbling of horse hooves, and there he was: an arthritic, liver-spotted old man astride a fiendish black horse. Marquis didn't bother to dismount. He steered his horse through the merchants' blankets and stalls, knocking over stacks of brooms and barrels of wine as he collected his monthly tithes. The horse deposited his own stinking loads wherever he wished.

Suddenly Marquis was struck by a spectacle that warmed his flint-chiseled heart: a budding maiden sitting on the ground humming, a litter of kittens in her lap, climbing up her shoulder, and even nesting in her tousled hair.

Marquis pulled the steed to a stop in front of Garnet and dismounted, no easy feat given his brittle bones.

"Who have we here? I thought I knew all the beautiful girls in Sughero. My spies have been neglectful."

Garnet knelt before nobility, the kittens tumbling off her and mewling displeasure.

"Are you married?"

Garnet looked at Marquis's feet. "I am married to God."

"To God?" The old man gripped Garnet's chin in his hand. "Such a waste. And you know it's a sin to be wasteful." He turned Garnet's face this way and that. "I shall remedy this."

He mounted his horse and galloped away, shouting over his shoulder, "Oh yes! I shall remedy this indeed!"

Two days later, the family back in their hill cottage, there came a messenger from the marquis requesting Garnet's hand in marriage.

Her parents would be moved into a stone house with valuable pastureland and given a larger herd of goats and two peons to help with the work.

Father and Mother held their breath.

"I am married to God," Garnet said, and her parents exhaled in relief.

The next day the offering was a larger house with double the servants and a treasury of gold so the family would never again have to labor.

"I am married to God," Garnet said.

The third day it was a villa with even more gold, plus a vineyard and a resident artist (sometimes Michelangelo, sometimes Caravaggio—the wrong century entirely, but hey, it's Nonna's fantasy).

(It's-a no *fantasia!*)

(Anyway.)

Garnet's response was the same. "Umm, God."

The fourth day there came not a messenger, but a sheriff, who dragged Father away and confiscated the herd of goats.

God, the girl chose, even in the face of her mother's streaming tears.

The fifth day the house was set ablaze, and as Garnet's mother was lugged off in shackles, she gazed beseechingly at her daughter. "He isn't so ugly, dear."

The sixth day the sheriff heaved Garnet up from her bed of leaves and took her to Marquis's estate, where a priest was waiting to not only annul Marquis's current marriage but also pronounce Garnet and the fiend man and wife.

"No-no-no-no-no! I am married to God!" she said to the priest, who was supposed to be married to God too. But the squirmy toad's neck was bent under the weight of a leather pouch bulging with coins that would buy his service and silence.

"No-no-no-no-no!" Garnet wailed for so long that the priest kept losing his place even as Marquis prodded him to hurry up, visions of his wedding bed engorging his lust.

"Mary, Mother of God, save me!" Garnet cried.

Finally the priest slammed his prayer book closed. (Apparently even palm-greased Church officials have souls. No offense.) *"I can't do it unless she is willing."*

"You want her willing? I'll make her willing." Just then Marquis looked out a window and saw Mount Etna bubbling. His astronomers had predicted that the volcano would erupt that night, and his black soul devised a black plan.

"Minions!" he shouted.

Within seconds, he was surrounded by a band of knee-bending syco-phants.

"Take her to Mount Etna and climb up as high as the heat will allow. Tie her to a stake and let her face the ash and lava. Soon enough she will agree to marry me."

"Yes, my lord," they said, drooling.

"No!" Garnet howled as they bullied her out and tied her to a mule. They climbed up first through green forest, but soon the soil hardened with pumice stones and dried lava. The volcano belched sulfurous ash and air that singed their eyelashes.

"Close enough," one of the minions said.

They pounded a stake into the scarp and bound Garnet to it. Etna emitted another belch, which sent the minions scrabbling down to safety.

"Mother of God, save me!" Garnet prayed as the volcano gurgled. Its rumbling resembled the howl of demons; its fiery glow the very furnace of Hell.

When Etna finally erupted, Garnet closed her eyes. She could feel her body being pelted by lava balls that burned her clothes but, oddly, not her flesh. She prayed to Mary for strength and mercy, even as magma gushed by on both sides.

And then our heroine fainted and dreamed of twenty-four fat-bellied cherubs fluttering around her, each holding a ladle and a bucket filled with cool spring water, which they doused her with over and over.

The next morning, under a cloud of ash, the inhabitants of Sughero gathered at the village's center fountain, now clogged and useless. News spread of Marquis's meanness, and the villagers trekked to Mount Etna to discover the fate of the girl. All of them went: winemakers; olive-pressers; laundresses; the town harlot; the minions; the sheriff; the neck-bent priest; Garnet's parents, who had been released from jail, both spilling waterfalls of tears.

When they reached the base of the smoldering mount, they found it was as devastated as they had feared. Rivulets of lava still glugged down the hillside, incinerating everything in their path. Tree stumps and animal carcasses were reduced to steaming humps. Mother and Father wept at the presumed death of their daughter until one of the minions pointed at something tumbling toward them from high up on the volcano. It wasn't a giant lava ball; it was a girl, totally nude, sprinting over the red-hot sludge, which did not appear to burn her feet. She tried to cover her nakedness as she neared, and suddenly every male spectator, from the priest to the sheriff to the snarling town mutt, was struck blind. Only the women were left with their vision so they could witness the miracle unfolding: a girl unburned by Mount Etna.

Which is not to say she was unmarred.

Her body was speckled with red blotches, but when her mother ran to her, she saw the blotches were not open wounds, neither blistered nor painful. As the women spun Garnet around to study the smooth, odd shapes, the mapmaker's wife shouted, "She is the world!" For indeed, God had tattooed Garnet with His creation.

As if that weren't miracle enough, the town harlot cried, "Hey!"

Everyone swiveled to watch as she lifted her dress and parted whatever undergarments a harlot wore under her skirt. "Well, what do you know? It's gone."

"What's gone?" the women asked.

"My rash. I've had this burning and itching for over a month—ruining my trade—and now it's gone!"

Just then, half a dozen of the men, including the sheriff, the beer maker, and most of the minions, yelled, "Hey!"

Though they were still blind idiots, they began rubbing their crotches and doing little jigs. "It's gone!" Clearly, the harlot had been spreading her glee.

Mother draped her cloak over her daughter, thus restoring the men's sight, and just in time, because right before their eyes, the olive-size mole on the broom maker's nose shriveled to the size of a chickpea and fell off. The three-year-old burn on the blacksmith's face disappeared. The baker's palm calluses de-callused. Even the mangy town mutt lost his mange.

The priest fell to his knees before the girl, unlooped the bag of coins around his neck, and pressed it into her palm. "The girl is a holy agent sent from God!"

The townsfolk fell to their knees in adoration, but Garnet protested. "No! Stand up! I am just a child!" She flung the coins into a huddle of beggars.

"You are much more than that," the priest said. "Get thee to a nunnery!" (I know, I know, but nothing else worked.)

"He's right," Mother said, visions of Marquis's determination whirling in her head. "She will be safe there." Together, she and Father whisked Garnet toward the convent on an adjacent hill. The residents of Sughero followed, gloating that their village had produced such a miraculous child. Their chests deflated when they saw a black steed racing up to them: Marquis coming to review his handiwork. When he saw the girl, he dismounted and hobbled to her. The townsfolk prayed that his black heart would soften at the miracle standing before him, and his chin did drop, but not for the reason they hoped.

Marquis leaned in to assess the marks on Garnet's face. "Away from me! You are too ugly to be in my presence."

The townsfolk gasped at his cruel words, but Garnet was not stung. She understood that in order to save her, God had hidden her beauty deep inside, like a pearl in an oyster, or the solid core at the center of the earth.

Marquis turned to leave.

"Wait," Garnet said. "God has a revelation for you."

Marquis refused to look at her, as if her face offended him. "And what is that?"

"Look."

Marquis lifted his head just as Garnet unwrapped her cloak so that he could fully view her mottled body.

"No!" Marquis cried, rending his hair at the defilement of such a beauty.

Before the townsfolk could blink, they witnessed Marquis's once-piercing black eyes drain of color and sight, because what good are eyes if they cannot see inner beauty? His bleached irises stared blankly at the girl as he raised his fists to the heavens. He opened his mouth, but before one word slipped out, every inch of skin, from his earlobes to his little toes, was overtaken by oozing rashes and boils. Marquis scratched at his stomach, his legs, his back. He peeled off his tunic and tights and scraped up handfuls of ash to rub into the sores. Nothing would relieve his pain, so he scrabbled like a lunatic up the smoldering volcano, where he lived out his days trembling and itching in the Cyclops's cave.

Garnet was saved from a horrible marriage, and because the villagers no longer had to suffer the marquis's tyranny, they insisted she move into his manor. They hoisted their saint onto their shoulders and carried her to the hilltop mansion, where she lived with her family, doling out Marquis's fortune to charities. The residents of Sughero reported that when their children were stricken with skin disorders—measles, mumps, roseola, flea bites—if they prayed to Saint Garnet (whom, according to Nonna, they proclaimed a saint, even if the Vatican did not), their children would be healed. And so they were.

Garnet became the unofficial patron saint of prostitutes, stray dogs, hummers, volcanologists, and, of course, cartographers, who marveled at the map on her body, which spontaneously changed to reflect explorers' discoveries, environmental upheavals, and the outcomes of wars.

Mating Habits of the Ferrarus Disgusticus

Archibald:

It's a stormy day in our smudge on the map. I'm impressed you visited, since getting here involves a series of ever-smaller planes—jets, turboprops, hamster-powered Cessnas—topped off with a spiraling drive up to my door. Even you commented on West Virginia's low status, its reputation maligned thanks in part to industrialists, Johnny Carson, and Virginians—our Siamese twin still fuming over that nervy Civil War split.

You asked why I stay when I could live anywhere—Neuschwanstein Castle, for example. I stay because it's home, Archie, a place of both mystery and mayhem that has cast a spell over me. A lesson I learned during my ten-year banishment when all I wanted was to return to this patch of dirt, even with all the horrid memories buried beneath it. Oddly, West Virginia is not present anywhere on my body, and I have searched every inch.

I also stay for Nonna, who is as devoted to Sweetwater as she is to Sicilia. She'll be joining me any minute because of this thunder, which, for her, is too reminiscent of Grandpa's booming tirades. I, however, love a good storm and often hike up to the widow's walk, which is topped with a lightning-rod-equipped cupola, and hold up my arms begging for a sky-blinding jolt.

After years of wedded anguish, Nonna finally made it back to higher elevation—not her beloved Nebrodi Mountains, but close enough. For decades she pleaded with Grandpa to buy a house up on Dagowop Hill, but even here in West Virginia, there's a strain between hill and valley dwellers. Of course he refused, Calabrian shore hugger that he was, and kept his bride chained to a level lot down in Sweetwater Village until the day the hill got its revenge.

Here comes Nonna with her crochet needles—always with red yarn to ward off evil spirits; a potent color, apparently. I have a hundred-plus crimson afghans, not to mention the hats and scarves and mittens.

(Another afghan, Nonna?)

(Sì, but no is for you. For the Padre.)

Did you hear that, Archie? You will soon be the proud owner of a coverlet sure to keep you safe from the evil eye.

(Tocca ferro. Ptt-ptt-ptt.)

There she goes again with the keys, which of course means I have to yank the tangled ring from my own pocket and join her.

(Jangle-jangle-jangle-jangle-jangle. Better, Nonna?)

(Sì, much-a much.)

This morning I read through your reams of questions, the first dozen delving into great-great-great-grandparents and seventh-generation cousins. Archie, most of these people died before I was born or were KIA or MIA, and I refuse to burden others by dredging up memories they want padlocked in the sarcophagi inside their closets. I'll do my best on my own, but be forewarned: I plan on tumbling related questions together, often out of order, and I am happy to be possessed of an unwieldy imagination—question seventeen on your list, I see.

Today I'm going to expose the courting rituals of the species *Ferrarus disgusticus*, which is why I'm tucked in bed in the bridal chamber, now with Nonna beside me. *(No, I won't hold your yarn.)* I feel like a bride lying here, the tulle canopy my veil, the flouncy bed skirt my train, though my Frank Zappa T-shirt would be an affront to the previous occupants, whose sheddings still cling to the bed linens.

So here goes: My grandfather Dominick Antonio Ferrari—

(Riposi in pace.)

(Whatever.)

—entered the world fists-first on April fifth, 1888, in Villa San Giovanni in the province of Reggio Calabria, Italy, at the tip of the boot. His first word was probably *Vaffanculo!*, and if he owned a dog, I bet he routinely kicked it. If so, I like to think the dog wised up after a spell and sank its teeth into the punk's hand. *"Vaffanculo!"* Fuck *you!*

Archie, don't bother raising your hallowed brows at my use of profanity in front of Nonna. She's used to it, I assure you.

(That's a-true.)

Nicky and I had to invent a childhood for Grandpa Ferrari, because the only pieces of information we possessed were the aforementioned date and place. Plus the fact that he disobeyed his parents' directive and married that dimwitted Sicilian whore.

(Bite-a you tongue!)

(I know you're not, Nonna.)

Nonna was neither dimwitted nor a whore (*see?*), but as my years on the planet have taught me, everyone needs someone to kick. Thus, Northern Italian Tuscans spat upon Neapolitans, who razzed southern Calabrians, who scorned Sicilians. Shit does indeed roll downhill—even in West Virginia, where the northern half of the state thumbs its panhandles at its southern-coalfield kin.

I have no idea how Nonna and Grandpa met or how he induced her to marry him, and Nonna still won't confess.

(None-a you business, wiseacre.)

I began spinning a fantasy about their first encounter on the day Nicky had his tonsils out and I was left in Nonna's care. I had been rifling through the junk in their basement, but a siren song lured me to Nonna's room. I stood outside her door and watched as she hummed a familiar note while sitting on the edge of her bed, head wrapped in a towel, body swaddled in a chenille robe. I'd never seen Nonna in anything but the shapeless jersey dresses she always wore—and still does—so to see her that way was like watching a seraph.

(So a-sweet.)

She unwrapped the towel and down tumbled three feet of white tresses. Nonna untangled the locks with a comb and reached for the bottle of Fiore Pergusa water on her nightstand. Countless times I'd watched Nonna pick the red Pergusa flowers from the strip of garden she cultivated in her backyard. In her kitchen, she would pluck the petals that smelled of roasted almonds and nutmeg and drop them one by one into a water-filled perfume bottle. Overnight, the color and scent would leach from the petals and turn the liquid the color of blood. The smell was even more concentrated, and one drop could aromatize the whole room. I didn't know the perfume's official use until Nonna poured a puddle into her palm and massaged it into her mane as lovingly as any caress I'd ever seen. I don't think Mary Magdalene could have anointed Jesus with as much tender care. I wondered if there was ever a time when Grandpa Ferrari hovered outside the door in awe.

Perhaps that's how she captivated him. Maybe one day she ambled down from Sughero to spend the day sunning in Messina. Nonna spread out her blanket and lounged on the shore combing her hair, though it would have been red then. Right, Nonna?

(Red-a, for sure.)

Three kilometers away across the Strait of Messina was Villa San Giovanni, home of foul-mouthed, dog-kicking punks. But on that day, Dominick Ferrari held a telescope to his eye and saw a vision: a Nereid combing tangerine locks. For centuries people on both sides of the strait had claimed they'd spotted the Pining Nereid, one of fifty sea women who helped the Argonauts navigate through those monster-strewn waters. Forty-nine had returned to the Aegean, but the red-haired one stayed behind for the love of a Calabrian who, though smitten, could not return her affection. Undeterred, she paddled those epic waters for so long that eventually her lower half evolved into that of a silvery fish. Through the years, thousands of men claimed to be the descendants of that original Calabrian, each avowing he was the one who would at last fulfill the nymph's heart's desire and thus restore her legs.

"I am the one!" Dominick said, so captivated by his own importance that he dropped his telescope and walked into the strait—six-headed Scylla and whirlpooling Charybdis be damned. The water rose to his knees, waist, neck, and finally he started floating, and then began swimming as fast as he could, lungs laboring as he tried to reach the Sicilian side, home of slow-thinking, humpbacked, feral gnomes.

(No gabbo! Ptt-ptt-ptt.)

Sorry, Padre. I forgot about the cursed humpback, or *gabbo, jettatura* extraordinaire.

Grandpa's feet touched the mucky sea floor, and he trudged up the coast, water streaming down his five-feet, four-inch bricklayer's body, his own locks dripping, briny water stinging his eyes. He had to blink to clear his vision to see if the Nereid was still there. She was. But she wasn't a sea nymph. Neither was she a humpbacked, feral gnome. She was a girl, a beautiful, finless, rose-lipped wonder as glittery as her name, which he would soon learn: Diamante. She sucked in her breath when she saw her own marvel: a man rising from the sea. When their mismatched Sicilian and Calabrian eyes met, they forged a pheromone-torqued bond that no parent, topographic snobbery, or watery strait could dissolve.

Nicky's version of their courtship was less romantic and involved dear Nonna getting knocked up behind a dry-docked fishing boat. I reject this account.

(It's-a no true!)

As does Nonna.

In my fantasy, the couple had a few good years of cooing and cuddling before Nonna's spell wore off. Maybe Dominick's love for her faded along with the color of her hair. Perhaps the red luster was her hypnotic totem, her *portafortuna.* Or perhaps, like Samson's strength, Grandpa Ferrari's allure and good nature were rooted in *his* hair, and he had a mop of it, as evidenced by the few photos we have of him as a young man.

But by the time his first child, my uncle Dom the Mighty, was born, Grandpa had only a Capuchin monk's fringe, and seven years later, when his second and last child, my father, Angelo the Lesser, was born, every hair on Grandpa's head had been blown away by the wind, picked up by birds to weave into their nests. His pate was shiny and bald as an onion, a phrenologist's dream, which was why he always wore that dumb newsboy cap, though he neither delivered newspapers nor read them.

When Nonna and Grandpa paddled the pond to America, Grandpa smuggled out in his coat pocket a clipping of a Gaglioppo grapevine from Calabria. Nonna's valise was packed with the Old Religion and a jumble of evil-eye remedies. She is always on the lookout for a squinty-eyed *jettatura* who might rob good fortune and health from her loved ones. Over the years she has pointed out likely culprits. Anyone with a hawk nose or unibrow was suspect. Beware of leers, direct stares, or compliments. Barren women were the worst — so envious. Barren women with an eye affliction — *ay-ay-ay*.

Enter Aunt Betty, the Mighty Dom's wife, sporting a too-black bouffant and sweaters so tight you could see her white bra through the strained knit. Unable to conceive, her first husband dead when she was twenty-two, Betty also had a spectacular wall-eye. (It still leaves me wondering if she is talking to me or the island of Malta on my left earlobe.) Her left eye not only drifted like a disconnected orb but also had a keyhole pupil, a lethal cocktail. If all that weren't cross enough to bear, Betty was forced to raise her dead husband's son by his first wife (also dead): my only cousin, who is no cousin to me, Ray-Ray.

We often heard Nonna muttering, "Why you marry this girl, Dominick?" It was clear to us all, even if it wasn't to Nonna: two double-D reasons perched above a narrow waist and, as Uncle Dom bragged, "an unimpeachable ass."

Betty was such a gross disappointment to Nonna and Grandpa

that Angelo the Lesser's pick for a wife could only be an improve-ment—or so they all hoped.

Just last week, after I plied Aunt Betty with a pint of peach schnapps, she described the day Dad brought Mom home to meet the folks.

In anticipation, Nonna had scrubbed the entire house for that girl Angelo met up in Massachusetts. It was 1948 and one of Dad's former army buddies had gotten him a six-month construction job at Wellesley. Working on a new wing of a library, perhaps. A vault for all those blue bloods' tiaras. I could imagine Uncle Dom's barb. *This is your last chance to go to college, bucko, even if it is a girls' school.*

Grandpa Ferrari's one paternal mandate was that his sons should attend college so they would die with the uncallused palms of aristocrats. Grandpa had barely scrounged up enough tuition for Uncle Dom, so he'd muscled my father into the army, not to topple Mussolini, but for access to the GI Bill. Thus, it was a colossal disappointment when Dad got out of the army and then flunked out of Vandalia U., a state college less than an hour from Sweetwater. He preferred to spend his days fiddling with Grandpa's furnace and water heater or sawing tree limbs that didn't need pruning.

The saw was Nonna's only inheritance from her father, a man her two boys had never met. Nonna wept when she pulled the thing from the packing crate, Dad and Dom rubbing the foreign postmark. Grandpa harrumphed. "Pah! I no want that Sicilian crap next to my American tools!" When he stomped off, Nonna called my father to her side. "It's a-yours," she whispered, handing it over. "But find a safe place for it." Dad raced upstairs to carve elaborate curlicues into the handle with an ice pick. He hid the saw under his bed, and from that day forward, his dreams were filled with the construction of ever-grander estates built by his own hands.

Fifteen years later Dad flew to that Wellesley job just to get the hell away from his torture chamber of a fam-i-ly who never let him forget his academic failure.

Up in Massachusetts, Dad was lectured on appropriate behavior toward those women of a higher caliber than the dinette and hat-check girls back home. He kept his whistles to himself the day he spotted Mom with her *Mayflower*-descended Episcopalian nose tucked in an English literature book. He did, however, scoop up her notebook and *The Faerie Queene* when she dropped them as she slipped on an icy patch while crossing campus. There was an injury of some sort: a scraped knee, a sprained ankle. She rested her arm on his three-inches-shorter-than-hers shoulder as they hobbled to the infirmary. Father was immediately smitten with this blond beauty who also penned poetry—sort of. Marina, her name, was shorthand for aquamarine, the blue-green of Mom's eyes when the sunlight hit them just right. They certainly hypnotized my father—that lump of earthy clay—whose heart immediately dropped anchor in the blue-green harbor of her name.

Mother, however—hmm. I know she was smitten with his wavy pompadour, but it's also possible she had just returned from a tense visit home to Charlottesville, a city in a state much higher up the social scale than West Virginia, regardless of the conjoined-twin-separation scar. Maybe Grandma Iris had invited some hand-picked beau for Dom Pérignon and cucumber sandwiches and made sweeping references about his and her daughter's rococo-decorated futures.

I imagine Mom back at Wellesley, her five-carat irises glowing brighter and brighter as Angelo spilled the glass marbles of his life: a flunked-out, blue-collar, West Virginia–dwelling Catholic. A toxic brew that would kill Grandma Iris, or so Mom hoped.

Six months of threadbare dates ensued. (Eating hamburgers at lunch counters. Feeding ducks on Lake Waban, where Mom could stare into her reflection. She was always staring into her reflection and not for the reasons you might think.) Mom's semester ended at the same time as Dad's job and that's when he took her home to meet the folks, with one detour first.

It was a Sunday afternoon, Aunt Betty said, and she, Dom, two-year-old Ray-Ray, and Nonna sat in the living room with their hands on their knees, waiting. Grandpa was in the backyard pruning his Calabrian grapevine, which he loved more than his Sicilian wife.

Nonna kept popping up to straighten lampshades, recenter doilies, and stir pots in the kitchen. She also kept running next door to Celeste Xaviero's house, because Nonna was cooking in her oven too. Celeste was a lock-picker of family secrets, a pastime made easier by the scant space between houses and her propensity to leave her windows open even in winter. I imagine Celeste prodding, *Is she here-a yet? What's she like? An improvement over Walleye, no?* Betty confessed that everyone had high hopes for this girl, thought that maybe Angelo had found the virginal *one*, hopefully not a deflowered, castoff widow like Betty.

Finally the happy couple burst through the door with their luggage and a bottle of cheap champagne. The family was captivated. Never had five feet, nine inches of such breeding crossed that humble threshold. Uncle Dom practically licked her hand. Nonna kept brushing Mom's cheek. *"Bellisima! Carina! Bella!"* She fawned, no doubt envisioning bassinets full of beautiful heirs, not like wailing Ray-Ray, a booby prize of a nongrandchild who was increasingly harder to love.

Grandpa Dominick came through the back door wearing his most tattered dungarees—*I no have to get slicked up for some girl*—his mud-caked boots, and his number-two newsie cap (number one reserved for special occasions), which Grandpa rarely removed, not at the dinner table, not in the presence of women, not even during Mass—when he went.

He entered the living room mashing dirt clods into the rugs that Nonna would have to pick out for weeks. "Where is this *ragazza?*" He looked up and saw my Anglo mother towering over my dad, my father's arm wrapped around her waist as if she were the best prize he'd ever won. Grandpa shivered from head to foot. *"Ragazza immagine,"* he said with a sigh, meaning "cover girl," because in those first sublime moments, even Grandpa could not deny her beauty. Grandpa looked at Angelo as if he had finally done something right, and he had. Years later, Nicky and I would stumble upon a hidden stash of girlie pictures taped beneath Grandpa's workbench in the basement. Like my mother, all the women were blondes: Jean Harlow, Marlene Dietrich, Marilyn Monroe.

(I no see what's a-so spesh about the blondie hair. Red is a much-a more rare. And-a lucky!)

(Indeed, Nonna. Indeed.)

Dad heaped one more scoop onto the virtual sundae he was assembling. "She's a college girl. Just finished a year at Wellesley."

A low wail erupted from Grandpa's lips. Suddenly solicitous, he waved his arm toward the dining room. "Come," he said to my mother. "Humble food, but what is ours is a-yours."

Grandpa excused himself as the fam-i-ly scooted around the table. When he returned, his face and hands pink from a brisk scrubbing, he was wearing his best shirt and his number-one newsie cap.

They all rammed their napkins into their collars. Except Mother, who draped hers across her knees. When Grandpa saw this refined gesture he tugged his napkin from his collar and flattened it across his lap.

"Angelo," he said. All eyes bounced from Angelo to Grandpa and back. "You do the fam-i-ly proud by bringing home such a jewel. You should marry this girl."

Dad and Mom looked at each other, then at Grandpa, and Dad announced, "I already did!"

Yup. During that short side trip on the way home, Mom and Dad had exchanged for-better-or-for-worse vows that they both probably meant at the time.

"What?" Nonna said.

"Yes!" Mother held up her hand to flash a modest gold band. Dad hoisted his champagne glass.

Betty jumped up and hugged her new sister-in-law. Mom remembered that hug. She said Betty clamped on to her as if my mother were a life preserver someone had thrown.

Grandpa sat there grinning, tears in his eyes, as if he couldn't believe his good fortune, until Nonna uttered the phrase that collapsed everyone's bliss.

"Who was-a the priest?"

"The priest?" Mom said.

"Who perform the Wedding Mass?" Nonna asked.

Dad really should have warned Mom. He should have taught her a few lines of Latin, trained her to genuflect, drilled her with the name of a made-up Catholic church: Saint Prosciutto's. Saint Mortadella's. But he didn't.

So Mom blurted out, "We eloped. Went to a justice of the peace in the middle of the night. He was in his *pajamas*," Mom bragged, as if it were all just too corny. "My father would have loved it," she added, making him seem a suspicious character, a shadiness only slightly lessened by the fact that he was already dead. "Of course, Mother would have a stroke," she said, eyes sparking.

"No priest?" Nonna's hands clapped the sides of her face. "Then you no married."

My mother looked utterly perplexed. "Well, of course we are." She again held up her ring finger. "And we didn't need a priest, because I'm not even Catholic."

I'm sure the walls in that room bowed inward from the mass sucking-in of breath.

Nonna stood up, sat down, stood up. "A Protest-ant? You married a Protest-ant?"

Celeste Xaviero's sentiment drifted through the open window. *"Dio mio!"*

Dad grasped at denominational straws. "She's Episcopalian. They have priests. And incense."

Mother, used to shock-value candor with her own mother, said, "Oh, I'm not Episcopalian anymore. I no longer believe in all that God hooey."

The roof should have blown off, Betty said, from the sheer volume of howling and railing. Nonna nearly fainted, and Betty had to bring her a glass of Marsala to calm her nerves.

(I no drink-a too much.)

(I really and truly do not care, Nonna.)

Grandpa stood up, his forgotten napkin sliding to the floor. He strapped his arms across his chest and offered his own direct bluntness. He walked over to stand in front of his once-again failure of a son, now also standing. "Have you consummated this?"

Angelo opened his mouth, but Mom wedged herself between father and son. "Don't you dare answer that, Angelo. That's none of his business." She looked at her father-in-law. "That's none of your business."

Grandpa scowled at her, teeth bared. She wasn't beautiful to him anymore. "Angelo. Tell this *puttana*—"

Dad's fist flew up to strike his father for calling his new wife a whore, but Grandpa grabbed Dad's wrist in his bricklayer's grip. He slapped his son across the face, leaving a red handprint on his cheek, a different kind of port-wine stain that vibrated deep into my father's wrenched body and settled into his sack of seed, into one feisty sperm that would one day beget me, born with my grandfather's hand slap tattooed on my face.

At that exact second, after only two days as a five-foot, six-inch husband, my father started shrinking in my mother's eyes.

"You bring shame on this fam-i-ly." Grandpa dropped Dad's wrist and left the room, dragging behind him a trail of words that mortified my father. "You are no son of mine and you are not welcome in-a my house."

Oh, the dejection. Oh, the misery . . . for about three months.

Our fam-i-ly is no melodramatic Italian opera filled with decade-long feuds and deathbed reconciliations. Okay, maybe we are, but not at that moment, because Mom and Dad were back in Grandpa's house not twelve weeks later and all because of three words spoken over the phone that held more power than Grandpa's decree: "Marina is pregnant."

Nonna's Mojo Risin'

Archangel Archie:

It's Tuesday evening and I'm reclining on a settee in the hall outside the den—a room from which I have been banished. Nonna is in there indulging in her weekly trifecta of extravagances, beginning with her Barcalounger that could seat four Nonnas—those squat legs dangling a foot from the floor. On the table beside her is decadence number two: a bottle of Marsala. And in her lap, number three, a Whitman's Sampler that will hold nothing but empty slots and a hint of remorse by the eleven o'clock news. I have been banished because it's TV night, and I have an annoying habit of chattering too much during her favorite program—

(Hush-a you mouth out there!)

—Maude. Of course, Nonna rants at Maude's liberal views. *You should no speech to your husband so mouthy! That's a-no way for a wife to behave! Look! Walter is wearing an apron!*

It's a good time to tell you about Nicky's charmed birth. I wouldn't dare if Nonna were beside me. It might propel her into a ritualistic tizzy—all that misplaced guilt—a weird Catholic-*malocchio* blend that I also shoulder. Before Nonna's only grandson surfed into the world on a salty wave, she guaranteed a sound delivery by insisting that Angelo and Marina move out of that garage apartment Dad's day-laborer salary afforded and into Uncle

Dom's boyhood bedroom—much larger than Dad's, which was the size of a porta-potty.

Before they moved in, Nonna painted the walls red. Red curtains, red throw rug, red bedspread. Dad made a bassinet that Nonna slathered red too. Then she unpacked her valise of good Sicilian magic—branches of rue, horn-shaped (penis-shaped) coral amulets, silver crescent moons, horseshoes, ankhs, blue-eyed glass beads—lucky talismans that she tucked in drawers, nailed over doors and onto walls, and sewed into drapes. Nonna also slid a four-tooth chisel that held special powers beneath Mom's mattress.

You might be wondering where Mom's mother, Grandma Iris, was during this prenatal hullabaloo; this was her first grandchild too. Mom was practicing her own preventive hoodoo by keeping her marriage and pregnancy a secret for reasons best known to her.

As Mom's belly grew, the rest of her languished. Incubating an angel apparently takes a toll. Finally, her stomach was too outsize for her hips, and the doctor relegated her to bed rest. Mom spent hours holed up in that room reading library books and scribbling poetry. She filled whole tablets and then resorted to grocery sacks, envelopes, drawer liners. No one could unscramble Mom's inner thoughts erupting as verse that sounded more like Chinese fortunes incorrectly translated: *Cursed perfection perfects my curse. O shiny seed, a dissecting world awaits. Growl the toady barfly.* I used to think I was too untrained to appreciate Mom's obscure lines. I know different now.

One might think Nonna would resent having an impenetrable poet in the house, having to haul trays of tea, bowls of pastina, up those steps five and six times a day. Quite the opposite. Nonna thrived on her duties, which enabled her to ward off envious visitors, particularly walleyed Aunt Betty, who might jinx the birth, the baby, or both.

Grandpa's gift to the couple was his temporarily moving to an army cot in the basement, where he was surrounded by bottles of his homemade wine, oily tools, and girlie pictures. Thank God Mom didn't have to see him parading to the bathroom in his dingy boxers, scratching his bum, rearranging his Calabrian lug nuts, which would have been enough to jinx anyone's birth.

Uncle Dom's gift was securing my father a blue-collar job stoking the furnace at the Plant, where Dom worked in personnel in the air-conditioned front office.

On February fourteenth, 1949, Nicky began gently tapping on his amniotic sac. The timing must have felt like winning the lottery to Nonna. Could there be a luckier, more red-hearted day to deliver a child? The feast day of Saint Valentinus, our martyred Roman cousin? Grandpa Ferrari sped to Scourged Savior Hospital, Nonna next to him, leaning over the back of her seat and dangling holy medals above Mom's belly. Dad held Mom's hand and smoothed her hair. At the hospital, he kissed her forehead before they rushed her through the swinging doors to the delivery room.

The fam-i-ly settled in the waiting room, prepared for hours of pacing and glugging cup after cup of bitter coffee. Nonna had brought her embroidery kit so she could stitch red crosses into my soon-to-arrive-brother's diapers. She didn't make it through even one cross because twenty minutes later, my brother slid effortlessly out of his brackish cocoon and into an oxygenated world eager to receive him. According to the nurses, Mom didn't even have to push. He did cry, but it wasn't shrill, more like a chorus of heavenly hosts or wind chimes tinkling in the breeze.

They brought him to the waiting room for a quick perusal by the fam-i-ly: flawless alabaster skin, aquamarine eyes, a halo of blond ringlets. An Aryan dream that would have made Hitler weep, or my father, who at that exact moment probably uttered to his son the three words I would be chasing for years: *I. Love. You.*

Nonna leaned over the baby, spit into his face (*ptt-ptt-ptt*), and blubbered her deflective chants with flip-flopped pronouns because the *malocchio* is much less interested in girls, the lesser sex. Grrr. Wonder what Maude would think about *that!* "Such a homely bambina," Nonna cooed. "Ugly as a toad. Ought to send her back to cook a while longer."

While the others fawned, Grandpa snuck to the nurses' station and filled in the birth certificate, forever burdening my brother with the cursed moniker Dominick Antonio Ferrari, Grandpa's own name, despite the fact that my parents had settled on Donald Joseph, after Mom's father. My mother exploded, although quietly, given her meager strength, but Dad acquiesced to the name, shaving off another inch of height.

Days later, Mom and Dad brought Nicky home and ushered him into his red bassinet, where he was again protected by a web of good magic. Nonna had a drawer full of baby-girl dresses to disguise Nicky in, confounding my mother. The Italian neighbors—including snooping Celeste Xaviero—understood the cross-dressing. They dropped by with casseroles and stuffed monkeys, hand-knit blankets and rattles, that Nonna accepted before slamming the door on the gift bearers' resentment.

Aunt Betty had to wait two weeks to see her nephew. Nonna refused her admittance, so Betty chose the morning when all the men would be at work and Nonna would be chanting her monthly rosary at Saint Brigid's—a prayer chain she wouldn't dare break. Betty described how she gripped Ray-Ray's mittened hand while she boarded the bus and how, when she got to the house, she slid the key from beneath her in-laws' doormat. Inside, she tiptoed upstairs for her first peek at not only the baby but that hallowed red room, which startled her into yelling: "Holy crap!" Mom wrapped her arms around her sister-in-law, a buoyant ally who might keep Mom afloat in this fam-i-ly. Betty sat in the rocking chair as Mom placed Nicky on her lap. Aunt Betty cooed and fussed. "Such a beautiful baby boy! Such a perfect, lovely baby boy." Ray-Ray sat on the floor plucking every strand of red yarn from Raggedy Andy's head before biting off his plastic eyes.

Betty was still chanting when Nonna hustled up the steps, too early, her rosary half prayed, because she had had a premonition. It was a disaster Betty and Mom recounted numerous times, telling it through Nonna's eyes. When Nonna entered, she found the demonic tableau—Ray-Ray surrounded by a pile of plucked yarn, yawning (the first sign of the presence of a *jettatura*); Mom sitting on the edge of the bed rubbing her temples because of a recently descended headache (the second sign); and Betty uttering pronoun-appropriate praises that invited the *malocchio*'s ire, her green keyhole pupil scouring every inch of Nicky, who had just gotten the hiccups (the third and worst of all signs)—and Nonna knew the babe had been hexed.

Nonna went spastic with signs of the cross, whirling around the room—all that iron jangling—pulling a knot of coral horns and scapulars from around her neck, bobby pins flying as she scooped Nicky up. "Ugly baby! Horrible! Pitiful! Pig-faced swine of a baby girl!" She plunked him into my mother's arms before scooting Ray-Ray and Betty from the room, down the stairs, and out the front door, where she batted them off the porch with a broom.

Such a tornado of holy cures! Mom was a prisoner in that chamber of undoing as Nonna performed ritual after ritual involving bowls of oil and water. She burned rue leaves and smeared the ashes on Nicky's face. She hid salt crystals in his ringlets. Flashing her hand signs, index and pinkie fingers extended like horns, Nonna recited her antidotal prayer: *"Malocchio che causi tanta miseria, noi ti caviamo l'occhio e ti mandiamo sulla luna! Distruggete il malocchio!"* Nicky's hiccups ceased, as did Mother's headache, but to ward off future enchantments, Nonna rolled out the heavy artillery: urine. Exactly whose, I'm not sure, but she collected spaghetti pots full to dribble outside along the property line. Even worse, she sprinkled droplets in every room in the house, even trickled a circle of it around Nicky's crib and Mother's bed. I imagine Mom's arched eyebrows, her horror as she stared into her reflection in a butter knife. *What kind of hell have I married into!*

I'm impressed that she endured it for so long, one postpartum month of breathing in those fumes; she lasted until Grandpa Ferrari reclaimed his room across the hall, where his sardine burps and pig-knuckle farts mingled with the miasma hovering above Mom's bed and kept her awake, and Nicky too; he finally started bawling like a real child. Not to mention that Mom began to suspect that Nonna's cooking was laced with pee too.

"Get us out of here!" Mom yelled at Dad one evening when he came home from work. "Get us the hell out of here now!"

Dad, bless his henpecked heart, slunk over to Uncle Dom's to beg for a down payment on a house.

"Goody!" Aunt Betty remembers saying. "The house two doors down is for sale!"

Dom wrote Dad a check, but it wasn't large enough to secure a house in swanky Grover Estates, where Dom and Betty lived a flat-lotted life. It was, however, just enough for one of those squat Monopoly houses up on Dagowop Hill. Mom flew to that cracker box and kissed every concrete step as she hiked up to her new pee-free home.

My Cursed, Cursed Birth

Padre:

It's a gusty day atop Dagowop Hill. I'm sitting in the whippet room, so named because of the painting over the mantel of a golden boy in a Little Lord Fauntleroy suit with a doleful-eyed whippet by his side. The house came furnished, so I don't know who the boy is, but I like to pretend it's Nicky in the alternative childhood he always wished for himself, one surrounded by titled pets and the accouterments of privilege Grandma Iris would have gladly provided if given the chance.

The room is circular with gobs of windows offering a three-hundred-sixty-degree view. Most of the leaves have blown from the trees, so I can see nearly every Monopoly house spiraling beneath my feet, even the one my father purchased all those years ago.

But long before that, this swatch of West Virginia was bought by a robber baron who shall remain nameless because his heirs have lawyers cocked and pointed in my direction. When Le Baron's workers began poking and prodding the soil, they discovered, not coal, as one might expect, but lead, mercury, and nickel. To process the loot, our tycoon immediately opened the Plant, a smoke-belching factory with pipes that glugged waste into the Ohio River.

Le Baron's town also boasted the sweetest water for miles.

When he found the source—a spring that bubbled from the top of a hill that stood like a pert nipple in the river valley—he built a springhouse over it, the slate roof topped with a whippet weathervane.

Le Baron also broke ground on the mountaintop for an estate that copied the Biltmore's chateau-esque style, though a quarter of the size, with asymmetrical wings and round towers. When Le Baron finalized the plans, I doubt he could have imagined that one day a trio of Italian women would run barefoot through the halls and slide down the banisters in their pajamas. Lucky for us, he also installed a heated reflection pond on a slice of earth below the springhouse.

Sweetwater Village was established at the foot of the hill to support Le Baron's employees: cottages for the craftsmen and mill workers; a grocery store to feed them; a pub for them to avoid their nagging wives; and, because most of the workers were Irish immigrants, a Catholic church and a school dubbed Saint Brigid of Kildare. Le Baron benevolently allowed his sweet water to drain downhill into his workers' pipes. He even had them construct a stone basin and pump in the town square where they could wash their necks and collect gossip.

The majority of West Virginia is Protest-ant, so Sweetwater is plunked like West Berlin inside East Germany, a papal haven for Cat-lickers, without Checkpoint Charlie or the Berlin Wall. Maybe the wall of animosity between the Prods and Cat-lickers will topple if the actual Berlin Wall ever falls. Oddly enough, although I was born with bisected Germany on my left thigh, West Germany decidedly less mulberry than its eastern cousin, after I recovered from German measles, when I was three, I saw that the countries had melded into one unified magenta blotch. This was my earliest recollection that someone or something was tinkering with my personal geography, an awareness that kept me perpetually looking over my shoulder.

When Le Baron died, the property went to his widow, a purported witch, who enjoyed her secluded lifestyle until eminent domain pulled the hill, like a rug, out from under her feet. City planners left her the house and a scrap of land, which, except for the oddly situated reflection pond, she immediately contained within a wrought-iron fence. An asphalt road spiraled up the hill, streetlights placed along it intermittently to illuminate the more dangerous curves. On one turn in particular, dubbed No-Brakes Bend, a leak in the natural springs washed over the road and froze every winter, making for treacherous driving. The land was chopped into dinky Levittown parcels to accommodate returning World War II vets, like my father, who didn't care about that frozen spot in the least.

There was always a smattering of grape stompers in Sweetwater, and they laid the grid of streets. The widest was Appian Way, which led from the foot of the hill through the village and up to the dogleg in the Ohio River, passing one perpendicular street where the Italians lived, called Via Dolorosa.

After the war, those Dolorosans flung their progeny up onto the hill, and then word spread outside of West Virginia and dozens of *famiglie* flocked upward, where they flushed boot-shaped turds in the villagers' direction. Suddenly O'Grady's Grocery had to stock salami and capocollo. Paddy's Pub (where the stout was served warm) had competition from Dino's Lounge (where the Chianti was served cold). Those Dagowop Catholics started attending Saint Brigid's, lopping off the *of Kildare* and redubbing this Brigid their Tuscan saint. They even installed a dark-haired statue in the narthex across from the Irish version, so it was a regular Battle of the Brigids.

It was a war of epic proportions: Eye-talians claimed one side of the church, Irish the other. Same with the grade school: bogtrotters on the left, macaronis on the right. The taunting was merciless:

Get on up Dagowop Hill where you belong, you oily-haired, guinea ragùs!

Up yours, you shillelagh-hugging, leprechaun-spawning, village tater tots!

Aware of the rift, the diocese appointed a cross-pollinated priest: Father Luigi O'Malley, who sported a massive, peculiarly shaped cantilevered mole on the side of his face that the children dubbed Abraham Lincoln. Father could guzzle whiskey with half of his flock and homemade wine with the other, which made him enormously popular but did little to fuse the congregation.

Enter my mother, that aquamarine jewel sparkling amid all the coal hunks on the hill. The Italians loved her because they believed her light coloring was superior to their own swarthiness. Whenever Mom traipsed downhill to the village for a loaf of bread or a wedge of cheese, silken ponytail swaying, the Italians, men and women alike, would stop changing sparkplugs or hanging laundry to admire her beauty.

Irish shopkeepers loved Mom because she was their British Empire kin—never mind the Protestant/Catholic turmoil—and because of the aforementioned superficial reasons. They displayed their awe in practical ways: a pound of bologna when she'd paid for only a half. A head of cabbage tossed in with the onions. Which was a good thing, because although she was smart, she never brought enough money with her to town, nor could she balance a checkbook.

Each time Mom strolled Nicky around the hill, the housewives fawned over him in ways they never did over their own dun-colored children. The wives squealed and followed them, offering nickels and Walnettos, and all the Old Country nonnas who lived in their children's spare rooms shuffled after them, clanging cast-iron skillets, spitting, and praying because, like Nonna, they had been trained in the Old Religion.

I hope life on the hill was initially good for my parents, their days filled with cups of coffee over the back fence and comparing tools in neighbors' garages. No Mom diving into her reflection or penning weird poetry. I don't know how Mom kept her location a secret from Grandma Iris during her first twenty months of marriage, but eventually Grandma tracked her only child down. Nicky and I, our heads swimming with too many film noirs, wrote our version of the events in a short story we titled "The Pearl-Onion Dame" (exhibit B), which I'll read for you now.

It was a rainy night in Charlottesville. The kind of night where—wait! I forgot. Bear with me as I run downstairs to the conservatory.

(Where are you off to in such a rush, Garnet? Oh! Are you making one of your tapes?)

(Yes, Aunt Betty. What is that thing?)

(It's a lampshade I mail-ordered. Don't you just love it?)

(That's a lampshade? But it's all—)

(I know! It's going in the carcass room.)

(Ah. Well, that explains it.)

Okay. I'm here. I have to dodge the piano and harp. Let me set the tape player down. I'VE GOT A JAZZ RECORD LINED UP ON THE VICTROLA. JUST HAVE TO PUT DOWN THE NEEDLE. There. I'm back. Listen to that horn. Saddest sound I've ever heard—next to my saw. Okay. Here we go. Take two, in my best Humphrey Bogart voice:

It was a rainy night in Charlottesville. The kind of night where a dame's chilling scream might pierce the skinny hours like a train whistle. The Cadillac pulled up in front of Jake's Place, a seedy tavern where merchant marines were routinely cheated in poker games. The chauffeur eased from the front seat and opened the rear door. Out slid a pair of well-formed gams attached to a shapely package in a mink coat, felt hat concealing her face.

"Get the door, Cedrick," the doll growled.

"Yes, ma'am." The driver obliged, protecting her with an umbrella.

Inside the bar, the private dick sat slouched in a booth in the back, facing the door so he could spot the broad he'd spoken to only once, on the phone, when she hired him. He didn't trust her, but he needed the work or he'd be flicked out of his third-floor walkup like a cigarette butt from a car window. And there she was, blowing in with the wind, red rose in her décolletage—their prearranged sign—clicking toward him in her high heels, a man wearing a chauffeur's hat behind her. She paused at the booth.

"Dirk Derringer?"

He nodded. "Mrs. Ruetheday?" Her name was an alias, he was certain, but so was his.

"Dust the seat, Cedrick."

Cedrick pulled the silk scarf from his neck and wiped the wooden bench as the moll peeled off her hat.

Mrs. Ruetheday was older than Derringer had imagined, maybe fifty, but well preserved, every blond hair in place, diamond earrings the size of roulette balls. He didn't bother to stand and he could tell that irked her. He was glad. She slid into her seat and commanded Cedrick: "Vodka martini. Extra dry. One pearl onion."

"Yes, ma'am," he said, and slithered away.

Ruetheday plucked off her gloves, one finger at a time. "Did you get it?"

The detective reached into his pocket and pulled out a folded slip of paper that contained the address and phone number. Sid the bartender appeared and dealt down a coaster and then Ruetheday's martini, the pearl onion on the bottom bobbing like one of Saint Lucy's plucked-out eyeballs.

The doll ogled the slip of paper in Dirk's hand, tinking her manicured nails against her glass. "Is that it?"

"Got the money?"

Mrs. Ruetheday groaned, as if discussing money were just too gauche, but she rifled through her clutch and pulled out an envelope.

Derringer paused before sliding the information across the table. He could overtake Mrs. Ruetheday if there was nothing inside that envelope and she was trying to skip without paying. The hovering silkworm he could lay out with one punch.

The dame took a sip of her martini, unfolded the paper, scanned the address, and choked on her vodka, coating Derringer in an alcohol mist. "There must be some mistake!" Ruetheday was dumbfounded to see that her crown jewel of a daughter had landed in godforsaken West Virginia. "My Marina would never live there!" Then she read a one-sentence addendum and her eyes rolled back in her head.

Mrs. Ruetheday slumped in her seat, swooning at the indignity of it all, the improbable address, the secret. She might have fallen and melted

*into a vodka puddle if Cedrick hadn't leaped forward to catch her, and
as he did, Derringer scooped up his payola, bolted to the door, and shot
out into the night like a .38 slug.*

It was the Wednesday before Christmas, Dad said. He had just
come home from work and found Mom in the still-unfurnished
living room changing Nicky on the carpet, her mouth full of
diaper pins and an overripe secret she was waiting for Christmas
morning to deliver. Dad was about to kneel when the phone rang.

Mom handed Nicky to Dad. "I'll get it."

She lifted the receiver, my father close beside her blubbering a
glut of *I love yous* into his son's ear.

"Hello?" Mom said.

"Marina? Is that you, darling?"

Mom swayed backward as if she'd been punched. "Yes,
Mother."

Even Dad could hear Grandma's rant charging through the
phone line, ruffling Mom's hair.

"Marina! I've found you! Why would you shut me out of your
life after all I've done for you? The best of everything, and you
married that—*Italian*—and moved to West Virginia! You will
rue the day, Marina, for making such a colossal mistake. Absolutely rue the day!" Mother held the phone away from her ear as
Grandma fumed.

"And I had to learn from a complete stranger that you have
a son! We have a Caudhill-Adams-Rutledge-[ad infinitum] heir! A
male successor at last!"

Dad would later understand the full import of this. Grandma's
fortune flowed matrilineally and could be traced back to the *Mayflower*, her bank accounts stuffed with generations' worth of inheritance, she being the only-child daughter of an only-child daughter of an only-child daughter and having birthed an only-child
daughter, my mother. The various husbands' surnames stacked
up like postscripts, but the money was uterally bequeathed.

Grandma jabbered about the deprivation her grandson was

surely suffering. "It's not too late. Come home now. Bring the baby. We'll say you married a war hero who died in Iwo Jima." The math was all wrong, since that invented husband would have died four years before Nicky was born. "Come home, Marina. Please. For the sake of your child. Your father would agree. Don't be melodramatic. Enough of this tantrum. Now, come home!"

Mom, face crimson, finally let loose. "I wouldn't dare bring up my child in that gilded hellhole! I love my husband" — good news for my father, and at the time it was probably still true — "and besides, I'm pregnant!"

"What?" said Dad.

"What?" said Grandma.

"Don't call me anymore!" Mom shoved in the last word before slamming the phone down.

That's right. For three months I had already been stewing in Mom's uterus. I was probably as pink and spotless then as my brother, and according to evil-eye lore, I might have remained so if Grandma Iris hadn't gate-crashed my development.

Grandma Iris never let anyone have the last word. Two weeks after her call, a delivery truck backed into our forty-five-degree-angle ice-covered driveway. Before Mom could sputter dissent, two teamsters unloaded a brand-new living room suite. I imagine her noble-poor resolve shriveled as the suite was followed by children's bedroom furniture, a washer and dryer, seven massive gilt mirrors, and a dozen wooden crates marked FRAGILE: HANDLE WITH CARE. Grandma never would divulge how she knew which home furnishings Mom needed (Dirk Derringer, private eye, no doubt).

Twenty minutes later, an even more prescient delivery arrived in an aquamarine, tail-finned Cadillac Coupe de Ville. Grandma Iris had somehow navigated the hundreds of miles from Charlottesville to arrive at our door. She hustled past my mother — "What in the world are you wearing?" — and ordered the teamsters to pry open one of those FRAGILE crates, the one that held two dozen bottles of vodka, several jars of pearl onions, and a martini-mixing set. Grandma guzzled a cocktail down and hugged her stunned daughter. "Now, where is my grandson?"

Hours later Dad arrived and found his house jammed with high-end furniture, a Stonehenge of crates, a mother-in-law snoring away on the sofa, and a martini-hammered wife squiggling nonsense — *Hold tight, flyman; bolster the balustrade* — on her bedroom wall.

The next day Grandma traipsed from gilt mirror to gilt mirror, one hung in every room now, though they were ridiculously outsize for our walls. Mom began unloading the rest of those crates, likely squealing when she unearthed selected volumes from Grandfather Postscript's library: Shakespeare, Milton, Austen, the Brontë sisters. Grandma had also had the forethought to include her dead husband's beloved reference sets: *Encyclopaedia Britannicas*, various editions of *Webster's*, even an *OED*, which I'm sure Mom and Grandma pored over as they sucked the vodka out of pickled onions.

When Nonna is pickled with her alcohol of choice, she offers an alternative explanation for my condition that has nothing to do with Saint Garnet del Vulcano and everything to do with the rest of those HANDLE WITH CARE crates. According to Nonna, anything the mother is startled or captivated by during her pregnancy can mar the developing fetus. Back in Sicily, Nonna swore, a toad had leaped from a pond and landed in front of her withchild friend Camelia, and her baby was born with a toad-shaped birthmark on his cheek. A meteor shower rained from the sky outside the bedroom where Nonna's cousin was delivering, and a Leonid shower of freckles speckled the newborn's shoulder. Abri the bachelor tipped his hat at Leta the milliner, and when Leta's daughter was born, Abri's profile was etched on her palm. Leta was soon divorced.

Imagine my mother's fascination when she tore into the back row of crates to find choice specimens from Grandfather Postscript's other obsession: globes. Mom hauled out world globes made of leather, globes made of marble, globes inlaid with malachite, mother-of-pearl, lapis lazuli, and bloodstone. There were styles galore: Franklin, Lancaster, Westminster, Queen Anne. Sherbrooke floor globes, desk globes, illuminated globes, globes that dangled from the ceiling with counterweights, globes held up by statues of Atlas, flip-top globes hiding decanters of brandy.

Grandma had calculated wisely. The detritus of her late husband's passions so entranced my mother that she happily handed over her son. I don't know how Dad endured the invasion, but I imagine that was the minute he flew to the basement, pulled out a beloved saw with a curlicue-etched handle, and began filling the house, and my prenatal ears, with a rhythmic sound that was sweeter to me than any lullaby.

Grandma found a practical application for Dad's carpentry skills: she had him build shelves for the reference books that would go into Nicky's room and for the globes that would go into baby number two's. Grandma picked up the first volume of the *Encyclopaedia Britannica*, A to Anno, and started reading to Nicky pronto so he could catch up to all the well-nurtured aristocratic Virginian babies. When she wasn't stuffing his gray matter, she held him in front of various mirrors, taming his forelock or centering his bib. "One must always look one's best, Nicky. You don't know who might be watching."

Mom had a love-hate relationship with the mirrors, by turns dodging them like Nonna dodged evil-eye *gabbos* and peering into them for hours picking at imaginary imperfections. *There she goes,* Nicky and I used to say whenever we caught her diving into herself.

Mom also spent hours in the globe room rearranging planets, spinning a dozen Earths. It was an innocuous distraction, or so everyone thought. Mom was not weakened or nauseated during this pregnancy. In fact, she was ravenous. Nicky said her cravings included slug livers, blue skink tails, turtle eyes, and canine testicles. I question this menu because I have never had a yen for dog balls in my life.

Grandma Iris had been excluded from Mom's first pregnancy,

and the Ferrari mob was barred from her second. Partial blame goes to Grandpa and Uncle Dom, who refused to haul their non-driving wives up Dagowop Hill. The rest goes to Mother, who forbade any visits from her pee-dribbling in-laws.

It would take a miracle—or a calamity—to bring them together. After supper on June twenty-third, 1950, Mom sat in my soon-to-be room palpating a three-inch 1890 Abel-Klinger wooden globe, the varnish shiny with the oils of a thousand caresses, including Grandfather Postscript's. Then Mom's inner ocean gurgled.

"It's time!" she called.

In dashed Dad and Grandma Iris cradling Nicky. Mom held tight to the Abel-Klinger—the one world she could control—and they skedaddled to Scourged Savior, where Dad again kissed Mom's forehead before they whisked her through the swinging doors to the delivery room.

Ever the dutiful, if shrinking, son, Dad phoned his father, and soon the elevator doors clanged open. The Ferrari clan (sans Ray-Ray and Betty, whose walleyed presence had been prohibited) tumbled out and landed at Grandma Iris's Ferragamo-shod feet. Though Grandma Iris was a towering blonde like my mother, Grandpa would not be suckered by beauty again. I bet Nonna couldn't help comparing herself to this sparkling rival who was only a decade younger but centuries apart in looks, language, and deportment. Nonna ultimately crept to the shadows in her limp jersey dress, coiled white bun, and swollen feet rammed into sensible shoes.

Dad tried to keep the peace. "It won't be long. She's probably delivering right now. Anyone for coffee?"

Finally they took their seats. Nonna hadn't brought her embroidery kit this time since she assumed I would be as considerate as Nicky and enter the world swiftly on a pain-free wave.

Au contraire. For twenty-one hours, Mom writhed in anguish, sweating and cussing and ruing the day, especially ruing the drugs that did nothing to dull the pain. Her shrieks pierced the waiting room—the expletives, the threats to Dad's manhood—and then, suddenly, nothing. Not a peep, just a foreboding silence.

I was not presented to the fam-i-ly in the waiting room. Once Mom and I were situated in her room, a nurse brought the fam-i-ly to her, the Abel-Klinger globe resting on a water glass on her bedside table. The mob rushed toward me, filled with anticipation. Mother's face bore an expression that must have hinted their hopes would be dashed. She peeled back the pink blanket to reveal a port-wine globe of a girl, flaming hair coning up like a volcano.

I imagine Mom looked for a shiny object to dive into, but she couldn't, so she held me toward them, tears of something in her eyes. "Isn't she beautiful? Isn't she absolutely beautiful?"

Perhaps it was hormones talking; more likely, those were the words of a desperate woman who couldn't fathom the monster she had knit together in her womb. But I was *her* monster, and if she didn't claim me, nobody would.

When the fam-i-ly members caught their first glimpse, a collective gasp erupted, along with a shriek from Grandma Iris. "Nooo!" she bawled before fleeing the room in search of a martini. Grandpa Ferrari and Uncle Dom tiptoed backward out the door to upchuck their gnocchi. Nonna spun around, certain that Aunt Betty had snuck in and cursed me. No Betty, but Nonna soon discovered the Abel-Klinger globe. Her eyes bounced from the orb to me and back as she recognized landmasses.

"Dio mio!" She scooped up the globe and tucked it in her purse. "Why you no let me visit and prevent-a this!" Nonna tugged amulets from around her neck, flashed those hand signs, offered her prayer. *"Malocchio che causi tanta miseria, noi ti caviamo l'occhio e ti mandiamo sulla luna!"* She lunged out the door and ran home to her arsenal: the rue branches, the blue-eyed glass beads, the spaghetti pots full of pee.

Which left only my father, admirer of fair Nordic traits, choking on the ball of *I love yous* he'd been gestating just for me, most of which, now, would never be born.

The (Abridged) Life of a Saint

Archie:

I've barricaded myself in my bathroom, so I apologize for the sound quality; lovely for saw playing, not so much for tape sessions, but tonight I needed to soak in a hot tub. I'm in hiding because Nonna and Betty are determined to give me a haircut. "You look a bit haggard, dear," Betty said, but I know what she's up to. I caught her sobbing over a stack of letters this morning. She is so gullible—she married Uncle Dom, after all. Sometimes I want to insert one of my skeleton keys into Betty's keyhole eye and unlock the mysteries behind her bad, bad choices. She believes I can fulfill every request I receive. *Dear Saint Garnet: Just one strand of your healing locks and my son's harelip will de-hare,* or *my daughter will grow an earlobe,* or *my sister will ungrow a third nipple.*

(Garnet! Open up, honey.)

(Go away, Aunt Betty.)

(Just a little trim. I promise.)

(If you don't leave I'll shave my head and flush every bit down the toilet. Pubes too!)

(Oh, dear.)

I would never do it, of course. I've grown quite fond of my free-spirited tresses. Now when I'm luxuriating in a hot bath, I delight in coifing them into ever grander beehives. I'm a sucker for bubble baths, Padre, where I can add topography to the secret landmasses few ever see. I suppose I shouldn't detail female anatomy to a celibate man, not that anything about me would inspire a manly twinge, and that's okay by me. With the help of the only explorer who fully traversed my globe, I have learned to appreciate this earthly vessel: one hundred forty pounds of red Carrara marble. As my intrepid surveyor said, "Imagine what Michelangelo could have sculpted out of you."

Today I'm going to tackle question twenty-three: *Earliest manifestation of miraculous signs?* My quote-unquote powers didn't surface until I was four, though I suppose I did perform one trick just by being born: I made Grandma Iris disappear.

What Dad and Grandma had in common was an appreciation for corporeal beauty, and while Dad could retreat to his saw in the basement indefinitely, Grandma could stew in her vodka for only so long. After just three days she slurred, "I'm leaving."

Mom probably said, "Thank God." A similar sentiment rose from the basement, Dad's "About time!" wafting with sawdust through the heater vents.

Grandma packed everything into the car herself, except for one Vuitton valise, which she protectively clutched during the farewells at the door.

Dad was suddenly solicitous. "Allow me."

"No, no. I'll carry it." Grandma held on tight, rushing outside and down the steps. "No need to see me off. Get back inside now." She was anxious to make a clean getaway and might have succeeded if she hadn't dropped her Vuitton. Out spilled Nicky's Roy Rogers pajamas and math flash cards.

"What the hell?" Dad rushed down the steps to the car and found his son wiggling in the passenger foot well.

Dad lifted Nicky out. "How dare you kidnap my boy, you son-ama-beetch!"

Grandma jumped in her car, rolled down her window, and squealed away, yelling, "You will rue the day, Marina! Absolutely rue the day!"

I think maybe, years later, Mom did.

After Grandma skedaddled, Mom warped under the weight of two infants at once and a husband who worked all day and fussed over only his son. Mom reluctantly allowed Nonna to help so that she could continue to compose the weird verse she'd taken to tapping to her bedroom walls: *Err well, wellborn heir, cast off your forebear's fate.*

Delighted, five days a week, Nonna schlepped her valise of incantations to our doorstep so that while Mom tended to Nicky or wrote, Nonna could work her magic on me. Day after day, she sat in my room surrounded by globes she could do nothing about because Mom refused to let Nonna haul them to the curb.

During those crucial months, my pre-sentient eyes scoured globes lining shelves, standing on pedestals, dangling from the ceiling; a solar-system mobile spinning over my crib matched the tiny system swirling on the underside of my right wrist—the only celestial masses I sported, Pluto barely a pinprick. Nonna scattered her own talismans around, all those ankhs and horseshoes. That four-tooth chisel that once protected Nicky's prenatal room was now hidden beneath my bassinet. She burned rue—a slightly better kind than Grandma Iris's—smeared me with ashes and salt, practiced her olive-oil arts, embroidered my diapers with red crosses, and even broke out the ceremonial pee, though in much smaller doses. Nothing worked. Finally she held me to her bosom, illuminated globes casting eerie shadows on the walls, and cried rivulets of tears that may have washed away my original sin but wouldn't rinse away my geography. Nor would they soften my father's heart, because he still refused to even tuck his finger under my chin.

Nonna swiped the wetness from her cheeks and started spinning the fable that she hoped would earn me favor with Dad, the golden threads coiling me in a cocoon that I was swaddled in—and believed—for far too long:

O*nce upon a time in the village of Sughero a baby girl was born. With pale skin and blue eyes, Garnet was destined for greatness . . .*

• • •

I picture Mom ducked down outside the door as Nonna spouted her fable, Mom muttering, *Sainted lobes budding amidst globes.*

In my infancy, I was introduced to the sound of Dad's sawing and to a comforting hum that would be the soundtrack of my life. It was more distinct when Nonna held me in her arms but present even when I was on the hill and she was down in her village kitchen. Eventually I understood that Nonna heard the note too: all her humming perfectly matched the vibrating *mmmmmm* in my head. Apparently no one else heard it, though as I grew, I asked whoever was in proximity time and again, "Don't you hear that?," a question Nonna had been asking all her life. Over the years I tried to find an instrument that duplicated the noise and finally heard it on *The Ed Sullivan Show.* A man in a tuxedo played a theremin, or, more specifically, his fingers stroked the air between two perpendicular antennas. His hands acted as grounding plates, producing a woeful sound that eventually included our note, which I would later identify as a low E.

Nonna remembers when the neighbors got their first look at me. It was a fall afternoon when she and Mom tried out the new strollers. Mom went first, pushing Nicky, with Nonna and me several paces behind. The hill women had not seen their flaxen-haired boy in months, and they had never seen his cloistered little sister. They raced forward with offerings, their own children toddling beside them. "Where is our beautiful boy?" Nonna sputtering *ptt-ptt-ptt.* Next they veered toward me; Mom and Nonna hoped decorous manners would prevail.

They did not. When the women inspected me, their hands flew to their mouths. "What's wrong with her? Is she contagious?"

"Of course-a not!" Nonna said.

But the children bawled at the sight and ran home, chased by their mothers who slammed their doors, windows too, and then the drapes.

Mom could have run home also, but that brave soul directed Nonna to take Nicky's stroller. Mom would steer mine and they would continue their walk. Mom held her head high as if I, antithesis of everything about her that was comely, were her Cracker Jack prize, yelling at the top of her lungs, "Behold, cruel hearts, untampered loveliness!"

Mom might have been content to snub the neighbors for good, but Nonna understood the power behind communal belief.

She wisely waited until Mom hustled Nicky to the village for a doctor's appointment, snarling at all the young housewives squealing after my mother, nickels and Walnettos in their outstretched hands once they realized the cursed one was not present.

During the previous weeks, according to Nonna Moretti, my nonna had been priming all the other hill grandmas over their afternoon Marsala, etching my bedtime story into their Old World brains. When the day arrived, a secret signal went out: white smoke from a chimney, a flapping of venetian blinds. All at once every nonna on the hill funneled into our house and to my drapes-closed bedroom decorated with lit candles, Nonna's talismans now in plain view along with Grandfather Postscript's globes. Nonna sat in the rocker and held me in her lap, my face hidden beneath a blanket, as the old women shuffled over, holy flames trembling in their eyes.

"Here she is," Nonna whispered. "The descendant of Santa Garnet del Vulcano, born to my son, *my* son, *grazie a Dio!*"

"*Grazie a Dio!*" the nonnas chanted.

Nonna peeled back the covering and I grinned at them, red hair shooting up, purple landmasses pulsing.

The nonnas couldn't stifle their disgust. "*Porca vacca! Santo cielo!*"

Nonna's eyes teared as her protective fantasy evaporated. She was about to re-cover me when Nonna Petraglia nudged her way forward, parting the other nonnas with her cane.

"*Mi perdoni. Mi scusi,*" she mumbled until she got to me. She bent deeply over me, her eyes just inches from mine. The scapulars around her turkey-wattle neck dangled in my face, making me burble.

"It's-a her," Nonna Petraglia declared. "Dere is a painting of Santa Garney in the Museo de Siracusa back in Sicilia. Dis is-a her! Es-atta replica!"

I'm sure my nonna looked up at her with deep gratitude. She was the only other Sicilian in the room, so I always wondered if there was some complicity. And by the way, I did contact the Museo de Siracusa and they have no record of any such painting, though they say it's possible it burned up in the wing that caught fire in the 1928 Mount Etna eruption.

Regardless, Nonna Petraglia's proclamation was proof enough for the other nonnas, who swallowed their revulsion along with their doubts and chanted, "Santa della Collina"—Saint of the Hill—already conspiring about how they could rub this into the potato heads in the village.

This time it was Mom who came home early, stumbling in on the bevy of old women slipping coins into my globe piggy bank, draping holy medals over my crib. One by one they left, bowing to my mother, the blessed incubator, kissing the back of her hand. Mom was too bewildered to compose a disjointed limerick. The women scrambled to their homes, and the gossip about Santa Garnet del Vulcano quickly spiraled up and down the hill. The result was more than the assurance that I would not be an outcast (at least not among old women). That evening when Dad stepped onto the front porch for his postsupper White Owl cigar, he found jars of pickled cauliflower, cans of Vienna sausages.

"Marina!" he called, mystified.

Mom padded to him, saw the bountiful offerings, clasped his hands, and spilled the Saint Garnet beans about me.

Whether he believed the story or not, from then on, Dad agreed to give me the occasional bubble bath, the real reason I adore them. One time, Dad filled the bathroom sink with sudsy water, slid in my rubbery body, and then so strategically coated me in bubbles that only my pinkest flesh was visible, and my aquamarine eyes, which reminded him of the woman he loved. He smiled broadly and I giggled at this anomaly he'd kept hidden from me. I pounded my fists in the water, splashing us both, delighting him so much that out of his mouth popped three marvelous words: "I. Love. You." I pounded my fists even harder, and the geysers rinsed off the sudsy camouflage, reminding him of everything I was not, and his smile vanished.

Subsequently, even in my baby state, I tried to re-create the bath-time ritual that had produced not only his loving look but those words. Unfortunately, the baths ended shortly thereafter, when I could no longer fit in the sink. That meant I would have to find alternative means to re-create the memory tucked in the heart-shaped box in my chest.

After witnessing the significant impact Nonna's Saint Garnet spiel had had on the neighbors and (to a lesser extent) her husband, Mom felt her heart soften. She saw, perhaps, a spark of God in her mother-in-law, and, I confess, so did I. Like youngsters who effortlessly absorb second languages, I learned the language of faith and the *malocchio* from Nonna. In exchange for Nonna's beneficent gift, Mom presented one of her own: she allowed Nicky and me to be baptized, a rite she had previously doggedly refused, causing Nonna nightly angina.

One day when I was playing Pick-Up Sticks in Nonna's driveway, Celeste Xaviero leaned out her kitchen window and described to me just how tightly Father Luigi closed his eyes when he dribbled those cleansing waters over my stained head, and it wasn't because he was praying. Afterward, Celeste shadowed him to the parish hall for the reception. "I think we all know whose sin caused that poor child's deformity," Father whispered to his altar boys, nodding in my mother's direction. The impact of Celeste's gossip was only slightly lessened when she added, "Wonder whose-a sin caused the rutabaga growing out of *his* face?"

It's a good thing Mom didn't hear Father's condemnation or she would never have given her second gift: allowing us to attend weekly Mass.

Dad (sans Mom) proudly displayed his son to Saint Brigid's parishioners, both Italian and Irish. He was always surrounded by a herd of young women, some married, some single, drawn not only to Nicky, but to Dad's bounteous hair and enthralling plight of being married to a non-saved wife.

Nonna came too, and she flaunted me, though she drew a markedly different demographic: the hill nonnas, of course, but also the Saint Brigid nuns, who flocked to me, headgear flapping like ravens' wings. When I was teething, they let me chew on the oversize rosary beads draped around their necks or waists. I don't know if at that time they truly believed I was a saint. More likely, they could see into my future school years, when they would be my teachers, so they knew the mean truth wiggling inside most children's mouths.

I loved those nuns. Sunday after Sunday I sat behind them in church on Nonna's lap, a strategic proximity that helped avert rude stares — and there were plenty. When the nuns pressed their hands together, I pressed my pudgy hands together too. When they bowed their heads to murmur Latin prayers, I garbled baby-speak versions of my own. I admired the veils that trailed down their backs like luxurious, holy manes, something my own coils would never do.

It was during those early treks to church that I was introduced to yet another sound that went on to trail my life: the wails of children. Not only sobs of fright, but a quavery "Mommy! What's wrong with—" The question stunted by a hand over the lips, or a nonna's knuckle to the forehead. "That's Santa Garney. Shut-a you mouth!"

I flourished under Nonna's and Mom's care, my physique expanding yearly as I went from the crib to the playpen to the high-chair to the stack of Sears catalogs piled on a chair when I was finally big enough to sit at the table.

Nicky was not immune to some envy over my most-favored-nation status with Nonna and Mom, even if he was the pulse that kept my father's heart beating. He was also the only male heir, the one who would perpetuate the Ferrari name. Not my non-cousin Ray-Ray Guttuso, who would always be a Guttuso even if Uncle Dom did adopt him and backhand him with our name.

Before I was born, Nicky got almost seventeen months of Mom's gooey-centered love. After I was born, my physical features were the only ones she extolled. "Is she the most beautiful baby you've ever seen? I think so! Is she the most flawless baby on the planet? I think so!" No doubt everyone within earshot asked a question about my mother: *Is she completely insane? I think so!* Mom praised Nicky's quick potty training and ability to read by age three, but after I was born, she never again commented on the thickness of his hair or the perfection of his smile.

The payback I suffered was a bruise on my right biceps in the exact shape of Nicky's fist, a new purple-green continent he dubbed Buttholia. Whenever he walked by, I'd get a jab. I retaliated by ripping pages from his *Britannicas* so that he would never know the national product of Uruguay or the meaning of the word *yashmak*.

Okay, Archibald. My fingers are pruney, and I don't see Nonna's eye at the keyhole, so I'm heaving out of the tub and schlepping to my room.

(Walleye! Getta the tubes!)

Crap. I forgot to drain the tub. Now Nonna and Betty will lock themselves in the bathroom with the ten thousand vials that Betty mail-ordered. She'll be on her knees for hours scooping up water, Nonna sitting on the closed toilet with her label gun shooting out *St. Garnet H$_2$O* tabs. If they were less upstanding, they could make a fortune, but they give all the *relics* away.

Two spirals down the hill is another holy relic, the grape arbor in back of our cracker-box house that Dad built years ago. Countless times I had been lured to the basement by the sound of Dad's sawing, had seen his palm gripping the handle enriched with his curlicues and sweat. The radio beside him crooned the torch songs he loved even if Uncle Dom called them sentimental crap. I loved them too, especially when my E note sounded. I secretly crouched on the steps the day Dad sawed the arbor posts, drawing the blade forward and back, the muscles in his arms flexing. His face bore the same anguished expression as the one Jesus wore on the crucifix over the Saint Brigid altar. I wondered what torment Dad was reliving in his head. Then I burped and he jolted as if he'd been caught shoplifting. His head swung toward me. "Go upstairs. This is private. *Private!*" I slunk away, stung.

The day the arbor was finished, Dad gathered us all outside to admire his handiwork. Mom even procured *store*-bought wine to celebrate. She and Dad set up lawn chairs that scooted closer and closer together as the sun set, Mom twirling Dad's hair in her fingers. Ah, alcohol. The great height-adding elixir. Nicky and I knew where this was heading, so we went inside, but an hour later I heard Dad bellowing, "I christen thee SS *Marina!*" after which he smashed the bottle against one of the posts.

After all the hubbub, Dad didn't do the actual vine planting. Nonna insisted that in order to ensure a plump harvest, Nicky and I should have the honors since we were Dad's little saplings. Unfortunately, Ray-Ray was also included.

The ritual had to occur in the spring just before sundown on the night of a full moon. I was only three. Nicky was four but already quite verbal since he'd spent so much time galloping through Grandfather's reference books. Nonna ushered us outside with a clothespin bag looped over her wrist. She reached inside and pulled out four sprigs from what I assumed was Grandpa's grapevine, cuttings she had planted in coffee cans and coddled all winter.

She also pulled out soupspoons and directed each of us to the base of one of the four arbor posts; she took the last. "Dig-a this high and this-a wide," she instructed with her hands.

We hunkered down. I jammed in my spoon, hoisted out my first load, and a porous stone popped out with it. I'd never seen one like it, and when I held it in my hand, it was ludicrously light. I dug my spoon in again, and another one popped out, and another, and another.

"What are these?" I asked no one in particular.

My genius brother loped over. "Where'd you get those?"

Maybe he wasn't so smart. "From the hole," I said, pointing.

"Did not."

"Did too."

"Nuh-uh."

"Uh-huh!"

Nonna came over. "What's all-a the fuss?"

"Garnet's filling up her hole with pumice stones!"

"Am not!" I didn't even know what a pumice stone was. "They came out of the hole. Look!" I dug my spoon in and out popped another one.

"That's not right." Nicky kicked the pile of stones. "Pumice comes from volcanoes and we don't live on a volcano. She must have buried them there earlier."

"I did not."

"Did too."

"What's-a the diff?" Nonna said. "We gotta get-a these in before the sun she goes down."

Before Nicky went back to his task he scraped dirt onto my bare foot, coating Antarctica and its glacial ice shelves.

Soon I heard Nonna mumbling, "Here-a too?"

She was pulling from her hole not pumice stones, but seashells. I crawled over and picked up a handful of pink scallops. I looked at her; she looked at me; we both looked at Nicky but decided not to call them to his attention. Especially since he was marveling at what he'd unearthed from his hole: a matchbox. He slid it open and discovered a toy station wagon completely demolished by some kid's rough play.

Then I looked over at Ray-Ray, who was not lifting an oddity from his hole but putting one in. He'd reached into his pocket and yanked out a dead bird, likely murdered by him. He slipped it into the grave, rammed his sapling on top, and scooped dirt around it.

Ray-Ray's clipping withered to a dry twig before morning. Nonna's and mine flourished and eventually produced the sweetest grapes of all, though they weren't the same variety as Grandpa's Gaglioppo. Though Nicky's vine grew, it was stunted and never yielded any fruit.

I understand now how bizarre these occurrences were, Padre, but swaddled as I was in Nonna's Old Religion, I thought everyone's life was filled with mystery. I often wondered what other children found in the holes they dug. And there were plenty of kids on the hill in those postwar years whose first words were probably "Mommy, what's wrong with—" I was never invited for birthday parties or sleepovers, and none of them would have had the courage to sleep in my much-talked-about globe room, which is why I never bothered to ask. Things changed when I was four and a little hill girl showed up at my door.

I was at the living room window watching neighbor girls decorate mud pies with buttercups when Dee Dee Evangelista hiked up my steps holding a baby doll. I instinctively ducked behind the drapes. When the doorbell chimed, Nonna came from the kitchen and answered.

"My doll needs a miracle," Dee Dee said.

Nonna's eyebrows pinched together. "Huh?"

"Nonna Lalia said Saint Garney can do miracles."

Nonna tugged the white hair on her chin. Finally she turned to me and held out her hand. "Come. It's-a time."

I had no idea what that meant, but I slid out and went to the door. Dee Dee's eyes rounded, and I could tell she wanted to bolt, but she looked at the sick doll and finally held Betsy Wetsy toward me. "She can't pee."

I had the same doll, Padre, only Mom had painted geographic splotches all over its skin with nail polish. How I loved that doll, and my mother.

Nonna clamped her hand on my shoulder, and the warmth from her palm seeped through my shirt and into my skin, where it radiated down my right arm and made my fingertips throb.

"Miracle her," Dee Dee whispered, picking at a pronounced sty on her eyelid.

I looked into Dee Dee's eyes, and Dee Dee stared back (the flaming sty also staring); her belief was so stern I took the doll, jiggled her, and heard liquid sloshing around in her belly. Even I knew the mechanics of Betsy Wetsy. You fed her a bottle of water and gravity took care of the rest, the water funneling through her and dribbling out a BB-size hole in her asexual mons. I lifted her dress and cringed at the brown streaks running down her legs, a hardened plug of it in her pee hole. I tried not to gag. "What did you feed her?"

Dee Dee's head hung low. "Hershey's syrup."

I handed back the doll. "Wait here." I ran to the kitchen and returned with Betsy's bottle filled with hot water, plus the dish of toothpicks Dad used to jab salami fat from between his teeth. I again lifted Betsy's dress to perform a delicate operation: I poked a toothpick in her stoppered pee hole while mumbling a prayer I had heard the Saint Brigid nuns utter countless times: "Sancta Maria, Mater Dei, *ora pro nobis peccatoribus, nunc, et in hora mortis nostrae.* Amen." I botched the Latin, but I was sure the Virgin Mary applauded my effort, because my body burned with fever at the same time that syrup oozed from Betsy, thick droplets of it. I fed the doll the bottle of hot water and soon Betsy Wetsy was peeing freely once more. Dee Dee's eyes widened as she took the doll and kissed its face, and that's when I noticed that Dee Dee's eye was suddenly sty-less.

Nonna crossed her chest three times. "It's-a true."

I looked twice to confirm, but the sty was definitely gone. I also felt wetness on my bare foot and was stunned to see that my recent hot flash had melted Antarctica's glaciers, the second instance of someone toying with my geography. I twisted around to see if some old *gabbo* had snuck into the room to toy with me, but it was just Nonna and Dee Dee, who looked at me in a way no child ever had.

An hour later, Arabella Bellagio appeared on my front porch. "Her eyelid is stuck. Heal my doll too."

She held the doll out, but I was captivated by Arabella's face, so peppered with freckles that I wanted to grab a pen and connect the dots. Nonna nudged me, so I took the doll and tipped her forward and back, the motion that would get her eyelids blinking. The right one winked at me; the left remained open, glued in place by Popsicle drippings, perhaps. Fizzies juice. I did what any healer would do under those circumstances: I spit in the doll's stuck eye socket, mashed the eye around with my finger, then dried it with the hem of my shirt while praying, "Sancta Maria, Mater Dei." Then I tipped her forward and back and—ta-da!—her eye was cured, and about every fifth freckle on Arabella's face had vanished. I rubbed my own eyes in disbelief and looked at Nonna, who was rubbing her eyes too.

That night after dinner I sat on the floor in my closet nurturing the hope that I actually was the reincarnation of Saint Garnet. I rifled through my cigar box of treasures: found marbles and buttons, a tire-mashed ring, a collection of bottle caps, cigar bands, and, from the nuns, an assortment of holy cards.

I fanned the cards—Saint Dymphna, Saint Agatha, Saint Germaine (another child whose birth defects made her a target for cruelty)—and wondered if it could possibly be true. Had I really healed those dolls and their owners? I didn't know the answer, but I felt holy, or as if I had to be holier than my natural tendency (all those fights with Nicky were certainly unsaintly). I hoped that one day my likeness would grace a four-color card that children would unwrap from bubblegum packs and trade during recess. Perhaps my father would collect them too. I understood that if I wanted to make the dream come true, I would have to clean up my act. The image of pews full of praying nuns sprang forth and that's when I got the idea.

I ran to the bathroom closet and reached for the stack of pillowcases. Because we didn't have black ones, I settled for a blue one, which I bobby-pinned to my head. I even used one of Mom's stretchy white headbands to secure it. The veil felt weighty around my shoulders and gave me courage, somehow, more like a superhero's protective garb than a nun's. The added bonus was that it tamed my hair.

I pointed my praying hands to heaven and walked down the hall imitating the nuns' measured gaits. I paused before the front door when I heard Mom and Dad on the porch, smoke from his stinky White Owl wafting in.

"Don't be ridiculous," Dad said. "It was probably a scab. Kids pick scabs off all the time."

"But your mother said she saw—"

"Not everything my mother sees is there."

"But Angelo! The freckles!"

"You're a college-educated woman, Marina. Don't get hysterical. There is no way—"

I don't know which puzzled me more: my agnostic mother's belief or my Catholic father's unbelief, both of which hung in the air as I banged open the door.

Dad muttered, "What in the—"

"Shush!" Mom said as I descended the porch steps.

I walked heel-toe-heel-toe in the center of the street, veil flapping as streetlights flickered on, powering me with courage as I lifted my chin for all my neighbors to behold my glory. Boy, did they ever. Every porch-sitting father and mother sipping Chianti. Every nonna doing supper dishes behind the kitchen window. Every cluster of girls making clover chains in the yard.

Nicky rode past me on his bike. "Who are you supposed to be?"

Immediately his left training wheel spun off and he toppled into the culvert in front of Mr. Gambini's house. I tried not to gloat since I was above all that now, ordained as I was Santa della Collina.

After that, other hill children brought me their tangled-up army men, their Mr. Potato Heads with stuck mustaches, their missing-eyed stuffed animals. Though I couldn't fix everything, I mended enough to establish my calling, and along the way I cured warts, bee stings, and ingrown toenails. Those were curious healings, occurring only when my back was turned, or when I blinked, or overnight. In the morning, a kid would come show me the pink spot on her heel where a roller-skating blister had once bulged.

Archie, I wish I could deny that those banal healings occurred. It would make life easier. But they happened, and since Nonna didn't question their authenticity, neither did I. Nor did I question who was genuinely responsible. Of course it had to be me, the landmassed replica of that original Saint Garnet, which Nonna thought would make me a target of jealousy. To ward off enchanters, Nonna insisted that pilgrims approach only when she was present to offer protection. She also set up two folding chairs in the garage and placed an upturned apple crate before them. More than once, I saw Mom watching through the basement's screen door, an enigmatic smile slicing her face. Nicky often pressed his nose to the mesh and mumbled, "Gimme a break." Dad stood there a few times grimacing, but I couldn't tell if he was looking at me or his saw on the pegboard, which he never once used when I was holding court.

Dad also suffered mightily when I insisted on wearing my veil to Mass instead of the stupid doily non-sainted girls wore. The first time I appeared, the nuns beamed at my divine imitation. Parents and older kids raised their unholy brows. "Who made Map Head queen?" The little girls stayed quiet, though, particularly Dee Dee Evangelista, who clutched her dolly and stored up all these things in her heart.

One afternoon when Mom and Nicky were gone, Nonna again closed the drapes and cleared the junk from the kitchen table. Someone rapped on the front door, and Nonna invited in four hill nonnas clutching packages.

Nonna ushered them into the kitchen, where we all sat down. The old women unwrapped their parcels and laid the goods on the table: half a dozen Pius XII–blessed gold chains, six tiny coral horns, six mini-crucifixes holding up wee Jesuses, and six nickel-size lockets with bubble glass on both sides. I wondered if I was supposed to bring something to this odd party until Nonna pulled a pair of scissors from her apron pocket. Everyone looked at me or, more precisely, at the hair beneath my veil.

Nonna stood and whispered, "We just need a few clips, Garney."

The nonnas smiled so sweetly, I couldn't refuse.

I didn't breathe as Nonna slid the pillowcase from my head, my hair springing free, and made the first careful snip, the old women gasping. Nonna held out the ringlet, which Nonna Petraglia took and inspected, the red hair coiling even tighter so it fit perfectly into one of the glass lockets. She snapped it closed, kissed it, and passed it to the next nonna, who kissed it as well. Nonna clipped off five more ringlets, and once the lockets were filled, the women formed an assembly line and strung each chain with a horn, a crucifix, and the locket holding the precious relic of my hair. It was an odd entwining of love for God and fear of the *malocchio*—their Old and New Religions colliding in a way that made complete sense to them, and me. They fastened the chains around one another's necks and then slipped the necklaces under their tops, where the talismans would rest in the valleys between their breasts. There was one locket left, and I wondered who the lucky recipient would be until Nonna presented it to me. I was thrilled to be in this exclusive club that had me at its center.

That night when Mom tucked me into bed, she caught sight of the relic. She lifted it close to her face and stared into the glass so intently that I thought she might claim it for herself. I prayed that she wouldn't, since I had a fantasy of that tiny crucified Jesus unlocking the bubble-glass locket and reaching inside so that He could tickle His nose with my hair while we both drifted off to sleep.

"Where'd this come from?" Mom asked.

I swallowed hard. "Nonna."

Mom's face was a strange blend of relief and incredulity. "She adores you."

• • •

I wish I could send you one of the lockets, Archie, but four of them are buried around the necks of their embalmed owners, Nonna fiercely guards the one she still wears, and though I wore mine for much longer than I should have, I eventually tossed it among brambles hundreds of miles from Sweetwater where it's probably a rusty, disintegrating clump.

Regardless of the nonnas' reverence, for two years I was the focus of ambivalent attention. *Is she or isn't she?* When I skipped down the hill with my pillowcase flapping I often had a train of girls tittering in my wake. Other kids lined the street to fling pea gravel and yell, "You big fake!"

One Sunday I slipped out of Mass for a drink. I was bent over the water fountain, right hand pressing the chilled button, left hand holding back my veil, when suddenly, from behind, someone pushed my face into the arc of water. I jerked up, sputtering, and found Eleanor Sweeney, the only girl my age with more residual baby fat than me.

"You look like a retard."

"I—"

"Take that stupid thing off." She reached for my veil.

I held on tight. "Hey!"

She was still grabbing for the fabric when the sanctuary door opened and out came one of the pretty hill housewives and my father, both giggling. Their smiles collapsed when they saw what Eleanor was up to. She darted back inside the church as Dad looked at me, though his face was beet red. The hill housewife tiptoed to the ladies' room.

Dad saw my wet veil. "Are you all right?"

Before I could answer, he tugged a handkerchief from his pocket, knelt, and blotted the water dribbling down my chin. He even cupped my face in his hand and tipped it this way and that.

As Dad ushered me back to our pew, I said a prayer of thanksgiving that he had not only intuited that I was in danger but also touched my face. Finally another treasure to put into the box in my chest.

• • •

When I started first grade I no longer needed Nonna as a baby-sitter. I hated losing my ally, and even worse than that, though I could hoist our garage door up by myself, I could no longer perform any miracles. Even my staunchest apostles stopped believing in me, which made those school years horrible.

Every morning I feigned a bellyache or fever, but Mom insisted I get up, saying, "You're beautiful just the way you are!," a refrain I chanted all the way down the hill and through town until I slid into school on a ribbon of howls from children who couldn't make sense of my skin. "Sister! What's wrong with—" No one wanted to sit near me, so I was relegated to the last desk by the door, where I drew cartoon Saint Garnets that might one day grace my holy card, Sister Agnes hollering, "Garnet! Stop humming!"

During recess I hid in the office of Sister Barnabas, the principal, but one sunny day she shooed me outside. "The sun will do you good." I was hunkered down by the flagpole digging holes, pumice stones popping out, when the Fabrini twins, Pia and Pippa, came over holding hands. I could hear Dee Dee Evangelista urging, "Go on."

The girls, identical except for Pippa's polio-withered foot, lived two spirals down from us. The impeccable hill acoustics allowed everyone to hear Mr. Fabrini's tirades. They weren't any louder than outbursts that erupted in about every fifth house in Sweetwater, but he was one a handful of fathers and mothers who also pounded their children (or spouses or nonnas) with boot heels or soup ladles.

"Can you heal me?" Pippa asked.

Other kids ambled over, boys and girls, some rattling pea gravel in their palms. I trembled at the immensity of this challenge, but I really had no choice. "I'll try." I inspected the foot.

"Not that," she said. "This."

Pippa rubbed a caterpillar-size wound on her cheek, a reminder of her father's belt buckle. With that shriveled foot, she was the easiest Fabrini to catch.

I wanted to cry as I imagined Pippa cowering in a corner, tiny hands trying to protect her face. At least my father never came after me in violence.

I yearned to give Pippa her heart's desire by removing the painful souvenir, but I also wanted to coat her in bruise-proof skin somehow so that her father would never hurt her again. I didn't have Nonna beside me, but I had something else. I pressed my hand to my chest, where I could feel the lump of my relic and the crucified Jesus beneath my top. "Close your eyes," I said. The twins obliged as I rubbed a pumice stone against the evidence of their father's cruelty. Three times I uttered, "Sancta Maria, Mater Dei," followed by a wobbly "Amen."

"Amen," said the twins, Dee Dee, and a few others.

When I pulled my hand away, the wheal was no longer red, but sooty gray.

Pia blurted, "It worked!," which sent Pippa's hand to her cheek. She rubbed at it, removing most of the dirt I had slathered there, unearthing the wound.

"No, it didn't," someone yelled.

"I told you she was a fake," another spat.

I felt the pelt of gravel as the crowd, except for Dee Dee and the twins, dispersed.

"It's still there?" Pippa asked, tears forming.

Pia nodded, and as the girls scuffed off, Pippa's chin sank; she was no doubt envisioning even worse scars in her future.

Which left only Dee Dee standing there, ready to withdraw her devotion.

She walked up to me and looked directly into my pupils. "I still believe."

The words rang in my ears as I lay in bed that night puzzling over my unreliable powers.

News of the disaster spread throughout the student body, so Sister Barnabas's salve was to appoint me cafeteria attendant. *Eat your cheese stick or I'll report you to Sister Barnabas!* Which was usually followed by high-pitched mockery: *Eat your cheese stick or Her Hiney Holiness will turn you into a booger. Poof!*

I knew Sister Barnabas's intentions were pure, unlike her cheeks, which were perpetually covered in red splotches. Which begs the question, Padre: Are facial anomalies a prerequisite for admission into Holy Orders? Your MoonPie, Father Luigi's Abe Lincoln, Sister Barnabas's rosacea?

Grandpa and Uncle Dom also thought I was a joke. Even Nicky drew an imaginary fifty-foot circumference around himself on the playground that I was not allowed to cross, not that I wanted to. Although there were a few times when I longed to be in his inner circle.

It was Palm Sunday after Mass, and Nicky stood in the narthex surrounded by admirers waving palms at him. All he needed was the donkey. Dad stood outside the ring beaming when Mrs. Valeri sidled over. "He's a beautiful boy, Angelo."

Dad nodded at Nicky and unfurled that smile.

"You must be proud of him."

Dad sighed the way he did only after eating Nonna's braciole.

Mrs. Valeri understood the sigh too. "You must love him more than anyone on the planet."

I waited for Dad's correction—at least I hoped it was coming—but all he said was "What's not to love?"

I knew the answer.

When we got home, I raced to the bathroom mirror and looked at my face, really looked at it. I pressed my palms over my cheeks, shut my eyes, and whispered over and over, "Sancta Maria, Mater Dei. Sancta Maria, Mater Dei." I didn't feel pulsing heat, but my desire was so earnest I felt sure that my stains would be gone. I peeled my eyes open, but the birthmarks were still there.

"No!" I said, louder than I intended. I closed my eyes and repeated the magic spell: "Sancta Maria, Mater Dei." I had never prayed for anything harder in my life.

I opened my eyes.

Nothing.

I again slapped my hands on my face and squeezed my eyes

shut, and this time I begged, "Go away! Please, please go away!" When I looked again, the birthmarks appeared, if anything, darker.

I heard sniffling at the door and there stood Mom, tears filming her eyes.

I held out my unholy hands. "Why can't I heal me?"

Of course what I meant was: *Why can't he love me?*

Corpus Christi

Archibald MacLeish:

The sun has set and the ladies and I are huddled around the barbecue pit in the backyard toasting marshmallows. I imagine Le Baron grilled hundreds of steaks on this spit; his witch wife must have rotisseried something else entirely. Nonna and I, carnivores extraordinaire, understand God's affinity for burnt offerings; all those sacrificial lambs and goats were a pleasing smell unto the Lord. T-bones are a pleasing smell unto us, even if it is forty-six degrees outside. Finally a use for Nonna's red afghans.

We're also warmed on the inside, courtesy of Betty's peach schnapps, Nonna's Marsala, and Guinness stout for me, though my few remaining *paesano* neighbors would disapprove. Tonight Betty concocted international hors d'oeuvres: egg rolls and nachos and baba gannouj—tidbits that would not have passed muster under the previous male regime. Nonna chose the dessert, s'mores. Her eyes never shine brighter than when she's roasting the perfect marshmallow. I often wonder if in her mind, it's Grandpa Ferrari skewered on her stick, the heat singeing his feet, his bulbous nose, and that dumb newsie cap erupting in flames.

I chose this locale because of question thirty-three. The first time I read it, Fresca shot from my nose. Was my father a strict disciplinarian? I mean, really. There was one time, however, when the paternal chain of command spelled bad news for me.

It was that sizzling June day of my First Communion. The entire Ferrari mob suffered through the pageantry at Saint Brigid's as the first-grade class paraded in: bogtrotters in the left column, macaronis in the right. Though we were supposed to process evenly spaced, there was an inordinate amount of space surrounding me. I didn't care, because Mom had finally bought me a proper veil made of tulle and lace to swap for the pillowcase. Before I donned it, I folded my novitiate headgear into a tissue-lined box and tucked it into the back of my underwear drawer, that holy of holies.

I should confess that after the publicly botched unhealing of Pippa Fabrini and my inability to heal my own stains, a wiggling seed of doubt had taken root in my soul. Not a doubt in God (yet), but a doubt in my sainted abilities.

When I questioned Nonna, she said, "God is-a the one Who decides who to heal and who not to heal. And besides, you no need-a the healing. You *perfetto*. You are Saint Garney. Santa della Collina. My granddaughter. *Mine!*"

On that first Corpus Christi day, as the children squirmed in the front pews waiting for Mass to begin, the side door opened three feet from me and in lumbered Mr. Giordano carrying his daughter, Donata, in his arms. Our class had heard about Donata's broken leg, and there it was, in a gigantic cast from her toes to her kneecap, still as pristine as her Communion dress, which was beautiful. But not nearly as beautiful as the way Donata's father carried her across the aisle and gently set her on the pew in front of me. Mr. Giordano arranged her veil around her shoulders, and before he left, he leaned down, cupped her face in his hands, stared straight into her eyes, and uttered the words "You look like a princess. I love you so much."

I was stunned by this fatherly display to a *girl* child. I wondered if I was the only one astounded, but when I looked down the pew at my lacy sisters, several seemed as awestruck as I, including the Fabrini twins. I had never felt closer to them in my life.

Soon Mass began and my thoughts turned toward performing

all the nun-drilled stage directions correctly. Then it was time to file up and kneel at the altar rail, where Father Luigi and Abe Lincoln made their way toward me.

Father's voice boomed in the distance. "The Body of Christ."

"Amen" came the meek reply.

We had been lectured about transubstantiation, how the bread and wine would change into the body and blood of Christ in our mouths. Classmates debated whether the hosts would turn into Jesus's fingers or toes, His eyeballs or earlobes, or just a hunk of raw flesh torn from our Savior's arm. I did not sleep well after that. On the big day I kept watching the girls ahead of me to see if Communion blood dripped down their chins. When Father stood before me, I stifled a gag—but no worse than the gag he stifled as he held the Necco Wafer–size host toward my face. He placed the disc on my tongue and I swallowed fast-fast-fast so that it would shoot past my taste buds before it morphed into Jesus's palm or upper lip. Imagine my relief when I didn't have even an aftertaste of blood.

Afterward the fam-i-ly came to our stifling cracker box on the hill. Before they arrived, Dad prepped the house. Emboldened by the vision of Mr. Giordano and Donata, I shadowed my father as he went from room to room to ensure all the windows were open before setting up the box fan in the kitchen archway. He knelt to plug it in, batting away my lacy veil fluttering in his face. Then we went out back to uncover the grill and fill it with charcoal. I kept fiddling with my hem. "This sure is the prettiest dress I ever wore. I feel like a princess. A regular princess."

Dad was having trouble lighting the charcoal, his pressing concern. I changed tactics and elaborately pranced around the yard looking for mole holes to step into and break my foot—well, a sprain would have been sufficient, since I didn't want to spend my summer in a cast. I couldn't find a hole so on my third loop around I just sat in the grass and grabbed my ankle. "Ow! My ankle!"

Dad was still hunkered over the grill, cussing the matches that wouldn't stay lit.

"I think I broke my ankle!"

"Damn charcoal." Dad finally looked over at me. "Go get my lighter and some newspaper."

I got up, shuffled into the house, and stood in front of the box fan to let the breeze billow out my petticoat and cool off the Cannibal Isles dotting my backside.

Dad yelled from outside, "Nicky! Bring me my lighter and some newspaper! And Marina, pull the meat from the fridge!"

Ah, meat. For this fam-i-ly meal, my father had procured thick T-bones. When Dad brought the steaks home the night before, he called us together to watch him unwrap them.

"Holy cow." Nicky had reached a finger toward the blood pooling on the butcher paper.

Mom stilled his hand. "They're beautiful, Angelo." I'm sure she ate them six times a week back in Charlottesville. "Your father will love them."

Dad's chest jutted out.

The next afternoon as I stood in front of the fan and waited for the fam-i-ly to arrive, Nicky started reciting information gleaned from his reference books. This tic had recently erupted whenever he was anxious, but it was better than memorizing his reflection or composing doggerel poetry. He sat on the floor behind one of the wingback chairs in the living room and rocked back and forth while recounting the history of the slingshot.

Uncle Dom's brood arrived first and he hauled in a grocery sack filled with cantaloupe and prosciutto. Ray-Ray thunked the back of my head. "Saint Varmint makes me want to vomit." Mom hauled Nicky from behind the chair as Betty entered. "There's my Nicky, and Garnet, our cherry-pie miracle worker." She rushed to the kitchen to scoop melon into balls and fasten strips of prosciutto around them with toothpicks. I took a piece of the cured meat when they weren't looking. Not as gross-looking as the capocollo Dom usually brought, thankfully, but it was extra-chewy and slick and salty. My baby teeth couldn't pulverize it, so I spit the wad into the trash. I wouldn't make the mistake of eating that again.

The potatoes were baking, the green beans were boiling, and Grandpa's car pulled into the driveway.

"They're here!" Nicky called from the front window. I ran to look out and so did Ray-Ray; he angled me out of the way like the pry bar he was. I muscled back to determine what kind of mood Grandpa was in, as if he had more than one.

Dad and Uncle Dom rushed out to genuflect to their king. Grandpa opened the trunk, and Nonna reached inside for a shirt box filled with her chocolate-dipped, pistachio-crusted cannolis.

Dad hooked his arm through Nonna's and she climbed up the stairs stoically. When she entered, she passed the box to my mother. Then her hands opened like rose petals and she looked at all of us lined up for our kisses, even Ray-Ray. She took our faces in her hands and smooched our foreheads. "Such-a homely children. It's a shame you so ugly." She slid a quarter into each of our palms, the real reason we lined up. Dad escorted her to the kitchen and settled her in the chair facing the fan, letting hot air blow tendrils of hair from her braid whorled into a bun.

Dad galloped back out to where Grandpa and Uncle Dom were standing in the street looking up at Dad's house, sour looks on their faces. Finally Grandpa labored up half the steps, paused, yanked a handkerchief from his pocket, wiped the back of his neck, and then forged upward.

When he opened the screen door I heard him moaning, "You trying to give me a heart attack with those steps, Angelo?"

Uncle Dom entered on his father's heels lugging a jug of Grandpa's homemade wine. "You need an elevator to get up this hill, Pop. It's even worse in winter, if you can believe it."

Dad came in last, glaring at his brother. He didn't say a word, but I bet he was looking for some excuse to hustle to the basement to saw wood.

"What I tell you about living up on this-a hill, Angelo?" Grandpa said. "Should-a been smart and bought a level lot you can mow without rolling over your foot." He walked straight to the kitchen, passing us kids as if we were tree stumps.

Ray-Ray slipped outside, probably to look for baby turtles to tape firecrackers to. Nicky slunk to his room to crack open the pocket *Webster's* he had bought that morning at Flannigan's Pharmacy. I leaned against the kitchen archway and watched Grandpa sit at the head of the table and demand a juice glass for his wine. Dad obeyed as Betty presented the prosciutto.

Grandpa again pulled out his handkerchief to swab his neck. That simple gesture made my hands ball into fists. Yes, it was insufferable in that kitchen with the oven pulsing and pots simmering, but the grand production of Grandpa wiping sweat felt like a dig at my father.

Mom pulled the tinfoil from the plattered T-bones. "Take a look at these." She held them toward Grandpa as if they were manna from heaven, or a stack of nudie pictures.

Grandpa's eyes widened and he held his index finger up to one to measure. "That's a two-inch-thick steak."

"*Spettacolare,*" Nonna said.

Dad wore a prideful expression I rarely saw, and then Uncle Dom opened his fat cannoli-hole. "Where'd you steal those, little brother? They fall off a truck? You certainly couldn't afford them on your paycheck." Uncle Dom would know.

Grandpa's eyes narrowed. "You no steal this-a meat, right?"

"Of course not." Dad's face was as red as the T-bones. What I didn't know at the time was that my father had bartered his labor for those steaks. He worked every night for a week at O'Grady's Grocery putting in a new floor. I often wondered why Dad didn't just tell Grandpa the truth.

Mom rushed to her husband's defense with a lie. "We used the birthday money my mother sent me."

Uncle Dom jabbed, "So the woman of the house puts the meat on the table."

I wanted to punch him.

"No!" Mom's apologetic eyes bounced over to Dad.

Dad grabbed the platter of steaks and went outside.

Uncle Dom followed. "Don't burn them! Your wife works hard to bring home the bacon."

"Shut up," Betty said, and I was glad.

The men congregated out back and Mom and Betty set the table. I sat on my stool watching Nonna peel an orange in one continuous spiraling ribbon, our E note drifting from her lips. Grandpa barked from outside, "Stop-a that damn humming!"

Half an hour later the fam-i-ly was called to the table, all except Dad, still at the grill with his tongs. Ray-Ray, born with some freaky internal alarm clock, returned from his expedition looking rumpled. Uncle Dom didn't notice the grass stains on his stepson's dress shirt, the dirt smudges on his cheek. He noticed his hands, though. "Go clean out under those nails. They're disgusting."

By the time Ray-Ray reappeared, the table was crammed with salad plates, dinner plates, bowls of cottage cheese, water glasses. Butter and salt and pepper and a basket of rolls. There was one empty spot at the center of the table, the most sacred space, where the meat would sit when Dad brought it in.

Uncle Dom aimed his head toward the window. "You're not overcooking them, are you?"

"No," Dad yelled back. "I just don't want them to be too rare."

"There's no such-a thing," Grandpa said. "You getta more iron when they are still bloody inside."

Bloody inside? The image made my stomach lurch. On the rare occasions when we had some cheap cut of steak or hamburger in patties instead of crumbled in a tomato-macaroni calamity, Dad would cook my meat to well done. The blacker the better. Any pink would send it back to the frying pan before Mom cut it into bite-size pieces for me. Mix that with the bloody clump of Jesus stewing in my belly and you'll understand my alarm.

Dad emerged bearing his weighty offering as if he were going through the Stations of the Cross, his first stop in front of Grandpa, who eyed the meat with great approval. Dad's second stop was Nonna, who pronounced, "*Magnifico.*"

When the dish was centered, Grandpa leaned in to claim the choicest one. Dom helped himself next, then plunked one on Betty's plate and one on Ray-Ray's. Then it was a mad scramble as hands reached for rolls and potatoes and butter. The steak pile was dwindling and I couldn't tell which was the well-done one; I kept looking at Dad, wanting to ask: *Which one's mine?* Someone tossed a baked potato on my plate, a spoonful of green beans, then a whole steak landed on my split-top roll. I had been gifted not only an entire steak, but a sharp knife as well; it lay atop my folded napkin. I had to kneel on my stool for better leverage, and when I stuck the knife in, blood seeped from the wound. "It's bleeding!"

"It's *perfetto*." Grandpa eyed the breathing cow on my plate. "It'll make you strong like me, see?" He speared a hunk of rare steak and rammed it into his mouth. I didn't appreciate at the time what a gift this was, Grandpa trying to placate me.

Still, watching him chew that bleeding bolus made me want to puke. Nearly. What I really wanted was my own well-done steak. "Where's mine?"

Mom jumped up and started to lift my plate. "I'll just throw it on the grill a few minutes."

"No!" Grandpa said, the magnanimous moment over. "You don't make a fuss for this child." He looked at me. "You eat what's on-a you plate."

"But Dad always cooks one special for me."

Grandpa glowered at Dad. "You coddle this child?"

"No!" Dad said, and that was the truth in everything except how I liked my meat.

And then I saw it, my nearly burnt offering on Nonna's plate, half eaten already. "That's mine! There's my steak!"

Everyone looked at Nonna chewing the food that should have been in my mouth. Nonna looked at me in horror as if she'd robbed the globe piggy bank in the back of my closet.

She lifted her plate and I reached out my hand, but Grandpa slapped it. "Don't you dare." He pointed at my plate. "You no take-a the food from your elder's mouth! Eat!"

Mom tried to intervene. "It won't take but a minute—"

Grandpa slammed his hand on the table, rattling all those glasses. "I said eat! Angelo, this is your house and you are her father. You make this child eat."

Dad looked at his father, and then at Uncle Dom, who wore a look not of sympathy but of contempt. Dad's eyes slowly found their way to me. "Just a couple bites."

I looked at Mom, now leaning against the sink, arms crossed over her stomach. She looked disgusted too. And outnumbered. Nicky began listing Neanderthal weaponry.

I don't know where the inspiration came from, desperation perhaps, but I pressed one hand over the relic beneath my bodice and the other over the mooing steak, closed my eyes, and recited my Sancta Maria prayer in my head so that Mary would elbow God to cook the steak to at least medium.

Ray-Ray said, "What the hell is she doing?"

I heard Uncle Dom smack the back of Ray-Ray's head. "Don't cuss!"

When I opened my eyes and lifted my hand, the steak was still a bloody mess, as was my hand. In desperation I prayed for Jesus to save me, for God to send a hurricane to end this horror, because I figured God owed me twice over: He hadn't removed my birthmarks and He had made me be born into this fam-i-ly. God did not save me, so I looked at Dad, hoping that whatever paternal drive had kicked in the day Eleanor Sweeney had doused me at the water fountain would again power up. But Dad stared at his lap, and I knew there would be no intervention.

Cannolis.

As I cut into that bloody steak, I tried to visualize cannolis. *Crunchy tubes stuffed with ricotta.* After this torture I would eat five in a row. I sawed at that steak for an interminable length of time until I finally held a hunk to my lips. I closed my eyes and rammed it in fast, *tiny chunks of pistachio that would stick in my teeth,* but all I could taste, feel, smell was blood. That copper-penny, rusty-nail, corrugated-toolshed smell of blood mixing with the Body and

Blood of Christ still undigested in my belly. Jesus's finger or toe prodding my spleen. It was a sacrilege beyond endurance. I spat the hunk out and it plunked on top of the saltshaker, knocking it over.

"*Dio mio.*" Nonna grabbed the shaker, spilled several grains in her hand to toss over her shoulder.

"I can't do it," I said, real tears springing to my eyes.

Grandpa picked up his knife and fork to resume eating, and I thought, *That's it?*

That wasn't it.

He took a forkful of potato and jammed it in his mouth. When he spoke I could see the starchy goo clinging to his teeth, his tongue. "Angelo. You spank this child and send her to her room. That'll teach her to obey."

"What?" Mom and I both said.

"You heard-a me. She need a good spank."

Nonna leaned back in her chair, shoulders slumped, as if she knew how this would end.

Dad knew how it had to end too. He stood up and actually came toward me.

"Angelo," my mother said in a voice that sounded like rushing wind as Dad shrunk another inch right then and there. "Don't you dare spank her!"

Uncle Dom sealed my fate. "Not only does your wife bring home the bacon, but she calls the shots."

That was that. Dad swooped over and scooped me up, but not in the tender way Mr. Giordano had held Donata. He sat on my stool and draped me belly-down over his lap, and the heart-shaped box in my chest tipped over too, spilling out the few warm memories of Dad to rattle around in my rib cage. Dad lifted my dress and layers of itchy petticoat, exposing my little-girl underwear and the Cannibal Isles mauling my backside.

I don't even recall the spanking, how hard or how many. I just remember the shame, my secret geography revealed to Grandpa, Uncle Dom, and Ray-Ray, who snorted the entire time.

I darted down the hall to my room when it was over, slammed the door behind me, and yanked that stupid dress over my head, along with the veil, which was tainted by proxy. I wadded up the unholy vestments and shoved them as far under my bed as I could, tangling them up with dust bunnies, stale sandwich crusts, dirty balled-up socks, unspoken *I love yous*, and my shrinking faith—not in God (yet), but in miracle-worker me.

Electricity

Son-ama-beetch! I just tried to sneak out to the grocery store, but now reporters from the *Sweetwater Herald* are camped outside along with the pilgrims. I'm glaring at them from the carcass room surrounded by stuffed bison and elk heads. An entire bear hovering in the corner. A musket hanging over the mantel, which I would love to aim at the press, because someone (a meddlesome priest from Baaston, perhaps?) spilled the baked beans about the Vatican's interest.

(Miss Ferrari! Just a sentence or two for the eleven o'clock news!)

They're using bullhorns now?

(Garnet Ferrari! Is it true you can cure shingles?)

(And conjunctivitis?)

(She can-a! I see it with-a my own eyes!)

(Nonna! What are you doing down there? Don't talk to them! On second thought, talk to them! She's the real healer, people. It's not me!)

(It's a-no true! She is the descendant of Santa Garnet del Vulcano. My granddaughter. Mine! Just look at-a her face!)

This is ridiculous. All I want is my Ding Dongs, and now —

(Pop! Pop! Pop!)

—shit! The light bulbs in the lamps just blew, all of them. I have to fumble around in the dark. Ow! Fucking humidor. CAN YOU STILL HEAR ME? I'M JUST . . . LOOKING IN THE CLOSET . . . FOR THE BOX OF BULBS I KEEP IN EVERY ROOM. JUST HAVE TO — OW! FUCKING HUMIDOR! Okay. Hang on a sec. There. Much better. I am so tired of burned-out light bulbs. I go through two dozen bulbs a month. I know, I know, impossible for you, maybe, but not for me.

Padre, I guess now's the time to tell you something, but please don't take it as a mark of sainthood. Though it's admittedly weird, it's not under my control, and it certainly hasn't healed anyone. It's yet more evidence that somewhere a *jettatura* is zapping a Garnet voodoo doll with jumper cables.

My initial run-in with electricity began after that First Communion when I stuffed under the bed not only my veil but all the miracle-worker lore that went with it. I couldn't heal Pippa Fabrini; I couldn't cure myself; I couldn't even heat up a stinking piece of steak. Whenever Nonna or Dee Dee or some other hopeful child tried to resurrect the legend, I'd plug my fingers in my ears and run away screaming. I lodged my supposed powers deep behind my pancreas and hoped that everyone would just forget about that made-up chapter of my life. Still, I couldn't deny that there had been healings, and that's when I realized that Nonna had been beside me for every successful cure. The next time I saw her, she was shelling peas on her front-porch swing.

I sat beside her and whispered, "Are you the real healer?" It felt blasphemous to challenge the fable she had concocted just for me.

"No!" Nonna's body quivered so violently that several peas spilled from the bowl, rolled across the slanted porch, and bounced down the front steps. "Why you say such a thing! *You* are the healer. No deny this-a gift or bad things-a will come!" She crossed herself three times and I caught movement next door: Celeste Xaviero crossing herself at her kitchen window too.

I knew better than to confront Nonna again, so from then on I watched from a distance whenever she hugged an ailing Saint Brigid girl or smooched some hill boy's scraped elbow or squeezed a napkin around her nicked finger. She didn't heal those kids or herself, but I knew she somehow fit into the miracle puzzle, a mystery I haven't solved but that I'm hoping you will.

I continued to wear my Saint Garnet necklace, however, because I couldn't shake the Old Religion belief that bad things would happen if I wasn't protected, especially since someone continued to fiddle with my geography while I slept, atolls emerging, coastlines retracting. Plus I still loved the idea of Jesus lulling Himself to sleep every night with tufts of my hair clenched in His hands.

When I was eight I sat on a stool in the kitchen archway clutching that necklace. I was watching Dad prepare to paint the living room, dragging furniture to the center of the carpet to drape with a paint-splattered canvas.

Though I was sitting right there, another splattered mass, Dad hollered, "Nicky!"

My brother was in his room memorizing *Webster's* letter-Q entries. Later I would rifle through his notebooks to see what sentences he had crafted to practice vocabulary. *Garnet is a quidnunc who better stop snooping or she'll suffer quid pro quo while she is quiescent.* My brother liked polysyllabic words, but I think he was also searching for the term to describe what was secretly happening to him that made him cower behind chairs and prattle factoids.

"Nicky!" Dad hollered again.

"What!"

"Get my flathead screwdriver!"

Nicky thumped down the hall, squeezed by me—"Look out"—and went downstairs to the garage. Soon he edged past me again—"Will you move!"—and handed Dad the tool. Nicky was about to dart back to his room when Dad said, "Wait a minute, son. I want to show you something."

Nicky rolled his eyes as Dad unscrewed the wall plates covering the electrical outlets above the baseboard and stacked them one by one in Nicky's palm. My brother eyed them as if they were a deck of turds.

"Set them on the kitchen table," Dad said. "Wait! Here are the screws." Dad was trying desperately to begin Nicky's apprenticeship as a jack-of-all-trades. My brother was a reluctant pupil. He slopped the rectangles on the table and they fanned out like playing cards, screws scrolling figure eights across the Formica before clinking onto the linoleum. I slid off my stool to gather them up, to show Dad who was the more attentive student. But when I looked for Dad's approving gaze, he was hunkered on the floor, his back to me, Nicky crouched by his side, both staring at a spot on the wall.

"Understand?" Dad said at the end of his private homily.

"Yeah. Can I go?"

Dad looked as if he just couldn't understand how the fruit of his loins could be so uninterested in home repair. "Yes."

Nicky went to his room as Dad began edging masking tape around the windows.

I was about to go remeasure Pluto on the solar system on my wrist. I always rooted for Pluto, that tiniest of planets, farthest from the sun and often overshadowed by its siblings.

Dad halted my retreat. "Garnet, go get my radio."

"Okay!" I ran to the basement, unplugged the radio, and brought it back up, the cord dragging behind me all the way to the living room. Dad was gone, but this was my chance to show him that I was in tune with his needs. I would plug it in and turn the dial until I recognized the downhearted sighs of Billie Holiday or Sarah Vaughan. I looked for an outlet and there it was, that naked box without a plate, wires twisted up inside. The hole Dad and Nicky were bent over not long before, Dad trying to impart his secrets about the power of electricity.

It was mesmerizing, those snaky wires coated in a web of frayed fabric, copper wires poking through here and there. I wanted to know the mystery behind those wires that enticed Dad to dismantle and reassemble lamps. There was power here, running through the walls, and I caught a hint of Dad's passion to maintain the inner workings of this house. His fascination with plumbing; his dutiful crack plastering. He was an attendant, an altar boy to a priest. I was kneeling before a portal to that private world of studs and insulation that few ever saw. I wanted a glimpse of the mystery, and that's why I jammed my finger into the wall socket that day.

I didn't see the mystery, but I felt it. A *bzzzzzz* that shot through my finger-hand-arm. I shuddered for what felt like hours but was only seconds until I pulled my finger out and ended the torture. I fell back on my bum, stunned, looking at my finger, which amazingly looked none the worse for the injury. I didn't cry as I stared at that exposed outlet with a new reverence. There was danger there. That's what Dad was imparting to Nicky just minutes before. I felt a second jolt that came with the question, Why hadn't Dad warned me?

That night another mystery surfaced. As I sat down for supper, Nicky reinforced Buttholia with an aggressive punch as retaliation for my Q snooping. Usually I suffered his blows in silence, but this time as I stewed, the bulbs in the wagon-wheel ceiling light began to flicker, and the socket Mom's mixer was plugged into went kablooey. Dad rushed to the fuse box, but nothing was amiss, so he blamed it on an external power surge.

Hours later while I was brushing my teeth, Nicky burst in without knocking and muscled me out the door, my mouth full of toothpaste glub. "I hab to spit," I garbled, pummeling the locked door.

"Swallow it, spaz."

Froth spilled from my mouth and splattered my new cowgirl pajamas. I growled and suddenly the slice of light beneath the door vanished as Nicky bawled, "Hey!"

Four months later my inner current sparked again. One Saturday before Christmas, Mom and I were in the kitchen squeezing out Spritz cookies. "You are such a good helper, Garnet." She kissed the top of my head. "You are my best-best, perfect-perfect girl." As I decorated angels and stars I felt someone watching and discovered Nicky peeping in from the hall. He wore the exact same expression I must have worn the Palm Sunday I saw my father beam over him in the Saint Brigid narthex.

Hours later I found Nicky sitting behind a wingback describing the parts of the Colt .45, because Uncle Dom, Aunt Betty, and Cousin Ray-Ray were on their way over for supper.

I wedged in beside him, something I'd never attempted before, and for some reason he let me. I took a deep breath. "You know she loves you."

He snorted, then pressed his forehead into the chair back. "How do you know?"

I didn't have any answer except the obvious one. "Because you're so beautiful."

Nicky cringed, as if being pretty wasn't enough, or maybe it was too much, especially for a boy. He opened his mouth, but car doors slammed outside, and the color drained from his face.

Uncle Dom barged in without knocking. "When are you going to move out of this dump? If Marina were my wife I wouldn't lock her up in this mole hole." He handed off his hat and coat to Betty, and then he and Dad sat at the kitchen table to conduct the business that always occurred before these meals. Uncle Dom pulled out the passbook for the college-savings account he'd set up for my brother. It was Grandpa Ferrari's directive, since "There's-a no way Angelo could afford it, and this boy has brains. Real brains!"

Dad swallowed his pride at these sessions, which wasn't easy with Mom watching her son's future being secured by a man who wasn't his father. For once Uncle Dom wasn't braggarty, and that night as Dad again mumbled his appreciation, Dom patted Dad's shoulder, saying, "It's okay, little brother. I'm happy to do it," though I noticed he was looking at Mom.

Afterward he pulled out the novels he'd brought for her. Soon Mom and Uncle Dom dove into a heady discussion, leaving Dad to mix drinks and Betty to apply lipstick.

Betty was not stupid; she could talk carburetors and expressed strong opinions about Chairman Mao and the recent death of Pius XII (Nonna was inconsolable—as devastated as Betty would be in a few months when Buddy Holly died), but she was not the intellectual equal of Mom, who had that one Wellesley year tucked under her belt.

Aunt Betty sat at the table, Nicky and I beside her; she tapped a Lucky Strike out of the pack and then waited for someone, my father, as it turned out, to light it. She and Dad traded chitchat, though both of them were more interested in their spouses engrossed in a discourse that might as well have been in Urdu. I had seen these blather-fests, but until that night I'd never noticed the look in the left-out spouses' eyes. Dad watched Mom, not only her lips, which he hadn't sampled in months, but her hands. It was as if someone had zapped her with five hundred volts. Her fingers jabbed Dom's shoulder as she argued about why *Lolita* was pubescent male-fantasy fluff. Uncle Dom was enraged but in an overcharged-battery kind of way.

That night in the kitchen I understood that Mom and Uncle Dom were flirting. As smarmy and offensive as Dom could be, he offered Mom cerebral stimulation that my father could not, especially since my public spanking, after which Dad stood barely five feet. That meant he could easily fit on the army cot he'd set up in the basement, where he slept more and more often, not with winemaking paraphernalia but with his beloved saw.

Dad poured the equivalent of a bucket of cold water on them. "Dom, did you bring the capocollo?"

Uncle Dom barked, "Ray-Ray! Did you bring in the capocollo?"

It's not that I'd forgotten about Ray-Ray; it's just that he always hovered in shadows around adults, a slag heap of quietude.

When Dom's voice boomed, I leaned back in my chair and looked at Ray-Ray over by the front door, cringing. He had forgotten his duty, but before Uncle Dom could rail further, Ray-Ray went outside to retrieve the meat.

Capocollo. Head and butt. The most disgusting Italian concoction in history. Though I have no idea what goes into it, Nicky and I made uneducated guesses: pig brains and slick intestines, snooty snout drool and hiney holes. I never let that stuff touch my lips, but as soon as Ray-Ray reappeared, Dad grabbed it and arranged the chapel-veil-thin slices on a tray already laden with eye-stinging cheese. Dad centered the platter on the table and everyone gathered around it, including Ray-Ray; he squeezed his chair between me and Nicky, who started naming Civil War battles.

Adult conversation turned to politics, specifically the conflicts over Vietnam that had begun tiptoeing into our news. I squirmed with boredom, since that particular land sliver had not even distinguished itself on the Indochinese peninsula on my right hip.

Mom served dry pot roast, and Ray-Ray hacked at it with his knife, his elbows ramming into my shoulder. He used these tactics to take potshots at Nicky and me when we were in front of our parents. Once they were out of sight his strategies became overt. The previous time he'd visited, Mom sent Nicky and me down to O'Grady's for a loaf of bread. Of course Ray-Ray had to come. We started our descent, Nicky and I shoulder to shoulder to create a sparse phalanx of two.

"God, you all live in a dump," Ray-Ray had said, shoplifted words that had no sting. He picked up a stick and waved it in our faces, trying to get us to flinch. We did not flinch, which irritated him, and soon he swatted the backs of our legs, our butts. Then he managed to poke the stick between Nicky's knees, grab both ends, and yank up as hard as he could, lifting Nicky a foot off the ground. Nicky screamed and when Ray-Ray let go, Nicky collapsed on a sewer grate and curled into a fetal ball, hands covering his crotch, but he managed to sputter, "King Tutankhamen became pharaoh when he was only nine years old!"

Ray-Ray stood over him, laughing. "That'll show you who's boss." I had the feeling he'd filched those words too. Then he reached his hand toward Nicky. "I'm just messing with ya." Nicky looked as confused as I was, but he let Ray-Ray help him up. Ray-Ray draped his arm over Nicky's shoulder and suddenly they were the phalanx of two trudging down the hill, leaving me the tagalong little sister.

Now it was December and Ray-Ray was back at our table mauling Mom's pot roast, ramming his elbows into my side. "Quit. Humming!" After supper Nicky sprinted down the hall to his books. Ray-Ray rolled out of his seat to follow and I brought up the rear, but as soon as Ray-Ray entered Nicky's room he slammed the door in my face. "Beat it, stain-ass!"

I went to my room as dishes were piled in the sink to make room for the poker game that always followed these meals.

In the morning I found cigarette butts floating in scotch glasses; poker chips in the French onion dip. Nicky and I usually scoured the detritus for leftover coins from the ante, and today I saw there were plenty. Nicky was still asleep, so I padded to his room, eased open his door, and saw him swaddled mummy-like in his blanket.

"Nicky," I whispered.

No response.

"Nicky!"

"A scorpion's venom paralyzes its predators!"

"There's over two dollars in change in the kitchen."

"Get the hell out!"

I backed away, stung.

Half an hour later I was counting loot at the table when Nicky finally emerged, blanket wrapped around him like a toga. I thought he was aiming for a cereal bowl, but he opened the medicine cabinet, pulled down the Alka-Seltzer, filled a glass with water, plopped in two tablets, and watched them fizz.

"Too much capocollo?"

If Nicky heard me, he didn't let on. I wondered if Ray-Ray had smuggled Uncle Dom's scotch into Nicky's room last night.

Mom emerged to make coffee, and Dad shuffled up from the basement, hair mussed, wearing the same clothes he had had on the previous night. He glanced at the curled, dried-up edges of capocollo and stifled a gag.

"Why do they always have to stay so late?" Mom scraped stiff pot roast and gelatinous gravy into an empty milk carton.

"You didn't seem to mind last night. *Have another scotch, Dommy.*"

"I was just playing my role. Isn't that why you married me?"

I leaned forward because I really wanted to hear the answer to that. Of course there was no answer, because Dad didn't know how to fight.

Mom jabbed him again. "Then let's talk about you and—"

"Don't be ridiculous."

You and who? I wanted to press.

Dad poured himself coffee and went back to his army cot, where he moaned and farted and burped for the rest of the day.

Later that night Annette Funicello came calling. It wasn't *Beach Party* Annette but Maureen Pasquali, who looked so much like my favorite Mouseketeer with her inky hair and perky disposition. This Annette lived next door with her daughter, Mary Ellen, a four-year-old with black ringlets and dimples for knuckles. Jake, Annette's husband, was a traveling salesman who sold prosthetic limbs. Rumor had it that fake arms and legs dangled from the rafters in his garage, which was windowless, so confirmation was difficult.

Annette had officially skipped into our lives a couple of years before. I was on the sofa fretting over South Africa. Once the lightest country on my thigh, overnight it had turned as dark as the protective chestnuts Nonna kept on her windowsills. I was rubbing an ankh over it as a safeguard against whoever was toying with me when someone rapped on the door. *"Jettatura!"* I yelled, certain that it was some old crone coming to appraise her handiwork. I froze, but the pummeling persisted, and Dad yelled from the basement: "Someone answer that!" I summoned the courage and when I opened the door, there stood Annette, eyes bouncing around my landmasses as if I were a pinball game. She swallowed her alarm along with her gum. "Is your daddy home?"

"My dad?" I would have expected her to ask for a cup of sugar. Maybe an egg.

"I have a plumbing problem and talk on the hill is that he's the man when it comes to home repairs."

My father had been dubbed top handyman? In his world there was no greater honor.

"Just a minute." I turned around and hollered, "Dad!"

Footsteps pounded up from the basement, and when Dad saw who was requesting his presence, he tucked in his shirt and fluffed up his pompadour. "Well, come in. Come in."

Annette declined, saying the baby was by herself, and described the leaking catastrophe in her bathroom. "Jake is all thumbs even when he is home."

Dad said, "I can take a look at it if you like."

"I was hoping you'd say that." And out they went.

After that, Dad spent as much time tending to Annette's abode as ours. The rewards were homemade pies and brownies, offerings Dad carted home as carefully as he might the sacred Eucharist. Mom never touched them.

The night of Dad's poker-party hangover, the telephone rang. Mom answered the wall phone in the kitchen. Her mouth puckered; she let the receiver drop, and it dangled on its yellow cord as she yelled downstairs, "Angelo! It's for you."

"Who is it?"

"Guess." Mom stomped down the hall and I could hear her lifting the sewing machine out of the table model set up in one corner of her room. Whenever Mom's brain was too frenzied to settle on a book or pen *poetry*, she worked on the living room drapes she'd been stitching for years.

Dad rushed upstairs and scooped up the phone. "Hello? Well, hi there. Sure, I can take a look at it if you like."

Ten minutes later, clothes changed, hair combed, he dashed out the door with his toolbox, and this time I clandestinely followed. I wanted to see what Dad and Annette were up to, plus I was hoping to get a peek of a battalion of wooden arms and legs inside Jake's garage.

I crept up Annette's front steps and cupped my hands around my eyes to look inside her storm door. Dad and Annette stood in the dining room and I could hear her high-pitched chirp. Dad laughed too, especially when she rested her hand on his forearm. Then baby Mary Ellen bounced in. Annette's hand still rested on my father's forearm, an innocent-looking gesture that gained significance when she turned and headed into her kitchen, dragging her finger down his wrist, then the back of his hand, and finally leaving a small gap between their fingertips, like the painting of God creating Adam in the Sistine Chapel.

Dad flipped open his toolbox, which was sitting on the table, reached for a screwdriver, and turned to look down at a wall socket. He knelt before the altar of electricity, and I wondered if he was going to call over his shoulder for Nicky to come and hold the plate and screws, the paten and hosts. He didn't have the chance because Mary Ellen bounded to him, apple slice in her hand. I expected him to call for Annette to come and fetch her girl child, but he just looked at Mary Ellen's dimpled knuckles, her unstained face, and proceeded to dismantle the outlet. He slid the rectangle into her palm. The screw he slid into his shirt pocket. My father tucked his finger under Mary Ellen's chin to make sure she was watching. Boy, was she ever, as he pointed to the exposed wall socket and then wagged his finger in the universal gesture meaning *Don't touch!* Mary Ellen mimicked him, wagging her finger, shaking her head. She was a quick learner.

It was a betrayal far worse than I could have imagined. Heat rushed through me from my toes to my scalp. A boiling wave flashed across my face as I gritted my teeth and suddenly sparks flew from that exposed box. Mary Ellen hid behind my father and squealed just as Annette's porch light exploded overhead; pieces of the shattered bulb rained all over me. I bolted down the porch steps completely oblivious to the Captain Hook arms and pirate peg legs and raced home clutching my chest, where a certain box had also exploded.

Inside, Mom was still in her room wasting thread and time on a ridiculous pair of drapes that she hoped would somehow make her house a home. "Is that you, Angelo?"

"It's me," I answered in a voice even I didn't recognize.

I ran to my room, table lamps and ceiling lights surging in my wake. I dove for my bed and pulled the covers over my head. Though I tried to stopper them, tears slid as the hum of Mom's sewing machine abruptly stopped, its power supply mysteriously cut, and I was glad.

SANCTUS INTERRUPTUS, UNUS

(Go ahead, Mother Ferrari. Say something.)

(It's-a on?)

(I pressed the Record button.)

(I speech-a now?)

(Yes, but hurry up, Mother. Holy moly. Garnet will be back any minute.)

(Okay-okay. Hold-a your horses [you evil-eye snake].)

(What's that, Mother?)

(Nulla, nulla, but you go now. I need private time in my Barkyloungy with the holy man.)

(Oh! Of course! I'll be in the solarium, Mother. Just call when you're finished.)

(Okeydokey. Bye-bye a-now [you key-eyed wicked a-witch].)

So here goes, Padre, and I hope it still counts if I sit in-a my chair. My feet are a-swoll up like salamis. So many stairs in this house. I keep asking Garney to get the elevator a-fix, but she no want any more workers in-a here. They keep snapping her picture and steal-a the silver.

Now we begin-a for sure:

In nomine Patris, et Filii, et Spiritus Sancti.

Bless-a me, Padre, for I have-a sin. It's been a long-a time since I make-a confess. I have been a bad *suocera*, uh, mamma-in-law. I harbor ill will in my heart for Walleye Betty. I pray so hard to have it remove, but it's still there, like a nail in-a my lung. I never ask for such a daughter-in-law. Yesterday I tole-a her there was no more Mallo Cups, but I hid the last one in-a my purse. Why she need the last Mallo Cup when she bring-a so much misery into our fam-i-ly with her *jettatura* jealousy and her—well, I no speech about all that-a now. Garney will tell you better than-a me.

I also must-a confess to easy-drop on Garney when she make-a her tapes. I no understand why she deny her gift, but now I'm-a gonna set the record straight. It is-a *not* me performing the *miracoli*. Okay, so maybe some funny things happen when I was-a growing up, but I never make-a the freckles or eye sties disappear like Garney do. Never. But here's some of-a the strangeness that happen to me if it help-a the cause.

Maybe you already know that my father was a poor goat herder who lived in the Nebrodi Mountains. When I was a bambina my mamma would put me in one of the goat pens to keep-a me safe while she do her chores. I keep her company with-a my humming, matching the sound I hear since-a birth that no one else seem to hear. I would dig-a the holes just like our little dog, and with every scoop, out pop the seashells. Mamma saw this and marveled, not only because we lived on a mountain but because when she and Papà dig-a the holes they only getta the dirt. Mamma say it's a sign of-a something, but she never say a sign of-a what.

My *papà* work-a so hard to keep food on our table, and I work right-a beside him since I was his only child even if, as he say, I was only a girl. My mother make magic when she cook since she know so many ways to prepare the goat, *stambecco brasato* still-a my favorite. When I'm just a girl Papà ask me to help him plant an almond tree as a surprise for Mamma. He hand me a shovel and when I jab in the blade, this time instead of seashells, the ground start-a to bleed. I drop the shovel and scream and Papà kneel and put his finger in-a the puddle to taste it, but I no think that's such a good idea. He look at-a me and say, "It taste like the red water of Lake Pergusa!" He would know since he make the trip to Siena when he was a boy to see that bloody water for himself. Again Mamma say it's a sign of-a something, but she never say a sign of-a what.

I also hear Garney tell-a you about the light bulbs she make-a go *pop-pop-pop*, but I tell you the truth, some of it's-a my fault. In Sicilia I also have the bad time with electric. I remember the night when I was-a twelve and all the people in Sughero gather at the center piazza at dusk to watch the mayor screw the first light bulb into the first street lamp. Everyone ooo and ahhh like it's a *miracolo*, even thirteen-year-old Angelo Ferrari, the boy who I—oh,

I guess I need to tell-a you about him, but it's-a no easy for me to speech about this. I never even tell this to my parish-a priest. But you are holier since you are the archbishop, so I trust you will keep-a my secret, except from God. It's okay now if you tell this-a to Him.

Our landlords, the Ciaffagliones, lived next door to us in the big-a house and they owned the finest vineyard for miles which produce Orgoglio della Sicilia, the best of Sicilia grapes which make-a the best-best wine. Signore Ciaffaglione was not-a so sweet as his grapes, however. We rent-a not only the land from him but the little falling-down house, which was just a stone's throw from the main one. My father had to give Ciaffaglione all our best-best goats, plus make sure the stone wall that kept our goats from the vineyard was always in-a good repair or we might get a stone through the window that conk one of us on-a the head.

Maybe it's because Signore Ciaffaglione was so bitter that he could produce-a no children. During harvest time he hired all his male relatives, including the two sons of Signora Ciaffaglione's sister who lived across the Strait of Messina in Villa San Giovanni: Dominick (the oldest) and Angelo Ferrari. The first time I met the brothers was the day Mamma take me to the strait for our weekly trading. I see the blue boat that brings the boys to Sicilia, and as soon as they disembark, Dominick rush up like he knows me all his-a life. He reach for my hair though we are just kids and said, "The Pining Nereid!" I think he's cuckoo for sure, even more because over the years I see he has it in-a his head that when-a we grow up we are destined to marry. I no understand where this *fantasia* came from. I never gave him any special favors, especially since he hated Sicilia, my beloved homeland, where he kicked the dirt and spit curses as if the soil had stolen his favorite sling-a-shot or his newsie cap that he wore even a-then. He hated picking the Orgoglio della Sicilia grapes, which, according to him, were no match to the Gaglioppo grapes from Calabria that his own-a father grew.

But he no want to live in-a Calabria either. So many times I hear him-a rant, "As soon as I save up enough money I'm going to America where I no have-a to pick the Orgoglio della Sicilia grape-a no more!" More than once he looked at-a me and say, "And you come with-a me, Diamante, and we build a beautiful life!" I know it's-a hard to believe he could say such-a prettiness, but he did, even if I always, always clamped my hands over my ears and ran away screaming, *"Noooo!"* Besides, Dominick lose all his money playing dice with the other pickers, so I don't think he will ever see the Liberty Statue. And double-double besides, my heart-a belong to his brother, Angelo, who was always such a sweet-a boy. He loved Sicilia and picking the grapes and popping them in-a his mouth and I loved watching him do it.

I loved watching Angelo even more when he served as altar boy at church during harvest season even though his brother make-a the big fun. But Angelo loved-a God as much as I did. Even when it was-a no harvest time I was often kneeling in-a that church with the pretty blue ceiling with the clouds painted on. I knew God lived on-a my mountain, in-a my church, even before I could crawl. I think Angelo knew that too because his face beam like an angel when he helped Padre Ponzo serve Communion.

When his work was-a done in the vineyard Angelo would climb up the trellis beside-a my bedroom window and whisper, "Diamante. Let's go make a picnic."

I would quick-quick grab a loaf of-a bread and some goat cheese, a handful of chestnuts, and race outside to our favorite a-spot, which was a flat rock in the woods at the far edge of the property. Someone—not Ciaffaglione, that's-a for sure—had placed a statue of La Vergine Maria in her own grotto on-a the rock. I love-a this statue, especially the braid that spill from Maria's head and dangle all the way to her feet. I remember the first time I see her I run-a my hand through my own hair that never grows more than-a six inches no matter what I do.

I even say to Angelo, "I hope one day my hair grows so long as La Vergine's."

Angelo reach over and touch the piece of my bang that always falls in-a my eyes. "It will. I know it will."

And you know, from that day my hair she grow and grow and I never cut it except for the ends when-a they get all frizzy.

We also love-a this spot because it is surrounded by a patch of wildflowers neither of us had seen-a before. The five-petal blooms smelled of roasted almonds and nutmeg and were the ex-act-a color of the Lake Pergusa blood water. I tell Angelo this and he name the plant Fiore Pergusa. Whenever we make-a the picnic I would inhale the aroma as he told me about life in Calabria, his apprenticeship as a stonemason, a trade both he and Dominick were learning from-a their father. Though Angelo wanted to master the skill that would provide a good-a life, his dream was to own a vineyard and develop a new grape that he would name after me. The day he confessed his heart's desire he asked, "Do you think it will happen?"

I stare into his eyes and could-a see a lush vineyard rolling across his hazel irises. "I do. I have-a the *profezia*. I see it."

I confess. I love-a this boy and his dreams but in a holy and innocent kind-a way. Of course we keep all this a secret from our parents, and especially from Dominick, since if I break-a his heart he might break-a Angelo's arm. I asked Angelo one-a time why he was so devoted to his brother who was-a so mean to everyone but me—at least back-a then. Angelo shook his head and lifted his shirt to show me his bony ribs and skinny-skinny waist.

"You see these bruises?"

I lean in close, but I no see the bruises. "No."

"Exactly. Dominick takes not only his beatings from our father but the ones meant for me too."

I am-a stunned. "Why would he do that?"

"He says that's what older brothers should-a do."

I ponder this thing that makes me look at Dominick different, but not different enough.

So now I get back to the night when our town, she gets the electric. It was the last night of the harvest so Angelo and I stood side by side in the piazza, but not too close since we were in-a public. We watched the mayor and other village officials prop a ladder against the streetlight pole. Mayor climbed up with the bulb in his hand as the brass band, she played. Once he screwed the bulb in and it glowed I was enchanted (but not in the evil-eye way) since it look-a like the bright heat I see bubbling so many times from Mount Etna. Angelo brushed his arm against mine and I felt a different type of electric. He must have felt it too, because he look at me and his eyes are so warm, but just then Dominick appeared with two gelatos in-a his hands. When he saw the sparks bouncing between his brother and me, he drop the gelatos and shove Angelo's shoulder so hard he stumble backwards. I was *furioso,* and that streetlight hum and buzz.

Then Dominick look at-a me. "You!" His face was filled with something, but it wasn't anger, at least I didn't think so until I saw him make-a the fist like he's gonna clock me for sure. But Dominick crack his brother in the jaw so hard Angelo flew five-a feet in the air and crashed into an ox cart.

I open my mouth to yell, my blood boiling like a pot of ragù on-a the stove, but before any words fly from my lips the street lamp blow up. The town is-a thrown into darkness and I hear Dominick's footsteps running away.

Eventually they fix-a the streetlight and string wires all over town. Ciaffaglione got a light bulb dangling from the ceiling in every room of-a his house, but he no put electric in our falling-down house.

The next harvest season the brothers return. Angelo and me continue to wink at each other during Mass and make-a the picnic by La Vergine in her own grotto. Angelo talk about learning to sculpt gargoyle drain spouts and how much money he'd have to save-a to buy the vineyard. This was also when I getta my *seni,* or, how you say it, breasts, and Dominick begin-a to stare at me in a funny way.

One night I'm in-a my bedroom making the sponge bath, so I'm-a strip to the waist, and I feel someone watching. I'm afraid someone has climbed up my trellis to spy, so I slip back on-a my dress. When I look out no one is-a there. Still, I feel the staring eyeballs, so I look over at the Ciaffagliones' house and see in an upstairs window a boy in a newsie cap holding a telescope to his eyes, the ceiling light bulb burning behind him. I hear Dominick calling in the distance, "Why you no love me and let me bury my face in those beautiful pillows!" My face, she boils, and soon that light bulb sputters and *pop!* outta she blows. In-a the distance I hear Dominick cuss. "Son-ama-beetch! I can no wait to move to America where the lights never go out!"

When I turn-a sixteen Mamma finally allow me to hike down to Messina by myself to watch for the boat that bring in the Calabrese harvesters for the season, including my Angelo. I take a blanket to sit on-a the beach so the sun can pink up-a my cheeks. I also like to comb my hair there because the salty air give me the nice-a curls. As I'm-a brushing and brushing I see the blue boat that I know will bring Angelo to me. I get up and run to the water and squint at the men in the bow. I look for Angelo's bushy hair, but I no see it, and I no see it even as the boat comes closer and closer and pulls up to the shore. I watch as the men disembark one-a by one, but there is no Angelo, only Dominick, who is lugging not only his own suitcase but Angelo's. Dominick laughs when he looks at-a me. "Stupid *bastardo* miss-a the boat, so now you're left with only a-me." He try to grab my hand but I yank it away.

"*Cretino* shouldn't be so gullible," one of the other pickers say.

The two men start the long hike up-a the hill, but when Dominick look over his shoulder at-a me, I only huff and stomp off.

I wonder what meanness Dominick do to make his brother miss-a the boat, the whole harvest season, and especially me! My heart sink as I think about having to wait another year to see Angelo. I trudge to the blanket and collapse, crying like the gulls that are hovering over me like kites in-a the wind.

When I can weep-a no more I dab the tears from my cheek with my hair. As I sit there coddling my sadness I stare across the water at Calabria in the distance, hoping that maybe Angelo is standing on-a the beach looking across at me. And then I see something bob in-a the water and I squint to make out if it's a dolphin or albacore or even the Pining Nereid. It looks more like a cantaloupe bobbling, but with arms and legs a-kicking behind as it swim toward shore.

I hold-a my breath and wonder if I should run away, but it's such an odd sight I can no peel my eyes from it. When it reach-a the shore it pulls itself up and I am amazed at the sight of a man climbing from-a the surf! And this man is as beautiful as Michelangelo's *David*. He's bare-chested and the muscles in his arms make-a my heart go thumpety-thump. His wet hair hangs down his neck, his pants clinging to his-a thighs. I feel a little guilty like I'm-a cheating on Angelo, who always was a small boy. But the man walks directly to me, his mouth opening, and out spills, "Diamante! Diamante!"

Then I know who it is. Angelo! Who grew five inches taller since the last harvest season and lay in his muscles that make-a my breath shallow.

I stand up as he gets to me and says, "Your hair has-a gotten so long!" He reach for my curls and I jump into his vineyard eyes. We are like magnets pulling together, but we resist the embrace since the fishmongers are watching. Instead we walk up-a the hill, his damp arm grazing mine, and I love him more than ever, but now also with a longing that is no longer so innocent. So, unlike the version I hear Garney tell-a you, Padre, that is the truth about the day I see a man rising from-a the sea. I no get the knocked up behind a dry-docked fishing boat!

Anyway, that night, even before the men begin to pick-a the grapes, Angelo and I make a picnic beside La Vergine. After we eat, Angelo pulls from his pocket a leather pouch stuffed with more lire than I had ever seen in-a my life. I was-a thinking it's a good thing Dominick didn't find that when he stole his brother's suitcase. Angelo had-a been saving all these years not only from his job as a grape picker but his job as a stonemason, since he'd begun to get paid for that too. He said this was our nest-a egg, and when he turned eighteen he wanted to start his new life with a-me.

"You mean you wanna marry me?"

Angelo reach over and pluck a Pergusa blossom to tuck into my hair. He lean in close to smell the red petals, then take-a my hand into his. "Yes. And we begin to build a big, big *famiglia*."

"Oh, Angelo. Yes-yes-yes! I hope to birth to you many, many sons."

"Daughters!" Angelo said, his eyes smiling so bright. "I want nothing but daughters so I can adore them all!"

I almost cry from the happiness, and I look up to heaven and wonder what I do to deserve such a man.

"I'll ask your father's *permesso* in the morning."

For the first time Angelo take my face in-a his hands and he kissed my mouth, his lips as plump and sweet as the Orgoglio della Sicilia grapes he had been eating for years. My in-a-sides go all wiggly and I nearly swoon from that kiss that is so long and a-deep, until I hear a rustling in the bushes. Angelo and I both look up just in time to see a figure running away, one hand holding on to his newsie cap.

The next morning Angelo no have-a time to ask my father's *permesso,* because during the night someone had torn down a part of our wall stone-a by stone so that every single goat got out and ran to Ciaffagliones' vineyard, where they ate more than half of-a the harvest. The goats' bellies were swollen, but they were still yanking down grape clusters as fast as they could, dashing and darting as we tried to herd-a them back home. It took several hours to round them up and mend-a the fence.

Afterward everyone gathered by the water pump between our house and the Ciaffagliones' so we could-a wash off the sweat and goat stink: my father and mother, Angelo and me, all the other male relatives. Except Dominick and Signore Ciaffaglione, who had-a gone missing a few hours before.

Soon out of the front door of the big house comes Signore and

Dominick. I hold-a my breath because I know my father has to figure a way to pay Ciaffaglione for the damage. My father take-a the deep breath and walk over, Angelo and I following close behind.

Before Signore has the chance to speak, my father remove-a his hat. "Of course I will pay restitution-a, sir."

A little smoke shoot from Ciaffaglione's mouth. "You bet-a you will. But just how do you propose to do it?"

My father stares at the ground because there really is-a no way.

Signore looked my father up and down. "That's what-a I thought. I'm going to have to take all of your goats and put you and your *famiglia* out, since I could rent-a this property for much more than-a you're paying now."

"No!" Mamma cry, though she speech very little in public because of her missing a-teeth.

"But Signore," my father pleaded, "we have no place to go."

"That's not-a my concern. But I am not heartless. Is there no one who has-a the money to pay for this a-loss?"

My father shuffle his a-feet because there was no one for sure.

Dominick looked at me funny and nudged Signore in-a the ribs. Signore brushed him off. "Be patient."

There was this spooky silence without even the sound of a bird until my mother starts-a to cry as she, like me, wonders where we will go.

And then Angelo opens his mouth. "I'll pay, Uncle."

"You?" Signore said as everyone swivel around to see Angelo pull our nest-a egg from his pocket and hold it out.

I wanted to cry at his kindness, but also for our future going up in a-smoke.

Dominick rushed forward and grab-a the pouch from the little brother who is now taller than him and raced back to hand Angelo's hard-earned money to their uncle.

Signore opened the pouch to poke his finger through the coins. Drool spilled from his mouth, but again Dominick jab his uncle in-a the ribs. "I no forget," Signore says. He rifles through the bag and begin to tsk-tsk. He look at-a my father. "This will cover some of-a the loss, but not all. I'm-a still going to have to kick you out of the house and put in new renters who can pay much-much more."

Again Mamma screech, "No!"

Father put his arm around Mamma's shoulder. "Signore Ciaffaglione. Is there nothing we can-a do?"

Signore look at-a me. "Yes. The slate, she be wiped clean if your daughter marries my nephew."

For a second I'm-a confuse and then happy, since I think he means Angelo, but then Angelo yells, "No!" and I understand which-a nephew Signore mean.

I look at Dominick, who can't even look-a me in the eye.

Mamma, she collapses all the way to the ground. "You no take-a my daughter!"

My father also falls to his knees in a-beseech. "Signore. Please. Not-a my only child."

Signore flaps his-a hand as if they are squabbling over a pound of a-cheese. "It make a-no difference to me. Either your daughter or your house."

Mamma's head, she flops down, but my father looks at me with such-a love, my heart nearly splits in two. He opens his-a mouth and I know he's-a gonna say, *Take-a the house.* But really, where they gonna go when they no have-a the money or strength to start over?

Before he can-a speech I say, "I'll do it."

Angelo shrieks, "No!" and falls to his knees, holding my hands in his. "Don't do this-a thing!"

I look into his hazel irises with the vineyard inside. "I have to, Angelo."

Now his head flops down because he knows he would do the same thing for his mamma if he was in-a my shoes.

Then Signore, that son-ama-beetch, reach in-a the pouch and pull out several coins to plunk in Dominick's mean hand. "That should-a pay your way to America, and your new wife's too."

Mamma and Angelo melt into puddles on the ground.

Two days later I'm-a standing before Padre Ponzo facing Dominick, who I hardly recognize because he's-a scrubbed so clean and wearing a new suit, but no cap. As Padre make us repeat the wedding vows I confess that in-a my head I swap Dominick's name for Angelo's. I even close my eyes and pretend it's Angelo sealing my lips with a kiss, looping his arm-a through mine to walk out of-a the church.

But on the way to the boat I remember whose arm is-a claiming me and I start to cry when we walk up the gang-a-plank onto the boat that will bring me and Dominick to America. It was dusk when-a we set sail; the street lamps' glow bounce off the *famiglie* on the dock who wave-a bye-bye from the shore to their kin they will never see again, and I see my parents and my Angelo, who is crying a waterfall. Then I'm a-weeping too, the tears filming my eyes so I no see so good, the street lamps going fuzzy and I hear them crackling even from the boat until they dim and fizzle out one-a by one.

For two weeks in the steerage I chant Angelo's name over and over like a rosary so Dominick no try to sleep with-a me. He let me have our only blanket and every day after he went up on deck he'd come back with some gift: a hard-boiled egg, a bar of-a soap, a satin ribbon. But then came the night when he got under the blanket with-a me and I know what he want. He even wrap his arm around me and make-a confess I never expected to hear. "Diamante. I have been in-a love with you since the first time I see your red-a hair." He run his fingers over my head and pretend not to see me wince. "This is the only way I know how to make-a you my wife. I promise to give you a good life and be a good-a husband."

Then he reach to tug up-a my nightgown, but I can't do it, and I can't do it, because all I see is his brother's face. "Angelo! Oh, Angelo!"

That's when Dominick clamped his hand over my mouth and chanted his own rosary into my ear. "It's Dominick. Dominick-

Dominick-Dominick-Dominick!" he say over and over as he takes from me that thing I was saving for Angelo.

Later that night I stand on the ship's deck and consider the choice-a before me: jump into the ocean and let it swallow me or make a life with Dominick until the day my real husband and I could be reunited. I looked at the waves for an answer and suddenly a school of dolphins rise from the water and swim right below me beside-a the boat. They chirp and whistle but I no understand why they are so happy when I am-a so, so sad. As I watch them breach over and over I see something bright in the middle of-a the pod, a giant silver fishtail glinting in the moonlight, the Pining Nereid swimming with the dolphins offering me safe-a passage across the Atlantic. I no see her arms or a-head because of the blackness, but in-a my heart I'm sure it is the creature who turned half into a fish to survive. Then I know what I have to do: turn into a dutiful wife so I can-a survive this marriage. From that moment on, for the rest of the voyage and then when we land in New York, whenever Dominick wanna sleep with-a me, I close my eyes and pretend it's Angelo's hand on the small of-a my back. It's Angelo's lips on that spot on my neck that make-a me crazy. It's Angelo's lunch I fix and laundry I scrub, and eventually my secret life is not-a so bad, since Dominick thinks I'm doing all of this-a for him. But in-a my head I am hiding inside the shell of a dutiful wife, and it is Angelo wearing his brother's a-skin.

Over the years, with all that pretending, I forget about my trouble with the electric back in Sicilia until Garney is-a born and then it all comes back and the wiring in-a my house goes kaboom. It drive Dominick crazy since he cannot find-a the source. He rewire mostly the whole house but still can no find-a the prob. Good for me we already had the piped-in gas. After Garney move away from Sweetwater, a dozen years ago, my electric return, and I think that is-a the end of that, but I was-a wrong. Maybe she no tell-a you yet about why she left Sweetwater. I was-a so sad because I know our separation is all-a my fault. My heart hurt so much since from the minute I hold her in-a my arms when she was a bambina, we had a bond that I didn't have with her brother, though he was our male heir and a beautiful one at-a that. But with her, there was that humming in-a our heads. Plus there was something about the way Garney look at a-me that had nothing to do with Saint Garnet or *miracoli*. Whenever I hold her it felt like I was hugging myself, or the sister I always wanted. Impossible, I know, but maybe that was a *miracolo* too.

And here is one-a more thing I must speech about. I hear Garney tell-a you the big fib. She say she no longer make *miracolo* once she get to school, but that is-a no true. I don't know why she lie about this, because many Sundays when I go to Saint Brigida, when Mass-a end, before I even shuffle out, some nonna or mamma would-a pull me aside.

"Nonna Ferrari. Little Carlo is home with the measles. Here's his teddy bear for Garnet to pray over." Or "Baby Linda has the mumps. Here's her favorite blankie." Sometimes they brought the actual child. "Nonna, Carmella has a wart on her finger. Look! Look! Please ask Garnet to pray over a-her."

Who could-a refuse such-a pleading? I would go find Garney and tug her behind the statue of Saint Brigida (the real one). She would take the stuffed toy or the favorite blanket or the child and hold it in her hands. She burn so hot with a-fever when she perform the *miracolo* that it runs up-a my arm too. The healing no happen right then. It take a few hours, maybe a day.

Okay, so to confess all of-a the truth, not everyone believe in her. We get the snub from some *famiglie* who think she make it all up, but who need-a them anyway? Garney no make-a this up. I have a-proof from parents of the children she heal who send me letters and thank-you cards with pineapple upside-down cakes or no-bake cookies. Some send me the pictures to show me the healing, which I send to you now. Look on the back and you see where I write the name of the healed and the date. Sometimes I write-a the ailment, like a-scabies or heat rash, all now gone. Listen as I read this-a one from Mrs. O'Greenie down in the village. It was not easy for her to cross the Saint Brigida aisle and ask for Garney's help, so you know I no make-a the fib.

Dear Nonna Ferrari: Jesus-Mary-and-Joseph bless your family for the healing your granddaughter has brought to our Dickey. Since she prayed over his diapers and ointment his rash has completely disappeared. May your home always be too small to hold all your friends. God is good, but never dance in a small boat.

I no understand the small-boat part, but I think it's a-sound advice. Anyway, why Garney resist her gift I do not know. She could a-heal so many more people if she wanted. She even heal people when she don't even know about it. I tell-a you the truth because I saw it one time with my own-a eyeballs. It was when she was wearing that pillowcase that embarrass her father to no end. I make-a the speech to him, but he no want to hear that his daughter was a *santa*, something I never understood.

There was a little girl who just move-a to Sweetwater and none of the other kids liked her. Her name was Potty, but I think that was a bad name the children called her because she make-a the pee-pee down her leg all the time. Not only did she always smell like the pee, but she pick-a the boogidies. Every time I see her she has a finger rammed up her nose digging for the boogidies. One day she ram the finger in too far I guess and get a bloody nose that drip and drip for months. Her parents were a-poor so they no take her to the doctor, and from then on that kid always had a bloody handkerchief stuck up her nose like a plug. It was a Friday morning when Garney and I walk down the hill to the village for the sausage casings. Little girls follow her like chicks after the mama duck asking her to touch-a the stuffed bunny or torn paper doll. Except for Potty, who leap from bush to bush and squeeze skinny-skinny behind the telephone poles so none of the kids see her and start pelting her with rocks, even Garney, I hate to say, but I saw her do this a few times, and yell, "Snotty Potty! Snotty Potty, go home!"

We reach the bottom of the hill and several village kids surround Garney too, begging for a healing. They all stop and then I see Snotty Potty behind the corner mailbox. She tiptoe over so that nobody see her, and I no make-a the fuss because I think she need the healing more than these toys do, especially since the handkerchief that plug her nose hole had fallen out and blood trickles down her lip. She sees me and starts to run away, but I nod for her to come forward. I even shield-a her with my body as she crawl up behind the crowd and reach her hand between the kids and touch Garney's veil. The minute she stroke it I feel-a the spark and when I look down at Snotty Potty, her nose no bleed-a no more! She look at me and grin and I see her bad teeth, but that no matter because she is one happy little girl who skip away shouting "Wheeeee!" I scoop up Snotty Potty's handkerchief and when I open it, the blood smears look just like-a Mount Etna. I fold it up and tuck it in-a my purse as-a proof. Garney never knew a thing and I hold that secret to my chest until now.

You see? There is too much God working through my grand-daughter, *my* granddaughter, which is why Walleye and me take matters into our own-a hands. We collect Garney's holy rel-ics—especially her toothbrush, so we can pluck out every bris-tle—and dole them out to the pilgrims outside. But no tell-a Garney. It's-a no right for her to keep her holy art to herself.

I will say the rosary for my penance today, Padre, and make a real confess at Saint Brigida's next First Friday. I promise, and you rest a-for sure I would never lie to a archbishop.

Okay, so. Amen.

(*Betty! Come and turn off this-a machine [you green-hearted* jetta-tura *who no deserve the last Mallo Cup].*)

Make-a that two rosaries, Padre. In-a Latin.

Doll versus Doll

Padre:

It's Wednesday afternoon and I'm in the library unpacking the newest *World Book* encyclopedias—a smorgasbord of illustrated knowledge. Nicky would have flipped out over the pictures of the recently unearthed terra-cotta army in Xi'an. I think he wished he could have been protected by a bevy of bodyguards too.

You already know about the ambivalence roiling around Sweetwater regarding me—sainted or stained, especially since I was out of the miracle business—but Nicky also elicited varied sentiments. Hill parents adored him for his beauty, the epitome of everything their russet-tinted offspring were not. School-girls adored him for the same reasons. They hid gifts in his desk: Woody Woodpecker key chains and Pluto (the dog) erasers, candy cigarettes and licorice pipes. The boys, however, despised him. In addition to siphoning away the love of *their* secret crushes, Nicky was a delicately boned, pink-cheeked sweet pea. Plus he had me for a little sister.

If Nicky couldn't hire a clay army, he could stay sequestered in his room soaking up knowledge. By the time he was eleven he had read all of Grandfather Postscript's reference books and had begun badgering Dad to buy him the newest *Britannicas* for Christmas.

"My set is over twenty years old!" Nicky wailed at the dinner table for the tenth night in a row. "It doesn't even mention Hiroshima" (bringing this up was a wise tactic, given our veteran father). "There are gaps in my knowledge. Wide gaps!"

"We just can't afford it," Dad said. It must have been excruciating for him to deny his son. "However," he added, making us all look up as if he were going to pull an erudite rabbit from his hat. "I think we can swing one volume a year. The salesman said you don't even have to buy them in order, so pick any letter you want, Nicky. Even Z."

Mom and I thought it was a brilliant compromise, but Nicky bawled, "One at a time? There are twenty-three volumes; it'll take twenty-three years. Twenty-four if I get the index too. And by then they'll be out of date!"

I understood his urgency; the ratio of kid time to adult time is roughly one kid week for every adult day, which is why Christmas is always so long in coming for kids.

"I want them all now!" His cheeks flushed as he stormed, as much as his lithe frame could storm, down the hall.

Dad's chin sank, but Mom proposed a solution none of us had ever expected to hear. "I suppose I can ask my mother."

Ever since Grandma Iris had tried to kidnap my brother, she had been banned from our home. Mom refused Grandma's phone calls, so she resorted to letters, the first containing a check so obscene that Mom, understanding the strings attached to all those zeros, tore it into pieces. She also refused deliveries of additional home furnishings, though I'm sure waving ta-ta to the window air conditioner was brutal. Sometimes I wanted to shake Mom and say, *What the hell are you thinking?*

Over the years Mom softened a bit, as did Grandma. She stopped sending appliances and started sending reasonable amounts of cash. She probably asked her accountant to calculate the appropriate exchange rate for lower-middle-class birthdays. Like kid time and adult time, currency had to be converted from wealthy to poor.

The night Nicky stomped to his room, Mom made the difficult

phone call to Charlottesville. Of *course* Grandma would buy the *Britannicas*, with one caveat: she wanted to deliver them herself. Remarkably, Mother agreed.

On Christmas Eve Nicky and I gazed out the front window as snowflakes drifted through the streetlights' funneled beams. We were on guard duty, watching not for Santa or even the mighty Christ Child but for Grandma, a woman we didn't remember but whose name prompted shudders from our folks. At the first glint of chrome we yelled, "She's here!" This was followed by a collective tightening of orifices. We watched her sleigh of a Cadillac pull into our steep driveway, tailpipe sparking against the cement. Dad came up from the basement, shoulders slumped inside his work shirt. Mom wore her perpetual skinny pants and sweater set, hair in a ponytail, but more makeup than usual. She and Dad shrugged on their coats and went outside, Nicky and I close on their heels.

Grandma, encased in mink, emerged from the car. "Darling" —she clasped Mom's face in her hands—"I see someone has been neglecting her skin care." Mother picked at her eyebrow as Grandma held her gloved hand toward my father. We expected him to kiss it, but he just gave it a pump. Grandma looked beyond Mom and Dad in search of Nicky. "There he is!" She engulfed him in a furry embrace. Initially he squirmed, but he relaxed as Grandma crooned, "My beautiful, darling boy. My handsome, perfect grandson." If Nonna were there, she would have dowsed us in a *ptt-ptt-ptt* shower. Remarkably, Nicky closed his eyes, perhaps pretending it was Mom.

Eventually Grandma's gaze landed on me and circumnavigated the globe. "It's even worse than I imagined." Mom socked her in the arm. "And there's Garnet," Grandma said, aggrieved at having to look at my face. *Out, damned spot, out!*

When I was younger, and much more gullible, I had asked Mom when she was going to tell Grandma about my sainted lineage. I had pitifully dredged the lore from my pancreas just that morning while Mom scrubbed the scum ring from the tub. "Does she know I'm Saint Garnet?" I fingered the glass locket beneath my shirt. "Does she know I'm special too?" Mom wiped her forearm across her brow. "Garnet, some people will never believe, no matter how many miracles they see."

There was also a time when I thought Grandma might be the *jettatura* toying with my geography, electrifying me, folding her hexes in with her letters, but ultimately I understood that she wouldn't have bothered.

After the awkward niceties, Grandma opened the trunk to reveal a display of gross overindulgence. Presents heaped upon presents, all store-wrapped, back and passenger seats piled high too. I may not have been her primary target, but I would gladly eat scraps from Nicky's table.

It took several trips to unpack the spoils, including a case of vodka. Dad stacked the wrapped boxes of encyclopedias that Nicky still knew nothing about in a corner. Nicky and I tucked the lighter ones around the tree, a sea of commercial gluttony washing aside the few sad presents Mom had placed there days before.

Dad hauled his mother-in-law's suitcases to my room—I would happily take the pullout couch—Mom and Grandma on his heels, Grandma catching glimpses of herself in various mirrors along the way, cautioning Dad, "Careful with that one. Do be careful, dear."

When they headed back to the living room, Grandma was in the lead muttering something about one bathroom for five people being beyond the comprehension of civilized society, and on top of that we were putting her in the *globe* room, of all places. "I might as well be in your father's study, for God's sake."

"You could always go to a hotel," Mom said.

Grandma stopped so abruptly Mom slammed into her, and Dad almost slammed into Mom but managed to ram on the brakes in his work boots.

"Don't be ridiculous," Grandma retorted. "I came all this way to be with my family, and I can certainly put up with a little substand—"

Dad didn't wait for her to finish, just plowed past his mother-in-law, another woman taller than him, and bounded down the basement stairs. He was sawing wood within seconds.

Mom dove for the case of vodka. "I need a drink."

"Make that two!" Grandma eased into the wingback across from the tree. She turned off the table lamp beside her, and she did look pretty with the Christmas tree lights glistening in the diamonds decorating her.

Mother returned carrying two martinis complete with pearl onions.

"Thank you, dear." After Grandma's first sip, the tight scrunch in her face relaxed.

Mother sat in the other wingback and I could see the striking similarities between them: the stunning features, the aristocratic bearing.

Nicky and I lay on the floor as Grandma blabbered about skin specialists and grapefruit diets for me (earning shin kicks from Mom), though I was only mildly pudgy, and a prep school for my brother that would ensure his admission to an Ivy League college. Nicky lifted his head. We all knew Uncle Dom's college fund would buy him only a state education at Vandalia U.

"Nicky is not going away to boarding school," Mom said.

I looked over at Nicky, who scrutinized our humble digs, which no doubt compared poorly to the ones he was conjuring in his head.

That night after brushing my teeth I came out of the bathroom and heard Grandma and Nicky mumbling in his room. I tiptoed forward and saw them standing side by side in front of the mirror over his desk, she flattening his forelock, he trying to appear taller by lifting his heels in a new pair of men's slippers. He was also wearing a pair of pajamas I'd never seen. "One must always look one's best, Nicky, even while sleeping. You never know when a house fire might force you into the street."

The next morning the family gathered in the living room, Mom and Dad on the sofa, Grandma in her wingback. I lost the coin toss so Nicky got to open his presents first. Grandma's gifts to him were eclectic: binoculars, safari hat, microscope, toiletry kit, miniature vault, board games that might subtly direct his career path and social status: Camelot; Monopoly; Finance; Easy Money. The grandest of all were the *Britannicas* and after the first peel of paper he shrieked, "Oh my God! Oh my God! Oh my God!," his voice getting higher and girlier, and I hoped none of the hill boys could hear him. He dove for Grandma. *"Thankyou-thankyouthankyou!"*

Grandma luxuriated in her expensively purchased embrace. Mom and Dad watched stoically, no doubt wondering what the real cost would be.

As Dad and Nicky hauled the books to his room, I unwrapped Grandma's gifts to me, which had a unified theme: Barbie. I had seen hill and village girls playing with that coveted doll during the past several months, but I never understood the fixation. She certainly wasn't on my wish list, since my obsession, as you know, was globes. When I tore the paper from the Barbie, I tried to act pleased.

Grandma leaned forward. "Don't you just love her? I hear all the girls do."

"Sure." I studied the doll's lissome frame, its blond hair and blue eyes oddly familiar.

Next came a two-foot-tall Barbie home in the Greek Revival style, which Grandma Iris had had built. The roof lifted off to reveal a posh interior with a bedroom and walk-in closet with metal rods and tiny hangers. Then a handmade, doll-size Cabriolet Mercedes convertible painted aquamarine with pink interior. There was also an excess of Barbie clothes: tennis outfits and tea dresses, evening gowns and sleepwear, and the crowning glory: a wedding dress complete with lacy gloves, a veil, and a bouquet.

"Oh, put it on her! Put it on her!" Grandma commanded.

I fumbled with the packaging and tried to skin off Barbie's swimsuit. My fingers weren't working fast enough, so Grandma scooted down on the floor and wrenched the doll from me. "Let me, dear."

I obliged and unwrapped my own board games: Sorry and Why.

Mom saw the disappointment oozing from my pores. "Mother, did you remember the—you know?"

Grandma was shoving a wedding glove up Barbie's arm. "What, dear?"

Mom nodded toward me. "You know. The thing I asked you to bring."

"Oh! I thought that was for you, dear. It's right there." She pointed to a square box.

Mom fetched it and handed it to me. "Here, honey."

I unwrapped the best present I received that year: a P. D. Windrem celestial sphere cherry-picked from Grandfather Postscript's collection. Resting on a wooden base was a clear plastic ball with constellations and stars labeled on it in white. In the center of the orb, speared diagonally through with a rod, was the Earth, a small blue ball with white continents. The constellations were printed so they looked correct if one was gazing up at them from Earth. But seen from outside the clear sphere, from God's perspective, the constellations were reversed. It was empowering to feel that omnipotent, to squint through the heavens and find North America on that blue ball, to narrow in on the United States, then West Virginia, and then one sixty-year-old flea booger whom I could flick off without batting an eye.

I took the globe to my room to find the perfect shelf space and soon Mom came in holding a broccoli-shaped present. "I forgot to put this under the tree."

I palpated it mightily before tearing off the paper and unearthing a ten-inch, orange-haired troll doll. Not sleek and leggy, but squat and rubbery, wearing caveman togs, its plastic blue eyes pressed into its face. Like she had with my old Betsy Wetsy, Mom had painted my geography all over its skin, but this doll I just couldn't love.

"Isn't it adorable?" She yanked the thing from me so forcefully a welt formed on the Isle of Lesbos in the crotch between my finger and thumb.

Mom sat on my bed and rubbed the doll's belly, spiraled its hair. "I just couldn't resist."

I left her alone to play with her doll and stood in the hall watching Grandma in the living room playing with hers. I also eyeballed the gross discrepancy between Nicky's loot and mine. If only I had been gifted the binoculars and safari hat so I could gallivant around Snakebite Woods, a plot of undeveloped forest on the backside of Dagowop Hill where truant boys hid to chug beer and smoke cigarettes. Nicky had warned me countless times never to go there, but that only intensified my curiosity.

After breakfast Dad hustled to the basement with the bottle of port and pricey cigars Grandma had gifted him. Mom's present was too large for Grandma to bring, so it was being delivered later that day.

"Who would make a delivery on Christmas?" Nicky asked.

"Anyone will do anything for the right price." Lesson number one Grandma wanted to impart while she had the chance.

Mom started to clear the table. "I hope you didn't overdo it, Zelda," a nickname I wouldn't understand until a high-school literature class.

Grandma walked up behind Mom and pulled her shoulders back. "Do watch your posture, dear."

Nicky paraded to his room to OD on rote memorization, and while Mom washed dishes, Zelda unpackaged Barbie clothes to hang in the dollhouse now set up on the kitchen table. I pretended to help by rearranging Barbie's living room furniture in the same configuration as ours. I was also using the opportunity to probe Zelda about Grandfather Postscript, a shadowy figure because Mom rarely spoke of him. Over the years, Nicky and I had pummeled her with questions about our book and globe benefactor, but whenever she tried to relay her fond memories (the time he took her to the horse track, or V-E Day, when he gave her her first taste of champagne), her eyes would tear up and she'd race to her room to compose more odd poems: *Fly high, Flyman, softer land-*

ings await. At that point all I knew about Grandfather was that his marriage to Grandma was scandalous because of their age difference—he being five years younger—and because he was unmoneyed, a far more grievous offense. He died at age thirty-nine under mysterious circumstances. Sometimes Mom said it was a train accident; other times it was drowning or heart failure.

The only photo I'd seen of him was a grainy black-and-white Mom kept on her bedside table. Grandfather was handsome in his three-piece suit with a high stiff collar. A bowler hat was cockeyed on his head. One foot was propped on a stack of books. His right hand was shoved in a trouser pocket and his left held the Abel-Klinger globe Mother had been looking at before she birthed me. He looked directly at the camera, one side of his mouth curved up into a dimpled grin. He looked fun, making it difficult to imagine him selecting Zelda as his bride. It also made me wonder if, like Mom, Grandma had had her own wild-oats tantrum by marrying beneath her station. I imagined her doing the Charleston in a beaded dress with Grandfather at a speakeasy before the cops burst in and dragged them off in the paddy wagon, she and Grandpa laughing at the hilarity of it all. How I wanted this romantic fable to be true.

"Marina, didn't you used to have this dress?" Zelda held up Barbie, now squeezed into a strapless silver gown with a bottom that fanned out like a fishtail.

Mom glanced over her shoulder. "Mine was a tad larger."

Barbie looked so much like the Pining Nereid Nonna had always told me about that I wanted to yank her from Grandma's hands, hurl her into Mom's dishwater, and see if she would sink or swim.

Because the moment felt right I sputtered the question I'd been working up the courage to ask. "What did Grandpa do?"

It was a grown-up query I picked up from Uncle Dom. Whenever he met a person, that was the first thing he asked. *What do you do for a living?* Or if it was a woman: *What does your husband do?* The answer would prompt a respectful head nod for doctors and lawyers, a shake of disdain for pipe fitters and gas-station attendants.

"He lived well," Zelda said.

I did not understand her answer. "But what did he *do*?"

"He was a professional dreamer," Zelda said. "And spender," she added, an odd comment, since I thought that was her job.

Mom scrubbed hash-brown crust from a pan. "He was a poet."

"He was?" I blurted, thinking, *Aha!*

"Pah," Grandma said. "He was no Tennyson."

"Perhaps if he'd had the right muse —"

"He found plenty of inspiration in starlets' dressing rooms."

Mom spun around from the sink. "*And* he was a philanthropist."

Grandma snorted. "He certainly gave a lot of my money away, though I doubt the women he gave it to were in need."

"He certainly gave you what you needed."

Grandma's mouth hung open, exposing several twenty-four-karat crowns. "You should be grateful for that, my dear, or you wouldn't be standing here with your hands in dishwater." At that moment, Dad belched from the basement. "I suppose you got what you wanted as well." She added one more stone to the pile. "I'm going to send you some of my neck cream, Marina. It'll work wonders for those jowls."

Mother's hand flew to her neck. I couldn't see any jowls — she was just thirty-one — but she frowned at her reflection in the kitchen window, pinching and probing her skin with rubber-gloved fingers. Finally she just stared at herself as if she were in a trance. It was at that moment I comprehended the there-she-goes pose I had seen hundreds of times over the years: Mom holding up the shiny base of an iron, a copper-bottomed pot, a steel spatula, and all those damning mirrors. This wasn't vanity.

An hour later I found Mom in her room scribbling in a notebook. *Souls need no finery. Wounds will do.* She tore out the page and taped it beside Zelda's mirror before leaning so close to her reflection that her breath clouded the glass.

At three o'clock the doorbell chimed. Mom's gift had arrived. Dad came up from the basement speckled with sawdust, stinking of cigar smoke and port. Even Nicky emerged from his cave. Zelda appeared with Barbie's mini-Mercedes in her hands.

The doorbell rang again.

"Well, answer it," Zelda said.

Mom chewed her lower lip and complied.

On the porch, blocking our view outside, stood a dapper man in a trench coat, silk scarf tied around his neck.

"Is this the home of Miss Marina Caudhill-Adams-Rutledge—"

"Ferrari," Mom corrected. "I'm Mrs. Angelo Ferrari."

"This is for you." He proffered a chunky envelope that sounded like it was filled with loose change.

"Merry Christmas." He stepped aside to reveal, in our driveway, a full-size Cabriolet Mercedes convertible, aquamarine with pink interior, the top down even though it was thirty-four degrees.

We all looked from the real car to the toy one in Zelda's hands, eyes darting back and forth to make sense of it all.

"Oh my God." Nicky pushed past us to run down the steps. Across the street, drapes ruffled as neighbors looked outside to gawk at this Christmas miracle. For a brief instant I thought this might be the one jewel that could earn Nicky the respect of the hill boys.

"Oh, Zelda," Mom said, and not merrily either. "You know we can't keep it."

"But why?" She looked at my father for support.

"We can't keep it," Dad grumbled, but he, too, was captivated and joined his son for the inspection.

I should tell you that at the time my family did not own a car. Every Monday through Friday Dad trudged down the hill carrying his lunch pail to the Plant. It was cause for ridicule from Grandpa and Uncle Dom, whose cars Dad had to grudgingly borrow on occasion. The price was to endure the ribbing "D'ya bring your groceries up the hill one lima bean at a time?"

Nicky was already behind the wheel as Mom, Zelda, and I made our way down.

"I had it custom painted," Zelda said. "It's not something I can return."

"The car has two seats, Mother."

I hadn't considered that as I scanned the cramped space that held two narrow seats, a substantial gearshift between them.

"But it's perfect for you and Nicky!" Zelda said.

Mom might have slugged her if those neighbors weren't watching.

Nicky twisted knobs as Dad lifted the hood. "That's some engine."

The deliveryman sidled up to him. "She can go one hundred miles per hour."

"Let's go for a ride!" Nicky yelled. "Can we go for a ride?"

Dad looked at Mom and I saw a hint of the gooey eyes that might have appealed to her when they first met.

"Just one ride," Mom conceded. "Then it has to go back."

Dad slammed the hood down as Mom opened the envelope and handed him the keys. He raced to the car door. "Scoot over, son." Nicky hopped awkwardly over the gearshift as Dad started the car. They might have screeched off if Mom hadn't insisted, "Take Garnet too!"

Dad and Nicky eyeballed me, then the available space in the car.

Mom read their minds. "Squeeze her in, for God's sake."

They did, though I had to wedge between them, the gearshift ramming my thigh. Dad's shifting was rough since he drove so seldom, but he managed to back out, tailpipe scraping the ground, Mom yelling, "Button your coats! And don't drive too fast!"

It was frigid, the wind stinging our eyes, but we didn't care as we barreled down Dagowop Hill, Dad honking to draw attention to the absurd display of a top-down joy ride in glacial weather. We spiraled around and around, Dad driving too fast, but he was going to make the most of this. I loved watching his feet work the pedals, his hand on the stick shift, my shoulder bumping into his in a rare moment of closeness.

On the third circle down, we hit No-Brakes Bend, the icy patch in front of Mr. Dagostino's where that natural spring crossed the road. It was a perpetual hazard in winter, for automobiles and foot traffic alike. More than one car had slid over the curb and bumped down the hill into the hedge Mr. Dagostino had planted as a buffer to protect his garage. Those experienced drivers all had sense enough to at least slow down to avoid serious damage. Not my father, however, and when the front of the car started sliding, I held on to the dashboard and gritted my teeth. But Dad smoothly corrected—elevating his driving skills in my estimation—and we were safely on our way, zipping through Sweetwater Village. All the stores were closed, but lights were on in apartments above the pharmacy and grocery and tavern as Irish shopkeepers prepared fourteen different types of Christmas potatoes.

"Where are we going?" I whispered to Nicky as Dad passed Saint Brigid's and Via Doloroso.

I felt my brother's shrug, and when I recognized the stone entrance to Grover Estates, the ball of joy in my gut exploded. Nonna and Grandpa were spending the day with Dom and Betty listening to Caruso on the new console Dom had been bragging about. Though I wanted my Christmas presents from Nonna and Betty, I did not want to spoil this glorious ride by suffering through Grandpa, Uncle Dom, and Ray-Ray.

Dad started honking before we approached Dom's split-level rancher with a two-car garage. He stopped in the middle of the street and let the horn wail.

Ray-Ray appeared at the window, his mouth flapping, and I imagined him saying: *Uncle Angelo is out there in a convertible!*

Dom angled beside him, hands on his hips as he surveyed the improbable spectacle of his little brother in a better car than his.

Betty burst through the door in her maxi-skirt and leopard top, chest bouncing as she rushed to us. "It's beautiful! It's gorgeous!"

Nonna followed, wiping her hands on her apron, grinning. *"Guarda la macchina!"*

"Holy smokes." Ray-Ray loped forward and circled the car before stopping on Nicky's side. He leaned close to Nicky's ear and whispered something I could only partially hear: "The inside's as pink as . . ." followed by an image apparently so foul my brother's body went rigid as he clasped his knees.

Ray-Ray slogged off, cutting between houses instead of going back inside.

"What'd he say?" I asked my brother.

"Anacondas constrict their prey to death before swallowing them whole." The joy ride had been ruined for him.

"Merry Christmas!" Dad yelled to the fam-i-ly, his chin lifted.

Uncle Dom and Grandpa ambled forward, both smirking, loading ammunition into their clabber-jaws to ruin it for Dad.

But Dad jammed in the clutch and revved the engine. "It sure as hell didn't fall off a truck!" He punched the gas and peeled out. I hated leaving Nonna and Betty in our gritty wake, but I loved the streak of rubber Dad laid down that Dom complained about for months.

I hope it was worth it, that fifteen-minute ride and two minutes of gloating, because how was he going to explain himself to the fam-i-ly once the car was gone? I could already hear Dom: *It did fall off a truck,* or, *You could manage only one payment, bucko?*

As soon as the three of us were back up the hill, Mom and Zelda rushed outside, Mom with her hand out to take the keys. "I could hear you honking all the way down in the village!"

Dad said, "You should have heard me in Grover Estates!"

"You didn't." A devilish light flared in her eyes that added an inch to Dad's height. Still, she knew what had to be done. When Nicky got out of the car she put her hand on his shoulder to steady him while she delivered the bad news. "Nicky, we can't keep it. It's too expensive and utterly impractical."

Mom, Dad, and I all held our breath, but Nicky just said, "That's okay."

It was like waiting for that cherry bomb that turned out to be a dud. Whatever Ray-Ray had whispered to Nicky apparently tainted the entire car.

We were about to head inside when Zelda said, "If this one is impractical, how about that one?" She pointed across the street at a line of cars more numerous than usual because of holiday company.

"What?" Mom said.

"The station wagon," Zelda forced out, as if the words were an affront to her luxury-car sensibility. She pointed to a white Dodge Polara, shiny as porcelain, which had been there all day as far as I could remember.

The prissy deliveryman again appeared with another envelope, the prize behind curtain number two if Mom was willing.

"Are you kidding?" Mom said.

"Darling, it's inconceivable that you and Angelo don't have a car. What if one of the children has an emergency and needs to get to the hospital?"

Mom looked at Dad, who amazingly did not look as if his manhood was in question. In fact, he was scratching his chin and walking toward the station wagon, the perfectly reasonable family car, no doubt mapping out his drive to and from work. It would also make things easier with the fam-i-ly when he had to explain the absence of car number one. *It was impractical, Pops. Only two seats. Not to mention the color.*

I looked at Nicky, who tapped his foot and mouthed, *Say yes!*

"It's not even top-of-the-line, dear," Zelda said, her wealthy-to-poor conversion kicking in. "And it holds an awful lot of groceries."

Mom looked at Dad. Dad looked at Mom. Something transpired telepathically between them because Mom said, "Okay."

"Wonderful!" Zelda said. "Let's have a drink!"

Mom walked over to inspect our first car. Dad took her hand as they squinted through the windows and opened the front door. They scooted inside like a couple of teens borrowing the old man's car for a night of necking, which I think might have done them both good.

Zelda handed the deliveryman the keys to the Mercedes, which he would be driving back to Charlottesville that night. "Don't go above the speed limit, Cedrick. And be sure to wash and wax it before you put it in the third bay."

As Zelda sauntered up the steps, Cedrick pulled up the Mercedes's leather top, fastened it in place, and squeezed inside for the cramped ride home.

That night I lay on the sofa listening to Mom and Zelda in the kitchen dissecting the people from Mom's former life. They had cartoon names like Bunny and Bowler, Chompers and Skiff. They yachted and golfed. They sipped champagne in exotic locales.

Barbie's dream house was now beside the Christmas tree where a crèche should have been, Barbie lying in her bed in a shorty nightgown, eyes wide open. In my dream state, I saw a human-size Barbie sitting stiffly in the kitchen as Zelda programmed her life. *Next year I'll bring Ken, darling. We'll have a legitimate wedding with your beautiful gown and a three-foot cake topped with real flowers. I'll buy you a split-level rancher and a car large enough for you and Ken and baby Nicky too!*

TAPE NINE

La Strega

Archie:

It's Sunday morning and I'm lying on a pew in the mansion's chapel, a room I visit more often than you would believe and not to commune with the Man Upstairs. It's a hexagonal space built in one of the towers with a marble altar in the center flanked by pews. Stained-glass windows ring the room, five of which depict Gethsemane with olive trees and a van Gogh sky. In the last window Jesus kneels in perpetual anguish, poor soul. Sunlight is speckling the ceiling with colors—the real reason I come here—so it feels as if I'm meditating inside a kaleidoscope.

Growing up I never would have believed that Le Baron's widow, or La Strega, as the Italians called her, had a Christian chapel in her lair. Most of us imagined a dungeon festooned with pentagrams and *cimarute* where she stirred caldrons of the same rue branches, salt, and olive oil that were in Nonna's evil-eye recipes. With their shared pagan roots, the Old Religion and Italian witchcraft have some crossover, but don't say that to Nonna. I once made the comparison and she dropped her Marsala, crossed herself thirteen times, and sputtered, "I use-a these things to ward off-a the *malocchio*! La Strega use them to bring-a them on!"

For years La Strega was the primary suspect regarding my pumice stones, electrical short circuits, and mutating geography. She certainly had reason to loathe us land-grabbing trespassers, though I didn't know why I should be her primary scapegoat. I never thought she was responsible for the healings, however, since her malevolence toward us was well documented. Though we seldom saw her, the neighborhood often *heard* from her in the form of unstamped letters that mysteriously appeared in mailboxes regarding lax snow shoveling, house-paint choices, or loud mufflers. She always knew which brave hooligans had TP'd her hedges and dumped Jell-O into her reflection pond on Halloween. She also topped the list of suspects when neighborhood pets went missing, though I would later deduce who the real culprit was.

Those who lived below the front of La Strega's house, like my family, felt as if she were cursing their backyard barbecues with ptomaine potato salad. Those who lived on the back of the hill felt as if she were mooning them every minute of their lives.

An electric gate guarded La Strega's driveway, which led up to the carriage house where her chauffeur, an old man who was also the groundskeeper, lived in the apartment upstairs. Few people bothered to learn his name, and children needled him mercilessly whenever they spotted him running errands in the village or raking La Strega's leaves. He wasn't much thicker than the rake he held, all legs and arms, a head shaped like a Brazil nut—or a nigger toe, as Uncle Dom called the nut. He called the chauffeur that too, though he wasn't a black man. Unfortunately, once the neighbors heard Dom's offensive slur, the nickname stuck.

The first Saturday of every month, that massive gate clanked opened so Nigger Toe could steer La Strega's Packard down the hill, the old bat in the back seat prodding him with a cane, hill nonnas lining the curb to rattle keys and clang skillets as she passed.

Cars are rumbling down the hill right now, in fact. Folks are heading to Mass at Saint Brigid's, newly equipped with fourteen stained-glass windows—one for every Station of the Cross—thanks to Nonna. She pestered me daily for a year to donate the funds to replace the mustard-colored glass that made the congregation look jaundiced.

"It's-a my dying wish," Nonna said, stilling her palpitating heart with one hand, hacking *soppressata* phlegm into the other. How could I deny her? Of course she danced the tarantella after I said yes.

Can you hear the tintinnabulation of the bells, bells, bells? It's Nonna's favorite song, "Ave Maria," and the sounds were long in coming, since Saint Brigid's steeple had sat bell-less for sixty years. It wasn't until 1961 that Father Luigi decided it was high time his church filled the air with a more melodious sound than the Sabbath belches and snores of its hung-over congregation.

It was a tough sell to the parishioners who barely had a grip on the lowest rung of the lower-middle-class ladder, so Father Luigi equipped every student in Saint Brigid's with a roll of raffle tickets to be sold at twenty-five cents a pop. The lucky winner would be the proud owner of a two-foot-tall, hand-painted statue of the Virgin Mary of Lourdes (French and thus nonpartisan). She was nestled inside her own plaster grotto that would protect her from the elements. The double lure was an as-yet-to-be-named prize for the kid who sold the most tickets.

The wound-up students, which included me, were let loose, and by the end of the month we had turned every Sweetwater citizen upside down by the ankles and jangled the last coins from pockets or bra—excepting only one spooky hill resident, whom no one had the courage to approach.

It was a Friday when Sister Barnabas gathered the students in the cafeteria, her wimple looking particularly bright against her rosacea. Beside her, the statue of Mary was propped on a table next to a fishbowl filled with ticket stubs.

Sister clapped her hands to stifle our chatter. "I'd like to introduce our special guest, who will relay the results of the raffle: Father Luigi O'Malley!"

Father rushed in bowing, Abe Lincoln jiggling on the side of his face. He paused beside the statue and bellowed, "I'm delighted to report that you sold nearly twenty-five hundred tickets."

A collective roar rose from the students.

"And now I'm going to draw the winner of this magnificent prize."

He tugged up his sleeve and reached deep inside the bowl. "And the winner is . . ." He jumbled the tickets interminably as I gripped my chair in the fifth-grade section. Nonna had been praying fervently for the statue, and with me as a sainted granddaughter, she felt certain she would win. She had even cleared a spot for it in her Fiore Pergusa garden, and after weeks of pestering she had coerced Grandpa into pouring a two-foot-square concrete slab to offer it a stable foundation. Though Grandpa grumbled, Celeste Xaviero overheard Nonna offer her ultimate threat: "God give me the *profezia* and if you no comply that slab will be the death of-a you!" My superstitious grandpa complied.

Finally Father pulled out the winning ticket and announced: "Maureen Pasquali!"

That's right. Annette Funicello. My father's crush, the woman whose daughter was more of a daughter to him than I was.

A scream from the first-grade section as Mary Ellen jumped up and down. "We won! We won! We won!"

I remember thinking: *Boy, did you ever.* Fluorescent lights overhead began sputtering, but Father squelched that with his next declaration. "I have in my hand the name of the pupil who sold the most tickets."

I again held on to my chair because I hoped it would be me. After all, so many hill nonnas had slipped me their quarters along with the holy medals and scapulars for me to bless. Even in my nonbelief, I didn't mind offering a few gibberish words if it would sell more tickets.

"And that person is Nicky Ferrari!"

Well, of course. When all those mothers were down to their last coins and it was between Nicky and their dung-beetle children, Nicky batted his aquamarines and skipped off with the loot in his mitt.

A wave of shrieks from the girls, a thunder of groans from the boys. I spun around to scan the sixth-grade section. Nicky's face was an odd mixture of delight in winning and mortification at having to walk up the aisle to collect his prize. Girls fanned their faces as he passed; boys hissed and lobbed spitballs. I bet in his head, Nicky was reciting various inventions in body armor. When he arrived, Father handed him a twelve-by-fourteen-inch framed reproduction of the most gruesome, flesh-ripped, thorn-pierced crucified Jesus I had ever seen. Several first-graders began sobbing. My hand instinctively clamped over the locket beneath my shirt so that I could shield Jesus's eyes the way I wanted to shield mine, and also Nicky's, since he looked as if he were about to puke as he stumbled back to his seat.

Then Father delivered the bad news. Even after our doe-eyed coercion, we were still six hundred and seventy-five dollars shy of the price tag on the bells.

We slunk back to our classrooms deflated, but after school, as Nicky and I ran down the hall, Sister Barnabas stepped out of her office directly into our paths. We skidded to a stop to keep from knocking her down like a bowling pin.

"May I see you two in my office?" She ran her hands along the wooden rosary beads at her waist that still had dents from my teething. I wasn't afraid of her office; that's where I had sought refuge those first difficult school years. I had also been sequestered there during various geography tests, since I was a virtual, if somewhat scrambled, cheat sheet. Nicky, however, quivered and mumbled something about bamboo shoots and fingernails.

We sank into the visitors' chairs and Sister sat across from us teetering a swizzle stick from Dino's Lounge between her finger and thumb.

"Nicky, I want to congratulate you on selling the most raffle tickets, and because of that I have a special assignment. As you know, we need several hundred more dollars to buy the bells, and there is only one person with that kind of money."

I knew where this spiraling path was leading. "La Strega!" I yelled. "We can't go up there. She's a witch!"

Sister jiggled her swizzle stick. "She is no such thing, Garnet."

"But Nonna—"

"Has been misinformed, and may I remind you that gossip is a sin."

I slumped back in my seat, chastised.

Nicky's teeth chattered. "Maybe Father Luigi should—"

"We have tried, Nicky." By the pinched look on her face, I could tell Sister still felt the sting of La Strega's door slams and perhaps the rosacea-colored effects of her incantations. "Father and I both feel that if anyone can do it, you, with your charm and intelligence, can."

I couldn't believe she was sending a child on such a dangerous mission. I again opened my mouth. "But—"

"She has quite an impressive library, Nicky," Sister said.

A brilliant move.

"She does?"

"It's far more extensive than the school library."

Nicky's head tipped back at the weighty image unpacking in his head. "I guess I can try."

Sister stood. "That's all we can ask, but please do your best, as I know you will. You really are our last hope."

Outside, as Nicky and I walked along Appian Way and up the hill, I felt an odd mix of slight (why wasn't *I* their last hope?) and relief (thank *God* I wasn't their last hope). Nicky was cataloging mythological Greek heroes. When we reached our house I started climbing the steps but Nicky walked past me and forged ahead.

"Where are you going?" He didn't answer, so I bounded after him, heart stuttering. "Nicky! Where are you going?"

"La Strega's."

"You're going now?" I thought I would go with him after we'd spent the evening arming ourselves with Nonna's protective amulets.

"Yep." His face blanched, so I hustled beside him. If La Strega was going to chain Nicky in her dungeon, I wanted to be able to run for help. As we marched toward the pinnacle I looked in neighbors' windows in case the nonnas were watching, torn between wanting their blessing and not wanting them to spread word to *my* nonna, who would have a seizure if she knew where we were headed.

Finally we stood before the mansion with its two fanged gargoyles overlooking the door and its pointy-hatted towers and turrets where I bet La Strega had installed hired guns. We scanned the brick pillars by the gate looking for a doorbell. Nicky spotted a wooden hatch in the right column and reached for the garbanzo-size knob. I stilled his hand.

"It might be a trick." I looked at the ground to see if there was a trapdoor waiting to spill us into a chamber of horrors.

"It's not."

His fingers trembled as he opened the hatch to reveal an intercom like the one Uncle Dom liked to show off in his home—*Betty! Bring me a scotch* (or *ham sandwich,* or *toilet plunger*)—and that I'm sure the neighborhood punks used to harass La Strega. *Your house is on fire! Nigger Toe is wearing your underwear!* Years later, the intercom is still an annoyance. *Saint Garnet, please cure my blepharitis.* But back then, Nicky held his finger above the buzzer, counted to three, and then punched the button. "Good afternoon, ma'am. My name is Nicky Ferrari. I'm one of your neighbors and I'd like to speak with you."

No response.

"I promise I won't take up much of your time."

Continued silence. Not even a *Get away!*

Nicky attempted a few more angles, all fruitless.

"You tried," I said as we ambled down the hill.

"I'm going back tomorrow."

The next morning I accompanied him as he again sought admission. It didn't work. Nor did he have any luck on Sunday, Monday, or Tuesday, which is when I stopped schlepping up beside him, because even if she was a witch, I had my pride. For two weeks, he went every day without success.

On the first day of the third week, it became intolerable to see my brother once again shove outside to grovel at her door. We had come home from school only so he could comb his hair, and that day, for some reason, it angered me. Though I hated the way Nicky hogged the bathroom and claimed the front seat whenever Dad took us for joy rides, he was still my brother. By the time I swapped my uniform for play clothes, I was boiling. I galloped down the hall and ran outside to catch up to Nicky. "This is the last time!"

Nicky didn't say a word, such was his desire to gain admission to La Strega's library.

Once again Nicky pressed the intercom buzzer. "Hello, ma'am. It's Nicky Ferrari. I just need a couple minutes of your time."

Surprise: no answer.

"Five minutes. That's all I'm asking."

Nothing but the cold silence of hell.

Nicky exhaled, closed the intercom door, and turned around to make the defeated trip home. I was about to follow but I took one last look at the house and saw a female figure peeking out of the window by the front door, though she didn't look like either a shriveled *gabbo* or a hawk-nosed sorceress. I nudged Nicky. "That's her!"

"That's where she always stands."

"What? She just stands there?"

"Yep. Let's go."

Strega or not, she had made me *furioso*. "No!" I yanked open the intercom door, rammed my finger on the buzzer, and said in my best Grandma Iris imitation, "How rude of you to just stand there when you have guests. My grandmother would never treat her company this way. Her ancestors came over on the *Mayflower*, her money is older than yours, and her house in Charlottesville is bigger!" (At the time I had no idea what Zelda's house looked like.) I slammed the intercom door and turned to leave. The intercom crackled and a voice grumbled, "I suppose you'd better come in."

Nicky looked at me in disbelief as the gate started humming, gears clanking, and then, amazingly, we were in. My brother straightened his tie and as he marched toward La Strega's, I dissolved into a quivering milquetoast.

Nicky looked over his shoulder. "Hurry up!"

We reached the massive entryway and I cowered beneath those gargoyles that seemed ready to eat me alive. Nicky raised his hand, but the door opened before his knuckles hit wood. I expected a vampire or zombie, but it was Nigger Toe, apparently the butler in addition to his other positions, wearing the same yard-work ensemble he always wore. For some reason, this disappointed me.

"Good afternoon," Nicky said. "I'm here to speak to the lady of the house."

Nigger Toe cleared his throat as if he spoke so seldom he needed to lube his vocal cords. "Madame will see you in the parlor."

Nigger Toe secretly scoured my face while I not-so-secretly scoured his.

I was prepared for guillotines, iron maidens, and head crushers, but what I noted on our shadowy walk to the parlor were oriental vases, Persian carpets, and velvet curtains blocking out the sun, sights you may remember from your visit here, Padre, though I've removed the heavy drapes. Nicky's shoulders straightened and his chin lifted as if he were the reincarnation of the original Baron. He didn't hesitate one second as he glided across the threshold to where La Strega, a lumpy, lace-clad form, was sitting on a clawfoot settee, a blanket draped over her lap.

"Do come in."

Nicky walked up to her as if he'd done it all his life. I wondered if she had already cast a spell on him.

"You're Dominick Ferrari. Angelo Ferrari's son." She sounded disappointed, as if the balance of Dad's meager bank account were tattooed on Nicky's forehead. "Your father makes that sawing racket at all hours of the day and night. What in the world is he building?"

Nicky had no answer, but if I'd had the courage I would have shouted: *That's private. Private!*

"And you're the—daughter"—she leaned forward unabashedly to inspect my stains, perhaps her handiwork—"who used to parade around in that ridiculous pillowcase. Thank God your parents put an end to that."

"Yes, ma'am," Nicky answered for us, thankfully, since my face was beginning to throb.

"You live next door to Louis Bellagrino."

"Yes."

"And the Pasqualis."

"Yes."

"Then you're a liar!"

Nicky flinched. "No! The Bellagrinos live on our left. The Pasqualis on the right."

"That's not what I mean. I know your poor Italian father, and I know his bricklaying father sailed here in steerage, not on the *Mayflower*. You have no money, nor will you ever."

That's all I needed to jump-start my ire, and Nigger Toe tapped a lampshade to steady a flickering bulb. "We do too! It's on our mother's side." I rattled the family tree. "Our mom is Marina Caudhill-Adams-Rutledge-[ad infinitum], born to Donald Flyman and Iris Caudhill—"

"Your mother is one of the *Mayflower* Caudhills? She's a Caudhill-Adams?"

"-Rutledge-[ad infinitum]!" I corrected.

La Strega adjusted her wide bottom. "Was it your grandmother who visited over Christmas?"

"Yes," I answered, perplexed by her intimate, if incomplete, knowledge of our lives.

"Of course," she said, probably dredging up images of Zelda's diamonds and Cadillac. "This is all very interesting." She assessed Nicky as if he were a glass vase on the mantel that she'd just been told might be Waterford. "You look like your mother. And . . ."

She paused and I wondered who she was dredging up in her head. Nigger Toe cleared his throat as if he were used to these reveries.

"So the priest has sent the beggars for alms," she said.

Nicky swallowed hard, no doubt wondering how she knew our goal. "Yes, ma'am."

"And for what purpose?"

"We need a donation to buy church bells . . . that would be dedicated in your honor."

Smooth, though I wondered if she would contribute to a religion at odds with her own spiteful one.

She harrumphed. "You should be attending a private academy, not that third-rate parochial school."

Nicky could only nod, because he thought the same thing.

Whatever crystal ball La Strega used to peer into our shabby world below also enabled her to read minds. "Say no more. How much do you need?"

Nicky swallowed hard. "Six hundred and seventy-five dollars."

"Radisson! Bring my purse!"

So Nigger Toe had a name.

Radisson exited and reentered carrying a tapestry handbag crammed with whatever it was that witches carried in their purses: vials of blood, dried frogs, dismembered human fingers that wiggled. La Strega settled it on her lap, dug and dug, and eventually pulled out seven crisp hundred-dollar bills.

"I, I," Nicky stuttered. "I don't have change."

"I don't expect any. The extra twenty-five is for you."

"For me?" His eyeballs nearly popped out of their sockets and rolled across the floor.

"That should buy a lot of encyclopedias, yes?"

"Uh-huh."

"Though perhaps it's time I introduced you to the great books of lit-ra-toor."

"Sure." Nicky was still gawping at the greenbacks.

"Please show yourselves out."

Nicky and I walked around Radisson and we were about to make a clean getaway when La Strega added one more thing.

"Perhaps tomorrow you would like to visit my library, Nicholas? It's quite extensive, you know."

Reminded of his real aim, he ignored the errant forename and said, drooling, "Yes!"

As we were taking our leave I scoured the room for a crystal ball. How did La Strega know our parents? Our neighbors? Our reading habits? And then I saw it: a telescope pointing down on the saps toiling away their lives for her amusement. Before we reached the door, I heard what sounded like a slap followed by La Strega scolding: "How could you miss their pedigree, Radisson? Your research is shoddy. Shoddy!" A pause, then La Strega added, "That girl is hideous."

After school the next day Nicky bolted outside and raced to Flannigan's, visions of root-beer floats dancing in his brain. I tagged along because his pocket was bulging with twenty-five one-dollar bills. Sister Barnabas had been so bug-eyed she'd pulled out a fat wallet and made the change herself.

"What are you going to do with twenty-five dollars?" I called after him, panting.

"I don't know."

"I know what I would do."

I was hoping he would ask, because I had my eye on a heavenly nightlight in the Sears catalog that salted the ceiling with stars. He did not ask.

We galloped past O'Grady's and Paddy's and pushed open the pharmacy door, the bell overhead jingling. Mr. Flannigan was behind the counter in the back filling prescriptions. Mrs. Flannigan washed sundae glasses at the soda fountain.

Nicky sat on a stool and I took the one beside him, swiveling, hoping he might buy me a root-beer float too.

"Hello, Nicky," Mrs. Flannigan said. "And Garnet," she added, though, like many villagers, she didn't make eye contact with my skin. "What can I get you?"

"Two banana splits," Nicky said.

I was stunned by his generosity. This was the priciest item on the menu.

"We're celebrating the bells, I see." Word had already spread about how Nicky slayed our malevolent dragon.

It was the best banana split I ever ate. As I savored every spoonful I ogled the penny candy in the glass case beside me. So many Mary Janes, Atomic Fireballs, BB Bats, wax lips, and licorice whips. If Nicky's generous spirit held I might walk home clutching a bagful of decadence.

And then Nicky began naming Jack the Ripper's throat-slit victims. I followed his gaze and spotted the Four Stooges, a collection of local bullies, gathered on the steps across the street in front of Dino's Lounge, which is where they always loitered until Dino scattered them with the baseball bat he kept behind the counter. The thugs were an integrated collection of Irish and Italian teens, their miscreant blood thicker than the familial kind. They were the chief cigarette and beer thieves, egg lobbers and tire deflators, pee-ers in the town's water basin. Cousin Ray-Ray would have fit right in, and maybe he occasionally did. Their hideout was Snakebite Woods, another reason Nicky warned me to avoid that scary copse. My pretty brother was increasingly the Stooges' target. He would regularly come home splattered with the remnants of mud balls or crab apples.

Nicky hunched over his banana split hoping the Stooges wouldn't see him or that Dino would appear and crack a few skulls, but he didn't come and he didn't come even as our spoons clinked the bottom of our dishes. Plus Nicky was due soon for a tour of La Strega's library.

And suddenly there she was. Her car, anyway. Radisson parked the Packard in front of the pharmacy. He adjusted his chauffeur's hat, blew a pink bubblegum bubble the size of a coconut, and then sucked the entire thing back into his mouth. When he got out I expected him to open the rear door for La Strega, but the back seat was empty. Radisson pushed open the pharmacy door, looked over at me, and tipped his hat. He loped to the back coun-

ter, and as Mr. Flannigan waited on him, I watched the Stooges
cross the street and circle the car, rearrange the side mirrors, flip
up the wiper blades, twist off the winged-cormorant hood orna-
ment. I spun toward Radisson wondering if I should alert him,
but one of the goons did it for me by reaching in the open front
window and honking the horn.

Radisson turned around. Any damage to the car would likely
come out of his paycheck, if La Strega even paid the man.

"Hey!" He ran outside as fast as his stick legs would carry him,
shaking his fist at the boys, his jaw moving. The Stooges began to
bounce up and down on the bumpers, making the car rock, and
the tallest thug reached for the antenna that stuck out of the roof.

I looked back to see if the Flannigans were going to help, but
they hustled through the back of the pharmacy and soon their
footsteps pounded up the steps to their apartment. They had been
the target of the Stooges' shoplifting for years. Now the Stooges
started circling Radisson, taking jabs at his chest, trying to swipe
his hat.

"That's not right. We've got to do something, Nicky."

"Let's go."

I assumed that meant he was ready to take action, but when I
followed him outside I discovered that he was using this diversion
to slip away.

As we edged past the scuffle, the Stooges jabbed Radisson with
words as well as fists. "Hey, Nigger Toe. You're nothing but an
ass wiper, you know that? An old hag's ass wiper." They started
chanting, "Nigger Toe! Nigger Toe! Nigger Toe!"

I wasn't even thinking when I swiveled to face them. "His
name is not Nigger Toe! It's Radisson! Radisson-Radisson-Radis-
son!"

All sound disappeared as the boys glared in disbelief at a girl
daring to challenge them. They turned away from the car and toward me, hands balling into fists. "She's even uglier up close," one
of them said as they all inched toward me. "God, what a freak."
I genuinely thought this might be the end of me. And then I

glimpsed Mr. Flannigan on his second-story balcony with a phone to his ear, the cord stretched taut from all the way inside. "They're out there right now harassing my customers. You've got to come, Mickey. Come now!" And the blessed sound of a distant police siren racing to save us. The Stooges scattered like cockroaches, leaving Radisson and me trembling. He put his hand on my shoulder. "Are you all right, miss?"

I could only nod since a glob of adrenaline was jammed in my throat.

"Would you like a ride home?"

I nodded again and turned around to include Nicky, but he was nowhere in sight. Radisson started to open the rear door, but I jumped in the shotgun seat since I rarely had that privilege. Radisson got in and turned the key in the ignition. We didn't speak as he spiraled up the hill, passing neighbor kids who pointed at the spectacle of stain-faced me being ferried in such grand style. The only one who did not look up at the car was Nicky, who trudged not to La Strega's library but homeward, nose practically touching the blacktop, probably listing infamous cowards.

The Saint Brigid's Day Massacre

O Padre, My Padre:

I'm walking to the wine cellar, so bear with me as I negotiate these narrow and—eww—slimy passageways. Nonna is leading the way with a flashlight—

(Watch out for the wall sconce, Nonna!)

(Son-ama-beetch!)

I *told* Nonna I would get the wine for her—

(You no know which-a vino I need!)

But apparently I no know which-a vino she need. What's the name again, Nonna?

(Moot Rot-a-chile.)

That's it, the one and only wine that will go with her marinara, though I don't know what we'll do when that particular rack is cleared.

(I no drink-a too much!)

(I really and truly do not give a gnat's ass, Nonna.)

Nonna certainly deserves refined wine after enduring Grandpa's hand-pressed Gaglioppo swill all those years.

And here we are, another room I love because of the *ploink-ploink* of water dripping from the stone ceiling. It's also thirty-five degrees cooler, so I've been known to drag a folding chair here on hot July nights. Last summer Nonna began lobbying for central air-conditioning. I'm on the verge of acquiescing and not because it's-a her dying wish.

Nonna is marching us back, carrying her Rot-a-chile like a scepter. Can you hear that? She's humming—not our E note but the theme from *The Godfather*. When *The Godfather: Part II* came out last year, she made me take her to see it five times, and I had to buy out the Sweetwater Cinema for secrecy. Nonna blubbered when the actors spoke in her mother tongue and the camera panned the Sicilian countryside. *I been-a there!* She also claims she knew Don Ciccio: *I know that no-good son-ama-Ciaffaglione-beetch! Watch out for you life!* I didn't have the heart to tell her he was a fiction, but by now most of her memories of life in Sicilia are probably fictions too.

Now we're in Nonna's basement kitchen, several steps below the main one. The flagstone floor is terra firma for the butcher-block table Nonna hauled up from her old Via Dolorosa house. I'm rubbing my hand over the concave depression made after years of Nonna's kneading dough and cutting pasta.

(Pop!)

Here comes the red wine. One glass for me (grazie, *Nonna*), one for her, one for the marinara.

(*And-a one for Padre.* Salute!)

(Salute.)

A New York City scene in *Godfather II* resonated with me the same way the Sicilian ones must have with Nonna: the San Gennaro Festival in Little Italy when the young Vito Corleone offed the Black Hand.

One sweltering July, Sweetwater held its own patron-saint festival. The lampposts on the north side of Appian Way were decorated with Saint Brigid of Kildare gewgaws: reed crosses, like the kind Brigid fashioned when she was converting pagan chieftains, and papier-mâché red-eared cows, its milk the only source of nourishment for Brigid when she was a child. Their sidewalk was crowded with booths selling oatcakes and Guinness stout, plus tables where children could color pages that looked like the illuminated Book of Kildare, the original of which had been handmade in the monastery founded by that Irish Saint Brigid.

The south side of the street was decorated with Saint Brigid of Tuscany tributes. The streetlights were hung with flags of angels, like the ones who ferried Saint Brigid to her brother Saint Andrew's deathbed, and papier-mâché Apennine Mountains, where that Brigid lived out her life in a cave. Their booths sold cannolis and Chianti.

Residents lined the street waiting for the double procession that would bring the two Saint Brigid statues from the church, through the village, and to the town square. The occasion would also be the inaugural ringing of the newly installed church bells.

In the school parking lot, white-clad children gathered in rows: peat-pressers on the left, garlic-grinders on the right. At the end of the lines, directly behind the two statues, each in her own cart, was a third cart holding a throne upon which sat the one and only Saint Brigid Queen. The nuns conspired, yet again, on behalf of a certain hill girl who was as divided as the congregation: half Italian, half British; half healer, half charlatan; half pale pink ocean, half mulberry continents. The Kildare Brigid had disfigured her face to avoid suitors, and I was sure I was chosen because I already looked the part.

I was sweating in the bride gown hand-sewn by Nonna. A lace veil covered my face, and though just five years before I would have luxuriated in all the netting, that day I felt ridiculous.

Eventually Grand Marshal Father Luigi bellowed, "Forward ho!" He marched ahead of everyone, waving both arms as if he were a celebrity, followed by a formation of nuns whirling rosary beads like propeller blades. Next came the children scattering oats and reed switches or blowing rude noises from ram horns. Bringing up the rear were the three Saint Brigid carts pulled by church ushers.

Families on both sides cheered as we passed, and though I was shrouded in netting, familiar wails drifted from the toddlers held in their parents' arms: "Daddy! What's wrong with—"

Then I spotted Mom, mother of the bride; Nonna, mother of the bride gown; and Aunt Betty, mother of none. Beside them, Dad downed Chianti and longed to be in his basement sawing wood. Dom flirted with one of Dino's waitresses. Ray-Ray flicked lit matches at Paddy's dog before Paddy chased him off. Conspicuously absent was Grandpa, likely tending his grapevine.

Something glinted before me in the dark-haired row of Italian children: Nicky's blond head in the noonday sun.

I wasn't privy to what was going on behind the scenes, but I imagine that as we processed, the Four Stooges slunk into an alley and clambered up the fire escape to the connected store roofs of the Italian side of the street, with their leader, Moe, wearing a white sailor's hat. They carried burlap sacks as they wove through chimneys and pipes and crouched behind the three-foot-high brick façade of Italia Imports. The Stooges opened their sacks filled with hundreds of overripe tomatoes, Moe seething as he said, "We'll teach Map Face not to stand up for Nigger Toe."

Three minutes before noon, just as Father Luigi stopped in front of the basin, the Stooges lined up tomatoes on the ledge. The obedient nuns halted immediately but the inattentive children banged into one another like bumper cars; the ushers had a difficult time stopping their carts, and the two Brigids and I lurched precariously forward and back before tipping into place.

Father Luigi held up a starter pistol, finger on the trigger as the town clock ticked toward twelve o'clock.

Nicky later told me that it was at that point he looked longingly at La Strega's house and imagined her library, which he still hadn't seen. When he dragged his eyes away he spotted something bobbing on the top of Italia Imports, a white sailor's cap, then the top of the other Stooges' heads, and, most significant, a row of plump ammunition. He assessed the situation and followed the goons' line of sight to find their target: the Saint Brigid Queen.

Nicky started jostling toward me through the children, looking up at Moe, who pointed to the clock only seven ticks away from high noon. As Father Luigi's finger began depressing the trigger, all four goons stood and cocked their arms in my direction.

Nicky pushed children out of the way and stepped onto my cart. Initially I was angry at him for stealing my limelight. I lifted the veil. "What are you doing?"

"Get down!"

"What?"

Nicky looked up at the clock. It was exactly noon. Father Luigi squeezed the trigger, and at the same moment it fired, the Stooges lobbed their pulpy grenades. With superhero strength, Nicky sprang from the cart step and shot upward in front of me, acting as a spindly shield. I shouted, "What's going on?" as church bells began ringing.

Nicky took the first hit to the side of his face; the red gunk splattered into his ear, streaked his hair. The second hit him squarely in the back, the third his left butt cheek, the fourth his right calf. He was propelled completely over the cart and onto the other side, where he landed headfirst on the concrete sidewalk and was knocked unconscious.

I leaped down, protected from the red volley by the cart, and knelt beside Nicky, who lay belly-down. I opened my arms wide, looked up at the goons still firing into the crowd, and bellowed, "Why? Why?"

A photojournalist for the *Sweetwater Herald* snapped a picture of me kneeling over Nicky that looked amazingly similar to the one John Filo would take eight years later of Mary Ann Vecchio kneeling over that dead Kent State boy.

Their original target protected, the Stooges began firing at random into the children: irresistible, pristine targets. Parents dove into the mêlée to grab their youngsters and drag them to safety. The unflappable nuns surrounded Father Luigi, who cowered with his hands covering his (and Abe Lincoln's) head as the church bells clanged and clanged.

Mirror, Mirror

Archibald,

I'm being a naughty girl while Nonna and Betty are at the village beauty parlor. Betty *finally* convinced Nonna to have her hair styled, for the first time in her life. A horde of photographers has camped outside, flashbulbs flaring every time we sneeze, so Betty wants us to look perpetually photo-ready. The paparazzi increase daily thanks to you, Padre. Did you really have to speak with Mike Wallace?

I'm hiding in the Packard inside the carriage house ogling the empty space where Aunt Betty's Corvette is usually parked, my gift to her when she passed her driver's test last year. Just how many Hail Marys do I have to recite as penance for the half o' cake I just snarfed down that I don't want to share with my roomies?

I receive dozens of packages every month containing photos of loved ones' maladies for me to pray over, toddlers' nightgowns for me to bless, dog collars so I might heal Rover's and Fido's mange. Occasionally I get a thank-you parcel, like this German-chocolate marvel, for some healing that's been pinned on me.

I have an insatiable sweet tooth, a venial sin at least. During my early years I devoured penny candy from Flannigan's until a horrid association left it forever unpalatable to me. The first years of my life, my baked confections came mostly from Nonna (and

Annette Funicello), but there was a brief spell when I considered her cannolis too provincial for my palate.

It started after the Saint Brigid's Day Massacre when, thanks to my brother, I was the only kid who walked away un-tomatoed. Nicky sported a bump on his noggin from hitting the sidewalk. That earned him the prize of setting the box fan in his bedroom during his convalescence. In my view he deserved an even richer reward.

A week after the massacre I slipped into Nicky's room, where he sat at his desk reading about flame-retardant clothing. He must have felt my breath on his neck because he turned around. "What do you want?"

I cleared my throat, though I couldn't believe what I was about to propose. "I think we should go see La Strega's library."

Nicky was also stunned, his head jerking up, but such was the depth of my gratitude.

"You know she wants to show it off and you're the only person who can appreciate it."

His mouth started to form the word *no*, so I pressed on.

"Radisson won't care. I saw him at the festival and I could tell he was proud of what you did to save me."

"You saw him?"

"Yes!" It was a lie. "You have redeemed yourself!" That line had sounded so much better during rehearsal.

"You think so?"

"I do." I revved up my nerve so I could bolster Nicky's. "Let's go right now."

Amazingly, Nicky stood in front of his mirror to check his teeth.

Mom was in the kitchen mixing cream soup and canned tuna together. I coughed to camouflage the jumble of Nonna's protective amulets rattling in my pocket; I'd gathered them from my room. "Where are you going?" she asked. Nicky hadn't been outside since the festival.

"For a walk. Nicky could use some fresh air"—words Dad had

spoken the previous night while he smoked his cigar on the porch and Mom darned a sock.

"Sounds wonderful." She crumbled potato chips over the casserole.

Outside, Nicky and I spiraled up to La Strega's intercom button. I thought we were going to have to play one-potato, two-potato.

"You go."

"No, you."

"No, you."

Mercifully, the carriage-house door opened and out came Radisson steering a wheelbarrow filled with potted begonias. Nicky inched behind me as Radisson approached and set down the barrow.

"Good afternoon, miss." He looked over his shoulder to see if La Strega was watching from her parlor window. She was. "And sir."

Before I lost my nerve I said, "Radisson, Nicky would like to see the library if that's okay."

Radisson groaned as if he could already predict how this would end. Ever obedient, however, he walked to one of those stone pillars, opened a door on its back, reached in, and pulled out a telephone. "Master Nicky and Miss Garnet would like to see the library."

A pause as he listened and the parlor drapes rippled.

Radisson hung up, pressed a secret button, and the gate clanked open. "Madame will be happy to receive Master Nicholas, and Miss Garnet is also welcome."

I waited for Nicky to correct his name, but he didn't.

Nicholas stepped onto La Strega's property, but I couldn't move. "Come on," he said.

I shook my head. "I don't want to." And truly, it was as if the soles of my shoes were slathered with tar.

Radisson shot me a look that conveyed the message *You're making the right decision.*

Nicky adjusted his collar, flattened his hair. "Okay. I'll see you later."

As my brother walked toward the house, extra vertebrae seemed to appear in his spine, making him taller and taller. By the time he reached the house, he stood nine feet and had to duck to clear the gargoyles. I wished I'd slipped some *tocca ferro* charms into Nicky's pocket.

Radisson dipped into the wheelbarrow and pulled out a begonia. "For you, miss." Then he whispered something that sounded like "Run like the wind, Miss Garnet! Fly like the wind!"

I raced to our house, whirred up the blinds in Nicky's room, and squinted up at the mansion where my brother was being versed in black magic.

An hour later, he returned with two books under his arm: *Oliver Twist* and *Great Expectations*. At the time I didn't understand their significance.

Thus began Nicky's education under the direction of La Strega. For an hour each week she grilled him on his assigned reading and stuffed him with cookies. He smuggled back handfuls in his pocket for me, doughy sweets shaped like strawberries and pears and sprinkled with clear sugar. I wasn't expecting graft to keep his secret from Mom and Dad. We could both imagine their reactions if they knew about his forays.

Initially I was afraid to eat La Strega's food, which I imagined was laced with gopher piss and newt eyes, but they were too pretty to resist, those leaves made out of white chocolate.

Every week I hid in my closet and inspected each one before popping it into my mouth. I began to crave those pieces of heaven, *x*-ing out days on the calendar until I would get my next fix. I'm ashamed to admit that during that time, when Nonna visited with a shirt box filled with cannolis, centered it on the kitchen table, and pulled off the lid, I didn't squeal as I usually did. Suddenly they looked clunky and unrefined. "Provincial," Nicky declared, scraping away from the table. "So crude," I added, getting up to leave, grabbing two cannolis so I would understand what provincial tasted like. I'm glad I didn't look at Nonna's face just then.

Nicky started bringing home, in addition to cookies, trinkets La Strega had given him: a porcelain figure of a bowing, golden-haired boy in knickers, one arm trailing behind him, a hand clutching a plumed hat. Very much like the boy in the painting in the whippet room. "It's a Hummel," Nicky said, apparently implying that it had real value.

I was not impressed. "Gee. Wonder who this is supposed to be?"

I didn't envy him that statue, but I lusted after the fountain pen that sucked ink from a bottle. With it came a box of stationery. "Like you ever write letters." Over the next months he accrued a chess set with marble rooks and pawns, a key chain and money clip, tie tacks and cuff links, and hand-painted Chinese teacups.

When fall came La Strega started buying him clothes. A sleeveless sweater vest that screamed: *Punch me!* Argyle socks with diamonds running up the shaft. Dress shirts with button-down collars. Silk neckties. Every punk in the neighborhood, including all the Stooges, would have slammed Nicky with mud balls if he ever wore one of those getups in public. And that was the irony. He never could wear any of it outside. He had to hide them in the back of his closet. When Mom and Dad were out, however, he'd play dress-up, marching from gilt mirror to mirror to practice his new manners. "I'll take two, thank you. Please pass the cream."

Several times during those months I found Dad staring at his son, because dress shirts weren't the only things Nicky pulled from his closet. He donned an invisible crown bejeweled with superiority. He started taking potshots at our Italian heritage, Dad's profession, even the roof over our heads. "God, we live in a dump." How easily my brother had succumbed.

Dad and I were suddenly peons. At supper, Nicholas groused about our misplaced elbows and propensity to slurp. After the fourth correction Dad and I simultaneously blurted out, "Geez." We looked at each other, both stunned by our shared sentiment. Dad picked up his coffee mug and extended his pinkie. I did likewise with my milk glass, and then Dad let out one of his juicy burps. I laughed so hard I nearly peed as I savored that blissful moment.

"How vulgar." Nicholas retired to the living room with the Sunday crossword, though he no longer lay belly-down on the rug to do it. Instead, he sat in a wingback and snapped the paper's spine to attention as if he were a stockbroker.

That Thanksgiving he couldn't resist breaking out his new togs. Dinner would be at Uncle Dom's, and Nicky boldly wore the starched dress shirt, silk tie, and sweater vest.

"Where'd you get that outfit?" Mom asked as we slid on our old coats, a Saran-Wrapped bowl of orange-cranberry salad in her arms.

Nicky spouted a well-rehearsed lie. "Grandma Iris gave it to me last year for Christmas. Don't you remember?"

Mom's brow furrowed. It was absolutely a costume Zelda would have given him.

Dad eyeballed his son with a look that begged *Who are you?* Only I knew the answer: Czar Nicholas, a boy tethered to La Strega by a golden rope, a boy who was counting the days until she could tug him up for good.

We piled in the car to drive to Grover Estates, and for the first time I thought Nicky looked as if he belonged in that pricey subdivision. Uncle Dom laughed at the getup. "Who are you supposed to be, bucko?" Betty tugged Nicky's earlobe. "I think you look handsome. Like a real gentleman." I could tell she meant it by the pained look in her eyes as she no doubt considered the toads she had to live with. As if on cue, Ray-Ray farted. He was leaning against the china cabinet popping cocktail wieners in his mouth. When the adults weren't looking, he flicked a wiener at Nicky's sweater. Nicky dodged it, but Ray-Ray pointed a finger and mouthed, *You're in for it.* Nicky started reciting a chronology of execution devices. Back home he stood at the bathroom sink for an hour scrubbing grass stains, not cocktail-wiener sauce, from the sweater.

A month later Mom received an extraordinary phone call. I heard only her side of the conversation, but I could guess the rest. La Strega was inviting her and Nicky to afternoon tea. At first Mom thought it was a joke. "Betty, is that you?" But it was La Strega all right. Mom put her on our version of hold, letting the receiver bounce to the floor so she could ask what Nicky wanted to do, a democratic move on her part. Mom was as curious about our local witch as the rest of Sweetwater. Of course Nicky said yes.

"We'd be delighted," Mom said. "What time would you like the three of us to arrive?"

Three of you? I imagined La Strega saying.

"Why, Garnet, of course. I just assumed she would be welcome." A pause, and then: "Wonderful, we'll see you at three."

Nicky stood in front of his bedroom mirror trying on five different dress shirts. He even polished his shoes, Brylcreemed his hair, and splashed on some of Dad's Old Spice. Finally he leaned into Mom's room, where she was folding Dad's boxers. "What are you going to wear?" He actually asked her that.

Mom rolled her eyes; visiting the wealthy for high tea was old hat to her. She dressed up as much as she ever did, slacks and a sweater. She also swirled her ponytail into a bun and wore earrings. I appreciated this conciliation even if Nicky did not. He looked disappointed to see her in her same old duds and I was happy when she slapped his hand away when he tried to rearrange her hair. I purposely did not change out of my cereal-stained turtleneck. I did, however, tuck a lucky rabbit's foot in my pocket along with Nonna's talismans.

Radisson answered the door slicked up in a suit and wearing one of those sweater vests.

"Good afternoon. Follow me." We trailed him into the parlor, where La Strega was seated on her clawfoot settee, blanket draped over her legs.

She waved a hand to the three chairs arranged around her and a low table in the middle set with teacups and saucers, a bowl of sugar cubes, a miniature pitcher of cream, a plate of sliced lemons.

It was cold in that room, but Radisson sneaked up from behind, helped us shuck our outerwear, and carted the pile off for a de-lousing.

"Do sit," La Strega directed. Mom and Nicky sat on either side of her, leaving me between them to eyeball a three-tiered tray of finger sandwiches, another heaped with those fruit-shaped indulgences.

I imitated Mother as best as I could, crossing my legs at the ankles rather than at the knees, draping my arms in my lap instead of tightly across my chest. I thought I was doing well until Nicky pinched me when no one was looking and mouthed: *Stop humming!*

Radisson filled our cups, and Mom used tongs to pick up a sugar cube and add a lemon wedge. I did likewise, stirring with the silver spoon on my saucer, trying not to clink.

La Strega took her tea with cream, speaking as she stirred. "I apologize for not inviting you sooner, Mrs. Caudhill-Adams-Rutledge—"

"It's Ferrari."

"Yes." La Strega refused to utter the cursed name. "I had no idea anyone of such caliber lived on my hill." She smirked at Radisson, who stood in the doorway. I wondered what the penalty was for his incomplete research.

La Strega leaned toward Mother. "I believe we have mutual acquaintances. The Claymores. Edmund, that is, the one in shipping. Not his brother the actor. And the Bernards."

"They were friends of my parents," Mother said.

On and on they droned. I was beyond bored. I think Mother was too, but she held up her end for Nicky, who drank his tea exactly as La Strega did, soundless sips, occasional stirring, though he lapsed once and licked the tea from his spoon and I thought, *At last, Nicky with a silver spoon in his mouth.*

Then I made my grand faux pas by adding a splash of cream to my lemony tea, the mixture curdling into a clotted mess. "Gross!" I said, drawing everyone's attention.

Nicky looked mortified. "God, Garnet. We can't take you anywhere."

"Nicky," Mom scolded.

La Strega looked as if this was exactly what she'd expected of me.

Radisson crept up and removed the offense. "It happens all the time, miss." He poured me a fresh cup, draped a new napkin across my lap, and offered me the tray of cookies. I shamelessly took two, but Radisson slid two more on my plate. I wondered what other clandestine acts of rebellion he might be committing.

Mom and La Strega discussed Mom's year at Wellesley and the atrocious state of our public school system. The topic shifted to books and soon La Strega asked, "Would you like to see my library?"

"Yes!" Mom gasped, her cool demeanor shed.

Radisson again appeared to undrape the blanket from La Strega's legs; she did have legs, and sturdy ones. She marched us across the hall to the dim room half the size of our house. You may remember those mahogany shelves loaded with first editions. Ladders that rolled forward and back to fetch books from the upper tiers.

La Strega pulled down *Jane Eyre.* "I've always been an avid collector."

Mom shivered when she held the tome in her hands, then she sat to inhale the musty pages. Nicky sat in the leather chair by the window and crossed his legs. He wore a peculiar smile, as if he alone were privy to some joke.

I wondered if Mom planned on reading the entire novel in one sitting, but thirty minutes later she looked at her watch. "I have to start supper!" She gazed wistfully at the book.

"Come again next week," La Strega said. "By all means."

Mom gobbled the bait and I shook my head at how easily she, too, had succumbed. Apparently La Strega's sandwiches were indeed laced with bat wings and worm breath. For several weeks, not only did Nicky get to oxygenate his blood with better air, but Mom got her literary fix.

For Nicky's birthday La Strega invited us for lunch in the formal dining room, where she introduced us to fondue. The stinky cheese bubbled in a cauldron set over an open flame. She showed us how to skewer the bread and dip it in. It tasted as gross as I'd feared and as soon as I spit mine into a napkin, the cheese bubbled so aggressively it exploded on me (no one else, mind you), particularly on Portugal on one arm and its colonial territory of Goa on the other. I looked at La Strega, wondering if she had orchestrated this, but she just sipped sherry and looked on passively. It took months for the red spots to vanish, and when they did, Goa mysteriously rejoined the shore of India on my ankle, where it belonged.

I feared even worse tortures and started to claim appendicitis or toothaches before these visits, but Mom said, "It wouldn't hurt you to pick up a book." If I'd known there was a kaleidoscope chapel on the premises I might have been more agreeable. But Radisson, bless his Brazil-nut-shaped heart, once he discovered my passion, arranged a table with books about globes. He also brought me bologna sandwiches instead of the limp cucumber ones Mom had to endure. I brought him Bazooka bubblegum, and though I never again saw him blow a coconut-size bubble, I hoped he chewed the gum and stuck it under La Strega's furniture, which is what I did with mine.

Bits of La Strega hoodoo fluttered into our lives below, because Mom began spending more time in front of the mirrors before we ascended the hill, applying lipstick, spraying her hair. I once caught Nicky and her side by side staring into the bathroom mirror, he flattening his forelock, she checking her posture. "Shoulders back, dear." Things did not look good for Dad and me.

She also began staring into mirrors even when she wasn't primping. More than once I found her with her nose against the glass as if she were looking through it to the life she might have had in Charlottesville if she'd married that handpicked beau. I imagined the world on the other side was filled with dazzling sunlight and privilege. When Mom left, I would sneak up to the mirror and press my face against the glass, but all I could see were reflections of our low-ceilinged Monopoly house. I began to wonder if La Strega's witchery was powerful enough to rewind Mom's life all the way back to Wellesley so that she would sidestep that icy patch and never meet my father.

From then on I stuffed my pockets with not only the rabbit's foot and charms but spools of red thread. Maybe they couldn't erase the maps drawn on me, but perhaps they could keep my mother on this side of the mirror.

During a visit in March, after having my fill of bologna, I lumbered to a divan in the corner, lay down unabashedly, and snoozed while Mom dove into yet another book. I'm sure I let out a cacophony of snorts, one so sharp it woke me. Nicky was by the window in his chair, which by now was indented with impressions of his skinny butt cheeks.

I thought Mom and Nicky were alone until I saw La Strega standing in a corner surveying the tableau she had arranged. She wore such a smug look I wanted to smack her. My brother wore a similar expression, and then he turned his head toward La Strega and did the unthinkable. *He winked!* It was a conspiracy and I imagined the far-reaching implications of their plot. Mom and Nicky's visits would increase to two nights a week, three, then weekends, and ultimately they would move in to the old bat's cave, leaving Dad and me in the trash heap below. Maybe Mom wouldn't have to move all the way back in time in order to recapture her life of luxury.

Just then Radisson entered, carrying a tray. He set a china cup on the table beside Nicky, contents inside steaming. Radisson plopped not one, not two, but three giant marshmallows into the cup filled with hot chocolate. As he was about to back away my brother bawled, "I told you I wanted mini-marshmallows! Can't you ever get it right, Nigger Toe?"

Mother snapped out of her trance and stood. "What did you say?"

Ah, the question I hated most when it was directed at me. That day I basked in it.

Nicky tried to reel his arrogance back in his mouth. "I said I would like mini-marshmallows, please."

"Yes, sir," Radisson said. "Right away."

As Radisson walked by, Mom reached her hand out to stop him. "No," she said, softly.

I imagine a little *ping!* sounded in her head as she looked at her surroundings with new eyes—La Strega, Nicky, the lure of books, the stench of superiority—and I could see her mentally pounding her forehead. *How could I have fallen for this?*

Mother pulled Nicky by the wrist to his feet, walked to La Strega, and looked directly into her eyes. "My son is no longer permitted in your home. Do you understand me?"

"But—" Nicky said, cornered-rabbit look in his eyes.

"Do you understand me?" Mom repeated.

"Yes." La Strega never once broke eye contact.

Mom scuttled forward and stopped in front of Radisson. "I apologize for my son's atrocious behavior." She squeezed the back of Nicky's neck and he and I both knew what that meant. Nicky looked at his feet. "I'm sorry." The most insincere apology ever uttered.

I was elated that these outings had come to an end. I didn't bat an eyelash in La Strega's direction, but as I walked past Radisson, he held out his hand.

"It's been a pleasure, miss."

Without thought, I wrapped my arms around this broomstick of a man and hugged him as tightly as I would from then on hug Nonna whenever she made cannolis. He was stunned at first, probably because no one had touched him kindly in years, but he patted my back as I slipped a fistful of Bazookas into his jacket pocket.

No one spoke as we descended the hill. Within thirty minutes Mom had hefted every one of our gilt mirrors—and the secret world hidden within them—from the walls and hauled them to the curb, mumbling, "No gold-framed future; no gilded windows; no fall of man or boy." Now there was a vacant hole on her bedroom wall surrounded by scraps of poetry that fluttered in the breeze. By the time Dad got home from work, the mirrors had been scooped up by foraging nonnas, who never looked a gift mojo in the mouth.

Maybe Nicky stopped seeing La Strega, maybe he didn't. He certainly didn't stop inventorying the prized bounty that had trickled down the hill to him: the chess set, the fountain pen, the Chinese teacups, and the porcelain statue of a golden-locked boy forced to bow before his widowed queen for all eternity.

Sibling Rivalries

Well, Arch-Support, it's official. The country has lost its mind. A ghost writer called yesterday wanting to pen my autobiography, although with one tiny detail altered—the setting. "Couldn't we say you were born someplace sexier?" Apparently West Virginia is too provincial for her elite readership. I wanted to ram a fist-ful of cannolis down her throat. Provincial this! Her alternatives astounded me: Manhattan's Alphabet City. Chicago's South Side. The Gaza Strip.

Well, maybe Sweetwater isn't so dissimilar to the Gaza Strip, Irish and Italians squabbling over a sliver of land. People have fought over less, and right now I'm on the widow's walk looking at our old house below, cars lined up out front to get a peek at my childhood abode, Mr. Bellagrino raising his fist at a gawker who's blocking his driveway.

The people who bought our house, the Walczaks, posted a massive sign in the yard reading *Saint Garnet's Birthplace*. A red X on my bedroom window indicates where I snored during my for-mative years. My old neighbors must be ruing the day the Polacks moved in. How are those Polacks ever going to screw in a light bulb (change a tire, make ice, have sex)? One would think those West Virginians—and Cat-lickers to boot, the butt of so many lame jokes—would be more sensitive.

Pilgrims are bolting from their cars for a photo op with Mrs. Walczak, who's dressed like an old nonna, though she's only in her thirties. She's set up a booth in the driveway where she sells baggies of dust bunnies she swears are artifacts from my youth. Before she knew about me, a spooky face materialized in her borscht with the outline of Poland on its forehead. It scared her so much she dumped it down the sink. Once she was better informed, she understood the great value of what she'd tossed, and now she makes a hopeful pot of the purple soup every day. I don't know who appeared in her stockpot, but it wasn't me, since Poland is lodged behind my left knee.

Two men have snuck around to the back of our old house, brothers, by the looks of their regrettable noses. They're peeking into Nicky's window, and the kitchen, and—

(Stop that! Stop that!)

Archie, they're pulling up one of Dad's grapevines, the root Nonna planted, and they're fighting over it. It's a real shoving match and—wow!—the big one just punched the little one in the jaw, and he's down for the count as the victor scrambles off, leaving his little brother in the dirt.

Amazing, this sibling rivalry I'd like to think I was too mature for—but alas, I was not. Of course, I learned from the masters, Uncle Dom and Dad. I have no idea why Dom felt the need to engage my passive father in jousting matches with the ultimate prize of earning Grandpa's respect. Dad always lost to his big brother, as did I. I'll never understand what power Grandpa had over his adult sons.

One of his dictates was that every First Friday the entire Ferrari clan had to gather at his house for an hour of Caruso prior to schlepping to confession. Dad and Dom brought tangible offerings for Il Duce in addition to their deference and dread. My father offered pork rinds, jars of pig knuckles, a pouch of tobacco. Uncle Dom brought Grandpa's pricey favorites: a wedge of Fontina cheese, a bottle of sambuca, *Playboy* magazine, and the litany of off-color jokes he'd collected all month, usually beginning with "This ignorant nigger boy walks into a saloon . . ." or "This clap-infested whore walks into a saloon . . ."

I always watched Nonna's face when her son related these vulgar stories. She just swiped out espresso cups as if in her mind she was on a beach in Messina, combing her hair, watching a figure emerge from the surf, but this time when she caught sight of the kelp-covered ogre, she scampered the hell away. I wanted to tell her: *Run like the wind, Nonna! Fly like the wind!*

Shortly before my twelfth birthday I approached Nonna's threshold with more trepidation than usual. Two weeks prior, I had gone to bed flat-chested, but during the night a new mountain range had formed, straining my pajama top. I had bypassed the gradual swelling of breast buds, the uprising so intense the Soviet Union on my left breast stretched beyond endurance and broke into more than a dozen separate entities. I hugged a pillow to my chest and went in search of Mom. I found her clipping coupons alone at the kitchen table, so I let the pillow drop.

"Oh my God!" She stood to take a closer look until memories of her own pubescent self-consciousness surfaced. "Well. It looks as if we'll be going to buy your first bra."

Mom must have had a preemptive talk with Dad and Nicky, because that night at supper they barely looked up from their fish sticks, and when I asked for the salt, Dad handed it over while studying New Zealand on my temple, avoiding all terrain below my chin.

The next First Friday, when we spilled out of the car for our monthly dose of Caruso, the grand exhibition was held. When Betty spotted me, she leaped from Nonna's couch and squeezed me so tight I couldn't breathe, our bazoombas mashing together like grapes in a winepress.

"The daughter I never had," Betty cried. I never felt closer to her in my life.

Thankfully, like Dad, Uncle Dom couldn't look at me for long. I imagine he was thinking, *Such a waste.*

We wended our way to the kitchen, where Grandpa held court. Nonna brushed my cheek with her hand but said nothing about the new developments. Grandpa Ferrari kept his rheumy peepers to himself. He had more important matters to deal with.

After the obligatory greetings, Grandpa stared at his younger son, then looked him up and down, especially scrutinizing his empty, giftless hands.

Grandpa finally growled, "Did you bring those tomato stakes like I told-a you, Angelo?"

It was as if someone had taken a sledgehammer and knocked Dad in the forehead. "No," he confessed, a schoolboy in front of the principal. "I left them in the garage."

"You stupid son-ama-beetch!" Grandpa threw a half-eaten plum on the floor. "I was going to stake them right after supper. Now those tomatoes will rot all because of a-you."

Nonna stood by the gas stove. "What's another day?" she said; valiantly, I thought. "Angelo can bring-a them in the morning."

"Shut up, woman." Grandpa's forearm flew up as if he would like to strike her, and by the way she flinched, I wondered if she had to anoint more than her hair with Pergusa water.

"Go get them," Grandpa said. "Now."

"But the coffee is ready." Mom rarely spoke at these affairs, but clearly she was listening.

Grandpa's eyes pressed into slits. "Angelo! I tole you to go getta those goddamn stakes!"

Mom stood up to her full height, a sinewy Corinthian column. "Let the man drink his coffee."

Grandpa stood so fast his chair tipped over, and he might have lunged across the floor to choke my mother if Dad hadn't intervened.

"I'll go!" Dad said.

"You bet-a you will." Grandpa readjusted his number-two newsie cap, righted his tipped-over chair, and sat back down, a smug look on his face. I wanted to sock him, and by the look on Mom's face, so did she. Her expression changed when Dad edged past her to do his father's bidding. It became a look, not of pity, but of shrink-wrapped disgust. I wondered what Annette Funicello would have done at that moment—probably run after her substitute husband to offer syrupy words of consolation.

The fam-i-ly migrated to the living room and Uncle Dom boomed, "Ray-Ray! Get your ass in here now!"

Cousin Ray-Ray. Yikes. I wondered how many magazines I could hold up to protect my new topography.

Ray-Ray slunk up from the basement, where he'd likely been fiddling with Grandpa's winemaking paraphernalia and girlie pictures. Thankfully he didn't look at me, just sat in a chair dragged in from the kitchen and picked scabs from his elbows.

When Dad returned with the stakes, Nonna looked at the mantel clock. "You better hurry or you miss-a confess."

We all stood, except Grandpa, who almost never went. Even Nonna begged off. "What I have to confess-a now?" I could think of a few homicidal sins I would like to commit on her behalf.

Even Mom went, just to avoid Grandpa's stare. The men and boys stampeded outside, around the corner, and across the street to Saint Brigid's. Betty and Mom lagged behind, me even farther back since I didn't look forward to presenting my new embellishments to the parishioners.

Via Dolorosa was a dead-end street with a circular turnaround at the end. At the center of the grassy turnaround stood a marble fountain of a Nereid who spit water from her mouth, or so we had always been told. The fountain no longer worked, and wild grapes, or at least not Grandpa's beloved Gaglioppo, had taken root at the fountain's base and twined themselves tightly around the statue, obscuring her figure. A few years before that First Friday, Nicky and I were digging for marbles by the fountain, me popping out pumice stones, and I made a startling discovery. The grape coloring and clusters surrounding the Nereid were the same kind as the ones sprouting from the arbor behind our house. When I went inside to ask Nonna about it, her knitting needles quaked and Grandpa belted, "Those *bastardo* grapes are Orgoglio della Sicilia. Nothing good ever come from-a Sicilia, not even a grape!"

Grandpa's bungalow was built on the center lot of the cul-de-sac, facing the fountain and Via Dolorosa, which stretched out before him like a carpet runner. The brickwork in the street was the prettiest in town, with an inlaid pattern of ocher and black stones woven down the center like the skin of a diamondback snake.

That First Friday as I walked to church behind Mom and Aunt Betty I noticed that the cursed Sicilian grapevine that once twined around the fountain had been cleared, revealing the mythic sea nymph. I paused to inspect the craftsmanship, the grape-stained marble looking astonishingly like my stained skin, and saw the face, the familiar face. "That looks like Nonna."

"It is," said Aunt Betty.

Mom and I both stopped. "What?"

We all stared at the marble features: the plump lips and subtle nose, ample breasts, fish-scaled hips, and ethereal tail. The most striking feature was the braid curving all the way down her back carved in such high relief it sprang free in places. Someone had broken off a six-inch chunk at the end, leaving only a meringue-like hair flip on the base. As we stood there, Betty divulged a tale she had learned from Celeste Xaviero, that lock-picker of family secrets, about a pair of rival brothers; not Uncle Dominick and my father, Angelo, but Grandpa Dominick and his younger brother, Angelo, whom I had never even heard of until then.

When my grandparents first moved to America, they spent a few years crowded together with other immigrants in Manhattan's Lower East Side. Jobs were scarce, so when Grandpa learned about the opportunities on the Gulf Coast, he and his wife boarded a train for Louisiana that would take weeks to reach its destination since it stopped at every Podunk along the way. A few days into the journey Nonna disembarked at an outpost where the mountainous terrain reminded her of the land of her birth. As the scenery washed over her, Nonna's ears picked up a faint hum that she hadn't heard since she'd left Sicilia. She tried to match the tone, her vocal cords rusty, until Grandpa called from his window seat, "Diamante! Come on or you miss-a the train!" The locomotive whistled, drowning out the hum, but when Nonna put her boot on the step to climb aboard, she inhaled an aroma she hadn't smelled since her courting days in Sughero: roasted almonds and nutmeg. Nonna backed away from the train just as it lurched forward.

Grandpa bellowed, "Diamante! Come on! What are you doing?"

Nonna paced up and down the platform sniffing for the source of her nostalgia, and then she spotted red Pergusa wildflowers growing beneath the sign that announced the name of the town that had already grabbed her heart: Sweetwater, West Virginia.

"Diamante! Hurry up!" Grandpa called from the chuffing train.

"No!" Diamante said. "*This* is where I build a new life with-a my husband. I have the *profezia*. I see it!"

Grandpa disappeared from his window, but soon he jumped from the train, carrying his valise and Nonna's, and trudged down the platform to her. "I see it," she whispered, and remarkably, Grandpa couldn't argue with that.

Lucky for Nonna there was not only a smattering of Italians who welcomed the still-barren couple into their enclave but plenty of work for Grandpa. The bulk of Sweetwater was already laid out and those early *paesani* put their skills to use paving the streets. Grandpa distinguished himself as the most gifted bricklayer, which is why he got that choice piece of real estate at the end of his cul-de-sac. When he and Nonna were picking their lot, she discovered a patch of wild Pergusa in the back and declared that it was a sign of-a something, although she didn't say a sign of-a what. After the bungalow was constructed the couple had their first child, Dom the Mighty.

Several years later, Sweetwater saw the appearance of another Calabrian, Uncle Angelo, who showed up on his brother's doorstep uninvited.

Angelo had crossed the Atlantic in steerage, then boarded a train that delivered him to the Sweetwater station, where he disembarked with his brother's address on a piece of paper in his hand. In broken English he asked passersby to point the way, and soon he was tromping down Via Dolorosa, still a muddy, cart-wheeled mess. He arrived at Dominick's house and rapped on the door.

Nonna came out of the kitchen drying a bowl, five-year-old Dominick Jr. at her heels. When she opened the door and saw who was standing in her doorway, the bowl fell out of her hands and cracked in two, alerting her husband, who sprinted downstairs. "What did you break-a now!"

"It's-a you," Grandpa said when he saw his bushy-haired brother.

There was no embrace, no cheek kissing or neck hugging, but because Celeste Xaviero was gawking, Dominick said, "I guess-a you better come in."

As they made their way to the kitchen, Dominick Jr. kept kicking his new uncle in the shins and lunging for the four-tooth chisel in Angelo's shirt pocket, his most prized tool.

The brothers sat at the table while Nonna prepared *stambecco brasato,* braised goat, which she made only on special occasions. Angelo laid out his plan: he wanted to work in America just long enough to build a nest egg to bankroll some business venture back in Italy. He was hoping to live with his brother so that he could save every penny.

Dominick glared at his wife, whose back was to him. Then he looked at his brother. "Why you never marry after all these-a years?"

Angelo fingered the four-tooth chisel in his pocket. "*Sono sposato a Dio.* I am-a married to God."

Diamante craned her neck around as Dominick snorted. "You turn into the *omosessuale?*"

"No! I am-a celibate. *Celibate.* No *omosessuale!*"

Dominick again looked at his wife, who had turned her head to the stove, though her shoulders were shaking.

"Why you cry?" Dominick asked.

"I no cry. I cut-a the onions." But she wasn't cutting onions.

"You owe me," Angelo said cryptically to Dominick.

Dominick adjusted his newsie cap and exhaled. "Okay. But just until you save up-a the nest egg."

The men stood, and Grandpa led Angelo upstairs to the army cot in the spare room where baby number two's empty bassinet sat, although there was no second baby yet — an intolerable embarrassment to Dominick, given the size of most Italian families, a shame he intended to rectify. Diamante endured the coupling only by fantasizing about Angelo. She also hoped his conjured face would ensure that baby number two would have a better disposition than her firstborn.

That night, when Dominick was in the basement scouring his wine vats, Diamante passed the spare bedroom, where Angelo knelt before his cot in prayer. She was about to tiptoe away when Angelo opened his eyes and sighed. "Diamante, your hair. Your hair."

Diamante ran her hand through the red mane that she had just unwhirled from her bun.

"*E' molto bella.*"

"*Grazie.*" Diamante leaned into the room and whispered, "You really married to God? You really celibate?"

Angelo looked at her with sadness and held up his rosary beads as proof. "*Sì.*"

Diamante nodded and walked away mournfully.

Dominick got his brother a job working for Le Baron, so every morning Diamante waved bye-bye to the men, often running after them with Dominick's forgotten lunch bucket or Angelo's four-tooth chisel, which Angelo prized but frequently misplaced. Dominick's younger brother soon distinguished himself: he was a better bricklayer than his older brother, plus he was an exceptional sculptor. In his spare time, Angelo began carving grotesque waterspouts shaped like dragons and lions and Chimeras, which the Italians bought and attached to their bungalows. When the ever-watchful Baron saw the extravagance, he commissioned Angelo to create not only dozens of waterspouts for his grand chateau but two gargoyles to overlook the front door. Le Baron was so pleased with the craftsmanship that he gave Angelo permission to design and lay out the bricks for Via Dolorosa.

Angelo sketched for a week before he settled on his pattern. He made the bricks himself, and he pulled them still warm from the oven and laid them immediately, while they were still pliable, for a snugger fit, leaving the impression of three of his fingers on every single brick, a deliberate feature. He worked nonstop, beginning at Appian Way and moving toward the house of his brother, or, more accurately, toward his brother's wife. Because Angelo had indeed taken a vow of celibacy, but every day he spent under the same roof with Diamante chiseled away at his oath. Whenever they wedged past each other in the hall in their nightclothes or when Diamante brought a glass of water to Angelo working bare-chested in the street, something sparked between them.

Angelo also came home for lunch and helped Diamante set and clear the table and even wash up the dishes, their hands swimming like fish beneath the sudsy water as they felt for soupspoons and butter knives, fingers occasionally grazing, perhaps even clasping as their hearts thudded and their godly resolve slipped down the drain.

Having been commissioned by Le Baron to do another project and given carte blanche in its design, Angelo began work on a statue in his brother's garage. Every night he hammered and four-tooth-chiseled and smoothed. He ordered special fountain parts from Sicilia, which arrived in a crate accompanied by clippings of a Sicilian grape that made a smoother wine than Grandpa's Gaglioppo.

On the afternoon of the unveiling, Angelo called together all the Italians in the neighborhood; they skipped down their newly bricked street, the children marching heel-toe along the serpentine inlay as if it were a game. They gathered around as he revealed the fountain modeled after Botticelli's *Birth of Venus,* though of course this Venus was a Nereid standing on her giant seashell. Scallop shells discreetly covered her nipples; another jutted from her hair like a Victorian comb. She was also holding out seashells like patens. Father Kavanagh raised his hands just as a red-winged raptor swooped overhead screeching like a girl being murdered. The falcon released its bowels, splattering not only the beautiful nymph but Angelo and Diamante. The old women cheered, since everyone knows that being shat on by birds brings good fortune. Father Kavanagh interpreted it differently. He stared up at the receding falcon and proclaimed his divine augury: "Sometimes shit just brings shit." He mumbled a swift prayer, and when he gave the command, Angelo turned on the spigot beneath the base, which set off a spray of water from the Nereid's lips, much to the crowd's delight. All this attention on Angelo started a fire in Dominick's belly, especially when he noticed the townspeople begin to look from the Nereid's face to Diamante's in wonder.

Several weeks later, one day around noon, Dominick had a case of the trots. Because he was close to home, he rushed there and barely peeled off his union suit in time. When he came out, Diamante was dashing from her bedroom trailing a familiar fragrance, and he heard the back door slam.

"Who's that?" he said.

"Who's what?"

"The back door."

"Nobody. You hearing a-things."

"Hmmm." Dominick loped to his room to change. That's when he saw it: a four-toothed chisel on his bedside table sitting next to the bottle of red Pergusa water, a spilled puddle staining the doily beneath the lamp.

Dominick scooped up the chisel and ran downstairs to Diamante, who was in the kitchen.

Dominick's shoulders shook and his voice wobbled. "Haven't I given you a good-a life? What have I done-a wrong?"

Diamante's head hung as she whispered the truth. "You're not Angelo."

It had stunned me to learn that Grandpa once had tender feelings for Nonna, but that was the end of them. It was at that precise moment, under Diamante's brutal admission, that his heart compressed into a hunk of coal.

"*Puttana!*" he howled. "I'm gonna kill that no good son-ama-beetch!"

Dominick bolted outside and ran, holding the chisel like the Olympic torch, to the site where the Saint Brigid School was being built and where his brother was working. Diamante chased after him. "No! No!"

Angelo was stacking a pallet of bricks when his brother charged at him. "*Testa di cazzo! Bastardo! Figlio di puttano! Individuo spregevole!*"

Angelo spun around just as Dominick grabbed him by the throat. "You get outta my house! My city! My country! And go back to Sicilia where you belong!"

Angelo stared at his sea nymph and opened his mouth, but Dominick socked him in the jaw so hard that my great-uncle fell backward into the stack of bricks, toppling them over. Dominick threw the chisel at him, splitting his lip; the dripping blood was the exact color of the Pergusa water. Dominick heaved Angelo up by the front of his collar, spun him around, and booted his ass all the way down Appian Way to the train station. Diamante scooped up the chisel and followed in time to see Dominick hurl Angelo into a boxcar just as the two-thirty-five train pulled away, the shrill whistle blowing so loud it nearly drowned out Diamante's proclamation: "We will be reunited some-a day! I have-a the *profezia!*"

Dominick looked at his wife and balled up his fist. "You! Get back-a home or I'm gonna clock you for sure!"

Diamante went back to a house emptier than it had ever been, curled up on the army cot in baby number two's bedroom, and squeezed Angelo's chisel in her palm as she cried herself to sleep. That was the night a six-inch segment of the Nereid's braid went missing and water stopped pouring from her mouth.

Seven months later Diamante gave birth to her second son in the same hospital where that son's children would be delivered fewer than three decades later. Dominick went to Scourged Savior only to fill in a not-really name on the birth certificate: *Non Miniera,* "Not Mine." It didn't matter that Diamante kept assuring him, "He's-a yours, Dominick! He's-a yours," which was a distinct, if slight, possibility.

But before Dominick got the chance to assign the infant such a *bastardo* name, Diamante shuffled to the nurses' station to fill in her choice: Angelo, her second and favorite son, who was born with a tiny birthmark on his left shoulder blade in the shape of a four-tooth chisel.

When Betty finished her tale, Mom and I stared at the statue, stunned. Betty swore us to secrecy as we proceeded down Via Dolorosa, where Great-Uncle Angelo had left his fingerprints on every brick, a permanent reminder to Grandpa of everything else his brother had touched.

We turned onto Appian Way, passing Aventine Laundry and Del Pizzo's Florist adjacent to Saint Brigid's. Uncle Dom and Dad were just leaving the church as we crossed the street and marched up the steps. They all grunted at one another, but when Dad raced off to keep up with his brother, Mom stared at him with newfound interest. Perhaps as she watched his receding back, she pictured the tiny birthmark she had traced her finger over countless times during their honeymoon years.

Then Uncle Dom socked Dad in the arm, and Mom muttered, "No offense, Betty, but I will never understand Angelo's devotion to Dom."

"He never told you?" Betty said.

"Told me what?"

"When they were boys, whenever their father went after Angelo with his fists, Dommy jumped in to take the beating for him."

Mom looked as perplexed as I felt. "Why did he do that?"

Betty shrugged. "He always said that was the big brother's duty."

I wondered who had instructed Dom about his fraternal obligation. Could it have been Grandpa, who'd had his own little brother to protect? The prospect was mind-boggling.

• • •

In the narthex, Betty pulled mantillas from her purse for Mom and her to drape over their heads and took out a doily for me. As I pinned it to my hair I tried not to think of a blue pillowcase tucked in my underwear drawer. Inside the sanctuary Nicky was kneeling in a pew, head bowed, eyes shut. Ray-Ray sat behind him drawing anatomically correct stick figures in a hymnal. Mom slid into the last pew to read some novel, her crisp page-turning the only other noise in that hallowed nave besides the penitents clicking rosary beads.

Betty and I padded up the side aisle toward the confessional booths, three cell-like chambers, each with its own door. The larger, middle one belonged to Father Luigi. Red lights glowed above the two smaller doors, indicating that some poor schmuck was spilling his guts in one and another schmuck was waiting his turn. Finally, the left door opened and out came the sinner, eyes to the floor. Aunt Betty went in and I wondered, as always, what sinful thoughts she harbored. Lusting after muscle cars. Loving her dead husband more than this new one. Infanticide. I could easily imagine Uncle Dom's offenses crusting his soul, though taking beatings for my father absolved him somewhat. I had also keenly studied Ray-Ray's face whenever he exited the booth: he was always wearing a vacant ax-murderer scowl.

When it was my turn I entered and knelt, and eventually Father Luigi slid open the screen that separated us. I studied Father's shadowy profile (and Abe Lincoln's) as he made the sign of the cross. I began: "Bless me, Father, for I have sinned . . ." then admitted my failings: Fighting with Nicky. Not doing my homework. Before doling out his penance, Father uttered his usual prayer. "May the person *truly* responsible for this child's affliction repent of her sins." I suffered his dig at Mom and tiptoed out of the booth to begin my prescribed prayers, though I thought that suffering through Father Luigi and Caruso was expiation enough. My other penance was to loiter in the narthex and allow all the First Friday nonnas to brush my cheek or touch my hair, letting them have some tangible element that they would run home to smear on their ailing kin. I had learned that it was use-less to deny them.

Afterward, Mom and Aunt Betty walked home arm in arm. Nicky ambled somberly behind them with his hands in his pock-ets, as if he were still in the confessional booth or wishing he were because he'd left out one important thing. He'd been walk-ing around like that a lot lately, especially after Dom and Betty's last poker party at our house. Nicky and Ray-Ray had once again disappeared after supper, and not only did Nicky not come out of his room the next day for poker change, he didn't even come out for Alka-Seltzer.

That postconfession day, even Ray-Ray must have sensed that Nicky was not to be harangued. I lagged behind my brother as we crossed Appian Way and stepped onto the sidewalk. Ray-Ray zig-zagged around me, kicking a stone, racing to kick it again. Mom and Aunt Betty paused to check for traffic before crossing the al-ley between Aventine's and Del Pizzo's. Nicky looked neither right nor left, as if it would have been okay with him if he was flattened by a delivery truck.

I, however, had an aversion to being hit by fast-traveling steel bumpers. I looked left into the alley before stepping off the curb. Thus it was a complete shock to be rammed from the right, not by a vehicle, but by Ray-Ray, who pushed me into the alley with a shove so hard it slammed me down, grinding my right hip into gravel. It knocked the wind out of me too, and I couldn't even scream when Ray-Ray dived on top of me, yanked up my shirt, and ground my new breasts and bra in his gritty hands. "When the hell'd you get these honkers?" He eyed the landmasses on my torso he'd never seen. "God, you're a freak," he said, jumping up and racing away. It happened so fast that for a few moments I lay there, stunned, shirt still bunched up around my neck, head in a pile of putrid-smelling carnations tossed out from the flower shop. The neon sign in the window sputtered until both Zs in *Del Pizzo* burned out.

Minutes later I stomped down the center of that snake street toward Grandpa's house angrier than I had ever been in my life. My hands were balled into fists, and I was ready to punch Ray-Ray in the nose, gut, crotch—anywhere that would draw blood or induce vomiting.

I kicked open the door and found everyone in the living room, Ray-Ray standing behind his father. I pointed at him and shouted, *"Vaffanculo!,"* a word I'd heard seethe from Grandpa's lips a thousand times.

I was about to leap over the coffee table and rip off Ray-Ray's ears when Grandpa said, "What did you say?" He looked at my father. "What the hell did she say?"

Mom rose and clamped both hands on my shoulders to hold me in place.

Grandpa repeated, "Angelo. What did your daughter just say?"

I wasn't looking at Dad. I was glaring at Ray-Ray, sparks shooting from my eyes as I tried to impart nonverbally that as soon as Mom released me I would be kicking his balls up to his tonsils. Ray-Ray just stood there smirking, and when no one was looking, he lifted his hands, fingers splayed, and flexed those filthy digits just as he had moments before when he was mashing my breasts.

"Goddamn, son-ama-beetch, asshole!" I broke free from Mom and dove at Ray-Ray, who ducked into the dining room. I dodged Nonna's knitting basket and raced after him but was yanked back by Grandpa, who grabbed my wrist, making my already sore hip bang into his chair arm.

"What kind-a daughter you raising with a foul mouth like this, Angelo? No granddaughter of mine is-a gonna speech like that. See?" He looked at my father, and so did I, remembering that horrible Corpus Christi day when he'd draped me across his knees.

"But he pushed up my shirt!" I finally sputtered. "He touched my—" I couldn't finish, didn't want to expose my private anatomy to any more humiliation.

"What?" my mother said.

"He did what?" Aunt Betty said.

I looked down at my chest and smoothed the fabric over it

with my right hand, my other arm still clamped in Grandpa's claw. "He—" was all I could say.

Aunt Betty stood and ran into the kitchen. "Raymond!" she yelled in a tone I'd never heard from her. Even Uncle Dom pushed out of his chair, already whipping his leather belt from around his waist. "I'll take care of this," he growled, pounding after his step-son.

Grandpa released my wrist. "Well, it's a terrible thing, that's-a for sure."

Finally I could breathe, but then Grandpa added, "It's just as bad for a girl to speech that kind-a filth. Angelo," he said in a syr-upy voice, as if he really loved his maybe-maybe-not son, as if he knew what was best. "There's only one way that children learn, and that's with a firm hand." He held up the back of his hand as proof.

Nonna's knitting needles clicked furiously.

I shuddered as I looked at Dad.

"Angelo," Mom said as if she were trying to rouse him from a deep sleep. "Angelo!"

But he didn't budge; he just kept looking at Grandpa, who was drilling his *Don't you dare* eyes into Dad's, a look so fierce I could only imagine the punishment I was in for.

Instead of spouting indecipherable verse, Mom stamped across the room and looped her arm through mine.

"Come on." Mom steered me to the front door, voice urgent. I wanted to wrap my arms around her neck and kiss her, but first we had to make our escape. "You too, Nicky." I only then saw my brother standing by the front window, drapes wadded in his hands, naming murdered Romanov children.

The three of us pushed outside and started walking the four miles home. No one breathed until we turned the corner and passed the alley with all those rotting carnations. I rubbed the Indochinese peninsula on my hip—including the raised welt of Vietnam that had suddenly appeared on the eastern coast—which was now scraped and pulsing thanks to Ray-Ray. I spit on my finger, dabbed at the tender flesh, and wished I could airmail Ray-Ray there and strand him in the jungle without a map or compass.

As we marched onward Nicky kept looking behind us. I didn't know why until Mom said, "He's not coming."

My brother had been watching for the station wagon to pull up and for Dad to lean out his open window. *Get in,* he would say, *it's too far to walk home.* It reminded me too much of the long walk home Nicky had made the day he had tossed Radisson and me to the Four Stooges. Except Nicky had redeemed himself.

My father did not rescue his family and save them from the slog along Appian Way and up Sweetwater Hill, from the blisters on their heels and the balls of their feet from wearing the wrong shoes.

As we huffed toward our house, I pictured him, a thirty-seven-year-old husband and father of two, kneeling in Grandpa's backyard staking the old man's tomatoes. I imagined him bent to his work, Grandpa standing over him, arms crossed, barking orders. Dad obeyed and he once again started shrinking, bones shortening, vertebrae compressing, pant legs bunching around his ankles, shirtsleeves swallowing up his hands until he was a timid six- or seven-year-old whimpering under his father's might. Little Angelo kneeling in the dirt, holding back tears and sniffling up snot because he hopes this time, for once in his life, he might get it right.

Portafortuna

Father:

I'm sipping Alka-Seltzer so forgive the fizzing. I have a queasy stomach, which started when Betty brought Nonna back from the hairdresser several nights ago. I knew something was amiss even before they returned, because it was after six o'clock and supper wasn't on the table. Finally Nonna schlepped into my bedroom in tears followed by Betty, who blubbered, "I'm sorry. I'm so, so sorry." Nonna wore a headscarf, though I saw pink bangs poking out. I actually groaned. Nonna clutched a Whitman's Sampler to her bosom, so I thought she was consoling herself with decadence number three. She opened the lid and I reached for a caramel, but what I found was Nonna's lopped-off white braid coiled inside like a snake.

I pulled my hand back as if it had bitten me, and I swear it did, Archie. Two pinpricks of Pergusa blood beaded on the tip of my thumb.

"I just ran out for a minute to get cigarettes," Betty said. "I told Sherri not to do anything drastic, but by the time I got back—"

Nonna tugged off the scarf to expose tight pink ringlets covering her head like flower petals on a swim cap.

"Pink?" I said, flabbergasted.

"It was supposed to be strawberry blond," Betty said. "And just a trim. Nonna, I am so, so sorry."

Nonna sank onto my bed and held the braid in her hand as if the essence of her being were woven inside. "It took-a my whole life to grow and she lop it off in-a two snips." She cried for half an hour, enough tears to fill the Strait of Messina. Betty and I patted her shoulders and her brutalized locks.

Eventually Nonna shrugged us off and pulled a hankie from her bra to sop up the wetness. "We have to bury this in-a the backyard."

Though it was dark outside, Betty and I wouldn't dare deny Nonna.

We snuck to the garage, Nonna in the lead with a flashlight since we didn't want to give our mission away to the pilgrims. Betty followed with the Whitman's Sampler. I grabbed a shovel and Nonna led us into the yard, her arms outstretched like divining rods. Nonna wove us around the birdbath and the barbecue pit and finally stopped at the patch of Fiore Pergusa she had planted and where stood a statue of Mary of Lourdes nestled in her own grotto.

Okay. Let's get this over with:

Bless me, Father, for I have sinned. It's been thirteen years since I last make-a confess. The only thing I want to admit besides a heart filled with unbelief is that two years ago I stole a holy statue from Annette Funicello's backyard. To be fair, it was no longer Annette's backyard. Turns out, Jake had been having an affair with a woman in Peoria with a prosthetic hand. The new homeowners are Baptists who don't believe in saints and they let the statue become overgrown by wild morning glories. And to be doubly fair, it wasn't my idea. Nonna had had her eye on the statue from the minute she did *not* win it all those years ago. Betty helped me lug the thing up the hill in the middle of the night, so half of the penance rightly belongs to her. And, umm, we'd been drinking.

But on the Night of the Braid, Nonna knelt before Mary and made the sign of the cross. Betty and I knelt and crossed ourselves too. This was Nonna's ritual, after all. She whispered a smattering of prayers, handed the flashlight to Betty, and heaved Mary to her chest.

"Move-a the grotto," she instructed me.

I obeyed as Betty shone the light on the flattened disc of earth beneath the base where startled centipedes and potato bugs scampered into shadows.

"Now dig," Nonna said.

I jammed the blade into the earth; its damp smell was rich and musty. I wasn't sure if I needed to make a six-foot-deep rectangle, so I just kept heaving pumice-speckled dirt to the side until Nonna said, "At's-a good." We knelt before the gaping wound as Nonna took the cardboard coffin from Betty. More tears slid down Nonna's cheeks as she laid the cord of herself into the grave and scraped earth over it, dirt raining on the yellow lid like a drum. We helped her fill the hole and tamped it down with our hands before setting the grotto back in place and nestling Mary inside, the roasted-almonds-and-nutmeg smell of crushed Pergusa blossoms wafting through the air.

Later that night I found Nonna in her bed raking a four-tooth chisel through her hair as if it were a comb. "Angelo. Oh, Angelo," she muttered before tucking the chisel under her pillow. I cleared my throat, made my way to her, and pressed my lips to her forehead. "Now you look just like Maude."

Nonna's feet wiggled beneath the sheets.

The next morning I went out to make sure it wasn't all just a dream. I saw the raw dirt around the statue, the forgotten shovel leaning against the forsythia. I was about to walk away when I glanced at Mary and spotted a long plaster braid snaking over her shoulder, though I didn't remember her having one. I spun around looking for someone to ask—Annette Funicello, perhaps—if the braid had been there all along or if it had sprouted overnight.

I'm sitting before the statue right now, Archie, in a lawn chair pulled up for the occasion. It's November tenth, Betty's birthday, but instead of blowing out candles together we have all gone our separate ways. Betty no longer celebrates her birthday, and with good reason. It's dusk and I can't ignore the tang of freshly dug earth that overpowers even the Pergusa blossoms, a stench that brought on yet another wave of nausea that no Alka-Seltzer will cure. I've been putting off question forty-seven long enough. It's time to get into that horrible chain of events, so here goes.

For five months after the head-in-the-rotting-carnations incident, Mom not only barred Dad from her bedroom but also refused to let Dom and Betty and their monster cross our threshold. I'd thought the ban was forever, but that Saturday in November I watched Mom frost a caved-in sheet cake with lemon icing. She had even borrowed Mrs. Bellagrino's pastry-chef gizmo to blob on orange flowers.

"What's going on?" I asked.

Mom stopped and looked at me. "It's Betty's birthday, honey. I invited them for cake and coffee this afternoon. Just cake and coffee."

"But Mom!"

"I know." She offered an adult admission I couldn't rebut. "Honey, she's my only real friend."

The compromise was that I would get to stay in my room with a box of Froot Loops. Plus I got to write *Happy Birthday, Betty* on the cake, though it looked more like *Holly Barfly, Bebby*, which was still nicer than the message I wanted to leave: *Vaffanculo, Ray-Ray!*

I was rinsing frosting from my fingers when Dad came up from the basement. "I'm heading to the pharmacy for cigars."

As he shrugged on his coat Mom said, "Take Garnet with you."

Dad looked at her, then me, and he hesitated only a second before saying, "Get your coat."

I seldom rode in the car alone with Dad. Usually Nicky called shotgun and I ended up in the back ramming my knees into his seat. That day, though Dad and I didn't utter one syllable, I relished that up-front drive.

The bell over the pharmacy door sounded as we entered. Mr. Flannigan was in the rear dusting the display case that held sundry last-minute gifts: aftershave and cotton handkerchiefs, costume earrings and brooches, an assortment of rosaries.

He called to my father, "White Owls and your *Play—*" He switched gears when he saw me. "Howdy there, Garnet. How about a cherry Coke?"

I looked up at Dad, who said, "Sure. And coffee for me."

Dad sat on the stool Nicky had swiveled on the day we celebrated the bells. I sat beside him, though it felt, frankly, weird.

Mr. Flannigan made his way to the soda fountain, slid a box of White Owls onto the counter, and served us our drinks. He and Dad started yammering about the Cuban Missile Crisis, which had been at the forefront of every adult conversation for the past six weeks. The Cuba on my left elbow had been at the forefront of my attention for the past six weeks too, since it had been itching like the dickens. I still wasn't sure if it was La Strega or someone else playing tricks on my skin, but I glided off my stool to peruse the ointments lining the back shelves that might offer relief. I also drooled over the penny candy, spun the comic-book rack, scanned the rows of greeting cards and the display case of baubles Mr. Flannigan had been dusting. Amid all the trinkets I saw something that stopped my breath: a heart-shaped charm on a bracelet, exactly like the one Mr. Giordano had given Donata last spring when my class made its confirmation. It was really too much; first the holy day he had carried his broken-legged daughter into church, and then the bracelet with a silver charm inscribed with my heart's desire: *I love you*. All the girls tittered, especially when Donata added, "He's going to buy me a charm every year until he walks me down the aisle on my wedding day." As I stood in Flannigan's I wondered what charm Mr. Giordano would buy Donata next: a horse, a four-leaf clover, a ballerina. It lifted my spirits to think that the bracelet had been a last-minute purchase while Mr. Giordano picked up shaving cream or Preparation H.

Just then the back of the display case slid open and Mr. Flannigan smiled across the crowded shelves at me. "See something you like?"

"That bracelet," I whispered.

"It's a nice one." He picked it up, walked out from behind the case, and slid it into my palm. "The heart opens up too."

I wedged my dirty thumbnail between the two halves and easily pried it open to reveal the slots where two tiny photos could go, or perhaps a piece of hair. I closed it and studied the back, imagining an improbable inscription.

"What's that?" Dad asked, now standing beside me.

I wasn't even thinking when I handed it over. He held it close to his face. "It's a beaut."

This was my chance. "Mr. Giordano just gave one to Donata. Lots of fathers do. Give their daughters charm bracelets."

"That so?"

"Want me to ring it up?" Mr. Flannigan asked. "Free engraving included."

For a minute it looked as if my father was seriously considering it. "Maybe later. We need to get going. Don't want to miss the big party."

I lagged behind as Dad pushed outside clutching a brown shopping bag.

The drive home was wordless and not because I was pouting. I was bubbling inside because Dad had left the little door open. *Maybe later,* he had said, words I polished on the ride back, since Christmas was coming, that season of miraculous births and of so many things.

When we got home Dad dashed to the basement with the bag that held the spoils we all knew about: his stinky White Owls and a splayed-blond-bombshells men's magazine.

Hours later the phone rang. Mom answered and I eavesdropped. Apparently Uncle Dom's car wouldn't start. God *does* answer prayers, I thought, until Mom said, "Angelo can come and get you, Betty. No! It's no trouble!"

"Traitor." I scuffed outside fuming at Mom and at Grandma Iris, who had foisted upon us a stupid car that would ferry my tormentors to my home. And then I had an idea. I slunk down the steps and approached the car as if it were a timid dog. "It's okay," I cooed, hand stretched toward the grille. I had watched my father lift the hood countless times to check fluid levels and belts. I thought I could easily open it and pull out some gizmo that would keep the machine from starting. I reached my fingers under the hood and tugged. Nothing. I pulled again and the car jiggled, but still the hood would not lift. "Open up!" More furious yanking. The car stared at me, all that chrome smirking, so I kicked the bumper. I was about to slink away when I remembered the car's secret.

The first day Dad drove us all over to Nonna's and Grandpa's to show off this car, Nonna had circled it, saying, "*Guarda la macchina!*," as she'd done with the Mercedes convertible. She clapped her hands on Dad's face and smiled. "I make-a the *portafortuna.*" She looked at Nicky and me. "Come. I need-a you help."

Nicky and I followed Nonna upstairs to Dad's old bedroom, which she had converted into an anti-*malocchio* chamber. His chest of drawers was stuffed with skeins of red yarn, boxes of saint medals, dried rue branches, jars of I-don't-even-want-to-know.

She filled her apron with a jumble of ingredients and sat at the card table to cut a three-inch square of red fabric. In the center, as she muttered a litany of prayers, she sprinkled grains of rice, a dash of salt, a tiny gold horn, a Saint Christopher medal, and two drops of yellow liquid from an old iodine bottle. She gathered the four corners and twisted them together, making a pouch. "You hold-a," she said to me. She twined red thread around the top of the pouch, counting all the while. After she tied it off, she kissed the bundle and held it to our lips for a final consecration.

Again we followed as Nonna carried the *portafortuna* downstairs and outside to the car. Nicky opened the passenger door so Nonna could scoot inside.

"Open the glove-a box," she said.

Nicky obeyed and Nonna shoved the lucky pouch as far back as she could. She rearranged several maps and a single mitten over it and made the sign of the cross before closing the compartment. "At's-a good. Now you are-a protect from the fender-bend or the run-out-of-gas." So far, the talisman had worked.

All of that could change, however, and I yanked open the passenger door, popped open the glove box, and pulled out road maps, the still-single mitten, gasoline receipts, and that detailed logbook Dad kept about the car's repairs. And then I found it, the red bundle, a bit dusty but still wrapped tightly with Nonna's loving care. I rammed it into my pocket, stuffed the detritus back inside, and hightailed it to my room just as Dad emerged from the basement. "I'm going to get them!"

"Don't start. Don't start. Don't start," I chanted.

Of course the car started right up. I felt the lumpy *portafortuna* in my pocket. "A lot of good you do."

Forty minutes later Dad still hadn't returned. I heard Mom open the front door. "Wonder what's keeping him?" I hoped against hope that my *macchina*-tampering had finally kicked in.

But eventually he arrived with his brother's family. I dove into the closet with my Froot Loops but could still hear every word when they entered the living room, Uncle Dom blabbering, "If Marina were my wife . . ."

Apparently Aunt Betty had Nicky in her big-bosomed headlock. "Where's your sister?"

Mom answered for him. "She's not feeling well, so she's going to stay in her room."

A pause, then Aunt Betty said the thing that made me love her even more. "I don't blame her, Marina. If I could quarantine Ray-Ray for the next thirty years I would. That boy, I swear."

That boy had probably spent the day hurling cats off the train trestle into the Ohio River.

Soon I heard the fam-i-ly singing "Happy Birthday" followed by a cheer as Aunt Betty blew out candles. Silverware clattered on dishes, then Ray-Ray's clodhoppers pummeled down the hall toward Nicky's room. "Come on," he called. I listened for my brother's acquiescent footfalls also heading toward his room, but instead I heard the front door creak open and then closed.

"Where're you going? Wait up!" Soon Ray-Ray was clomping down the front steps too.

I kept waiting for Mom to announce, *Okay, now. Time for you to shove off.* But she didn't, and she didn't, even as the afternoon light began to fade.

I heard kids cavorting outside, so I burst from my closet and knelt on my bed to look out the window at the litter of children circling Mr. Julietto, our candy man, who paraded around the hill passing out goodies he pulled from a World War I military satchel. One time I was in Flannigan's as he rattled off his list — Mary Janes, root-beer barrels, candy peanuts — and I watched Mrs. Flannigan dumping whole boxes full into his sack. Candy Man was like a migrating bird; he disappeared into his home around Thanksgiving, when arctic weather slid in.

That November day, he must have sensed an early winter, because it seemed he was doling out all of his remaining treats. As I peeked through my blinds and watched him, I really did feel ill; obviously, God was punishing me for fibbing and perhaps because of the stolen *portafortuna.* I started plotting while buttoning up two sweaters. I would have to tiptoe past the party, but I heard Betty laugh in the way she did only when she was tanked, so I knew the scotch and schnapps were blurring everyone's vision.

I've heard stories about mothers lifting cars to rescue babies, the superhuman adrenaline surge that allows mere mortals to perform heroic feats when faced with a catastrophe. I was faced with a disaster — missing out on Candy Man — and I cracked open my door, tiptoed down the hall, zipped by the kitchen, and eased outside undetected. I followed the trail of candy wrappers and pushed myself to the forefront of the children.

"Garney!" Mr. Julietto said. "I wondered where you were, honeydew."

There are times when port-wine stains evoke sympathy, which is sometimes welcome, sometimes not. That day I embraced it, because along with his pity came the biggest fistful of confections Candy Man could pull from his satchel. As I pushed back through the kids, someone whined, "How come she always gets so much?"

"Because she's a saint." Dee Dee Evangelista sighed, visions of a Betsy Wetsy miracle swirling around her head.

"'Cause she's so ugly," Tony Panatela said, the barb stinging less with the loot in my paws.

I headed to my favorite spot for savoring penny candy: Snakebite Woods, a cemetery for BB-gunned squirrels and birds and the hideout of the Four Stooges.

Streetlights buzzed on up and down the street as I circled around and around and down the backside of the hill, but before diving between the trees, I leaned forward and listened for any sign of the Stooges: cackling and snorting, loogie-hawking.

Though the coast seemed clear—the Stooges hopefully in the village getting their skulls cracked by Dino's baseball bat—I avoided the downhill path that led to their ground-level box fort, which I had seen during previous expeditions. Instead I darted onto the upward path that crested a rise and snaked down the other side. Twigs snapped under my feet as I aimed for the four-trunked sycamore, its bark peeling off, revealing naked white skin. I contorted myself into the center of the trunks, my own kind of box fort, and dumped an entire mini-box of Mexican jumping beans into my mouth while looking up at the lacy crosshatch of branches already stripped of leaves.

I peeled off the waxy Necco Wafer wrapper and before shoving the first chalky disc in my mouth I chanted, "The Body of Christ." I ate one after another until the package was empty.

The Sugar Daddy took real effort, and as I warmed the taffy in my mouth, I peeled off more strips of sycamore bark and rubbed my hand against the smooth, cool trunk. My mind reeled back in time as I imagined the Adena mound builders who'd once lived here. Perhaps the ground the tree stood on was one of their mounds, and underneath it rested the skeleton of an honored chief wrapped in deerskin or fox fur or whatever they used to preserve their dead.

My Sugar Daddy finished, I angled out of the tree, squatted down by its base, and picked up a sharp stick to scratch at the earth. I scraped away layers of matted leaves, the smell of mushrooms drifting up. I dug, hoping to find a yellowed human tooth or a pottery shard, some connection to Sweetwater's original residents. I unearthed acorn caps and worms and pumice stones, of course, but no artifacts, so I unwrapped gumballs and rammed one after another in my mouth. The blending flavors of sour apple, cherry, grape, and dirt congealed into a gritty wad the size of a nectarine. Soon my jaw became sore so I spit the glob into the freshly dug hole, sprinkled in all my candy wrappers and the sucker stick, and started covering it over. Maybe in a thousand years some Judy Jetson girl would unearth them, flatten all those wrappers, and read *Necco Wafers* and *Jumping Beans,* words that would have no meaning to her, and she would wonder what message the long-dead person who had buried this treasure had hoped to convey.

It was a sad cache, and because I could, I reached in my pocket and pulled out the *portafortuna.* I tugged at the thread and unwound it, going around thirteen times. The square sprang open in my palm, revealing the salt and the rice, the holy medal and gold horn. I sprinkled the contents into the hole, laid the red square on top, and was scooping dirt over it when somewhere in the woods a voice wailed, "Stop!" My hand stilled and I feared that somehow Nonna had discovered me undoing her good magic. I tilted my ear up and heard a sharp crack and then a muffled cry.

"Quit!" a thin voice pleaded, a voice decidedly not Nonna's.

I fell back on my bum but then jumped up and started running toward that word lingering in the air because I knew that voice intimately. Then everything was quiet except for the wind in the trees. I froze, willing my eardrums to pick up any hint of sound, and I heard it: not voices, but bodies jostling. I knew exactly where it was coming from and tiptoed toward the Stooges' box fort with the four trees serving as corner posts. The goons had filched lumber and nails from various construction sites, but the trees' asymmetrical growth cycles left wide gaps between the planks.

A sound like sheets flapping on a clothesline came from inside the fort. I crouched low and tiptoed toward the widest gap between the slats, wondering what torture the Stooges had cooked up now.

I held my breath and peered in, though I didn't think I'd be able to make out much since the sun was nearly gone. Nearly. At first all I could see were stripes of dim blue light filtering in from the opposite wall. Then movement below, a triangle of something white and as smooth as the skin of a sycamore that had shed its bark. And it was skin, a shoulder. Not one of the Stooges', but Ray-Ray's bare shoulder blade, though he was mostly facing away from me as he knelt and hovered over whoever it was he was wrestling with, a figure almost completely hidden by Ray-Ray. I wondered what game this was and then, when I saw the other boy's bony knees, his pants tangled around his ankles, wondered if it was a game at all. A tinny voice inside my head started chanting, No-no-no-no, because I didn't want the other boy to be who I already knew it was. Ray-Ray gripped a handful of the boy's golden hair and yanked his head back. "Be still!" The boy tried to wrench free, twist his head out from under Ray-Ray, and I saw his porcelain cheek streaked with dirt, a petrified look in his eyes, a look that I've tried to gouge out of my brain ever since.

A hot wave rushed over me, under me, through me. I ran away, branches whipping my face, scratching my skin, as I careened forward and found myself crouched before that four-trunked sycamore, a tree sturdy enough to lean on while my head flopped forward and I puked onto the grave I had so recently dug. I vomited up all of Mr. Julietto's candy, the jumping beans, the Necco Wafers, innocent delights I had just indulged in so fully but that I would never be able to enjoy again.

Then my body started shuddering as the ground rumbled beneath my feet. I don't think I imagined water leaking out of a fissure in the dirt. I heard what sounded like percolating coffee from inside the earth and I started to run.

I burst out of Snakebite Woods just as something exploded at the top of the hill. Whatever it was, I wanted it to blow us all to smithereens: Me, Mom, Dad, Nicky, and most of all, Ray-Ray. I raced up the hill feeling mist on my face, not rain exactly, not snow or ice. It was dark by then and I tripped and stumbled more than once. The neighbors' porch lights pinged on all along our street as I scrabbled up the middle of the road, seeing the image of my brother's petrified face, that look in his eyes, and Ray-Ray. Something surged from the pit of my gut and shot from my fingers, eye sockets, mouth until every streetlight on the hill began humming and sputtering. They surged as I ran under them and one after another they exploded, sparks and glass shattering on the now-wet road, crunching under my sneakers. Porch lights popped like gunshots, neighbors rushing outside: "Hey! What's going on?" I charged upward, around and around, panting, lungs burning as I left a trail of darkness in my frenzied wake. I scrambled up our cement steps, skinning my shin on one sharp edge before banging through the front door, not caring about our own crackling porch light, or the table lamp, or the overhead hall light, all sizzling and then snapping us into darkness.

"Oh my!" Mom slurred, too drunk to care, as poker chips clattered on the floor.

"Get a flashlight, for God's sake," Dad said. "I'm winning!"

Amid all that chaos, the dangerous blend of water and electricity, the world exploding and imploding, and that horrid image in my brain, my parents were concerned only about their stupid card game.

I ran to my room, stomach churning, and slid under the covers in my leaf-littered sweater and mud- and glass-crusted shoes. The burn of vomit still in my throat. I lay there, shivering, and not just from the frigid air that had suddenly whirled around Dagowop Hill.

Soon I heard footsteps out front. I knelt on my bed and looked out into the blackness as Nicky made his way up one slow step at a time, golden ringlets dripping from whatever had poured from the sky. The front door opened and then closed behind him, but my parents didn't notice him any more than they had noticed me. He went into the bathroom across the hall from my room, and I lunged to my keyhole and squinted out. Miraculously the bathroom lights worked for him. He closed the door, punched in the lock, and yanked the shower curtain back. The faucet in the tub cranked on full blast, water rushing and gurgling, pipes moaning. Then the plunking sound as he eased himself in, and I imagined water swirling up to the rim. He stayed in there for half an hour, furiously scrubbing, occasionally sniffling, and I pictured his bony white knees gleaming in the box fort.

Finally my brother came out, and as he went to his room, I wondered if I should follow. *What did he do to you?* But his bedroom door closed on my opportunity. I tiptoed to the bathroom, where Nicky's sepia-tinted bathwater glugged down the drain, as if the answer might appear in the ring of dirt circling the tub.

I felt bile rising and rushed to the toilet, but my nausea vanished at the sight of rusty water. I went to the sink, turned on both faucets—stained water splashed into the sink.

The front door opened. I ran to the hall and tried to plant myself there like a sturdy, four-trunked sentry. I leaned against the wall for strength, but when I heard Ray-Ray's footsteps approach the hall entrance, I ducked back into my room and stood next to the doorway, peeking out with one eye. He loomed at the end of the hall, oblivious to me, his eyes aimed at Nicky's door. Ray-Ray's soaking torso swayed toward it, but then he turned slowly around and sat in one of Mom's wingbacks, the fabric of his clothes rustling as he settled in, claiming ownership.

The following morning, a fresh layer of snow blanketed our hill, suffocating our Monopoly roofs, our streets, our lawns. Mr. Julietto had correctly predicted an early winter. The snow wasn't blue-white but gray, like fireplace soot. I knew that beneath it, remnants of streetlight glass circled the base of every creosote pole up and down the hill. Just one day before I would have marveled at the powdery swells. But as I looked out my bedroom window I imagined Snakebite Woods were covered too, my four-trunk sycamore, my candy-wrapper-filled mound, and a box fort hoarding dark secrets beneath the ashy snow.

I sat in my room listening for Mother's bed to creak, the little yawns and moans to slide from her mouth as they did each morning. Through the wall I heard her cough, the boards under the carpet whining as she walked to the bathroom. "Brr," she said.

I opened my door and listened to the tinkling sound as Mom peed. The toilet flushed and the spigot turned on. "What the hell's wrong with the water?" I heard her fumbling with the towel rack that often detached. "Stupid thing." She came out and saw me standing in my doorway.

"Morning. Don't drink the water." She untangled my hair and assessed my leaf-speckled sweater. Grimy sneakers. "Did you sleep in your clothes?"

I didn't answer, so Mom started walking toward the kitchen, toward loose poker change that I had no interest in. It would have been so much easier to spin around and hide under my covers, to pretend I hadn't heard, hadn't seen.

"Mom."

She turned toward me, face weary from years of life in this fam-i-ly. "What is it?"

"I have to tell you something." I looked at Nicky's still-closed door, imagined him bundled mummy-like in his sheets. "In here." I led her into my room, where I closed the door. Mom sat on my bed and dug sleep from her eyes. How I longed to dive into my closet.

"Garnet, I have a lot to do this morning, and now the water is screwed up."

My heart thumped as I pushed out the few words I could muster. "Ray-Ray hurt Nicky."

"What?"

I looked at my trembling hands and somehow found the language to describe what I had seen through the slats in the box fort.

Before I even finished, Mom burst into the hall, hands to her blanched face. I thought she was racing to her room to vomit up weird verse or dive into a hand mirror, but she ran to Nicky's room. I followed, breathless, as she barged in and over to his bed. Nicky jerked up, hands rushing up to protect himself as he began listing venomous snakes.

"What did he do to you?" Mom said, voice too high.

Nicky's eyes widened into that panicky look I had seen the night before.

Mom shook his shoulders, hard. "What the hell did Ray do to you?"

Nicky looked at me over Mom's shoulder. He understood that somehow I knew too, and his expression collapsed from terror to red-faced shame. "Nothing!" His voice issued from some narrow place. He rolled toward the wall, probably hoping he could fall through the gap and be swallowed up for good. "Leave me alone!"

"What's going on?" Dad stood in the doorway in his boxers and T-shirt. Black socks with a hole in the big toe.

Nicky buried his head deeper in the crevasse. Mom looked at Dad. "It's Ray."

"What?" Dad scratched his armpit.

I backed around him and moved into the hall as he entered. I couldn't bear to watch Mom's face as she searched for her own words to tell Dad what I had seen.

"Close the door," Mom said to Dad, though she was looking at me. As if it weren't already too late to protect me from this.

I sat on the hall floor as if I were waiting outside a confessional.

Until that moment, I had never heard my father truly angry. Over the years he had stuffed down his antipathy for his brother, his father, as if it were unthinkable to harbor ill feelings toward members of one's own family. As if blood kin couldn't wound one more deeply than anyone else on the planet. But that day, the groan started in the pit of his stomach and rumbled up to inflate his lungs before shooting through his throat in one long roar. I had never heard such screaming, such *goddamn, motherfucker, son of a bitch, bastard,* in all my days, and these were followed by Italian pejoratives: *testa di cazzo, bastardo, figlio di puttano, individuo spregevole!*

The door to Nicky's room flew open, the top hinge breaking, as Dad burst out, a maniacal glare in his eyes. He rushed toward the room where his clothes still lived but paused in the hall. I wondered if he was going to throw up too. He didn't. He clenched his fist, cocked his arm, and punched a hole in the plaster wall as if it were tissue paper. "I'm gonna kill that son of a bitch! Where are my car keys?"

I expected Mom to come out and placate her enraged, hungover husband. Instead, she dashed from Nicky's room and rushed past me cowering on the floor. "I'll find them," she hollered on her way to the kitchen. "Put on some pants."

Dad raced to his room to tug on a pair of trousers. He had one leg in and was about to ram in the second but he stopped, frozen, as if he'd just remembered something important. And then my dad started crying, real chest-heaving, gasping-for-breath sobs. Soon he shook it off. *"Picchiare selvaggiamente qualcuno!"* I understood that. He was going to beat the shit out of someone, though by then I wasn't sure if it was Ray-Ray, Uncle Dom, or both.

I slumped against the door frame, stunned, looking at a hole in the wall and plaster chips on the floor, wondering what I had set in motion. It looked as if Dad really might kill Ray-Ray, and Uncle Dom too if he tried to intervene. And there was Mom coming at him with the keys in her hand. "I found them! I found them!" She could have been offering him a knife or a gun. *Kill them good, Angelo. Kill them good.*

Dad started to barge out the front door, red eyes pulsing, uncombed hair shooting out like tongues of fire.

"I'm going too," Nicky said, which stopped all of our hearts.

"What?" Dad and Mom said.

Nicky stood in his bedroom doorway.

"No," Mom said. "Dad will take care of this. You stay home with Garnet and me."

Then my beautiful, delicately boned, fine-featured brother took a deep breath and said, "Dad, I have to go too."

Dad looked at Nicky. "All right."

"No!" Mom grabbed Dad's arm as he passed, trying to stall him.

Dad drilled his eyes into hers. "Marina, Nicky wants to do this. He needs to do this." I looked at my father, my brother, wondering where all this courage had sprung from.

It was definitive bravery, and Mom knew it too. By the way she stared at Dad, I could tell that he appeared a foot taller in her eyes. It was as if he'd disappeared after their courting days, had actually been gone, not merely sawing wood in the basement, but now she had found her husband again, a miracle in itself, and I immediately thought that if she could find him, maybe he could still find me.

Without breaking his gaze, he gently slid her hand from his arm and held it for one second, two. He offered a nod, which somehow bolstered my mother, and she backed away to let the two men in her life grab their coats from the closet and head outside.

Mom and I watched as they descended the ice-coated steps, Nicky nearly losing his footing.

"Careful!" Mom called.

They slammed the car doors and Dad backed out too fast, tailpipe sparking the ground. He peeled out, leaving two icy strips on the street, furious to get to Grover Estates.

I pictured Ray-Ray and Uncle Dom sleeping in their warm beds. They had no idea what was torpedoing toward them.

It sounded exactly as it should have. Metal and glass plunging into bricks and mortar. A screeching, crunching, grating roar. Alarmed residents yanked on their robes and galoshes to rush outside and down the hill, never mind the dirty water, the curlers and half-shaved faces, the teakettles keening on the stoves. They hurried outside, along with me and Mom, who squeezed my hand so hard it throbbed. We slipped and slid, because beneath the snow was a layer of ice. The natural spring that perpetually washed across No-Brakes Bend had frozen with a vengeance. It was a patch Dad could never easily navigate, but especially not while livid and speeding. We saw the tracks where our station wagon had skidded over the curb and then flown completely over the embankment and the row of hedges before plunging into the side of Mr. Dagostino's garage.

Mom let go of my hand and ran toward the hissing smoke. I started to follow—"Mom, wait!"—but someone yanked me back by my waist. Annette Funicello, who looked even whiter than the snow, her eyes rounder than mine. "No, Garnet!" She tugged me back up the hill, though I tried to wrench free.

"Let me go!" I wailed, but she was stronger than I ever would have imagined, that adrenaline surge of mothers protecting their young. She pulled me all the way to her house as neighbors kept pouring down the hill, all those old nonnas kissing scapulars and holy medals as they rushed forward in their fur-lined boots, their children asking Annette, "What happened? What's going on?" The questions went unanswered, but they would know soon enough.

Mary Ellen stood inside her front door. "Mom," she whined when we came inside.

"Just a minute, honey."

Though it was warm in her house, I started shivering, teeth chattering. Annette raced down the hall for a bedspread, which she wrapped completely around me before settling me on the couch in front of her picture window. She came at me with a brown medicine bottle and a spoon. I opened my mouth without protest and swallowed the burning liquid. I could still hear people outside crying and sobbing, a distant siren that grew louder and louder. I started to sit up to look out the window. "No," Annette said, pressing me back down. She tugged the drape cord;

the heavy curtains swished together, sealing out the light. They couldn't seal out the noise, though. I tipped my ear toward the siren so that its cry could pour into my ear and twist around like a cyclone with the siren that was screaming inside of me, because I was the one who had removed the *portafortuna* and emptied it of its good-good magic.

Hours later I awoke to the sound effects of cartoons: slide whistles and *ka-bongs* and plucked violin strings. Tom chasing Jerry with an ax. Mary Ellen sat cross-legged on the floor in front of the TV in the living room. A cluster of shadowy figures stood just inside the front door: Annette and my mother and Sergeant Mickey from the Sweetwater police, who handed Dad's wallet to Mom. She held it to her nose, inhaled, and I, too, smelled the musky scent of leather. I imagined holding the curved shape of it to my cheek, wondering where my father was that Mom was being entrusted with his billfold. I wanted to ask about Nicky, but for the moment all I could do was lie there, still swaddled in Annette's bedspread, holding my breath.

Sergeant Mickey offered Mom the keys to the station wagon. At first she took a step back from the ring of dangling metal, but then she held out her hand, and when he rested the keys in her palm, her hand sank under the weight of them. He left Annette to minister to my mother, her outstretched hand still cupping Dad's keys, which she had armed him with that morning. Her hand started trembling, the keys jangling, as if she were holding some dangerous thing in her palm: a wad of rusty razor blades, a blasting cap, a scorpion.

SS Edmund Fitzgerald

Archie:

I'm in the conservatory surrounded by the grand piano, a cello, and a honey-colored harp, though my preferred instrument, as you know, is the lowly saw. Specifically, a Sicilian import with a curlicue-etched handle stained with my father's sweat. Its melancholy wail fits my mood, since I've been conjuring ghosts. Now there are even more ghosts, because the SS *Edmund Fitzgerald* sank last week on, you guessed it, November tenth. I asked Nonna how a cargo ship hauling so much mystically protective iron could go under, drowning twenty-nine men, whose bodies they haven't recovered. She didn't have an answer.

After the Accident I felt as if I were trapped in an underwater world waiting for someone to reach down and rescue me. And the hill was a soggy mess. That night in Snakebite Woods, as volcanic pressure was building inside me, the pressure that had been building inside the hill finally found an escape, the mouth of a sweet-water spring. The belch thrust upward with such force it blew Le Baron's whippet-tipped springhouse to smithereens, spewing water and bricks down on the hill and village; it coated our phone lines, TV antennas, and trees. Slate shingles were found miles away embedded like hatchets in telephone poles. City workers soon stoppered the jet, forcing the water to find an alternative exit at the base of the hill beside the Plant, collecting who-knows-what along the way. Of course, all of this was the least of my worries, and Mom's.

After Dad's wallet and keys were returned, Annette escorted my mother home, one hand on her elbow as if it were a rudder. I followed in their wake, marveling at this pairing. Once inside, Annette lowered her eyes, establishing Mother as primary widow, with all the consolation prizes that would come her way.

As Annette walked home, where she would secretly mourn, several ladies congregated in the street even in that snow: Mrs. Bellagrino, Mrs. Evangelista, all the old nonnas making signs of the cross. They were organizing the hill's collective response: *You make the minestrone; I'll make the risotto; you take up a collection for the novenas,* their words coming out in puffs as they looked up at our home. They could have been watching a drive-in movie screen or an aquarium perched on a high shelf.

The air in our house suddenly liquefied, our footsteps sluggish against the wet weight of it. The phone rang and Mom went to the kitchen to answer. I heard mumbling and she hung up, but it rang again, and again, until Mom let the receiver drift to the floor with a muffled clunk. The front door opened though no one had knocked, and in tumbled Grandpa and Nonna.

Grandpa waited in our living room for Mom to stand before him. I cowered behind her as he swished that newsie cap in one hand and droned on and on, about what, I couldn't say. His words sounded garbled, each syllable encased in a bubble. Nonna stood beside him still wrapped in her apron, the strings floating up behind her along with the end of her braid, which she hadn't yet swirled into a bun. Clumps of tacky pasta dough in the crotches of her fingers. She was as inert and anchored as one of those underwater divers planted at the bottom of so many fish tanks. An oddly sweet look was imprinted on her face, as if in her mind she was a young mother bouncing a four-tooth-chisel baby on her lap, cooing and trilling as she predicted a future for him that she'd thought would last much longer than this. And so had I.

Not long after, Uncle Dom and Aunt Betty arrived. No Ray-

Ray. Dom was haggard and unshaven. Betty pushed past her father-in-law in an uncharacteristic display of boldness and dove for
my mother, who held both arms straight out to stop the advance.
Mom's mouth opened and a foghorn sound poured out that hammered our eardrums, and Betty froze cold when she learned the
truth about her not-really son.

I couldn't bear the look on Betty's face, so I swam down the
hall to Nicky's room and closed the broken-hinged door.

I looked at Nicky's unmade bed, the sheets rumpled just as he
had left them that morning, a rabbit hole where his legs had been
before he yanked them out in a moment of nerve. The divot in
his pillow where his head had rested. I reached my hand for it,
hoping the downy feathers would still be warm. It was cool to the
touch, no hint of the boy who had slept in that bed for the last
thirteen years. I felt absurdly sad for his mattress, an inanimate
thing that would never feel the bony weight of him again.

I mourned for all of it: his bedside lampshade decorated with
Heckle and Jeckle stickers, the on/off button Nicky's finger had
pressed countless times. I grieved for his desk, for the contact-
paper-covered soup can filled with pencils and pens he would no
longer grip. The shelves of *Britannicas*, the stacks of them too,
piled around the room. Pickle jars filled with marbles, a few steel-
ies mixed in that Dad had snuck home from the Plant. I felt a
fist in my gut at the thought of him. Dad. A tormented image I
pushed away from me as fast and as far as I could because I could
not yet face the full breadth of our loss, and my hand in it.

I felt weary under the weight of all that water and I sank down
on Nicky's bed, burrowed under his covers, and tried to inhale
the scent of him, because I could breathe this water, draw in the
stinging scent of Ivory soap, the pilfered aftershave Nicky had begun to splash on after his pointless attempts to use Dad's razor.

I nestled my face into Nicky's pillow, specks of my purple landmasses embedding in the cotton weave, and I imagined his fury at
this defilement. I rubbed my arm, Buttholia, and I longed for the
sharp crack of Nicky's fist, a purple bruise that would blossom

and eventually evolve into a muted yellow-green. A fleshy sea anemone.

My eyes burned and I closed them, let the tears soothe the grit, and I felt myself floating up, a surfacing buoy. Footsteps pounded down the hall and I was once again weighted to the bed. I just knew it was Nicky coming to thrust open the door and ask me what the hell I was doing in his room. I clutched the edge of his covers and giggled as the handle turned and the door eased open one inch, two, just enough for me to see Nicky's hand on the knob, then his shoulder, and finally his head leaning in.

Though of course it wasn't Nicky at all.

Mom rushed toward the lump nestled in her son's bed. "Oh my God! Nicky, is that you?"

Though of course I wasn't Nicky at all.

SANCTUS INTERRUPTUS, DUO

Dear Archbishop Gormley,

This is Betty Ferrari, Garnet's aunt. I have to whisper because I've just stolen Garnet's tape deck and I'm hiding behind the bromeliads in the solarium. I need to talk to someone because everyone here is so sad, crying at the drop of a hat. Mother Ferrari has been cooking like she's feeding an army, which I guess she is since we lug pots of spaghetti and pinto beans to all those people outside. We have to sneak the food out since Garnet forbids us. "Don't feed them or they'll never leave!" But they all look so hungry. Plus I think Nonna needs to cook for them, but even that doesn't stop her tears. Yesterday she wept into her apron for two hours straight, blaming it on the diced onions, but I know better. This anniversary is so hard on us.

Did you hear that? Even the pilgrims have been crying for days. About every four hours they start howling and there it goes again. It's as if a dark cloud has settled over this hilltop and we're all one raw nerve of pain.

I know where it's coming from. Garnet has been in the conservatory night and day playing the saddest songs over and over on her daddy's saw. Last week I was in the backyard and I overheard her telling you about, well, everything. I know you need to understand her history, our history, but really, is it necessary to dredge that up now?

Oh, dear. I know it's impolite to blow my nose like that. And there goes my mascara. Give me just a minute to blot up this mess. Do forgive me, but what I really need forgiveness for is bringing this tragedy into our lives. It's all my fault. I have been cursed from birth, just ask Mother Ferrari, who tells me so every other minute.

I take all the blame for bringing Ray-Ray into their lives. He was never a child I would have chosen as my own. I just know that if I had birthed any children they wouldn't be monsters. I didn't even choose his father, but it's not as if boys were knocking down my door to ask for my hand. But Louis, that was my first husband, was a widower who didn't seem to mind my eye malady, though sometimes I wish I were as brave as Saint Lucy and could pluck it out. Maybe then Mother Ferrari would love me like a daughter, because she is the only mother I have left.

Anyway, Louis was more interested in my cooking skills and the two thousand dollars my father scraped together for a dowry, money I had to use for Louis's funeral seven months later, leaving me to raise that child by myself.

Since it's just you and me here I need to confess that I never loved Ray-Ray. Maybe he knew. That boy was a terror, which is why I married Dommy. Ray-Ray needed a firm hand and Dommy surely had that. But Dommy is gone now too, and I don't miss him one bit. Is that wrong? And now Ray-Ray is halfway around the world and I confess I don't miss him either. I never was like all those other war mothers who wore those POW-MIA bracelets to show off their grief for their real sons. Wherever Ray-Ray is, shot dead in the jungle, locked in some bamboo cage, I hope he stays missing forever. God forgive me.

Father, sometimes I don't know why I do what I do, especially after Garnet invited me into her home after everything that's happened, not just with Ray-Ray, but with Dommy and Grandpa Ferrari, but I don't know if she told you about that yet. I'll say it again just like I told the bank and those thugs who showed up at my door: I don't know why I should be held responsible for Dommy's gambling debts or overdue loans, which I knew nothing about. Which makes Garnet's generosity so much richer since there is no family tie any longer. She could have tossed me to the curb . . . or to those thugs. And how did I repay her? I talked to Mike Wallace and his *Sixty Minutes* crew. I couldn't be rude, and I tried not to say anything Garnet wouldn't want me to, but honestly, people need to know about her healing powers, which are real. I've seen them. Anyway, the episode aired last night and it wasn't easy to keep Garnet away from the TV. She would have had a fit if she saw it. I'm not sure if you caught it, but Mr. Wallace's assistant said he'd send me a transcript. I'll mail you a copy just as soon as—

(*Aunt Betty! Have you seen my tape recorder?*)

Shit. I have to go now, Father. But please pray for us. Please pray for all this crying to end.

Transcript: *"The Reluctant Saint"*

MIKE WALLACE: The holiday season is in full swing as Christians prepare to commemorate their Savior's birth and as Jews celebrate the Festival of Lights. Not every child longs for a bicycle or plate of latkes; some long for the healing of an ailment or a birth defect. Over the past few years an increasing number of hopefuls have made a pilgrimage to see alleged miracle worker Garnet Ferrari here in Sweetwater, West Virginia, a lowly site for a saint, but no lowlier than a straw-lined manger.

Sweetwater's primary industry was once a metal-processing plant, but as you can see from the tchotchkes in storefront windows—Saint Garnet coffee mugs, volcano lighters, lava lamps—the town's chief product these days is its reclusive healer. Jimmy Katzenberger bought Flannigan's Pharmacy after the original owners passed away a couple of years ago. The pharmacy no longer fills prescriptions, but it maintains a candy counter and soda fountain that offers the Saint Garnet Float and the Mount Etna Fizz.

WALLACE: You sell a lot of these fountain drinks, Jimmy?

JIMMY KATZENBERGER: Oh yeah, yeah. People will buy anything with that saint stuff on it.

WALLACE: You were born in Sweetwater?

KATZENBERGER: No! Hell no. I'm from New Jersey, but I know a good thing when I see it.

WALLACE: Tell me, Jimmy. Do you believe Garnet Ferrari can perform miracles?

KATZENBERGER: Do I believe? Well, see this cash register? Two years ago it was empty and now it's full. I call that a miracle!

WALLACE: From sunrise to sunset, traffic crawls along Appian

Way, the only access road to Garnet's home at the pinnacle of Sweetwater Hill, visible there in the distance.

WALLACE: Sir! Roll down your window!

MOTORIST: *¡Oh, mi Dios!* You are Mike Wallace!

WALLACE: Yes, I am. And where are you from?

MOTORIST: New Mexico.

WALLACE: New Mexico! That's a long drive with, what, five kids you have in there?

MOTORIST: *Sí,* but we've got a sick little girl here. Mami, pass Mariquita up here. See this harelip? We can't afford surgery, so we were hoping—

MOTORIST'S WIFE: Praying, José! Praying!

MOTORIST: Praying that Saint Garnet would heal her. She healed a boy from Arizona born with only one nose hole, so we are optimistic.

WALLACE: Indeed, every person in this procession is hoping for a miracle, but the question on everyone's mind is, Can Garnet deliver? According to longtime resident Celeste Xaviero, Sweetwater inhabitants by and large had a long history of beautiful skin.

CELESTE XAVIERO: It's-a true. Before Garnet left, most of the people here had the prettiest complexions, people *born-a* here, I mean. People who moved here may have brought their disorders with them, oddly shaped moles and rosacea and-a the like, but after they lived here for a while, those things would clear up.

WALLACE: On their own or with the intervention of Garnet?

XAVIERO: I wouldn't want-a to say, since I don't like to gossip.

WALLACE: And what happened after Garnet moved away all those years ago?

XAVIERO: Everybody in town broke out in a rash! Our gums, they turned gray, and our teeth-a fall out. One itchy patch would clear up and another would appear.

WALLACE: And then Garnet moved back and the rashes disappeared?

XAVIERO: Not immediately, maybe after six months, but *si*, they disappeared.

WALLACE: And do you attribute *this* to Garnet?

XAVIERO: I don't really know, but I find it strange that she was-a born with the biggest skin disorder of all and she never healed herself. As far as I know she's still covered in-a birthmarks, though I wouldn't know since she never visits, and I was her nonna's closest friend!

WALLACE: Sitting on the steps outside of Dino's Lounge, three returning Vietnam veterans are more direct.

VET. #1: Hell no, she's no saint. Taking kickbacks from all the dipshits up there. And her brother was no saint neither.

VET. #2: Little faggot. We used to pound him but good.

VET. #3: And Map Face just gave everyone the creeps.

WALLACE: How did you know them? Were they your classmates?

VET. #1: No. I was older. But Bimbo was in Nicky's class before he dropped out.

WALLACE: Where is Bimbo now? Maybe I can interview him.

VET. #2: He didn't make it back from Nam. Fat ass stopped to get a ham sandwich out of his pack and got shot in the neck. Stupid ass.

WALLACE: I'm sorry to hear that.

VET. #3: Say, you wouldn't have a spare buck or two for a veter—

WALLACE: And here comes Dino the bar owner with a ball bat. Hey, where are you all going?

WALLACE: This is the scene outside of Garnet Ferrari's hilltop estate. Even in this cold weather, families have established a tent city along her fence. A section of the north side is jammed with votive candles and letters taped to the railings. Pier Paolo Vespucci traveled from Italy to sell ex-votos, mini versions of afflicted body parts offered to Saint Garnet in hopes of a healing. At his booth you'll find eyeballs and ears, kidneys and feet made of silver or tin, wood or bone.

WALLACE: You've come a long way to do business, Pier Paolo.

PIER PAOLO VESPUCCI: It's-a no business. It's-a holy work. These people need to make-a the plea for a healing and they offer a gift to Saint Garnet so she intercede on-a their behalf.

WALLACE: And it makes you a nice profit.

VESPUCCI: A man's gotta eat, Mr. Wallace. But I perform a service, see? And affordable too, so everyone can buy the ex-voto and be healed.

WALLACE: You have a nice assortment here, but what if someone comes and there is no votive to represent his or her affliction?

VESPUCCI: It's easy, see? I have the wax here and I can form-a almost anything. I even make-a one for your pock-a-mark cheek.

WALLACE: My—

VESPUCCI: You had the bad acne as a kid, but Saint Garnet can even heal-a this. I have seen myself once when I make the cheek with the pock-a-mark for a lady and she is healed in one week.

WALLACE: But—

VESPUCCI: I take-a the ball of wax and press and press until it's flat and I make it look like-a the cheek with the jaw and a tiny bit of-a lip. Then I take this-a tool and I bop-bop-bop-bop all the little marks. See? Then I punch a hole and insert the ribbon. Now you take this to the fence and say the good prayer that Saint Garnet intercede and God heal-a you cheeks too. And for you I make-a the good price. Just three dollars.

WALLACE: Three dollars?

VESPUCCI: Okay, two fifty.

WALLACE: As you can see by the numbers of ex-votos hanging from the fence, people have deep faith in Garnet's powers, and many claim to have been healed. With me now is Eddie Rangel from Oregon. So you've been healed by Garnet Ferrari?

EDDIE RANGEL: Yes!

WALLACE: And what was your affliction?

RANGEL: See this thumbnail? Ten years ago I got a fungal infection, but nothing would cure it. Then it migrated to the next finger and the next. Then it jumped over to this hand. I'm a dentist, Mr. Wallace. Who wants to open their mouth for a guy with funky nails?

MRS. RANGEL (offscreen): Tell him we usually look a lot better than this.

RANGEL: We've been camping here for a week. We may look a little grungy, but we wash up every morning in the reflection pond, and look at this nail bed. Look! The new growth is coming in just as pink and healthy as anything. Can you believe it?

WALLACE: Everyone bathes together even in this weather?

RANGEL: More of a sponge bath, and the water is heated!

WALLACE: Does it bother you to know that Garnet would like for all of you to go home and leave her alone?

RANGEL: That's what we hear, but we don't believe it. Why would she send her aunt and grandmother to pass out food and holy relics?

WALLACE: Why indeed? *Sixty Minutes* tried repeatedly to ask Miss Ferrari these and other questions, without success. Though we can't get close to the front door, there is an intercom system built into her gate. Let me just punch the button.

WALLACE: Miss Ferrari. It's Mike Wallace here with *Sixty*—

GARNET FERRARI: For the last time, *go away!*

WALLACE: This is the same greeting we've received for the past two days, but you can just make out a figure standing by the beveled window there. (Zoom in, Freddy.)

WALLACE: Some say Garnet's gruff behavior is an act to deter nonbelievers. Regardless, the longest line of all up here leads to a booth where pilgrims can get free food and blessings. Standing in line is August Delp holding his two-year-old daughter who has a prominent growth on her forehead. How long have you been waiting in line, sir?

AUGUST DELP: Three hours.

WALLACE: That's a long time to stand while holding a sleeping child.

DELP: It is, but she's got a melanoma and this really is our last hope.

WALLACE: What about surgery?

DELP: We're Christian Scientist — well, I am. My wife is dead set on surgery, but I have to show her . . . I need for her to see that . . . well, I need for her to believe in me again.

WALLACE: Believe in *you*?

DELP: It was my sin that caused this, sir. Not the baby's. Mine.

WALLACE: Let's hope August finds what he's looking for. Behind the table stands Garnet's aunt Betty and grandmother Diamante. Thank you for speaking with me today, Betty.

BETTY FERRARI: My pleasure, Mr. Wallace. I have always loved your TV show, and so has Garnet. Tell everyone out there that Garnet Ferrari loves *Sixty Minutes*!

WALLACE: Yes, yes. So besides minestrone, I see you're giving out . . . what have you got there? What's in all those vials? Water?

BETTY FERRARI: Not just any water, Mr. Wallace. This is water Garnet touched with her own, umm, hands.

WALLACE: And what is Grandmother Ferrari doing with the vials?

BETTY FERRARI: She offers a prayer over every one before handing it over.

WALLACE: That's a lot of prayers. And what's in the vials at the end there with the yellow tint?

BETTY FERRARI: Oh! That's for particularly difficult cases. Extra potent stuff, you know.

WALLACE: Grandmother Ferrari, I wonder if I could—

DIAMANTE FERRARI: Get away, you squinty-eye *jettatura*! *Ptt-ptt-ptt!*

WALLACE: Apparently Grandma doesn't like our cameraman.

BETTY FERRARI: Oh, dear. I'm so sorry, Mr. Wallace. She's funny about certain things.

WALLACE: I don't mean to be insensitive, Betty, but you have a rather unusual eye. Did you ever ask Garnet to heal you?

BETTY FERRARI: Heal me? Well, no. It never occurred to me to ask Garnet to do that, though it would certainly make life easier, especially with Mother here.

DIAMANTE FERRARI: Walleye old-a *gabbo*.

WALLACE: What's that—

BETTY FERRARI: There are so many people who deserve a healing much, much more than me.

WALLACE: Don't you think you deserve to be healed?

DIAMANTE FERRARI: I see you over there with-a you squinty-eye camera trying to steal-a the *miracolo* from this holy water. Shoo! Shoo!

WALLACE: As the sun sets on Sweetwater Hill, travelers snuggle together in tents, RVs, and cars. As it was for Mary and Joseph all those years ago, there's not enough room in the inn, and the overflow has claimed the parking lot of the vacant plant. Pilgrims call it the Pit, and the ones who are here don't get to bathe in the warm waters of the reflection pond. They rely on the foul-smelling liquid that trickles from the pipe at the backside of the factory. They may have come with visions of sugarplums, but they are leaving with dashed hopes and various disorders that, at least so far, Garnet has been unable or unwilling to heal. Their evening entertainment is sitting around the fire drums swapping tales of woe.

VISITOR #1: Garnet didn't heal me none. I still got this rash, and she didn't heal my wife's appendix scar neither.

VISITOR #2: She didn't heal my boy and it broke his heart. He told everyone back in Toledo his face would be normal again, but, well, I don't know what he's going to say to them now.

WALLACE: Why do you think you and your children weren't healed when so many others claim to have been?

VISITOR #3: I want to see those healings for myself, but I think it all boils down to money.

WALLACE: Money? Are you suggesting Garnet is selling her healings?

VISITOR #1: What do you think? It's the rich folk with the fancy cars that can make it up the hill that are the ones getting all the healings. Us poor slobs who maybe hitchhiked or came by bus or Amtrak and can't get up there, you don't see none of us being healed, do you?

VISITOR #2: That's right. Garnet doesn't heal the poor.

VISITOR #3: I don't think she heals anyone. I think she's a charlatan, that's what I think. Planted a few confederates to go around saying their rashes disappeared. Probably painted the rashes on with food coloring.

WALLACE: You really think she's a fake? That this is all a big scam?

VISITOR #4: Damn straight! We always heard nothing good ever came out of West Virginia. Shit. Here come those beggars again. *Hey! Get away from our fire! Go build your own!*

BEGGAR: But you took all the wood.

VISITOR #4: Not my problem, lady. Now go on back to your side of the lot. Git. Git!

WALLACE: Who are those folks?

VISITOR #4: Bunch of pathetic old beggars who have no business being here. Ugly as sin.

WALLACE: Ugly indeed.

WALLACE: Longtime resident Desiderata Evangelista, now Sister Evangelista, has made it her mission to tend to the disgruntled souls in the Pit as well as the camera-shy beggars. Every day she and her friend there with the pronounced limp bring pots of homemade soup and bread.

WALLACE: Sister Evange —

SR. DESIDERATA EVANGELISTA: Call me Sister Dee Dee. Everyone does.

WALLACE: Sister, apparently not everyone is a believer. Do you think Garnet can heal people?

SR. DEE DEE: Yes. Well, God is the healer, but He has been working through Garnet for years. I've known her all my life and she's been performing miracles since we were children.

WALLACE: What do you say to people who claim Garnet is a fraud?

SR. DEE DEE: O ye of little faith, Mr. Wallace. I saw Garnet's power with my own eyes. Of course there will always be skeptics, and to be perfectly honest there were instances when Garnet could not heal a physical affliction, but—

WALLACE: What do you mean?

SR. DEE DEE: Maybe you should ask Pippa here.

WALLACE: Forgive my indelicacy, Pippa, but by the looks of your foot, Garnet didn't heal you, and yet you continue to believe?

PIPPA: Garnet *did* heal me, sir, years ago when I was a schoolgirl.

WALLACE: She did? But your impair—

PIPPA: My foot? Oh, my foot never needed healing. It was my father who needed the healing, and after Garnet prayed over me, he never beat me again.

WALLACE: Your father hit—

PIPPA: I have to run now. The soup is getting cold.

WALLACE: One of the locals brought up an interesting point, Sister. If, according to you, Garnet can heal the skin afflictions of so many, why hasn't she been able to heal herself?

SR. DEE DEE: I've thought about that many times over the years. Perhaps erasing her birthmarks isn't the healing Garnet needs. Perhaps God put her on this earth to act as a magnet.

WALLACE: A magnet?

SR. DEE DEE: Have you seen her, Mr. Wallace? She absorbs the world's afflictions and takes them onto herself.

WALLACE: That's quite a burden.

SR. DEE DEE: Some might call it a blessing.

WALLACE: Tell me, Sister. Garnet has repeatedly insisted that she has no power, she is not responsible for the healings, and she would like nothing better than for the pilgrims to pack up and leave her in peace. What do you make of this?

SR. DEE DEE: That's the biggest mystery of all. But God has a pattern of using people who are at first resistant. That doesn't mean He can't still work through them. I pray every day that Garnet will finally accept her calling. Because with or without her consent, people are being healed. In one way or another, people are definitely being healed.

WALLACE: So we leave this hallowed ground with more questions than answers. Is Garnet Ferrari a saint or isn't she? I really don't know, but there are plenty of believers who think she is. If you listen carefully, you can hear an angelic sound drifting down from the hill, the pilgrims serenading their healer with "O Little Town of Sweetwater" in the hopes that she will continue to be God's healing saint, even if a reluctant one.

The Assassination of Abraham Lincoln

Most days I despise my captivity, Archie, but if I have to be a prisoner, it might as well be in a mansion with enough square footage to get lost in. Betty's mission is to sleep in a different bedroom every night, which she can do for six weeks before beginning the rotation anew. There's also the fur vault, cane closet, and hat room, with shelves of velvet heads topped with the history of millinery wear, from Victorian bonnets to Jackie Kennedy pillboxes. I often wonder where La Strega wore them, since she rarely left the premises.

After the Night of the Braid, Betty discovered a use for all those chapeaus. Every Friday, she, Nonna, and I pick out headgear and stroll to the game room for our newest vice, bowling. We're down here right now and Nonna is lining up her shot wearing a helmety toque complete with Mephisto feathers, though I can still see pink bangs. Betty is keeping score in a flouncy affair that looks like a spilled-out junk drawer: strands of pearls, silk flowers, a taxidermied sparrow nesting on top. I chose a maharajah turban with the eye of a peacock feather fastened in front by a brooch. Quite stylish, and, I must say, the pope would fit right in if he visited wearing his miter—tell him to bring his own bowling shoes, though.

(*I make-a the strike! I make-a the strike!*)

(*Attagirl, Nonna!*)

You should see Nonna and Betty, jumping up and down like little girls, pearls spilling off Betty's hat and rattling across the floor, no crabby husbands to rein in their glee. There was a time when I thought I would never see these women again, let alone share a mansion where they enjoy uninhibited bliss. After the Accident we were separated for too long by geography and grief. It took ten years and the alignment of several planets to bring us back together.

But first: the Great Schism.

Less than twenty-four hours after I lost my father and brother, Grandpa claimed Dad's chair at the kitchen table and ate our consolation food. Nonna hovered by the stove, tears dripping into the *pasta e fagioli*, her cooking made difficult by the foul water that poured from the pipes. I wanted to stop Nonna's busyness and make a full *portafortuna*-stealing confession, but it looked as if she needed to occupy her hands or she might fracture into a million pieces.

Even from the kitchen I recognized the sound of Grandma Iris's Cadillac pulling into the driveway, that grating tailpipe. Surprisingly, when I opened the door, she knelt and embraced me, her body a life preserver I tried to grab, but she withdrew it too quickly. Nonna crept up and I expected them to embrace over their shared losses, but Grandma just shucked her fur and draped it over Nonna's arms.

Nonna accepted her subservient station. "You wanna sand'? A cuppa coff?"

Zelda's eyebrows pinched together.

"A sandwich and a cup of coffee," I translated.

"No. No. I . . . darling," she said to me. "Where is Marina?"

I looked toward Mother's closed door, a sanctuary littered with untouched teacups, plates of saltines. Earlier that day I had slipped in and sat on the bed where she lay under covers, her body a crescent facing the wall. "Mom," I had said. "Mom." Her answer was gloomy: *"Stopper the ice floe; unforge the steel."* I nudged her shoulder, hoping to rouse her so that she would stroke my head and utter some rational comfort. But she was still sunk at the bottom of her own murky ocean and I thought: *There she finally goes.*

Zelda tiptoed down the hall, rapped gently on the door, and

eased inside. An hour later she emerged, face as blank as a washed chalkboard, to find her suitcases lined up in the living room thanks to me, Grandpa too busy picking cashews out of a can of mixed nuts. He did, however, lift his wide ass when I told him there were two crates of vodka that I didn't have the strength to haul in. That night I didn't have to take the pullout couch. Quite unexpectedly, we now had a bedroom to spare.

Our house became an old-timey luxury liner, our footing unsteady and slippery. The living room served as the upper-class deck, Grandma Iris in her wingback receiving visitors in place of her daughter, accepting meringue pies and High Mass cards that I had to explain. The kitchen transformed into steerage, where Nonna heated up dishes that Grandpa consumed. I became a porter navigating between these disparate worlds, bumbling around with trays loaded with coffee and biscotti and pain.

Mom had to attend the viewings at the funeral parlor, but only her disengaged body emerged from her room, thanks to vials of Grandma's pills. For whatever reason, Mother didn't want me to go to the viewings. Before she left she hugged me, the first time since the Accident, wearing a black dress compliments of Grandma, the fabric slick against my cheek.

"Stay here," Mom slurred. "This is going to be awful."

I didn't want to let go. I wanted Mom to tell me everything was going to be all right. That it wasn't my fault. Tell me my Saint Garnet story until we both emerged from this soggy dream. But she didn't, and Grandma had to peel my fingers off of my mother one by one.

They left me alone with a bowl of ice cream and my brutal imagination. I pictured the hubbub at the funeral parlor: mourners shuffling by the coffins, lids raised to reveal the tragic father and son. I wondered if the mortician had gotten everything right: Nicky's crisp collar and perfectly knotted tie. Dad's pompadour that had made so many women woozy. I didn't want to think about gashes and cuts filled with whatever compound miracle workers used to reconstruct loved ones' faces.

An image of Dad's callused palms sent me to the basement, where his sawhorses were still set up, a board across them waiting, swells of sawdust coating the floor. It was absurdly quiet without the sound of his sawing, the only light the flame of the gas heater flaring, illuminating Dad's cot against the wall, boxes of White Owls and stacks of girlie magazines shoved underneath. I pushed through the basement door to the garage and tugged the light string. The overhead bulb cast a circle of light on the spot where Nonna had once set up my Saint Garnet chairs. On the wall, the pegboard of tools that my father had meticulously organized. And there it was. His saw with the curlicues he had carved when he was a boy. I reached for it, but my hand shook so violently I couldn't touch Dad's most sacred possession. Instead I collapsed on the motor-oil-stained floor, the chilled cement stabbing my tailbone.

The coffins were closed at the funeral the next day. Mom stood in the narthex between the two Saint Brigids, a grim statue of a different sort, standing erect only because of Grandma's hand on her back.

"You can do this, Marina," Grandma said to bolster her. "You have to do this."

They took deep breaths and went up the aisle, followed by Grandpa Ferrari, number-one newsie cap in his hand. My knees began to buckle, but Nonna gripped my arm, leaned close to my ear, and whispered, "Hum. Just-a hum." We both made a sound so faint few people could hear it, but it was enough as Nonna ushered me forward. Another gift was that on that day I was not assaulted by the whispers of children, the *Mommy, what's wrong with* — that might have done me in completely.

Here's what I remember about the funeral: Rose-draped caskets at the front of the church, Father Luigi hovering over them, shaking his head at the shock of it all. Saint Brigid's was packed on both sides with Irish and Italians, the Flannigans and O'Gradys, our Dagowop neighbors. Whole rows of nuns, their habits tainted by the foul water. Three pews crammed with hill nonnas in jersey dresses, black mantillas covering sepia buns. They rubbed keys, flashed hand signs; bits of rue branches peeked from their sleeves to ward off the evil eye that had obviously been cast upon our fam-i-ly, but by whom? One of them mumbled, "La Strega," which ignited a vortex of prayers. It would have been easy to pin this on her, but perhaps the real *jettatura* was sitting right in their midst, humming. At the back of the church, leaning against a marble column twice as thick as him, a rake of a man with a chauffeur's hat in his hand. I did not see La Strega.

After the benediction, Father made the sign of the cross and we stood as the twelve pallbearers assembled, most of them church ushers and decidedly *not* Uncle Dom or Ray-Ray. No Betty, either, who must have been bawling in her room over in Grover Estates wondering how her life had ever come to this. Or perhaps she was gaping at the hole in the ceiling of Ray-Ray's room. Apparently when Le Baron's springhouse exploded, the geyser hurled the whippet weathervane miles through the air until it crashed through Uncle Dom's roof, the shingles and insulation and plaster, before plunging completely through Ray-Ray's mattress. If only he had been impaled there, my revenge would have been complete.

Grandpa Ferrari held the front of his son's coffin as if he were hauling a pallet of bricks. As the procession marched out, a woman's howl erupted from the back of the church. Mother squeezed her eyes shut because she and I both knew which secondary widow that shriek belonged to. I trudged by the confessional booths and started shuddering, wondering if I would ever have the courage to admit what I'd done by removing Nonna's good magic from the glove box, if there was enough atonement in the world.

After the cemetery, our house overflowed with hill and village dwellers. The blue-collar set — Dad's coworkers and his favorite mechanic; neighbors who had borrowed his tools; Mr. O'Grady, whose wooden floors my father had bartered for T-bones — gravitated toward steerage, the kitchen. They paid homage to Grandpa Ferrari at the head of the table, one of Dad's stogies plugged in his mouth, the smoke blending with sickly sweet flowers and simmering tomato sauce. He accepted their deference, as if he cared about my father. As if he gave a damn. All the while Nonna poured cream in their coffees, tears running down her cheeks.

Saint Brigid's white-collar congregants gathered in the living room around Father Luigi, who sat ex cathedra in one of the wingbacks. Sister Barnabas hovered behind to keep his wineglass full, his cookie plate heaped, her own tears glistening against the red splotches on her cheek. Mom, barely sentient, slumped in the other wingback; she'd been placed there by Grandma, who had instructed her on her duty on that horrid day. I leaned against the archway that straddled both worlds and watched the parade of old nonnas slip Mom envelopes containing the few dollars they could scrape together, a holy card, a pope-blessed scapular. After offering condolences they genuflected before Father Luigi and kissed his hand. Then they surrounded Nonna in the kitchen, gift bottles of Marsala clinking beneath their shawls.

Mom's eyes glazed as if she were replaying the last twenty-four hours of Dad's and Nicky's lives, as if she were trying to think of one thing that would have stopped them from bolting out of the house. She kept looking at the balled-up rosary one of the nonnas had pressed into her hand. I knew it wasn't beads she was seeing. I also knew she was wishing that when she found Dad's keys she had thrown them down the sewer grate in front of our house. I was rewinding my own actions, and in my mind I would have just given up after being unable to open the station wagon's hood. I would have clapped my hands and run to my closet. I would never have heard Candy Man, or if I did, I would have plugged my ears so that I would not be tempted, would not go outside and ultimately to Snakebite Woods. But that wasn't right either, because Nicky would still have been there, being brutalized by Ray-Ray.

Grandma Iris provided alcohol in obscene proportions. She

kept Mom lubricated and acted as hostess to the rest of the first class guests, trying to appear the epitome of grace under duress, mascara smudges giving her away.

In steerage, Dad's coworkers began telling stories about the day Dad saved Ernie Silva's life. There had been an explosion in one of the furnaces, and Ernie's clothes had caught fire. Dad knocked him to the ground and rolled him around until the flames were out. I remembered that day Dad came home with his shirt all smoky and his eyebrows singed. He never told us what happened. Al Malarkey recalled when Dad brought his family a week's worth of groceries after a steel sheet had sliced off Al's thumb. I watched Grandpa's face as the men paid homage to his honorable son. I couldn't decode the tight grimace.

Most of the guests didn't know what to say to me. "So how are you doing?" they asked, looking at my feet, my shoulder, my hair. Their pity and revulsion made me squirm, so I drifted down the hall, but my bedroom held stragglers ogling my globes. "They are real-a! I thought it was a big-a fable," Celeste Xaviero muttered. "Wait'll my sister hears about this!" They discussed issues unrelated to Dad and Nicky: the price of milk, their favorite soap opera. How long we would have to boil the water, though the Water Authority had announced that despite the color, it was safe for consumption.

There was only one person in my parents' room. Annette Funicello opened Dad's closet, tugged out the sleeve of one of his shirts and held it to her nose. It was such a brazen display, I couldn't be angry. She would never again call with the excuse of a home repair. I looked at her, and beyond her, to my reflection in the vanity mirror, the only one Mom hadn't thrown out. I was wearing the same impenetrable scowl Grandpa Ferrari was wearing in the kitchen. Only then did I realize that, like Grandpa, I didn't know my father. I didn't know he was capable of saving lives.

In the living room, alcohol had taken effect. Even Father Luigi's eyes drooped. I leaned against the wall and scanned the congregants who had gathered around him as if he were a deity, which he resembled even more when the conversation took a theological turn. *Why would God put a good man on the planet only to yank him so brutally away? Not to mention Nicky, who never had a chance to prove what kind of man he might have been.*

I had my own question: *What is the punishment for* portafortuna-*tampering that results in the deaths of members of your family?*

Mom had been so quiet, they forgot she was there.

The priest took another sip of wine, and after several clattering attempts, Sister Barnabas set the wineglass down on the table for him.

"It is not for us to question God," Father said. "Perhaps He could see even greater tragedies in their futures and was sparing them. This could have been a great act of mercy."

Mom's head lolled forward and then snapped back as she tried to rouse herself from Grandma's anesthetic. "Mercy? You call this an act of mercy?"

"W-well," Father stammered, surprised to see the grieving widow sitting right beside him. "God knows all and sees all. His time is not linear, so it's possible that—"

"God doesn't see shit," Mother said, not angry, voice not even raised. "And if this is what your God calls mercy, I don't want Him in my house."

The congregants gasped.

Mother stood, shaky, hand clutching the chair arm. "You're not welcome here either," she said to the priest. "Now get the hell out."

Father Luigi coughed under the scrutiny of all those onlookers witnessing his dismissal. Their eyes shifted to Mom as she wobbled down the hall, shoulder brushing the plaster. She paused before the fist-shaped hole in the wall.

Annette Funicello rushed past her, something bunched up under her coat. Mother didn't notice. I think in her mind she was crawling into that hole where she could hide with the wall studs and wiring and copper tubing. The intricacies of the house that so mesmerized Dad.

Of course she couldn't dive in, so she went to her room and closed the door, sealing the rest of us out. Except for Grandma Iris, who padded down the hall and slipped inside.

Drawn in by the sudden silence, Nonna edged into the room drying a ceramic bowl.

Father sputtered as he tried to reclaim his dignity. "She's in a great deal of pain."

"Yes," said Sister Barnabas.

"Of course you know she's a nonbeliever," he added, scooping up his wineglass.

It was the wrong thing to say, and the same surge I had felt in my gut as I raced home from Snakebite Woods began again.

"Perhaps God arranged this tragedy to bring her to belief."

"What?" I said, unable to fathom that the God I believed in would sacrifice my father and brother just to get Mom's attention, much less do it by using me as an unwitting pawn.

"If you don't answer God's knock, He may tear off your door," Father said.

Nonna looked at the front door. "What?"

Sister Barnabas tugged his sleeve. "Father."

"If you don't answer God's door, He may rip off your roof," Father said.

Nonna looked up at the ceiling. "What?"

"Father," Sister Barnabas said with more force, trying to remind him of the proximity of the kin of those door-torn, roof-ripped, car-mangled sacrifices.

Father brushed Sister's hand off. "I'm just saying that God must love this woman dearly if He'd go to such lengths to bring her into the flock."

The bowl in Nonna's hand fell to the floor and split in two. "God loves-a this woman more than-a my son? My grandson?"

"No!" Father said. "That's not what I meant—"

"He destroy my fam-i-ly for her?" Nonna looked down the hall at my mother's closed door. "*Jettatura!*" Nonna tore at her hair, bobby pins scattering, braid springing free like a garden hose.

Kitchen chairs scraped against linoleum as the entirety of steerage gathered around to watch the commotion, the house listing. Even Grandpa Ferrari stopped ramming cold cuts down his throat when he realized his wife was at the center of the tumult.

Grandma Iris dashed from Mom's room wagging her finger. "Will you be quiet out here? My daughter is trying to sleep!"

"*Your* daughter! *Your* daughter!" Nonna spat. "What about-a my son! She kill-a my son! That no-good son-ama-beetch with her no-priest, pajama-judge marriage that is-a no marriage! She kill-a my son and-a my grandson too!"

Grandma held out her hands. "What is she talking about?"

Father Luigi looked up, his face trembling at the scene he had caused, his cantilever mole trembling. "I—"

"He says it's-a your daughter's fault. God kill-a my son for her!"

Sister Barnabas, the bravest woman on the planet, hustled forward and tried to pat Nonna's hand, her shoulder. Nonna batted her away.

"Your daughter bring evil into this-a town, this-a house, this-a fam-i-ly. Now I wash-a my hands of a-you and of-a her!" Nonna scuffed her feet against the carpet as if she were wiping off the dust of our existence. I remember thinking: *She doesn't mean me. Surely she doesn't mean me.* I tried to catch her eye for assurance, but given her state, I don't think she even remembered she had a granddaughter. She lunged for the door. "I no set-a my feet in this house-a no more. You are a-dead to me!"

Grandma Iris stood there, stunned. When her composure returned she said, "Clearly the woman is unbalanced," before padding back to Mom's room.

Nonna banged outside, leaving her husband sucking fat from his teeth. He took his time adjusting his newsie cap and digging for his keys.

Eventually he shoved outside. I bolted to the door and looked at Nonna in the street grating her feet against the blacktop, flick-

ing her hand under her chin, offering *up-yours* gestures toward us
that had nothing to do with the *malocchio*. Her mouth blubbered
a foul curse that would shrivel our futures for good. Grandpa
walked up beside her, grabbed her arm, and dragged her to the
car. Once tossed inside, she cranked down the window, and as
Grandpa drove away she continued to cast her bad spell that settled over our house like a fishnet.

I had lost not only my brother and father but also Aunt Betty
and now Father Luigi and his soul-swapping God had sliced
Nonna from my life. I can only imagine what I must have looked
like when I pivoted toward him: a heap of pulsing-red flesh. I
glowered at the priest and at Sister Barnabas, who looked, frankly,
scared shitless as I inflated, bile gurgling inside. To her credit, she
once again angled herself in front of Father Luigi, but it was no
good. I opened my mouth and out roared a blast of the same
pejoratives my father had spewed about Ray-Ray: "Goddamn
motherfucker, son of a bitch, *testa di cazzo, bastardo, figlio di puttano, individuo spregevole!*"

Sister's veil blew straight back in my fiery explosion, as did
Father's hair, and the room grew hotter and hotter as I vomited
words that pummeled the pair of holy faces, their eyes squinting
against the barrage, Father's wineglass quaking in his hand.

When I finally clamped my mouth shut, it was as if we were
in a vacuum devoid of sound. Nobody moved. Except for Abe
Lincoln, who started quivering on the side of Father's face, not
just tremors, but wiggling like a cocooned caterpillar, the mini-
face imploding, the chin and nose caving in, and then, remarkably,
it fell off and plunked into Father's wineglass, where it fizzled, a
little tendril of bubbles drifting up.

Father raised the glass to inspect the pea-size bit resting at the
bottom. He gasped anew when he looked up at Sister Barnabas,
whose cheeks were no longer rosacea'd.

"Holy Mother of God." Father slid to the floor to kneel before
me. "It's true. I had heard rumors, but now I know it's true."

I backed away as the congregants, except for Sister Barnabas, gaped at me; Sister took off her glasses and squinted into the lenses to assess her now-flawless reflection. She spun to face me, tears in her eyes, and crossed herself.

"Saint Garnet," she whispered, collapsing to her knees, kissing the crucifix on the rosary that once served as my teething ring (but is now on display in a glass case in the Saint Brigid narthex along with shriveled-up Abe Lincoln). Though I implored them to stop, to please get up, Sister groveled with the rest of my followers, both first-class and steerage, who had also slid from their chairs to pay homage to me.

Acts of Contrition

Padre:

First of all, I did *not* kill Abraham Lincoln, nor did I cure Sister Barnabas. Maybe La Strega's spells had backfired with grief. Or the nonnas' collective evil-eye remedies had taken effect. Or Nonna's foot-scraping curse had scraped off those anomalies. It most definitely was not me, because I wouldn't lift one sainted (or stained) finger to heal Father Luigi, though I might for Sister Barnabas if I had the inclination and powers, which I do not.

Second of all, Abe Lincoln wasn't the only one to die that day. My reverence for the One True Faith also withered, an important artifact, but not so easy to display in the Saint Brigid narthex. Father Luigi's theology made me question what the hell kind of God that was. Perhaps, as Mom had once proclaimed, it was all so much God hooey.

After that moment of clarity in my living room, I raced to my bedroom, opened my underwear drawer, pulled out the box that held my pillowcase veil, and charged to the kitchen to dump it into the trash. It was a theatrical performance, but I wanted the gawkers, particularly the ordained ones, to see my own version of wiping their dust off the soles of my shoes. I didn't know that as I left, one of my neighbors rescued the box and tucked it into his underwear drawer, where it sat for over a decade. Now if you send twenty dollars to a particular Sweetwater PO box, you can be the proud owner of a quarter-inch square of my veil in a cardboard coin holder. Be forewarned: I have seen several of these quote-unquote relics and not only are a number of them the wrong shade of blue, some are dotted swiss, Padre. Dotted swiss.

However, I did not rip the Saint Garnet relic from around my neck, an external artery I just couldn't sever. Or, to be completely honest, a tiny bit of me still wanted to believe, not in the Church's ordained representatives, but in God.

Regardless of my sacrilegious act, the throng continued to kneel and began spouting the rosary, Father Luigi the loudest cantor of all. I ran to my room and dove into bed, held pillows over my head, but those repetitive words-words-words slithered under my door, up my box spring, through cotton weave and goose down, and into my ear. They must have wedged themselves under Mother's door too, because soon I heard Grandma in the living room. "What in the world is going on? Get out and leave my daughter in peace!" Though the mob left, they took up residence in the street, bringing in candles for the night shift. It was really too much. Three solid days of their reverence that had nothing to do with my dead family or live mother.

In moments of near lucidity, Mom would emerge from her room and slide through the house like a wan shadow. Occasionally she looked outside. "What are they looking at? Why won't they stop staring?" She plucked hair from the growing bald spot on her temple or searched for a steel spatula or brass light-switch plate, mumbling, "Bear the scrutiny, bear the freefalling pain." Grandma began hiding the cutlery. She repeatedly stormed outside and raised her fist at the mob, but they would not budge. Their chants grew louder each day until we were all sleep deprived, and, even worse, Grandma ran out of vodka.

On the fourth morning I dodged suitcases lining the hall and found Grandma firing directives at her peon Cedrick and a trio of hired muscles. I thought Grandma was making her great escape, leaving Mom and me to our limited devices.

She pointed to Nicky's room. "Gather all the books." Then she pointed to my room. "And all the globes."

I planted myself in my bedroom doorway. "No!" I had lost too much already.

"Garnet, let the men work!" Grandma said.

I held tight to both sides of the door frame, but one of the hired muscles reached under my arms, lifted me off the ground, and plopped me down in the hall. He snarled to indicate he meant business, so I sank to the floor and watched him pack up the spheres that had orbited me for years.

Soon the men began hauling luggage and boxes down the front steps to a moving van parked in the street, nudging pilgrims out of the way. They didn't take any furniture. No cookware or box radio. No board games or Barbie house. I couldn't breathe until Grandma led Mom from her room and said to me, "Come on, Garnet." I nearly cried when I understood we were included among Grandma's treasures. She steered Mom down the basement steps, to the garage, and into the back seat of the Cadillac. My heart thudded as I thought about everything we were leaving behind, and I almost ran upstairs to grab my cigar box of riches and Nonna's lucky talismans, but then I spotted the only worldly possession I needed: Dad's saw, drooping from the garage pegboard. I hugged it as I got in the front seat.

Someone — Cedrick — opened the garage door from outside, and Grandma began backing out. One of the nonnas outside pointed. "There she is!" The pilgrims rushed the car, but Grandma punched the gas, jerking my head forward as I traced my finger over the curlicue-etched handle, hoping that somehow Dad had embedded a three-word message there for me. We spiraled down past No-Brakes Bend and the caved-in garage where Dad and Nicky had landed. At the foot of the hill we careened around the pump where all those craftsmen had once watered their horses. We sped along Appian Way, past where Mr. Flannigan shoveled snow. I glanced up Via Dolorosa, where Nonna was no doubt preparing her husband's lunch, salting pasta water with her tears. The hair on my neck bristled as we passed Grover Estates, but my body went numb as we crossed the railroad tracks then veered onto Route 60 East, a road I had never driven on in my life.

I slipped into a dream filled with gum wrappers; deep-sea divers; musical notes crowding the sky like crows, their theremin caws ringing in my ears. A vacuum nozzle poked through the clouds and sucked up the birds, taking all sound with it, including my E note, and even in my sleep I felt suddenly deaf. Soon I was being hoisted up a four-trunk sycamore by a crane, voices mumbling, "My God! What's wrong with—" and "It's even worse than Cedrick described." Grandma's and Mom's voices bickered from a great height, Mom slurring, "If you put me back in that room I'll jump out the window!"

Hours later I awoke to impeccable quiet. I strained to hear, but the music was gone and I was lying in a canopy bed. Wherever it was I had landed, I think I already knew it was a place without magic. Still, I marveled at the expansive room appointed with hoity-toity furniture, not antiquated La Strega stuff but white French Provincial. I slid off the mattress still clutching my father's saw, and, remembering the power in Nonna's four-tooth chisel, I tucked the saw under the bed. I opened doors looking for an exit but found a walk-in closet crammed with shiny dresses, another devoted to shoes, and a bathroom with a clawfoot tub, a vanity lined with brushes and combs, and a wall made of mirrors. That's when I knew whose room this once was: Mom's. I went back into the bedroom and spotted pictures of her posing with Great Danes, or in ballerina gear, or playing tennis. Even then she wore her hair in a ponytail.

I again wondered why Mom had chopped off this limb of her family tree, why she couldn't at least have kept the fortune that would have made our lives so much easier. The four of us could have lived anywhere—Madagascar, Finland—and we wouldn't have had to endure Uncle Dom, Grandpa Ferrari, and, worst of all, Ray-Ray. I was angry at Mom for denying us this salvation and for diving into herself when I needed her most. I wanted to rail at her disengagement, so I slipped from the room into a blindingly white hall lined with closed doors.

I heard voices and tiptoed toward them along the railing that led to a wide stairway flanked at the top by two giant vases. I crouched behind one and looked down at the mini-replica of the Versailles Hall of Mirrors: gobs of gilded looking glasses, crystal chandeliers, Grecian women on pedestals. Nicky would have drooled; Dad would have immediately started looking for the basement. On the far wall hung a painting of Mom as a teenager standing beside a horse, one arm resting on its mane. She was wearing riding breeches and a velveteen helmet. It was hard aligning this image with the one of her on her knees in our bathroom, scrubbing the toilet.

Grandma stood beneath the largest chandelier of all, arms crossed as she dressed down the maid, a globular black woman of sixty or so wearing a crisp dress, a white apron, and a cap. I had met a black person for the first time just a year before, when Nicky and I drove with Dad to the Sweetwater lumberyard. We were in the pickup bay and Dad was tying two-by-fours onto the roof of the station wagon when a black man approached.

"Hey, Albert," Dad said. They shook hands, Dad's dark-skinned fingers meeting Albert's slightly darker-skinned ones.

"I want you to meet my boy—my kids," Dad corrected himself when he twisted around and saw me. "Garnet, this is Mr. Fulwood. We work together at the Plant."

Albert bent forward, holding out his hand. I stared at it for no longer than he stared at Taiwan on my knuckle. I was captivated by the wide plane of his pink palm, thumb the size of a kosher dill. "Pleasure to meet you, sugar snap." He shook my hand.

"That's Nicky." Dad nodded at my brother, giving him a *Come here* look. Nicky obeyed, and Albert also shook his hand, though he offered no endearment.

That simple memory of Dad, Nicky, even the stupid station

wagon that now looked like an accordion and was sighing in the village dump, made my chest ache. The tears sprang, silent ones, since I didn't want to give away my position.

"This is intolerable, Opal," Grandma railed. "Absolutely intolerable. Do you understand me?"

"Yes, ma'am," Opal said, eyes to the floor.

Grandma spun on her pumps, leaving Opal as stiff as one of those statues. When Grandma was out of sight, Opal crossed her arms and flapped her lips in a good Grandma Iris imitation. I adored her instantly, and even more when she tipped her head toward me. "Morning, honeydew. You hungry?"

I wiped my nose on my sleeve. "I want my mom."

Opal lumbered up to me and draped her arm around my shoulder. "Course you do." She led me down the hall to the east wing. "It was her daddy's suite." I was not surprised that Grandfather Postscript had had his own section of the house, four rooms in a row. The first was the mother of all globe rooms, where pieces from my collection had already been reshelved. The second was a library with Nicky's *Britannicas* stacked in a corner. The third was a study with a massive desk and walls completely covered with cocktail napkins, dry-cleaner receipts, matchbook covers, ticker tape, pages ripped from ledgers, all scribbled with phrases like *fly-fish the queen* and *succumb the lowly collier*. I remember thinking: *Uh-oh.*

The last room was the bedchamber with a sleigh bed that ferried my mother to what I hoped were blissful dreams. I climbed up and leaned close to her face, her closed eyes. She had always been thin but looked fragile now, and all my anger vanished.

Opal pulled a handkerchief from her apron to dab her eyes. "I helped raise your mama from the minute she was born. It's good to have her home, but not like this, Lord. Not like this."

"Mom," I whispered. "Mom."

Her eyelids fluttered, but they didn't open. I saw a pharmacy on the bedside table and I wondered if Grandma had induced a coma in my mother to prevent her making yet another escape.

"Better let her rest." Opal guided me off the bed and down a back set of stairs that led to the kitchen.

Sitting at the table was the cook, also dressed in maid regalia. Cookie was in her thirties, skinny as Radisson, and the third black person I'd ever met. Though her left hand was bare, her right was rammed into a too-tight rubber glove, which mildly impeded her task of peeling potatoes over a grocery sack. More fascinating to me was the cleft in her chin so pronounced that it made her chin look like butt cheeks. She was singing along with "Please Mr. Postman" blaring from the transistor radio beside her.

"I told you not to listen to that racket in here!" Opal said, shutting it off.

"Yes, ma'am," Cookie said, though she was eyeballing me.

"Ma'am says she's going to tan our hides if we streak up those mirrors again. I gave you that job 'cause I thought you could handle it. This is intolerable, Cookie. Absolutely intolerable. You understand me?"

"Yes, ma'am," Cookie said, eyes now on her potatoes.

Opal patted a chair, indicating that I should sit. "Cookie will fix you something to eat." She sashayed out, apron bow above her rear end swaying from side to side. I looked at Cookie, expecting a good Opal imitation, but she just started singing, not "Please Mr. Postman" but "There Is a Balm in Gilead." She stood and, still wearing that glove, cut a thick slice of bread, slathered it with apple butter, and handed it to me.

"Bet the kids back home gave you a time of it."

I was stunned by her directness.

"And plenty of grownups too," she added, pouring me a glass of milk. "It won't be easy for you here. Lord knows it hasn't been easy for me and I only got—" She swiveled around to see if anyone was snooping.

"Only got what?" I wondered if her butt chin was enough to induce Grandma's scorn.

Cookie sat beside me and slowly peeled off her glove. It took a moment for me to understand what I was seeing. Cookie had si fingers on that hand. Not a runty worm tacked on at the end, but a fully grown extra pinkie jutting out from the side.

My mouth fell open—not out of disgust, necessarily. Mostly I was picturing how that extra digit might come in handy playing jacks, or cat's cradle, or the piano.

"I know it's nothing, really, but kids can be cruel."

It really *was* nothing compared to the anomalies covering my body, but Uncle Dom's crude jibes pinged around in my head: *pickaninny, blue gum, nigger toe,* obscenities based solely on the color of Cookie's unmarred skin. With or without that extra pinkie, I figured, she suffered plenty.

"I used to think God was punishing me," she said, "but one day my mama told me a story."

Here we go, I thought. Another fairy tale to gloss over reality. Something about God having leftover clay from the *sweetness* bucket and tacking it onto His most prized girl. I wondered why He hadn't used it to fill in her chin crack.

I smiled politely, changed the subject. "Does it work like the rest of them?"

Cookie wiggled all six fingers like spider legs, both delighting and repulsing me. "God made us this way for a reason, honey. We just have to wait and see what that is."

I didn't want to contradict her since she was trying to offer solace, even if it was the God-hooey kind. Plus, a tiny molecule on the tip of my single right pinkie still wanted to believe.

For the next several months I felt like a museum specimen. Grandma never took me out, and I eventually understood that it had nothing to do with her grief. People catered to us, delivering vodka and pearl onions, fresh flowers and choice cuts of meat. Workers arrived with a load of iron bars to install over every window from the ground floor to the third.

Dr. Trogdon visited regularly to keep Mom's bedside vials full. He examined me several times, measuring continents, tugging the skin on my forearm so taut that Thailand vanished beneath a tidal wave of pale flesh. Grandma gasped hopefully, but that part of the landmass resurfaced when he let the skin relax. "It's a remarkable example of nevus flammeus," Doctor said. "She would make a fascinating study, the results of which I'm sure we could publish."

"Absolutely not," said Grandma.

He spouted something about surgeries and the unlikelihood of success given the extent of my birthmarks. After hearing that, Grandma immediately hired a seamstress. She showed up with patterns, swatches, and a tape measure; Grandma groaned at my pre-growth-spurt chubbiness. Within a month I had a new wardrobe of froufrou dresses, opaque leotards, slacks, and long-sleeved blouses that itched like the dickens. My old clothes Grandma hauled off to who-knows-where.

I refused to relinquish my Nonna-made necklace, however, since I longed for her white braid and cannolis. Countless times, I thought of calling her, had even picked up the phone once, but given the way she had so thoroughly wiped us off the soles of her shoes, I wasn't sure if she could suffer my voice. I was too afraid of permanent banishment to complete the call. There were also moments when I ached for Aunt Betty's hugs, for the sound of her gum-snapping, but I was still so angry at her for harboring Ray-Ray that I couldn't have stomached her voice.

Instead, I retreated to Mom's closet and pretended it was Nonna and Betty slathering me with caresses instead of just the hems of Mom's dresses. I even found the silver one with the fishtail bottom, its tiny cousin hanging in Barbie's closet back home. I tugged the full-size one from its hanger and hugged the Nereid skin to me, wishing I could morph into a fish and swim to some mythical place devoid of grief. But I couldn't, and it was in that dim closet that my yearning for Betty and Nonna became unbearable, so I looked for a place to lodge it until we were all ready for a reunion. Because I no longer had a cigar box to store hidden treasures, I looked to my own geography, where I found a safe haven. Iceland, on my left forearm, with a freckle on the spot where a volcano with an unpronounceable name jutted up. I bundled together my longing and pushed it down the volcano's mouth and then rammed in a cork to keep it in place until the time was ripe.

It was in Mom's closet that I began mulling over the dualities in my life: two wealthy widows, two mansions, two (Old, New) religions, two designations (charlatan, saint), two disfigured (one stained, one six-fingered) girls who had remarkably landed under one roof. I often wished I could split in two: one fully magenta Garnet, the other mere beige. A twin sister to shoulder some of the load. But there was no twin, and there wasn't even a Grandma Iris—a ghost who never sat down for a meal and who spent her time downing martinis in the west wing as she stared at Nicky's last-ever school picture. She was too distraught to remember the federal mandate that I had to attend school; I did not remind her. I frequently heard her offering regrets over the phone. "I'm afraid bridge is out, darling. I don't dare leave Marina yet. No, her *son* died in the car wreck. Her husband was a war hero killed in Iwo Jima."

Each morning Grandma sat beside my mother with a bowl of warm water and a washcloth. She scoured Mom's face and limbs before patting her dry and applying lotion. "This is where you belong, darling. Never leave me again." Mother would not have stood for this ministering if she were awake, but if it took lost consciousness to have her daughter back home, Grandma's expression seemed to say, then so be it. If only Mom and I could both squeeze into that Nereid dress. One time, however, after Grandma recapped her lotion, she cupped Mom's cheeks in her hand and gently squeezed them together so that Mom's mouth opened and closed like a fish's. She leaned close to Mom and begged, "Please say it. Just once, darling. *I love you.*" She pressed Mom's cheeks three times, her mouth popping open for each word, but no sound came out.

An image of me leaning over Dad in his coffin, my fingers gripping his jaw, pulling harder and harder until his mouth opened, but he spilled no words. Then I felt a wrecking ball to my sternum as I realized that they had never, not once, poured from mine.

Because that pain was too much, I hid it not only in Iceland, but beneath layers of distractions. Every morning I would hustle to the kitchen to eat breakfast with the help. Cookie bustled around in her one rubber glove refilling coffee cups and flipping eggs. Opal pored over Grandma's to-do list; Cedrick, whose official title was chauffeur, read the *Wall Street Journal*. Then there was Muddy, the English gardener, who hummed "God Bless America" while he ate. At least someone was humming, since I had lost the inclination, and the note. The help lived on the premises: the women tucked on the third floor, the men over the carriage house.

I spent my time exploring Grandma's eighteenth-century Greek Revival home with its gobs of white columns and its symmetry. The interior was also eye-piercingly white: walls, furniture, carpet—the antithesis of La Strega's dim chateau. Outside there were no longer ponies or Great Danes, but there was a pool and a clay tennis court. A three-tiered water fountain in the middle of the front circular drive. A shuffleboard pad. A knot garden, which Muddy coddled obsessively. At the back of the property I discovered foundations of the quarters for the slaves who had cleared the land and built the house. I looked from the narrow footprints of their shacks to the manor house, all that marble, those pillars, lugged in and installed by backbreaking labor. I added to my list of dualities half poor Italian, half descendant of slave owners.

I also spent hours in the study trying to decipher Grandfather's notes: *climb high, bright soul, your purchased future awaits; regret, victorious, dogs the idle days.* I recalled snippets of Mom's Sweetwater poetry: *steel pots waiting, steel wool scrubbing, steal far, far away.* I imagined the two of them sitting shoulder to shoulder when she was a girl, he penning the first line, *Whisper the golden joy that grates,* she scribbling an answer he would understand completely, *For she will swallow it whole.*

I wanted Mom to wake up so I could interrogate her about her chummy bond with her father that had resulted in a whole new language. The thought of Nicky carrying on the tradition by devouring Grandfather's encyclopedias reminded me that there was still a hole in my chest that only fam-i-ly could fill, even a brother who both loved and hated me.

Thus, on April Fools' Day, I slipped into Grandfather's library, sank into a leather chair, and began working my way through the first volume of the *Encyclopaedia Britannica*, A to Anno. It wasn't just about joining that well-read club, and in fact it was grueling to slog through entry after entry—but that was my penance for hurling my brother into Mr. Dagostino's garage.

I know, I know. Why would I offer penance to a God I no longer believed in? Please remember that I was still wearing a necklace strung with the remnants of my two faiths; my atonement was meant primarily to assuage whatever evil-eye spirits crisscrossed the globe. However irrational it was, I couldn't wipe off Nonna's Old Religion as easily as I could the mole-faced religious leader's Church.

One afternoon when I was in Grandpa's study, Opal came to do housework. I imagined she'd cleaned this room hundreds of times while Grandfather posted nonsense on his walls. It took three tries, but I finally asked, "What was Grandpa like?"

Opal stopped dusting and closed her eyes. "Lord, he was handsome." She checked over her shoulder before sitting on an ottoman. "He was known for his good looks even among the coloreds. He had this dimple"—she slid an index finger down her cheek—"and he knew how to use it." Her mouth crimped on one side. "Used it a little too well on the ladies," she said to herself. "Even some of the help, those weak-hearted fools."

Opal coughed. "Don't mind what I say. But this place livened up after he slipped in with that New York crowd. He just showed up for Sunday tennis one spring and never left." She went on to describe my grandparents' extravagant marriage, how green-eyed the women guests were and some of the fussier men. "How she snagged him I'll never know. Course he had that peculiar—" She looked at me in such a way that I wondered if he sported birthmarks that weren't apparent in the one photo I'd seen.

"That's neither here nor there, and it didn't seem to matter to your grandmother. Both her parents were dead and she was already twenty-nine. Uh, uh, uh."

Grandpa was also a thrower of legendary parties whenever Grandma slipped across the pond. He invited celebrated guests she would never have approved of: W. C. Fields, Charlie Chaplin, Ziegfeld *Follies* girls.

"You know that giant chandelier in the mirror hall?" Opal asked. "One time Fanny Brice rode one of the horses underneath it, grabbed hold, and swung back and forth on it like a monkey, crystals falling off everywhere. Like to never get that thing back together before the old bat got home. She still found out and had a fit. But your grandfather just smacked her on the behind and said, 'It'd do you a world of good to swing on that thing from time to time too!'"

I eyeballed Grandpa's weird graffiti. "Then what is all this?"

Opal stood and reached out to touch a scrap but thought better of it. "Your granddaddy was a wonderful man, full of pluck." She pointed a finger at me. "And he was a good father. I don't care what anybody says. No matter where he came from or what he did, he loved your mother and never would have left her alone with—well, I don't care what anybody says." Opal surveyed his desk, the letter opener and fountain pens. I wondered why Grandma hadn't cleared away the remnants of his life the way she had cleared away ours.

"But there was this other side of him," Opal said, face sullen. "He had the moods."

An image of Mom staring into a ladle popped into my brain.

"Locked himself in this room for weeks at a time writing that gobbledygook."

I heard distant thunder and it took a few seconds to realize it was my heart thudding in my ears. There was my mother, after all, locked inside herself. I opened and closed my mouth several times before whispering, "How did Grandpa die?"

Opal looked over at a window, or what was once a window; it had been bricked up and painted white to match the walls, though curtains still hung over the space to continue the symmetry. She looked over at me. "Nobody told you?"

I shook my head.

"How old are you again?"

"Thirteen. Almost thirteen."

Opal surveyed me up, down, sideways. "I suppose that's old enough. You see —"

A voice boomed from the heavens: "That'll be enough, Opal!"

My head swung to the doorway, but Grandma wasn't there. I looked at Opal to make sure I wasn't going cuckoo myself. She was already dashing around the room dusting like a lunatic.

"Did you hear that?" I whispered.

Opal nodded to an intercom speaker on the highest shelf. Then I knew: Grandma was snooping on me and probably had snooped on Grandpa and Mom for years.

From then on I spent as much time outside as possible. Grandma couldn't wire the trees or the air; at least, I didn't think so. My excursions led me to another penance that I stumbled upon accidentally.

One Friday while Cedrick was out ferrying Grandma around so she could buy more Fabergé eggs, or whatever it was she did, and Muddy was sweet-talking his garden, I went to the carriage house and found a horse buggy, a Bailey Electric car, an evolution of Cadillacs, and an aquamarine and pink Cabriolet Mercedes. I was sitting in the convertible punching pedals, recalling my first joy ride with Dad, when I spied a tableau that at first froze me solid: two sawhorses set up in the corner with a two-by-four balanced across them. Then my legs were no longer under my control as they made their way over. I slid my hands across the wood, pretending that Dad had placed it there. All I needed was the saw and I raced to my room and dug under the bed. I ran back to the garage and gripped the saw handle in both hands. The blade wobbled and I rested it about two inches from the end of the board and began my flimsy back-and-forth motion, the blade stuttering, board sliding and slipping.

I needed to master this critical skill, so I hoisted the saw over my shoulder, figuring that if I brought it down hard enough I'd gouge a furrow where my blade could grab hold. Then I could make enough noise to echo throughout the property and rouse my mother. But when I brought the saw down, my force was too strong. I didn't know to hold the board in place with one hand, since that was another thing my father never taught me. The board cartwheeled over, landing with a loud crack. The front sawhorse collapsed onto its side and lay there like a petrified animal.

Immediately my eyes teared up for my father, who no one else in that house seemed to miss, for not offering to him three holy words.

I would have started blubbering if I hadn't caught sight of Muddy standing with a shovel in one hand as he assessed my distress.

"You've got to treat the wood like a friend, missy."

Then that sweet man who smelled of manure and rosemary came over and wrapped my hand around Dad's curlicues, rested the other firmly on the righted board. He placed his hand atop mine and guided the initial timid strokes until I gathered momentum. "That's right. You've got it now."

Muddy did not ask why I was dotting the wood with tears, or what I was building, or why, from then on, I needed a stockpile of lumber. I loved him for that, and I loved him even more when I heard his reply to Grandma after she cornered him one afternoon and asked, "Has she lost her mind?"

"By no means, ma'am," he said. "It's for mulching the rhododendrons. They like a good bite of acidy pulp."

I sawed an hour a day, as if I were lopping off the end of my penance that stretched from the earth to the sun. With each stroke I muttered an endearment my father would never hear.

On the Fourth of July, Opal's daughter and grandchildren came for a visit, a yearly extravagance Grandma, astoundingly, permitted. I planned to camp beside Mom and nibble my way through a box of scones Muddy had mail-ordered from London. He gave everyone a sampler to show there were no hard feelings about that American War of Independence business. My reverie was interrupted by the sounds of children whooping outside. I looked into the backyard at a puzzling sight.

Just three weeks before, I had helped Muddy put water in Grandma's in-ground pool and line its perimeter with potted plants. Grandma lounged beneath a beach umbrella calling the shots. "The hibiscus should be spaced three feet apart. Three!"

It was inviting, all that cerulean water, but when Muddy urged me to change into my bathing suit for an inaugural swim, I discreetly nodded toward Grandma and declined. My new wardrobe intentionally did not include swimwear.

What I saw on that July Fourth were three spindly black kids splish-splashing not in Grandma's grand pool but in a round, three-foot-deep, ten-foot-wide plastic pool set up beside it. I mean, *directly* beside it. If those kids minded, they didn't let on as the two girls squirted water pistols and the boy snorkeled in that limited expanse. Opal and her daughter, another rotund woman, lounged beneath umbrellas in flowery muumuus. It delighted me to see Opal with her feet up at last, her feet up at last; thank God Almighty, she had her feet up at last. Muddy cooked hamburgers on the grill. Cookie appeared in her maid uniform, crisscrossing the patio to place dish after dish on the picnic table set up beneath a shady tree. I wondered why she didn't have her feet propped up too.

Opal saw me and waved her jiggly arm for me to join them. I shook my head, but she put her hands on her extraordinary hips and mouthed, *Get your butt down here.*

I kissed Mom on the cheek, said, "I love you, please wake up," and raced downstairs in pedal pushers and a blouse. Grandma had allowed no shorts in my wardrobe.

The kitchen was empty, but "Heat Wave" blared from Cookie's radio. She rushed in and saw me, or, more precisely, saw my extra pair of hands. "Thank you, Jesus. Garnet, put those gherkins in that bowl and grab the ketchup and mustard from the fridge." Even with one hand in a rubber glove, she could deal sliced olives onto deviled eggs like a blackjack dealer.

Opal hollered, "Cookie, I asked you to bring us more tea!"

"Only got two hands," Cookie muttered.

Cookie loaded me down and we carted our offerings outside.

Opal called, "Did you bring me my tea?"

Cookie went over with a pitcher, groaning, and I understood why. Charlottesville was suffering its own heat wave.

"Garnet," Opal called. "This is my daughter, Darlinda."

Darlinda's head snapped back when she saw my skin, but she managed a smile, revealing a quarter-inch gap between her two front teeth.

"And those are my grandbabies, Snooky, Lester, and Daisy." I eyeballed the kids in the pool as they eyeballed me, elbowing one another in the ribs. Daisy jumped from the pool, eyes tearing, and rushed to her mother's arms. "Mama, what's wrong with—"

"You've got better manners than that," Opal growled at them. "Say hello."

"Hello." They scanned my birthmarks that pulsed even redder in the heat.

"Hello," I echoed, before joining Muddy at the grill.

"How do you like your burger?"

"Burned," I said. "The blacker the better."

Opal again called for Cookie, telling her to fetch a fly swatter.

"The woman is busy, Mama. I can get it," Darlinda said, hauling herself out of her chaise.

Opal held out her arm. "Cookie doesn't mind. Do you?"

"Not at all, Miss Darlinda." I tried to decode the look on Cookie's face, but her expression was as impenetrable as the paper scraps in Grandpa's study.

When dinner was ready, Opal's family sat at the table, Muddy too, who cracked self-deprecating jokes: "How many Brits does it take to untie a knot garden?" He patted an empty seat beside him, which I accepted. Cookie stood behind us and filled her own plate, reaching between us with her gloved hand, the three brats nudging one another at the sight. Cookie just hummed her balm song, then slipped away to sit on a settee under a crape myrtle.

"There goes six-shooter," Snooky said.

"Butt-face," Lester added. "She really *cracks* me up." He laughed at his own joke.

"I heard she's contagious," Daisy said, round eyes looking as if she believed it. All three kids studied the sides of their hands, no doubt imagining an extra digit pushing through. Opal and Darlinda did likewise, their faces puckered.

I rose, took my plate, and sat beside Cookie, who kept dabbing sweat from her chin.

I noted the stains under her arms. "Why are you wearing your uniform?"

Cookie nodded at Opal in the same way Opal had once nodded at an intercom speaker. I didn't understand what power Opal had over her, and I guess Cookie sensed that.

"She got me this job when nobody would hire me."

"But you're a great cook."

Cookie held out her gloved hand and the secret inside. "Some folks are funny about who they want handling their food."

I looked at my own stained hands, then up at the west wing, where I assumed Grandma was passed out, and marveled that she would hire Cookie. But I saw the curtain was drawn back, the sun glinting off the martini glass in Grandma's hand.

The kids finished eating and skipped back to their pool while Opal and Darlinda played shuffleboard. Muddy traipsed off, leaving Cookie and me to haul plates and platters inside. Opal continued baying requests. "Cookie! Go get my sun hat! And bring down my word-search book!"

I washed dishes in the kitchen, bouncing to Cookie's transistor music. Every time she brushed by she'd say, "You shouldn't be in here scrubbing pans."

An hour later the kitchen was clean, but Cookie and I were sopping messes. Grandma's pool lured me to it like I was a spotted koi. The kids stopped splashing as I plopped on my bum at the side of the pool, shucked off my shoes and anklets, and slipped my feet into Grandma's cool, cool water.

I kicked and splashed, I oohed and aahed to show them I could have my own fun in a pool that was clearly better than theirs.

Opal called Cookie over, yet again, to send her on some needless errand, a coaster, a nail file. The perspiration stains under Cookie's arms had broadened substantially. When the errand was complete and she walked by me, I held out my arm as a gate.

"Put your feet in the water. It feels really good."

Cookie looked at my feet swirling figure eights beneath the surface and I knew she wanted to dive in, maid dress, rubber glove, and all.

"That does sound nice." She looked from Grandma's pool to the kiddy one. "It is the Fourth of July." She glanced over at Opal, engrossed in her word search, then up at the west-wing window, where Grandma no longer stood. Cookie hauled a lawn chair beside the wading pool.

"This pool." I patted the concrete lip beside me. "Sit here."

"Oh no, honey. No." Cookie again eyed the west wing. "I couldn't do that."

I was about to ask why, but she sat in her chair beside the plastic pool. Opal's grandkids scooted to the opposite side, cupping their five-fingered hands together for protection as they anticipated what was about to happen. Cookie slipped off her shoes and discreetly unhooked her hose from her garters. She rolled the nylons down into discs that reminded me of capocollo to expose legs that were as shapely as Mom's. That's when we all learned that in addition to her extra pinkie, Cookie had an extra little toe on her right foot, which made perfect symmetrical sense to me. All eleven toenails were painted bright red and it lightened my heart to imagine Cookie sitting on the edge of her bed, cotton balls between her toes, as she ministered to a part of her that most people would never see.

"Eww," screamed the grandkids.

Rather than cowering, Cookie peeled off her rubber glove to expose the extra pinkie, doubling their horror. Even I could hear them gasp.

Just as Cookie was about to dip in her foot, Opal sat up in her chair and yowled, "Cookie! Go get my — my — eye drops, now!"

Cookie froze, her big toe hanging in midair. If a toe could express yearning, that one certainly did, bowing toward the water like a dousing rod. The toe hovered there and then suddenly dove in, dragging the whole foot with it, including that purportedly contagious anomaly.

Darlinda stood and screamed at her children: "Get out of the water! Get out of the water!"

Cookie yanked her foot out, but it was too late; the grandkids jumped out of the pool. Each hopped on one leg and cupped his or her right foot, all of them wailing like hired mourners in biblical times.

"I'm sorry." Cookie scooped up her capocollo hose and shoes. "Let the kids come back in now."

The kids sneered at her when she wasn't looking, which pissed me right off. As Cookie skulked by me, I grabbed her arm and yanked her down beside me.

"Put your feet in the water." Only this time, I pointed at Grandma's forbidden pool.

Cookie looked at me as if I'd lost my wits. "I can't put my feet in there."

"I live here now, so this is my house, my swimming pool, and you are my guest."

"She's no guest." Opal rushed toward us. "Don't you do it, Cookie."

"Hush up!" I said to Opal in a voice that sounded too much like Grandma's, but I didn't care. I was doing this not only for Cookie, but for me. We needed these healing waters, each for different reasons.

I said more softly, "Put your feet in the water."

Amazingly, Cookie slid in first the right foot, then the left, all eleven toes wiggling with delight as Opal and the gang yowled, "No! No!" I don't know what alarmed them more: the fact that Cookie was putting her feet into a *white* pool or the thought that *I* might contaminate *her*.

I started kicking my legs to shut them up, and so did Cookie—she had probably wanted to shut them up for years. We churned the water, sloughing off our sweat and stains and extra digits; at least, that's what I was praying for. You heard me: praying. For a scant second I forgot about my shrinking faith in God as I begged Him to fulfill our deepest longings. I tugged the Saint Garnet necklace from beneath my collar, clutched it in my hand, squeezed my eyes shut, and began reciting my spell from so many years before: "Sancta Maria, Mater Dei. Sancta Maria, Mater Dei." I added internally: *This is it, God. Your last chance.*

I heard hammering and when I opened my eyes and located the source, it was Grandma pummeling her fists against the window, mouthing, *Get out! Get out! Get out!*

Cookie saw her too, but instead of yanking her legs out, she kicked even harder, whirlpooling the water, singing at the top of her lungs, "'There is a balm in Gilead!'"

I started bellowing with her, thinking that if my prayer didn't work, maybe her balm song would. We sang and sang, even as Grandma pounded the glass while Opal and Darlinda hollered, "Get out, Cookie. You've got to get out now!"

Of course, when Cookie finally pulled her feet from the water, she still had a sixth toe. I looked at her hand, and the extra pinkie wiggled there too. She didn't seem to care. I think something else inside of her was healed because she trotted back into the house with her head held high singing, "'Our day will come!'"

Maybe Cookie didn't care, but I did. My test had failed. I confirmed for myself once and for all that I had no powers, and neither did God.

I stood, tromped to the edge of the yard, yanked that stupid no-powers relic from my neck, and hurled it to the back of the property, where it landed in a tangle of briars. A startled red-winged raptor darted from the thicket and shot through the sky, screaming like a girl being murdered. In my head I screamed right along with it.

Mommy through the Looking Glass

Golden McArches:

I have brazenly escaped my prison and Nonna, Betty, and I are sitting at a table in Sweetwater's first-ever McDonald's. Okay, it's actually in Vandalia, a city fifty-three miles north with a much larger population, more square mileage, and a professional baseball team.

It's never easy for me to slip beyond my fence, and this time my disguise is one of Le Baron's old suits, a driving scarf wound up to my nose, saucer-size sunglasses, and Radisson's chauffeur's cap with my hair tucked inside. Betty and Nonna are incognito thanks to mail-order wigs. Nonna chose the Cher model, Betty the gigundo Dolly Parton.

I pulled out of the driveway, and the pilgrims and newshounds were thankfully more interested in determining who was in the back seat than in looking at the driver. As I chugged forward, one of the more environmentally aware mob members hollered, "Gas guzzler!," to my shame, but at least we bundled together several errands.

Down the hill we inched because I refuse to speed around No-Brakes Bend, though I'd paid to have a culvert inserted beneath the road so those natural springs would no longer wreak havoc on our lives.

Appointment number one was with the senior-most partner in

Sweetwater's only law firm. He's billing me a fortune to fend off Le Baron's nephews, who are bent on ousting me and the ladies from our chateau.

Appointment number two was with an architect in Vandalia, where I reviewed the plans for the Nicky Ferrari Library, which will be built over a plot of unholy ground in Snakebite Woods. I had no longer been able to bear looking out my window at that shadowy copse, so I bought the lot, and next spring crews will begin clearing the property of a *portafortuna*-spilled grave and a decaying box fort that should be shipped straight to hell.

Appointment number three is at McDonald's and I've just eaten a Big Mac. Betty is sucking on a chocolate milk shake, and Nonna is enjoying fries, wiggling her feet like a toddler, which we are surrounded by. One little girl just skipped over, pointed at my red hair, my mottled face, and asked, "Are you Ronald McDonald?"

"Indeed I am, little lady. Indeed I am."

She yelled over her shoulder to her mother, "It's him! It's really him!"

The mother nodded, but she was more interested in her fried pie.

The girl hugged me with more strength than I would have thought possible, but such was her delight at meeting a mythical hero come to life. I imagine I hugged my mother with the same exuberance when she finally came back to life in Charlottesville.

On July fifth, after hibernating for eight months, she simply walked into the kitchen in her nightgown, with her stringy hair and sour breath, where everyone except Grandma sopped up eggs with buttered toast.

"Is there any more coffee?" Mom asked.

I raced over and wrapped my arms around her, but I don't know if I was offering a life preserver or clinging to one.

Cookie, who had surprisingly not been fired after her previous day's rebellion, rushed to her. "Hallelujah! Thank you, Jesus!"

Opal kissed and kissed Mom's face. "My baby, my beautiful baby girl."

Muddy stood behind us crimping his napkin and trying not to cry.

Cedrick eased out of his seat and went in search of his queen.

Within minutes Grandma bustled in to find her daughter eating her way through several countries: English muffins, Belgian waffles, French toast.

Grandma shook her head back and forth. "But my plans are incomplete!"

We all gawped at her pronouncement.

Grandma sat beside Mom and draped a napkin across her daughter's lap. "Slow down, darling. You'll make yourself ill."

Mother ate for three days, skin pinking up, a little belly bulge forming, purple smears beneath her eyes fading. No one mentioned Dad or Nicky, since Mom still looked like she might collapse in on herself at the slightest sneeze. For weeks she wandered aimlessly, as if she were looking for a book she'd set down, or she lounged on a chaise in the solarium, where Opal and Cookie brought her rice pudding and sweet tea. I often curled up in a chair behind a topiary giraffe. If I were still enough, they forgot I was there and I could eavesdrop as Mom climbed back into the present rung by rung.

"Nicky and Angelo are gone," she whispered one day.

Opal was polishing silver at a table but stopped to look at Mom. "Yes, they are, honey. They surely are."

Mom slumped and I thought, there she goes, but she shook it off. "Garnet's okay in my old room? She's not . . . going wicky-wacky?"

"Lord, no. She spends most of her time in your father's suite or out in the carriage house sawing wood."

Mother groaned, but after a pause she asked, "Why did Mother bar all the windows?"

Opal glanced up into a corner where an intercom lurked. "Why does she ever do anything?"

Grandma was now in a flurry of clandestine errands, so I shadowed Mother with an imaginary rope I was ready to loop around her waist if she started slipping inside herself again.

Though Mom gained physical and mental stamina, she spent too much time in Grandfather's study reading those crazy walls, by turns laughing and crying, as if she recalled the inspiration behind every enigmatic word. One day she unpinned a paper doily and pointed at the scribbles. "Bluster the hatchet man who foils my whims!"

I must have looked as if I were counting the cartoon nut-birds circling her head.

"Bluster the hatchet man!" she insisted.

"Uh-huh. That's very nice."

That afternoon I caught her rifling through Grandfather's closet, sniffing his shirtsleeves the same way Annette Funicello had inhaled the scent of my father. It nearly split me in two to see my mother aching for her dad. The lid on my heart-shaped box began rattling. I was working up the courage to tell Mom how much I missed Dad. Before I could, she whispered into the shirt, "You would have loved Nicky."

A little squeal slid from my mouth.

"And Garnet!" Mom looked over at me. "I'm sorry. It's just, the *Britannicas*, you know."

I did know. Just that morning I had seen Mom scanning dog-eared pages to read notes Nicky had jotted in margins, a secret code of his own involving stars and ampersands, dots and dashes, his own SOS.

Maybe Mom was ready to mourn Nicky, but commiserating with me over the death of my father would have to wait.

Grandma became suddenly attentive and often joined us in the solarium for lemonade.

"Have you read any good books lately?" Grandma asked whenever Mom brought up the inevitability of picking up the pieces of our lives on the hill, the untended house, piling-up bills.

"I'll handle all of that, darling," Grandma would say. "You never had a head for business."

Grandma hauled in bags and bags of books to occupy—or distract—Mom's convalescence. One afternoon while delivering her offerings, she planted a seed. "Have you thought about finishing the degree you started at Wellesley?"

Mom's head jerked up, as if the largest carrot in the world dangled before her. She shook it off faster than I would have imagined. "I can't do that. What about Garnet?"

By the speed of her answer I knew Grandma already had plan B in the hopper. "You could always attend University of Virginia. You and Garnet could live with me until you're finished. We have plenty of excellent schools for Garnet too."

Blast. So she did remember that federal mandate.

"I brought a course catalog in case you're interested." Grandma slid it into Mom's hands.

Grandma's apple of temptation for me was less alluring, though I did take a giant bite.

I was in my room building a house of cards when Grandma came in with an overnight case.

"I have a surprise for you." She dashed to my bathroom, the breeze of her entrance collapsing my unfinished house. I followed as she turned on the lights over the vanity.

She pulled out the cushioned chair. "Sit, sit."

I obeyed and faced my reflection in the mirror.

Grandma charted the red map of my face and neck with her eyes, then opened the overnight case to reveal rows of foundations, concealers, and powders.

"I've never worn makeup." I wasn't necessarily opposed. I was thirteen, after all.

"You're a young lady now. Your mother wore cosmetics when she was your age."

"She did?"

"Indeed." Grandma opened a bottle and dabbed beige liquid onto a cotton ball. "And this isn't just any makeup, dear. This was specially ordered to help with your . . . condition."

Ah. There it was. Before I could rebut, Grandma gripped my face in her hands and began patting the liquid onto my cheek. I don't know if I was more mesmerized by Grandma Iris actually touching me or by watching the landmasses disappear. It was astonishing to see whole continents and archipelagoes vanish. All those grade-school taunts erupted in my head: Polka-Dot Mary, Map Face, Plague Hag. As my geography faded, so did the jeers, and I lost control over my eyes, tears carving mulberry riverbeds in my now-porcelain flesh.

"Don't cry, darling." Grandma daubed on fresh foundation and dusted me with powder. "You'll ruin the effect."

I certainly didn't want to do that, especially since for the first time in my life, Grandma was ministering to me, not with red Pergusa water, but with makeup. I luxuriated in her attention. Like my brother and mother in La Strega days, I, so easily, succumbed.

After Grandma left I gaped at myself in the mirror, but it wasn't with the same flaw-checking madness my mother engaged in. It was as if a new nonsainted, nonstained world had opened up to me—except for one thing: my volcano hair. But Grandma left a potion for that too. After hours of practice, I could tame most of it into a ponytail if I used enough Dippity-do.

I didn't reveal my new persona to Mom. Both Grandma and I knew that might be dicey, so, like Nicky playing dress-up with his La Strega duds, I furtively morphed into a spotless girl in my room.

One night Mom and I lounged by the pool, me perusing a *Britannica*, Mom underlining classes in the college catalog. She periodically closed her eyes and moaned. When I asked what was wrong she said, "Nothing."

Finally Mom closed her book and looked at me. "I got a letter today from Aunt Betty."

The cork in Iceland started quivering, and I clamped my hand over it.

"She misses us."

I swallowed hard. "What about Nonna?" The cork battered my palm.

Mom shook her head. "I don't know, honey. But I think that given time . . ."

I wondered if there was enough time left in the universe.

"Our life back home isn't much, and it's horribly complicated," Mom admitted, "but those women are your fam-i-ly."

This was a tremendous confession, or concession, though I noticed she didn't say *our* fam-i-ly.

She opened her mouth and by the look in her eyes, I could tell she was about to spill something significant. Just then Grandma rushed out with a shopping bag, dissipating Mom's clarity and stilling the cork on my arm.

"I got your books!" Grandma said, breathless.

Mom had recently begun compiling her own grocery lists of titles. She pulled out a stack of the books and shuffled through them. "Where's Ginsberg?" Her tastes had shifted from English lit-ra-toor to Beat poets.

Grandma pursed her lips. "I will not allow that obscenity in my house." She looked at me and set into motion a plan that we had been working on for days. "Marina, I want to throw a belated birthday party for Garnet."

Mom gasped. "Oh my God, Garnet. I can't believe I forgot!"

Mother had slept through my pivotal teenage birthday, as had everyone else.

"Tut-tut, darling," Grandma said. "Water under the bridge. Let's make up for it by having a soiree for our girl. She's all we have left now."

That was a dangerous maneuver, and Mom's eyes filmed over as she tallied up her losses. Grandma's eyes glazed briefly too, and I caught a glimpse of her own private mourning that she'd bathed in alcohol. She had lost her male heir. Her golden boy.

Mother sniffed and looked at me. "Would you like a party, Garnet?"

My head bobbled up and down.

"Okay, then."

Grandma flung off her gloom. "Goody!" She rushed toward the house to order elephants and trapeze artists or whatever she had in store.

"Nothing fancy," Mom called. "A simple party with the staff. Cake and ice cream."

"Cake! I must call François!"

Later that night I slipped downstairs for the bag of coconut marshmallows I had eyeballed in the pantry during lunch. Grandma was yelling in the kitchen, so I eased open the swinging door half an inch and saw her jabbing her finger into Opal's shoulder.

"I told you to destroy any letters from that woman. How could you let one slip by you? How? You must be more vigilant, Opal. Do you understand me?"

"Yes, ma'am."

I slunk upstairs marshmallow-less, saddened to think of Betty writing stacks of apologetic letters that Mom and I would never see.

During the following weeks Grandma was a dictator: concocting menus with Cookie; auditioning musicians, florists, and house polishers. Mom became increasingly agitated, her "Nothing too fancy! And just with the staff!" appeals completely ignored as evidenced by the RSVPs that arrived daily from Mom's old chums: Bunny and Bowler, Chompers and Skiff.

Mom groaned when she scanned the names, particularly Skiff's, a former beau who had never married, according to Grandma, though "what he'll do with his father's shipping money I don't know." Skiff was the prearranged mate Mom had been dodging when she ran off with my father, a man Mom had barely mentioned since she'd awakened. As Mom read and reread Skiff's name, she muttered, "Slipknot the Skiff slot." A bad omen.

The day of the party Cookie whipped up canapés and shrimp cocktails and oysters Rockefeller, directing the three sous-chefs hired for the occasion. Her gloved and ungloved hands blurred like hummingbird wings. Opal was in charge of the coat-check girl, the bartender, and the three waiters, all black. She instructed them on where to place the flowers, set up the bar, and arrange the rented tables and chairs in the Hall of Mirrors. A table for the three-tiered cake that was topped with real flowers but no birthday candles. I asked Opal why the rest of the table was bare.

"Why, honey, that's where the guests will put your presents."

Presents! I couldn't fathom what types of gifts these people would bring: bags of loose diamonds, barrels of oil, gold bars.

Also steered to the hall was a jazz combo; the musicians set up under that painting of Mom resting her arm on a horse, though I swear I saw her two-dimensional, oil-painted eyes roll at the intemperance of it all.

Mom tried to sidestep all the busyness. "It's all too much. It's just too much." Finally she escaped to Grandpa's bedroom and crawled into bed. I nestled beside her with my imaginary rope and watched her stare at her image in the silver bowl on the bedside table, a reflective pose I hadn't seen since we'd moved there.

An hour before the shindig, Grandma swooped in with two garment bags. She draped one over my mother's lap, the other over mine. "I took the liberty of buying you both dresses."

Mom stood and handed her bag back. "I'll manage."

"But look." Grandma tugged down the zipper and pulled out a pink suit. "It's not fancy."

"No, thank you." Mom inspected the fabric. "And besides, it's wool. You want me to wear wool in August?"

"But Jackie Kennedy just ordered the same suit! It's Chanel, Marina. Sometimes one has to suffer for fashion."

"Let Jackie suffer."

Grandma stepped toward Mom and held the jacket against her torso. "It'll look so pretty with your hair." She undraped the jacket from the hanger. "Just try it on." She tried to slip Mom's balled-up fist into one of the sleeves.

"Goddamn it, Mother." Mom grabbed the jacket, tossed it on the floor, and left.

"I just don't understand," Grandma muttered. "She would have looked so pretty."

Padre, three months later I saw that pink suit again. Not on Mom, but on Jackie Kennedy, who was wearing it on a monumental November day in Dallas. She must have been itchy in that wool suit in the Texas sun in that open convertible, but she was one who knew how to suffer.

Grandma zippered Mom's suit back into the bag and turned her eyes on me. "Certainly Marina couldn't object if you wore your new dress."

Certainly she could, but I shrugged.

The dress was pretty enough, but a little young for my teenage self. Pale rose with an oversize Battenberg lace collar. Grandma led me to my bathroom, where she daubed makeup on not only my face and neck but my ears. She fashioned my hair into an over-gelled ponytail and secured it with a velvet rose. I squeezed into lacy tights before stepping into the dress.

"You look very sweet." Grandma yanked down the long sleeves, eyeballing my midsection, until she caught sight of Cyprus on the back of my hand. "I almost forgot!"

She strutted out and returned with a pair of gloves with satin bows and cultured pearls sewn at each wrist. "They're highly fashionable."

I slid on the gloves, and my right pinkie extended, though I hadn't commanded it to.

"Don't get messed up before the guests arrive," Grandma said as she left.

I posed before the mirror, scrutinizing the geography-less girl staring back at me. She could walk the streets of Sweetwater or Charlottesville without drawing undue attention. Inside my gut, a clown juggled balls of both sadness and joy.

Soon I heard Mom thumping down the hall. "Garnet, are you getting ready?" I instinctively closed my bathroom door. "Yes!" I turned on faucets, flushed the toilet. I think I already knew how Mom would feel about my getup.

My room faced the circular drive in front of the house so I was able to watch the cars pulling in. Convertibles and glossy numbers with leather roofs circled the three-tiered fountain now spewing aquamarine water. Not a station wagon among them. I thought about Dad, who couldn't even afford to buy us a used set of wheels. I thought of him even more as young couples unfolded from their vehicles, the women with upswept hair and pastel dresses carrying beautifully wrapped presents. Every husband was taller than his wife and dressed in a pricey suit and polished shoes. I could identify a few by their nicknames: the big-toothed one had to be Chompers. The one who refused to relinquish his hat, Bowler. They handed their keys to Cedrick, who passed them to Muddy, who parked cars beside the tennis court. Only one man arrived without a companion. Judging from the way he primped in his rearview, I knew it was Skiff. He was also taller than my father, but the hair on his crown was thinning, a satisfying defect.

Mom called from the other side of my door: "They're here!"

"I'll be down in a second!"

"Oh God," she said before padding away. I rushed to my door, peeked out, and was disappointed to see her wearing her same skinny pants and an aqua shell, her hair in a ponytail without a velvet rose. She headed not to the grand staircase but to the steps that led down to the kitchen and the back door.

I crouched behind one of the two vases that flanked the top of the stairway and looked through the railing into the Hall of Mirrors. A black version of Radisson led guest after guest to Grandma, who was standing beneath the chandelier that Fanny Brice had swung from. "Zelda!" They offered hugs and kissy-kissy. Grandma didn't look offended by the nickname.

Opal directed her staff from a corner, sending envoys with trays of champagne and canapés. The women clustered around Zelda asking sensitive questions. "How is she doing really? No, really?" The men migrated to the jazz combo, tapping their feet, looking at my mother's painting. Chompers said, "She was a beauty." The rest of them sighed, particularly Skiff, who positioned himself at the back of the pack, a lone dinghy facing Zelda, who kept scanning the room for her truant daughter.

"Wonder what Zelda's got cooked up over there." Bowler nodded across the room at what I assumed was another portrait, hung directly opposite Mom's but covered in a white sheet with a pink bow at the top, a dangling cord at the ready for the grand unveiling. My heart ka-thunked and I was actually moved by the notion that Grandma clandestinely had had my portrait painted so that Mom and I could wink back and forth at each other in perpetuity. Then I wondered which version of me Grandma had commissioned: the au naturel me or the Kabuki one. The Kabuki one, no doubt, or at least—at that moment—I hoped.

Mom didn't come, and she didn't come, even as more guests arrived and my legs began to cramp. I wasn't about to go down there without her to hide behind, and besides, it didn't look as if any necks were craning in search of a birthday girl. Regardless of the presents now heaped on the table, I understood then that this party wasn't for me.

The men swapped champagne for bourbon and sat at the tables, where they pulled cigarettes from cases and tapped ashes into crystal bowls. Soon they began making blunt inquiries.

"I heard she flunked out of Wellesley and has been living in West Virginia. Why in the world would anyone live there, for God's sake?"

"I heard Zelda cut her off for marrying a Jew."

"What did her husband do? Does anyone know what her husband did?"

"I have a joke, Yummers. A Jew, a nigger, and a clappy whore walk into a bar . . ."

I was stunned that this fashionable set included versions of Uncle Dom. And I was even more shocked when they kept trading racist jokes while Black Radisson leaned in with their fresh drinks, his expression fixed. He went back to the bar for the next round and nodded at the bartender, who pulled a bottle from his vest pocket, unscrewed the eyedropper lid, and squirted a dose of something into each drink. I don't know for certain what the liquid was, but it was yellow and I think, in another culture, might be considered excellent counter-*malocchio* juice.

Finally Mom appeared from the kitchen, Cookie, her equal in

height, behind her, guiding her in by the shoulders, whispering in her ear, shoving a drink in her hand.

The women squawked like gulls and flocked to her. "Marina! You look stunning! How we've missed you!"

Cookie drifted to Opal's station as the women circled Mom. Even in her old clothes and uncoifed hair, Mom was striking. The women scoured her from stem to stern, some baring their teeth while pretending to be cordial. "I can't believe you've kept your figure after having children." The men stopped yammering and gawked at Mom, particularly Skiff, who crossed his arms and appraised the jewel amid this cluster of lesser stones.

Grandma had been sipping a martini but slipped off to the bar to knock back a few, leaving the women to interrogate Mom. "What happened at Wellesley? Why didn't you come to Monaco? So where exactly have you been?" The questions were relentless with no pauses for answers, thankfully, since I don't know what Mom would have said. *I've been scrubbing toilets and eating capocollo with Italians.*

"We were so sorry to hear about your son," a chunky woman said. It looked as if she genuinely meant it.

"Nicky." Mom's head bobbed ever so slightly, as if the God she didn't believe in were flicking her forehead with a giant finger.

Uh-oh, I thought. From the looks in Opal's and Cookie's eyes, I could tell they were thinking *Uh-oh* too.

But Mom shook it off. "Thank you, Bonbon."

A woman wielding a cigarette holder said, "Yes, Zelda told us about your son, and about your husband who died in the war."

"My husband didn't die in the war." Mom's eyes shot virtual flames at Grandma.

Grandma fiddled with her pearls and sort of tap-danced across the floor without spilling a drop of martini. "You must have heard me wrong, Taffy. I said he *served* in the war. *Served.*"

At the mention of war the men's jokes became militaristic, sort of. "Bumpy, remember that little bistro we celebrated in after we liberated Paris? One time a frog, a kike, and a pig-alley whore walked in and found a table of heil-heinies . . ."

Skiff inched over to Mom, clearly on a prearranged mission, judging from the way he and Grandma traded looks. I wondered what would happen to me if Mom and Skiff married. He would whisk her across the pond and I would be stuck with Grandma taking etiquette lessons.

Skiff nudged Bonbon and Taffy aside and cupped his hand around Mom's elbow.

"Marina." His voice was tinged with both yearning and spite.

Mom looked at his hand, and her eyes drifted to his. "Skiffy."

They did the kissy-kiss and Mom stared at the silver bracelet on Taffy's wrist.

"You look marvelous." Skiff scrutinized my mother in the same way the women were scrutinizing him. "You broke my heart."

Mom looked at him, and then at Grandma, who merely tilted her head in a way that communicated: *You did, dear.*

Bonbon started to sidle away, but Taffy held her in place. She recognized theater when she saw it.

Skiff slid a tendril of Mom's hair behind her ear. "One day we were canoeing and the next you were gone. Where did you go? Zelda was always a little dodgy on the details."

Zelda glared at him as if to say, *This wasn't part of our plan.* "What does it matter where she was *specifically?* If Marina had wanted you to know, she would have told you."

"Ouch," Taffy said.

"Touché," said Skiff. "At least tell us about your old man. What did your husband do?"

The glass in Mom's hand shook, its contents sloshing close to the brim.

I looked at Grandma to see if she would again rescue her daughter, but she just stood, another statue among so many.

Bonbon, bless her plump heart, tried to throw Mom an oar. She took the shaking glass from Mom's hand. "How did you meet him? What was he like?" She assumed those were innocuous inquiries.

I wondered how Mom would describe her choice of spouse: a

barely high-school-educated runt who wore paint-splattered work boots and carried a lunch pail.

I felt like a stranger floating above this superior set, a part of Mom's secret life that was so disconnected from this one.

"He was a wonderful man," Mom said. "And a hard worker."

A sob lodged in my throat.

"But what did he *do?*" Skiff wore the same expression Uncle Dom would have worn.

The light in Mom's eyes dimmed. She tugged at the hair at her temple and I imagined that in her mind she was replaying the movie of her life with that horrible ending.

This time I genuinely expected Grandma to dive in with some elevated lie, to save herself, if not her daughter, since Mom's choice of a husband reflected poorly on Grandma. *He owned a steel company. He was an oil tycoon.* But Grandma just stood there with a strange look on her face. Not embarrassment, which is what I would have expected. More like smug satisfaction. *Let's see how you're going to get out of this one, dear.* As if today's festivities were staged to show her daughter just how much she would rue the day.

Mom roused herself a bit. "He sawed the gnawed wood."

"What's that?" Skiff asked.

"What did she say?" Taffy whispered.

"He sawed the gnawed wood and inlaid the T-bone floor."

I don't know what stunned me more, that my mother was blurting her nonsense in public or that I actually understood it. Regardless, as I watched her silently backflip into herself, I uncoiled my imaginary rope to lasso around her waist. I genuinely thought I could be Mom's savior. I could be the savior of Dad's reputation too if I pranced downstairs in my fancy dress, tidy hairdo, and de-geographied face. I would show everyone how refined we all were, how well Dad had provided for us. So I stood, smoothed down my collar, sucked in my gut, and clomped my shoes on each step as I descended to draw attention away from my caved-in mother and place it squarely on me.

"My father was a lumber tycoon!" I bellowed. "Our house is on top of a hill; it's bigger than this one, and it has its own bowling alley and a room just for mink coats." I don't know where all that came from, since this was before I even knew about the bowling alley and fur vault in my current chateau.

"Is that the daughter?" Taffy's cigarette holder tipped limply toward the floor.

Bowler eyed my overly powdered face. "*That's* Marina's daughter?"

I could feel the oily disappointment oozing from their pores.

"Yes, I am." I stepped into the Hall of Mirrors.

All eyes were on me as the guests made their assessments and no doubt determined, even without knowing the secret beneath my war paint, that I was miles below their offspring. Skiff's eyes pivoted from Mom to me, probably in the same way my father's did on the day I was born.

I looked over at Cookie and Opal, bug eyes about to pop out of their heads, Cookie hiding her gloved hand behind her back.

Grandma and I looked at Mom, who looked at me but didn't see me. The spark of consciousness in her eyes was gone. I bet Grandma was thinking, *Whew.*

Grandma hustled over and yanked me offstage. "Well, now that you've all met, it's time for the unveiling."

She deposited me beside Mother and went to the giant painting. The guests murmured with anticipation. I was miffed that my grand entrance had fizzled to nothing. I wanted Mom to see my hurt, but she stared so intently into one of the mirrors across the room that I waved my hand in front of her face and whispered, "Mom? Mom?" She didn't even blink.

Grandma cleared her throat. "It is such a pleasure to have my family reunited."

"Hear, hear!" Skiff clamped his arm around Mom's waist. I don't think he cared that she was a shell of herself. She was a beautiful shell who looked smart on his arm.

"In honor of my daughter's return I took the liberty of commissioning a painting that will grace the Caudhill walls for generations to come."

I slipped my hand into Mom's ice-cold one to steady my nerves, since I knew that once again all eyes would be on me as they compared my face to, perhaps, a mulberry-stained one.

Grandma's eyes actually moistened as she wrapped her hand around the rope. I was moved by her newfound familial pride. "Ladies and gentlemen, behold."

I couldn't bear to watch, so I squeezed my eyes shut and listened to fabric swishing to the floor, the gasping awe of the crowd, the feet shuffling forward to better admire the vision.

"How beautiful. How stunning. It's Marina all over again," they said. I wondered how much license Grandma had given the artist.

Finally I peeled open my eyes, expecting to see a gentrified version of myself, but the figure staring back at me was Nicky.

The crowd mused: "Is that her son? That must be her son. How beautiful. And tragic."

"Nicky?" Mom's hand warmed in my grip. "Is that my Nicky?" Her fingers slipped from mine as she inched toward the painting. Skiff let his hand fall from her waist to watch the heartbreaking reunion.

It was a stunning painting, Padre, not with my brother holding a stupid plumed hat or wearing knickers but fashioned after his last school picture, when he wore his La Strega duds and held a chess castle in his hand. The flawless porcelain skin, the rosebud lips that had earned him slugs from the Four Stooges earned him respect here.

"Well," Skiff said. "*That* is Marina's child, for sure." I don't think I imagined the relief in his voice as he predicted what their own progeny would look like.

"Isn't he exquisite?" Bonbon said.

"Yes. He is," Taffy conceded.

My brother was the savior who would elevate my family. It would never be me.

Skiff went to congratulate Grandma on the painting. Mom crept forward and craned her neck to take in the full impact of her son painted monumentally out of scale with the delicately boned prince he actually was. The guests warbled amongst themselves.

"He was her only son, you know."

"He would have been the first male Caudhill-Adams-Rutledge heir."

"Yes. What a horrible, horrible loss."

I was stunned by the sentiment bubbling beneath their words. The presumed superiority of the male offspring was alive and well, as was the preference for beauty over, well, me. How easily they would have chosen to slip me into the front seat of the station wagon that day and tuck my brother safely between his sheets.

"What did you say?" Mom still faced my brother, so we all assumed she was communing with her dead son.

In one movement she spun to face the crowd, the sentient spark again ignited. "I said, what did you say?"

"We said he's a beautiful boy," Bonbon valiantly answered.

"He certainly got all of your looks," said Chompers.

The wrong thing to say, as it turned out.

"Where's Garnet?" Mom desperately scanned faces, bypassing mine three times before she understood what Grandma had done to my real face, which was the antithesis of everything lovely in that room.

"What did you do to her?" Mom looked from me to Grandma. "What the hell did you do to her?"

"It's, it's, it's just a dress, dear. Nothing fancy," Grandma sputtered, eyes frantic.

Mom raced to me and grabbed me by the wrist. "This isn't my daughter," she said, seething, to Grandma, to everyone. "This isn't my daughter!"

Mom pulled me across the hall and whisked me upstairs with the force of a hypercharged mother protecting her young, if that's what she was doing.

I could hear Taffy asking, "That's not her daughter? Then who is she?"

My feet stumbled as Mom led me to my bathroom. I expected her to order me to raise my arms so she could pull the offending costume over my head, but she turned on the hot water, grabbed a washcloth, and soaked it. She held the steaming thing to my face and scrubbed and rubbed until most of that opaque foundation and powder and rouge was off, mulberry continents resurfacing. When she was finished, everything was smeared, my ponytail was lopsided, and errant strands were springing every which way. There were beige streaks on my Battenberg collar, dripping down my dress.

I expected her to say, *Now go change,* but instead she once again yanked me from where I stood, this time taking me out of the bathroom and into the hall. I resisted but couldn't match her strength. She whooshed me back downstairs, hurried me across that cool marble, and stood me under Fanny Brice's chandelier.

It was horrible, all those gasps and cringes from the wait staff and guests. From Cookie.

"This is my daughter." Mom gripped my chin and twisted my face toward the guests so they could all get a good look. I tried to wrench free but Mom held me tight as she yelled at the spectators, and Grandma, "Isn't she beautiful? Isn't she!"

There was no sound for two whole minutes as the stares pierced my skin like a million blowgun darts. Then someone started whimpering. I scanned the crowd to find out who; perhaps it was Bonbon, or Cookie, or even Skiff (who was hurtling toward the door as fast as he could). But it was me blubbing like a three-year-old.

Cookie dashed up and pried Mom's hand from my face. "Leave her be!" It was the first time I ever heard her voice raised.

Mom looked at her hand still in a claw, makeup smears on her arms, her sweater. She looked at me, really looked at me, and understood.

"Garnet," she whispered, but I cowered behind Cookie, the only person I could trust.

"I . . . I . . ." Mom looked for someone, something to pin her actions on. "It's this place, this goddamn place! We've got to leave, tonight, and go back home."

Grandma clipped up beside us. "I'm afraid that's not possible, dear."

"What?" Mom asked.

"Your house went into foreclosure months ago. It's been sold, contents and all." Grandma no longer cared what polite society thought about this if it would keep her daughter under her barred roof.

Mom shook her head. "But you were supposed to take care of all that."

Grandma didn't have to answer. We all understood that she had done just that.

Mom looked at me and I read the apology in her eyes, not just for past omissions, but for what she was about to do. Inside her left iris, a minuscule version of her waved goodbye. She looked past me into one of those mirrors and padded to it, pretended to smooth down her ponytail, but she was looking into the glass, perhaps into our old life on the hill, the squat house, the lost fam-i-ly, maybe even into a version of herself trapped on the other side squinting into the mirror too. I heard it, the crack that sounded from inside her skull. Her hands balled into fists and she pounded her thighs, gently at first, then harder.

"Mom, stop it." I pictured the bruises that would bloom on her willowy legs.

Mom didn't hear me, or maybe she did, because she stopped pummeling herself and started pounding the mirror, the mirror, the mirror.

"Oh my God," Bonbon said. "Somebody do something."

Nobody stepped forward as Mom punched the glass, chanting, "No-no-no-no-no." Now using her fists, harder and harder, until the glass shattered, fragmenting her view, so she moved to the next mirror, pounding and shattering, cuts on her hands as she moved to the next and the next, until someone, Cookie, I think, screamed, "Someone do something!"

Grandma didn't come to her rescue. Neither did Black Radisson or Cedrick. Muddy appeared from who-knows-where. He wrapped his arms around Mom while cooing, "Shh. Shh. It's all right now, missy."

Mom struggled against him, but he held on tight. "It's okay now. I've got you."

Mom sank in his arms. He scooped her up and carried her upstairs as she bawled what was incomprehensible to everyone except me: "I put the kill keys in his hand."

"That's all right, dearie."

"And they weighed so little."

"So very little." Muddy ferried Mom to the east wing, to the sleigh bed, where she climbed back into herself for good.

The guests stood there goggle-eyed, as if this were the stunning coda at the end of the performance. Finally they collected their opera glasses and programs, crunched over all that shattered glass, and peeled out in their fancy cars to their fancy homes and telephones to call in their reviews so that impolite society would be informed of the madness.

Grandma called Dr. Trogdon and while we waited for him I sat on the stairs as Cookie and Opal swept up the shards of glass and taped cardboard over the broken mirrors, both women working in silence.

When Dr. Trogdon arrived I followed him to Mom's bedside; his pill vials rattled around in his case as he removed a syringe of brown liquid, which he injected into Mom's arm. Grandma stood over him with a look that was neither distressed nor fretful; it was pure content.

A decade after that party I sat in the whippet room examining the contents of Grandma Iris's safety-deposit box that had been delivered to me by the fiduciary of her estate. Amid the codicils, stock certificates, and many car titles were, I discovered, two clues that helped decode Grandpa Postscript. The first was a *Charlottesville Daily Progress* society column, which I'll include as exhibit C.

Confidence Man Leaps to His Death

On V-E Day, while the rest of America and her Allies celebrated the fall of the Third Reich, thirty-nine-year-old Donald Flyman (aka Reginald White) leaped to his death from a second-story window in the home of his wife, socialite Iris Caudhill-Adams-Rutledge, of the *Mayflower* Caudhills. It is unclear if suicide was his intent or if, according to a member of the housekeeping staff, he was attempting to flee after it was discovered that he had embezzled $400,000 from his wife's estate and was planning to leave the country with an unnamed woman.

Flyman was born in Tredegar, South Wales, the son of a coal miner who worked in Bedwellty pits. Young Flyman emigrated to the United States, where he initially sold encyclopedias and wrote greeting-card verse before infiltrating the wealthy class.

Flyman and Caudhill-Adams-Rutledge had a brief engagement that culminated in the most anticipated wedding of 1929, held on Saturday, October 26, just days before Black Tuesday and the stock-market crash that would financially devastate so many of the wedding-goers, but not the well-diversified Caudhills.

Nine months after the ceremony, the young wife delivered a daughter, Marina, who, according to the same source, "was the apple of her father's eye."

Mrs. Caudhill-Adams-Rutledge refused to allow her late husband's remains to be interred in her family's crypt.

Flyman was buried in Potter's Field with only the housekeeping staff and his daughter, now almost fifteen, in attendance.

The second item was a black-and-white photograph of Grandfather standing in that three-tiered fountain wearing a shirt-and-trunks-combined swimsuit with horizontal stripes that made him look like a convict. He's grinning broadly, his right hand waving, revealing a stunning anomaly: a second pinkie. Behind him, barely caught in the frame, one of the black maids smiles a bit too knowingly, one finger pressed to her butt-creased chin.

Get Thee to a Nunnery

Happy Holy Days, Archie:

The ladies and I just watched Perry Como's Christmas special, so we're feeling all gooey inside, thanks to Mr. C.'s cardigan and Nonna's ninety-proof wassail. Now Betty can't wait to buy our tree, and she's already ordered strings of pink-flamingo lights from the mail-order-crap store. I'm going to have to speak with her about her spending habits.

I said nighty-night and now I'm in the crystal-ball room, one of the towers fitted with bubble windows, which offer excellent viewing. We got a dusting of snow today and the village is gussied up: Saint Garnet angels hanging from street lamps—sheesh—colored lights rimming storefronts, Christmas trees in apartment windows above them. Even my hill neighbors have outdone themselves in case they make the national news.

The pilgrims still refuse to leave, though I had hoped this arctic blast would send them flapping back to Capistrano. They just pulled closer to the heated pond, where the steam works wonders on their pores. They've also somehow tapped into electricity since I see a number of space heaters, utility lamps, and pink-flamingo lights strung around luggage racks. *Betty!* They're never going to leave. In fact, Nonna is out there right now handing out candy canes, afghans, and swigs of something from a thermos; high-octane wassail, no doubt. She really needs to stop that, though she does look content tugging children's earlobes, muttering prayers, offering hugs and kisses. The children follow her as if she's the real healer—as I keep insisting.

There was a time when I thought I would never see her again, or Aunt Betty. And though the mood is ripe now, since I'm inside a crystal ball, I don't think I could ever have forecast our reunification, especially during my exile in Virginia, and after Mom obliterated Grandma's Hall of Mirrors, I was banished to even more distant lands.

Back in Charlottesville, after Mom's outburst, Dr. Trogdon and Grandma kept vigil by Mom's bed, the doctor redressing the cuts on her hands, Grandma pushing back Mom's cuticles, the words *I win* almost visibly scrolling across Grandma's eyelids. I sat on the floor in the doorway tending my own wounds. Cookie—Aunt Cookie, though neither of us knew that yet—checked on me regularly, urging me to whisper something into Mom's ear that might keep her from slipping so far away.

Honestly, Padre, I don't know what I would have said to Mom at that moment since I now doubted her maternal love. Perhaps, like her slog through the underclass, her love for me was merely a defiance of everything Grandma Iris held dear. I was a rue-the-day temper tantrum, that's all.

I wanted to jump somewhere too, through a bricked-up window perhaps, but mostly back to Sweetwater. I fingered that volcano in Iceland beneath which I had hidden my love for two women who I hoped would rush to embrace me, though I wasn't sure. I longed for a way we could live together without Grandpa or Uncle Dom peeing testosterone all over our lives. Then there was the issue of Ray-Ray.

Eventually I went to bed, but in the morning I discovered the next part of Grandma's scheme. I was eating breakfast with Opal and Cookie when Grandma came in and sat beside me.

I don't think I just imagined the difficulty she was having spitting out what was on her mind. Finally, she turned her chair toward me. "Garnet, I'm sending you away to boarding school."

Cookie and Opal gasped.

Grandma looked at them. "It's really for the best." She patted my wrist in a gesture she'd likely been practicing for months.

I withdrew my arm. "I don't want to leave Mom."

Grandma stood. "We must secure your future with a solid education. There's no telling what they've been teaching you in West Virginia."

My mind flew back to all those nuns who genuinely loved me.

Grandma added the final dollop. "I would have done the same for Nicky."

There was no rebutting that, even if her motives in each case were quite different.

Grandma tugged me to my feet. "I'll help you pack."

Upstairs, a trunk had already been placed in my room. In went the clothes, the makeup. No globes or *Britannicas*. Before I left I climbed onto Mom's bed, wrapped my arms around her neck, and whispered into her ear, "Don't let her send me away."

No response.

"Mustn't keep Cedrick waiting," Grandma said, though she'd kept the man standing at attention for decades.

She pried me off the bed and led me downstairs, past that painting of Mom in the Hall of Cracked Mirrors, her adoring eyes aimed across the room at Nicky—his heart's desire fulfilled at last. Grandma rushed me through the farewell lineup of Opal, Cookie, and Muddy, all snuffling, holding out mementos I barely had time to snatch: a feather duster, a transistor radio, and, from Muddy, thankfully, my father's saw.

Outside, as Cedrick opened the back door of the Cadillac, I heard Cookie singing, "'There is a balm in Gilead!'"

I looked back at the house and saw Grandma heading inside, clapping her hands as if I were so much chalk dust. Cedrick nudged me between the shoulders and I fell into the back seat, where I was surrounded by blackened windows and automatic locks snapping down all around. Bluster the hatchet man, indeed.

As the car sped away I performed my own disappearing act. I

imagined myself bouncing on a diving board, sproinging higher and higher before vaulting into the air, hugging my knees for the biggest cannonball of my life.

Suddenly, from the car radio, a voice announced Valentina Tereshkova's impending U.S. visit, and I thought that if she could blast into space, so could I. My rocket would be my own body, and in my mind I launched myself and flew ever deeper into the cosmos, planets flickering by as I set my destination for Pluto, that perpetually dark ball that would hide me. But when I looked to the solar system on my wrist, Pluto was inexplicably gone, leaving Neptune to bring up the orbital rear. I would have to drift aimlessly, but even that was okay. Grandma's war paint would protect my hull from stinging barbs, sideways glances, tragic deaths of sundry family members, even betrayals by one's own mother. I determined I would not feel anything. Period.

Archie, I'll burn through my refugee years in New Hampshire as quickly as I burned through your questionnaire — now a pile of soot at the bottom of the barbecue pit. Tell the committee it's a saint's prerogative, but really, that was tiresome stuff.

Grandma ensured that my home for the next several years would be a cramped dorm room that I shared with roommates who came and went as if the place had a revolving door, most of them lasting less than a week because my makeup would smear off overnight, giving them the crack-of-dawn fright of their lives. On those mornings, the traumatized child would be led from my room by our dorm monitor, young Sister Joanie, who scanned not only my smudged face but Dad's saw, which was hanging brazenly, if unused, above my bed (the curriculum at Saint Leoma's did not offer shop). Rumors spread among the students about who or what I was — a failed experiment, ax murderer — assuring my outcast status, but at least no one came looking for miracles. That sainted nonsense thankfully hadn't yet trickled outside of West Virginia.

Sister Walburga, the principal, was a German import who goose-stepped around campus spinning a Bakelite yo-yo, an innocuous-looking pastime until some girl wore her skirt too short or arrived late to morning Mass. Then Walburga would fling that yo-yo at the offender's head and reel it back in without batting an Aryan eyelash. I was her target more than once because, though I was never tardy to chapel, I spent the hour earplugged to Cookie's radio while perfecting my Etch A Sketch skills. God hooey, remember.

I thought about Nicky constantly, especially since I was living his boarding-school dream. No doubt roommates would have been lining up to share a dorm with him. Countless times I traded spots with him in the crumpled station wagon, my embalmed body buried six feet deep beside my father and his sewn lips. My own hell. How different Mom's and Nicky's lives would have been if my brother had lived. This only amplified my guilt—an emotion that could penetrate my hull—which sent me to a windowless carrel in the school library to resume my encyclopedic penance, and where you can probably still find my initials carved into the desk and gum wads stuck in secreted locales.

One academic requirement was that each girl had to master a musical instrument. By the time I made it to the music room for a private conference, the only choices left were cymbals and the tuba. Sister Joanie, also the music teacher, could tell I was uninspired. She put a finger to her lips and paced back and forth in her ugly nun shoes. Finally she looked at me. "Do you still have that saw hanging in your room?"

I nodded, dumbstruck.

"Go get it."

I raced back to my dorm, returned with Dad's saw, and hesitated just a second before handing it over. Sister bent the blade back and forth, scrutinized the curlicues. "It's quite lovely."

I bit my lip to keep from feeling. I bit it even harder when Sister lifted a bow from a pegboard, sat on a stool, tucked the saw handle between her knees, and drew the bow back and forth across the blade to sound a perfect E note.

"Do you know 'Good Morning, Heartache'?" I pitifully asked.

Sister looked at my puckered face. "No, but I'm sure we can figure it out."

Sister Joanie sat me on a stool, positioned the beloved instrument between my knees and hands, and showed me how to perform my new penance, replete with Dad's torch songs, which I continued in my room daily, even after lights-out. I ignored shoes hurled at my door and fists pounded on walls to get me to stop playing the music that tormented everyone's dreams.

I never heard from Opal, Cookie, or Muddy, who I later learned had no idea what hellhole Grandma had shipped me to. I did, however, receive care packages of makeup as well as allowance checks from Grandma, but no invitations to visit over the summer or holidays. I also never heard from my mother. Not once. Initially I tried calling Grandma's house, but the operator always droned, "The number you dialed has been disconnected." Letters to her were returned unopened. Finally Grandma had the decency to admit that she'd carted Mom off to a sanitarium, though she refused to tell me which one.

Eventually even that was okay. Call it self-preservation, but during those space-drifting years, I decided that I didn't need anyone. Not my mother, who had betrayed me. Certainly not Grandma Iris, who abhorred me. It was better not to risk relationships, since they would inevitably lead to pain.

I turned fourteen, fifteen, sixteen, seventeen, eighteen at Saint Leoma's, adding five inches in height, obliterating my prepubescent pudge. I was a voyeur to milestones other girls celebrated, like first dates and first kisses. I didn't attend mixers with our brother school, though I peeped into the crepe-papered gym to watch couples slow dancing. A weird feeling percolated as I watched all those mating rituals that had me smooching my pillow and practicing terrestrial exploration beneath the sheets—a carnal sin, I know—neither of which assuaged the yearning for human contact that was getting harder and harder to contain.

After I yanked my diploma from Heil Walburga I enrolled in Mount Sexton, a Catholic college five miles to the west of my boarding school, where most of the castoff Saint Leoma's girls matriculated. I again took up residence in a library carrel and in a frighteningly similar dorm room with a bevy of roommates who also couldn't suffer my saw playing and removable face. Not to mention the collection of anti-*malocchio* charms I had amassed that had the girls scratching their heads: metal street signs, bowls of rusty nails, jars of cat's-eye marbles that I hoped would protect me from even harsher penalties than the loss of my entire family—though what could be harsher than that?

Instead of making friends, I amassed credits toward my double majors: geography and library science. My other preoccupation was outer space. On July twentieth, 1969, I trespassed onto my dorm roof with a telescope to gape at the moon, hoping to spot the American flag planted there. I rubbed my hand across my stomach, wishing someone would plant a flag and claim me. I was on the rooftop four months later to gawp at Apollo 12. I bought a sleeping bag, put fresh batteries in my radio, and skipped classes during the Apollo 13 scare. Though the rest of the country was by then blasé, I hiked up again for Apollos 14, 15, and 16. Campus police busted my ass the last time and confiscated my telescope for six weeks.

I remained frequent grist for the rumor mill—*born skinless so she wears liquid flesh!*—but eventually I had competition. Yvette Guillaume transferred to the college in my junior year, a girl who had been bounced out of two dozen schools across the country, starting when she was in first grade. The nuns considered her an irritant not only because of her impertinence, but because of her political activism, her Sally Bowles haircut, and her military garb. I watched from a distance as she organized hunger strikes in the cafeteria on veal day and dive-ins during synchronized-swim meets to denounce the insulting smiles the athletes were forced to wear. Her unchecked fury both thrilled and frightened me.

To my apolitical shame, I did not sit-in with Yvette's antiwar set during the Vietnam protests, though my birthmarks participated. That little land sliver on the Indochinese peninsula on my hip was now inflamed and itchy. My scratching often drew blood, and though the area scabbed over time and again, I just couldn't leave it alone.

Nor did I join Yvette's feminist crew and picket the town's beauty pageant, or hurl my bra into a Freedom Trash Can to mingle with high heels and girdles. As the can was set ablaze I spotted Sister Joanie, who taught music at Mount Sexton too. It was fitting that she was there, since the older nuns had begun needling her when she opted for modern nun apparel: simple blouse and knee-length skirt, a veil that barely covered her hair—*Jezebel*. I was hoping she was going to toss in a starched wimple, but she just cheered the girls on. When she spotted me rubbernecking from across the street, she raced over. "You should throw away all that makeup, Garnet! You don't need it."

My face flamed at the idea of what those girls might do if they saw my undiluted geography, a less sympathetic abnormality than being born without skin.

I ran away without saying a word.

Charismatic Yvette was at the center of numerous crushes. Both town boys and doe-eyed college girls hovered around her on campus, socialist tracts clutched in their hands. Plenty of other girls hated her, since her teachings often countered their charm-school lessons, especially the ones encouraging them to act dumb. "Read the damn book instead of balancing it on your head!" Rumors abounded about why she had been shipped to the hinterlands: Ex–Manson Family member. Founder of the Weather Underground. She also had a revolving-door cast of roommates, and they left not just because she tried to indoctrinate them in her leftist ways, as parents claimed. Gossip circulated about Yvette's weird rituals; they upset some of the students as much as my melting face. Not surprisingly, the nuns devised a plan to kill two troublesome birds with one stone.

My favorite holiday during those years was Halloween, the one night when I could have paraded through the streets without makeup and fit in completely, though I never had the courage to try. I no longer had a taste for candy, but if I *had* gone ringing doorbells in my real face, I would surely have amassed the most loot of all. Instead, I attended the Halloween cult-film festival at the town's movie house, where patrons smuggled in Boone's Farm and joints. Year after year I went, and I began to recognize other folks who had made this their ritual too, especially the hippies who always sat three rows in front of me.

On October thirty-first, in my senior year, I sat in my usual spot enjoying the aroma of pot wafting up from the hippies. We laughed our way through various Frankenstein sequels, yelling "Yes, master," at inappropriate times.

Afterward I bumbled to my dorm, though I wasn't eager to arrive. I had been informed that yet another roommate would be installed that day. The moon was eerily bright; chilled wind gusts swayed my hair. Drunken teenagers wobbled by. A girl in a sandwich board painted like the new Pong game. A boy dressed in a rumpled Columbo coat. Several Richard Nixon and Chairman Mao masks because of Tricky Dick's recent visit to China. One Nixon bumped into me, the papier-mâché penis jutting out from beneath his coat poking me in the hip. He slurred, "Pardon my dick," slipped off his mask, and handed it to me as a goodwill gesture.

I strapped the thing on, though I could barely see through the eyeholes as I made my way to my room and slid the key in the lock. I opened the door and found Yvette Guillaume in her underwear sitting on the twin bed where I had thrown my dirty clothes, which were now heaped on the floor.

Her face was covered in white-white Kabuki paint, thick eyeliner, lethal eyebrows, little rosebud lips, much more dramatic than my own everyday makeup. I was trying to make sense of what she was doing with the length of Ace bandage unraveled on the bed. She was binding her right foot in a figure-eight pattern, looping the bandage around her toes and arch, then back around her heel. Over and over she crisscrossed until the bandage was used up and she secured the end with a safety pin. I wondered what her injury was until she pulled out another bandage from a silk bag beside her, unrolled it, and bound her left foot in the same fashion.

Finally she gazed up at the ceiling. "Are you going to stand there all night?"

I sputtered behind that Tricky Dick mask, trying to come up with a retort, but she shimmied under the covers without even removing her makeup and clicked off her lamp.

Her bed was empty the next morning and I stared at garish makeup smears on her pillowcase. I was as alarmed as all my ex-roommates who had awoken to a similar spectacle had been.

I didn't want to return to my room that day after classes, so I holed up in the library, pretending to read. I kept thinking of Yvette in my room, perhaps scheming about how to indoctrinate me, but into what? The library closed and I was freezing as I crossed campus in the rain, my own Kabuki makeup running. I bolstered my nerve and slid my key in the door, wishing I had that Nixon mask to hide behind. I prepared for the traumatized look on Yvette's face when she saw my dripping skin.

Yvette was plopped on her bed in her underwear, and though she wasn't wearing Kabuki makeup, she was again binding her feet. Afterward she slid beneath the covers and before clicking off her light she looked directly at me.

Here it comes.

She stared into my eyes and without a hint of revulsion, even with my face melting, said, "Are you going to stand there all night?"

Again she was gone when I woke the next morning. I loitered around campus until midnight, but this time when I opened our door, I was confronted by a four-panel Chinese screen positioned around Yvette's bed to offer privacy for her and whomever she was passionately embroiled with, she screaming, "Rebel! Oh, Rebel!" He grunting, both making so many sloshing/bumping/skin-slapping noises that I couldn't move. Finally the climax, which rippled through me too. The mattress springs stopped creaking, the breathing settled, and Yvette called out, "Jesus Christ! Are you going to stand there all night?"

A hand reached out and folded back one of the Chinese panels so that I could fully see Yvette, Kabuki makeup smeared, her mate yanking the sheet up to his waist. Rebel fumbled for a cigarette on the nightstand. Finally he looked at me. "The chick from the balcony! Far out."

I was stunned to see one of my art-house hippies in my room.

"You know each other?" Yvette stood, impeccably nude, and slipped into a silk robe.

"Yes, master," we both said, which cracked us up.

Yvette settled a pan of water on her contraband hot plate.

Rebel pointed to my face. "You staging a paint-in too?"

Yvette whipped around. "No! No, she's . . ." She didn't know how to finish, and from the look on her face, I could tell she'd heard the rumors surrounding me. I felt suddenly mythic, in the best possible way.

"What's a paint-in?" I wondered if this was a club I had already joined.

"Well," Yvette began. As she fixed us tea she revealed that her diplomat father had accompanied Nixon to China. Appalled by the treatment of Chinese women, Yvette began binding her feet and wearing Kabuki makeup in protest. Her father was so humiliated that he yanked her out of American University and flung her into our gulag, where he would continue to pay tuition if she stopped her antics. She gave up the makeup—except during Halloween and sex—and trussed her feet only in our room.

Every night I was treated to Yvette's rituals: bowls of oolong tea, x-ing another square on the calendar that counted down to her December graduation, and binding her feet before walking clumsily around our room on her heels to perfect the lotus gait, the hobbled step of foot-bound women that was supposedly an aphrodisiac. Neither Yvette nor I found anything sexy about taking away a woman's ability to walk without pain. We understood the real aphrodisiac was utter dependence.

Though I hate admitting this, given my burgeoning feminism, I began waking an hour earlier so that I could slather on makeup before Yvette emerged from behind her screen. I also bought seven pillowcases, not to wear as nun headgear, but to swiftly swap out so that Yvette wouldn't see the remnants of my previous day's face.

Throughout the following weeks I stood at the back of Yvette's rallies, where she whipped her followers into a radical frenzy. At night she made good use of her Chinese screen, whipping various partners into another kind of frenzy. Sometimes it was Rebel. Or that dude from the record store, or the anarchist from DC who had tracked her down, or Rosie the Brazilian exchange student. Though they seemed uninhibited by my presence on the other side of those papered panels, all that copulating only reminded me of my own longing, so I would grab my stargazing kit and head up to the roof.

If Yvette wasn't inciting a riot or engaged in sex, she would sink into a pool of despair. I often found her on her bed rifling through two decades' worth of postcards from her divorced, jet-setting mother: *Having a wonderful time. Wish you were here.* Or *here.* Or *here.* Yvette wishing she were there-there-there too.

Worse still were the letters from her father, which held special powers. "Why would he say that to me? Why?" she muttered to herself over and over in tears. Given how much I longed for an accumulation of my father's words to tuck into a certain box, I couldn't imagine what Yvette's father had written that could so crush his fearless daughter. I also couldn't understand why she continued to pore over those pages that obviously caused her such pain. Countless times I considered wrapping my arms around her to offer solace, but I was too afraid it would make Yvette reel in the life preserver of friendship she had so recently cast.

I was also too anxious to play my saw in her presence—*Stop that racket!*—so I performed that penance while she was in class. One afternoon, however, when I was perfecting "Is That All There

Is?" I heard sniffing at the door. I swiveled around, ready to whip the saw behind my back and impulsively shout, *Go away. This is private. Private!,* but Yvette begged, "Please don't stop."

I couldn't refuse, and from then on, every night I serenaded Yvette, particularly when she was holding her father's words to her chest. Though hall mates pounded walls and hammered fists against the door, Yvette would yell, "Shut up! This is beautiful!.," a word I never thought would genuinely be connected to me.

On December eleventh, I prepared for Apollo 17, the last moon landing for who knew how long. Yvette was draping a silk scarf over her lamp and setting out massage oil for whoever would be arriving to offer a sensual diversion. I didn't think she even noticed me gathering my gear, but as I opened the door to leave she said, "Plant a flag for me."

On the roof, I sat on a campstool and gazed through my telescope at the Taurus-Littrow region, where the astronauts had landed. Though the view was as stunning as always, my eyelids began to droop. I spread my unzipped sleeping bag beside the heat-emitting ductwork and folded myself inside, where I fell into a sound sleep bathed in moonbeams.

Hours later I heard the door to the roof creak open. My heart thudded since I thought it might be campus police busting my ass yet again. A spectral figure bobbled toward me, closer and closer; my heart shuddered and then, sweet relief, I recognized the lotus gait.

Yvette approached with no coat or proper shoes, just her bandaged feet without even socks to keep them warm, a bundle of her father's letters clutched to her stomach. Yvette's paramour must have been a no-show.

She hobbled toward me, hands out in anguish. "Why would he say that to me? Why?"

"I don't know." I considered running downstairs for my saw, but the sight of our leader with no one to distract her made my heart ache.

In one sweeping gesture, I flapped open my sleeping bag and

invited Yvette into the warmth emanating from the ductwork, and from me, as I began my descent back to earth.

Yvette did not hesitate; she knelt and slid deftly beneath the covers. I folded the sleeping bag over us both and she faced me. Our eyes locked as she put her hand in my hair to pull my mouth toward hers and then buzzzzzzzzzzzzzzzzzzzzzzzzzzzzzzzzzzzzzzzz
zzzzzzzzzzzzzzzzzzzzzzzzzzzzzzzzzzzzzzzzzzzzzzzzzzzzzzzzzzzzzzz
zzzzzzzzzzzzzzzzzzzzzzzzzzzzzzzzzzzzzzzzzzzzzzzzzzzzzzzzzzzzzzz
zzzzzzzzzzzzzzzzzzzzzzzzzzzzzzzzzzzzzzzzzzzzzzzzzzzzzzzzzzzzzzz
zzzzzzzzzzzzzzzzzzzzzzzzzzzzzzzzzzzzzzzzzzzzzzzzzzzzzzzzzzzzzzz
zzzzzzzzzzzzzzzzzzzzzzzzzzzzzzzzzzzzzzzzzzzzzzzzzzzzzzzzzzzzzzz
zzzzzzzzzzzzzzzzzzzzzzzzzzzzzzzzzzzzzzzzzzzzzzzzzzzzzzzzzzzzzzz
zzzzzzzzzzzzzzzzzzzzzzzzzzzzzzzzzzzzzzzzzzzzzzzzzzzzzzzzzzzzzzz
zzzzzzzzzzzzzzzzzzzzzzzzzzzzzzzzzzzzzzzzzzzzzzzzzzzzzzzzzzzzzzz
zzzzzzzzzzzzzzzzzzzzzzzzzzzzzzzzzzzzzzzzzzzzzzzzzzzzzzzzzzzzzzz
zzzzzzzzzzzzzzzzzzzzzzzzzzzzzzzzzzzzzzzzzzzzzzzzzzzzzzzzzzzzzzz
zzzzzzzzzzzzzzzzzzzzzzzzzzzzzzzzzzzzzzzzzzzzzzzzzzzzzzzzzzzzzzz
zzzzzzzzzzzzzzzzzzzzzzzzzzzzzzzzzzzzzzzzzzzzzzzzzzzzzzzzzzzzzzz
zzzzzzzzzzzzzzzzzzzzzzzzzzzzzzzzzzzzzzzzzzzzzzzzzzzzzzzzzzzzzzz
zzzzzzzzzzzzzzzzzzzzzzzzzzzzzzzzzzzzzzzzzzzzzzzzzzzzzzzzzzzzzzz
zzzzzzzzzzzzzzzzzzzzzzzzzzzzzzzzzzzzzzzzzzzzzzzzzzzzzzzzzzzzzzz
zzzzzzzzzzzzzzzzzzzzzzzzzzzzzzzzzzzzzzzzzzzzzzzzzzzzzzzzzzzzzzz
zzzzzzzzzzzzzzzzzzzzzzzzzzzzzzzzzzzzzzzzzzzzzzzzzzzzzzzzzzzzzzz
zzzzzzzzzzzzzzzzzzzzzzzzzzzzzzzzzzzzzzzzzzzzzzzzzzzzzzzzzzzzzzz
zzzzzzzzzzzzzzzzzzzzzzzzzzzzzzzzzzzzzzzzzzzzzzzzzzzzzzzzzzzzzzz
zzzzzzzzzzzzzzzzzzzzzzzzzzzzzzzzzzzzzzzzzzzzzzzzzzzzzzzzzzzzzzz
zzzzzzzzzzzzzzzzzzzzzzzzzzzzzzzzzzzzzzzzzzzzzzzzzzzzzzzzzzzzzzz
zzzzzzzzzzzzzzzzzzzzzzzzzzzzzzzzzzzzzzzzzzzzzzzzzzzzzzzzzzzzzzz
zzzzzzzzzzzzzzzzzzzzzzzzzzzzzzzzzzzzzzzzzzzzzzzzzzzzzzzzzzzzzzz
zzzzzzzzzzzzzzzzzzzzzzzzzzzzzzzzzzzzzzzzzzzzzzzzzzzzzzzzzzzzzzz
zzzzzzzzzzzzzzzzzzzzzzzzzzzzzzzzzzzzzzzzzzzzzzzzzzzzzzzzzzzzzzz
zzzzzzzzzzzzzzzzzzzzzzzzzzzzzzzzzzzzzzzzzzzzzzzzzzzzzzzzzzzzzzz
zzzzzzzzzzzzzzzzzzzzzzzzzzzzzzzzzzzzzzzzzzzzzzzzzzzzzzzzzzzzzzz

ZZZZZZZZZZZZZZZZZZZZZZZZZZZZZZZZZZZZZZZZZZZZZZZZZZZZZZZZZZZZZZ
ZZZZZZZZZZZZZZZZZZZZZZZZZZZZZZZZZZZZZZZZZZZZZZZZZZZZZZZZZZZZZZ
ZZZZZZZZZZZZZZZZZZZZZZZZZZZZZZZZZZZZZZZZZZZZZZZZZZZZZZZZZZZZZZ
ZZZZZZZZZZZZZZZZZZZZZZZZZZZZZZZZZZZZZZZZZZZZZZZZZZZZZZZZZZZZZZ
ZZZZZZZZZZZZZZZZZZZZZZZZZZZZZZZZZZZZZZZZZZZZZZZZZZZZZZZZZZZZZZ
ZZZZZZZZZZZZZZZZZZZZZZZZZZZZZZZZZZZZZZZZZZZZZZZZZZZZZZZZZZZZZZ
ZZZZZZZZZZZZZZZZZZZZZZZZZZZZZZZZZZZZZZZZZZZZZZZZZZZZZZZZZZZZZZ
ZZZZZZZZZZZZZZZZZZZZZZZZZZZZZZZZZZZZZZZZZZZZZZZZZZZZZZZZZZZZZZ
ZZZZZZZZZZZZZZZZZZZZZZZZZZZZZZZZZZZZZZZZZZZZZZZZZZZZZZZZZZZZZZ
ZZZZZZZZZZZZZZZZZZZZZZZZZZZZZZZZZZZZZZZZZZZZZZZZZZZZZZZZZZZZZZ
ZZZZZZZZZZZZZZZZZZZZZZZZZZZZZZZZZZZZZZZZZZZZZZZZZZZZZZZZZZZZZZ
ZZZZZZZZZZZZZZZZZZZZZZZZZZZZZZZZZZZZZZZZZZZZZZZZZZZZZZZZZZZZZZ
ZZZZZZZZZZZZZZZZZZZZZZZZZZZZZZZZZZZZZZZZZZZZZZZZZZZZZZZZZZZZZZ
ZZZZZZZZZZZZZZZZZZZZZZZZZZZZZZZZZZZZZZZZZZZZZZZZZZZZZZZZZZZZZZ
ZZZZZZZZZZZZZZZZZZZZZZZZZZZZZZZZZZZZZZZZZZZZZZZZZZZZZZZZZZZZZZ
ZZZZZZZZZZZZZZZZZZZZZZZZZZZZZZZZZZZZZZZZZZZZZZZZZZZZZZZZZZZZZZ
ZZZZZZZZZZZZZZZZZZZZZZZZZZZZZZZZZZZZZZZZZZZZZZZZZZZZZZZZZZZZZZ
ZZZZZZZZZZZZZZZZZZZZZZZZZZZZZZZZZZZZZZZZZZZZZZZZZZZZZZZZZZZZZZ
ZZZZZZZZZZZZZZZZZZZZZZZZZZZZZZZZZZZZZZZZZZZZZZZZZZZZZZZZZZZZZZ
ZZZZZZZZZZZZZZZZZZZZZZZZZZZZZZZZZZZZZZZZZZZZZZZZZZZZZZZZZZZZZZ
ZZZZZZZZZZZZZZZZZZZZZZZZZZZZZZZZZZZZZZZZZZZZZZZZZZZZZZZZZZZZZZ
ZZZZZZZZZZZZZZZZZZZZZZZZZZZZZZZZZZZZZZZZZZZZZZZZZZZZZZZZZZZZZZ
ZZZZZZZZZZZZZZZZZZZZZZZZZZZZZZZZZZZZZZZZZZZZZZZZZZZZZZZZZZZZZZ
ZZZZZZZZZZZZZZZZZZZZZZZZZZZZZZZZZZZZZZZZZZZZZZZZZZZZZZZZZZZZZZ
ZZZZZZZZZZZZZZZZZZZZZZZZZZZZZZZZZZZZZZZZZZZZZZZZZZZZZZZZZZZZZZ
ZZZZZZZZZZZZZZZZZZZZZZZZZZZZZZZZZZZZZZZZZZZZZZZZZZZZZZZZZZZZZZ
ZZZZZZZZZZZZZZZZZZZZZZZZZZZZZZZZZZZZZZZZZZZZZZZZZZZZZZZZZZZZZZ
ZZZZZZZZZZZZZZZZZZZZZZZZZZZZZZZZZZZZZZZZZZZZZZZZZZZZZZZZZZZZZZ
ZZZZZZZZZZZZZZZZZZZZZZZZZZZZZZZZZZZZZZZZZZZZZZZZZZZZZZZZZZZZZZ
ZZZZZZZZZZZZZZZZZZZZZZZZZZZZZZZZZZZZZZZZZZZZZZZZZZZZZZZZZZZZZZ
ZZZZZZZZZZZZZZZZZZZZZZZZZZZZZZZZZZZZZZZZZZZZZZZZZZZZZZZZZZZZZZ
ZZZZZZZZZZZZZZZZZZZZZZZZZZZZZZZZZZZZZZZZZZZZZZZZZZZZZZZZZZZZZZ
ZZZZZZZZZZZZZZZZZZZZZZZZZZZZZZZZZZZZZZZZZZZZZZZZZZZZZZZZZZZZZZ
ZZZZZZZZZZZZZZZZZZZZZZZZZZZZZZZZZZZZZZZZZZZZZZZZZZZZZZZZZZZZZZ
ZZZZZZZZZZZZZZZZZZZZZZZZZZZZZZZZZZZZZZZZZZZZZZZZZZZZZZZZZZZZZZZZ
ZZZZZZZZZZZZZZZZZZZZZZZZZZZZZZZZZZZZZZZZZZZZZZZZZZZZZZZZZZZZZZZZ
ZZZZZZZZZZZZZZZZZZZZZZZZZZZZZZZZZZZZZZZZZZZZZZZZZZZZZZZZZZZZZZZZ
ZZZZZZZZZZZZZZZZZZZZZZZZZZZZZZZZZZZZ.

Three on a Match

Bless me, Father, for I have sinned:

First of all, I am not a lesbian.

Second, I know you're feeling cheated by the abrupt ending of my last installment, but if Nixon can erase eighteen and a half minutes from his Watergate tapes, I can erase a segment of mine. I'm not even going to pretend it was Nonna performing an arthritic Rose Mary Stretch.

Third, did I mention that I am not a lesbian?

Okay, maybe I was, for thirteen days, but I chalk it up to those experimental college years, to six weeks of being a torqued-up, peeping Garnet to the calisthenics going on behind Yvette's screen, but mostly I pin it on loneliness. On enduring a decade without a warm embrace or a kiss good night. That evening on the roof while I was swaddled in my sleeping bag, under Yvette's well-practiced hands, nuts and bolts sprang free as my outer hull exploded. By morning I was a flesh-and-bone girl again, filled with carnal bliss and absolute terror, since I didn't want Yvette to see my makeup-less face.

Though it pained me to do it, as the morning sun crested, I unwrapped my arm from Yvette's waist. She groaned as I stood, but I tiptoed across the roof and down to our room so I could apply fresh camouflage and return before Yvette knew I was gone.

In the bathroom, I lined up the foundation and concealer as I had done for so many years. I held a steaming washcloth to my face to scrub off the previous day's remnants, and when I looked in the mirror to check if I'd missed any spots, I saw Yvette standing behind me. I felt as exposed as I had in the Hall of Mirrors, my face gripped in Mom's hands as she brutally put me on display.

My eyes swiveled to Yvette's reflection. "You weren't supposed to see me!"

I grabbed the foundation, the cotton balls, daubed like a maniac. Maybe if I applied it quickly enough, she would think it was all a dream.

Yvette stepped forward and stilled my hand, the tinted cotton ball falling into the sink.

We looked at each other in the mirror until I slumped over. "I didn't want you to see me."

Instead of turning on her bound heels and retreating, Yvette cupped my face in her hand and lifted it up so that we again looked at each other's reflections, my mulberry stains open for scrutiny. Rather than pronouncing, *You're beautiful just the way you are,* which I would never have believed, Yvette uttered the honest truth: "You don't have to hide anymore."

I broke under the weight of that statement, but instead of tumbling to my knees, I fell into Yvette's arms and bawled like a twelve-year-old who had just lost her father and brother. I wailed for the fam-i-ly I had avoided grieving over by blasting into space. Even that Icelandic volcano erupted, and I cried for Nonna and Betty. For my regret at never telling my father I loved him. For those same words I would never hear from him again. Mostly, however, I wept for myself, and for my once staunchest ally — my mother, my mother, my mother.

When I was wrung dry I glared at all those vials of makeup. Maybe they weren't Dr. Trogdon's pills, but suddenly they were poison to me.

I swept the bottles and tubes into a hand towel. Yvette followed as I burst from our room and stalked down the hall, girls flattening themselves against the walls as we passed since they had never seen me without the clown paint. Instead of cowering, however, I lifted my chin and stared them straight in the eye.

Outside, Yvette and I marched to the biggest trash receptacle on campus, next to the dining-hall picnic tables meant to catch our wrappers and soda bottles. I didn't hesitate one second before tossing into this Freedom Trash Can, not a bra or girdle, but the goop that had been concealing me for years.

The cherry on the sundae was that at that moment, Sister Joanie dashed out of the dining hall and galloped toward me, cheering, "It's about time!"

Yvette looked at me, a prideful spark in her eye, which bolstered my courage to bolster her nerve. "Go get your father's letters." Her eyes rounded, but she nodded, fetched them, and I applauded as she tossed his hurtful words into the trash one page at a time.

From then on it was me behind Yvette's Chinese screen. Since my face was just the tip of my secret, I slowly revealed my personal geography to her, my anxiety dissipating when she did not run away screaming as I exposed one shoulder, then the other. My chest, then stomach. Feet, ankles, knees, thighs. "You're a work of art," she said, surveying the full breadth of me at last, and for the first time in my life, I believed it.

Yvette traced coastlines and minor continents with her fingertip. Landmasses that had not been altered since I'd left Sweetwater except for the occasional Vietnamese rash. Apparently La Strega or whoever had been tinkering with my mapped body had short-range powers. It became a game. "My mother has been there, and there, and there," Yvette would say. "I've always wanted to visit the Balkans!"

"Why don't you ever go with her?" I finally asked.

Yvette shook her head. "She never asked." Another child banished from her mother's world.

Maybe Yvette longed to make a home with her mother, but

for a brief spell, she staked a claim on me. She even made it official one night when she pulled a tiny American flag from her robe pocket, stuck its toothpick pole into a wad of chewing gum, and planted it on my solar plexus. "One small step for woman-kind," she said, but it was a giant leap for me. Those were blissful days. Made even sweeter because we knew full well that when the semester ended, Yvette would snatch her diploma and disappear from my life just as quickly as she'd entered it.

And that is exactly what happened.

On December twenty-third, I watched Yvette bind her feet for the last time and apply the Kabuki makeup that she could once again wear publicly. I helped her carry her suitcase and folded Chinese screen to the train station, though the walk was excruciatingly slow, given her lotus gait. We arrived just in time for her to catch the train that would rumble her to San Francisco, where antiestablishment vibes lured her. Like the final scene in *Cabaret*, as Yvette hobbled down the platform in her Sally Bowles haircut, she raised her hand and wiggled her fingers as a final ta-ta.

It was the loneliest Christmas of my life. Now that I was human again, and earthbound, I was forced to confront weighty matters, not only my longing for family, but the issue of where I would settle when I graduated in the spring.

When the new semester began, I perused maps lining the geography department. I would close my eyes and jab my finger, hitting at various possibilities: Saskatchewan, Natchitoches, the Bermuda Triangle. As January bled into February, I finally admitted that the bump of ground I longed for was Sweetwater. But after years of no contact, I didn't know if I could still consider it home or if the people there would consider me fam-i-ly.

And then fate intervened.

February fourteenth, on what would have been Nicky's twenty-fourth birthday, while lovebirds crossed campus holding volumes of Keats, I was summoned to the dean of students' office, where a bevy of suited men with briefcases were waiting.

The dean was overly solicitous, offering me a breath mint, a bottle of Tab, both of which I declined.

The six suited men took seats in the dean's office on two couches that faced each other. The three men on the right were smiling; the three on the left were not. All six simultaneously set their briefcases on their laps and flipped them open as if they'd choreographed that move.

The man with Brezhnev eyebrows cleared his throat. "Miss Ferrari, Mr. Billheimer has a remarkable story to tell you, so I think you'd better sit down." He waved his hand at a chair pulled up just for me. I sat, wondering if Grandma Iris was trying to program my post-college life. This time I was prepared for a fight.

Mr. Billheimer was the senior-most member of the smiling group. "Miss Ferrari, I'm afraid we have both good news and bad."

Behold:

Two Saturdays before that Valentine's Day, back in Sweetwater, Radisson had clanked open the gate and then steered the Packard downhill, La Strega in the back encased in fur, since it was an especially frigid morning. Witnesses claimed that Radisson and La Strega were fighting, she leaning over the seat swatting him with a cane, he parrying her blows with his chauffeur's cap, all while the Packard gained speed as it spiraled around and around the hill until it hit ice-coated No-Brakes Bend. The Packard flew over the curb and through the brick wall Mr. Dagostino had had built there ten years before, after our station wagon had flown over the curb in a similar manner. The Packard toppled the brick wall and then it, too, plunged through the garage.

La Strega was killed on impact. Unconscious Radisson was rushed to Scourged Savior, where he died fifty-two minutes later.

La Strega had left no children, so her three nephews, born to Le Baron's sister, flew in for the funeral and, more important, the reading of the will. Though the nephews were indeed listed as heirs, they were contingent beneficiaries. The primary inheritor was the person who had known La Strega more intimately than anyone on the planet during her widow years: Radisson.

Can you friggin' believe that? The old bat had a soul after all.

Because La Strega died first, her complete fortune was passed onto Radisson for exactly fifty-two minutes. I can only imagine what kind of hilltop monarch he might have been, but I bet his reign would have involved Ferris wheels and dodge-'em cars for the local children.

When Radisson died, his will superseded La Strega's. He had bequeathed all his worldly possessions, which now included his fifty-two-minute fortune, to the only person who had ever been kind to him in his life: a mottled girl who'd once filled his pockets with Bazooka bubblegum and who had actually called him by name.

Thus, like so many orphans and spinster-governesses in all those great books of British lit-ra-toor lining La Strega's library, I was rescued by an inheritance I never even knew I was in line for.

The three smiling lawyers who represented Radisson's wishes were grinning, since their hourly rate was *huge*.

The nephews' lawyers, all frowning despite their fat hourly rate, were contesting Radisson's will and the fifty-two-minute gap that to them was far worse than Nixon's eighteen-and-a-half-minute one.

Radisson's attorneys advised me to take possession of the mansion immediately; they had a limousine waiting, as well as a moving van. I raced to my room and grabbed the only thing I wanted: my father's saw.

It was my turn to wiggle my fingers in a farewell ta-ta to the little patch of earth that had been my home for nearly half my life. I also left behind an unfinished education, since I was sixteen credits shy of my dual degrees. I do not regret that decision.

Twelve hours later, under the radiance of a full moon, me sitting shotgun beside Benny the limo driver, we crossed into West Virginia. I heard a faint hum that grew more pronounced the closer we got to Sweetwater: a blessed E note that hadn't played in my head for ten years. We crossed the railroad tracks and turned onto Appian Way, and I growled as we passed the entrance to Grover Estates, the G on the sign crooked, both Ts missing. We drove down snake-bricked Via Dolorosa and circled a Nereid statue not spitting water and stopped in front of Nonna's house, where the windows were dark. The note in my head rung loud and clear and soon a lamp went on in Nonna's bedroom. I was stunned to see her porch light illuminated too, with an actual bulb. I wanted to race up and pound on the door, but it would likely be Grandpa Ferrari answering in his underwear; the image made the bulb flicker, and I thought, *Shit.* My weird circuitry still existed, at least in Sweetwater. I urged Benny onward and we coasted by Saint Brigid's and through the village, where most of the businesses were boarded up. Thankfully, the neon Sweetwater Cinema sign still blinked, as did the one for Dino's Lounge. The Plant where my father had labored, however, was now defunct, with broken windows and graffiti spray-painted on its shell.

As we began our ascent up the hill, all my *portafortuna*-opening deeds resurrected themselves. I closed my eyes when we passed the silhouette of a toppled-over brick wall because I didn't have the courage to face it, or our old house either.

We arrived at the pinnacle and that massive gate, where Benny stopped the car. A spindly figure loped from behind the brick column. For an instant I thought it was Radisson coming to hand me a begonia, but it was Mr. Billheimer, who also closed the gate behind us. He opened my car door and handed me a ring of skeleton keys, which I rattled without thinking to clear out La Strega's ghost.

"Welcome home," he said, adding a caution: "Lie low for a while, and though it may be tempting, don't do anything rash."

For two weeks I didn't venture beyond my gates. Initially I slept in Radisson's apartment above the garage, though I tried not to look at the mangled Packard that had been towed inside and that I have since had restored. Upstairs I found a welcoming armchair by the fireplace and a twin bed beside a window that overlooked a mulberry tree. My benefactor apparently spent his off-hours reading Barbara Cartland romances and crafting model

World War I biplanes, which he had strung from the ceiling with fishing line, so it was as if I were falling asleep beneath dogfights every night.

Mr. Billheimer visited daily. We sat in La Strega's parlor, where he divulged the extent of my holdings, which unfurled from his mouth like adding-machine paper. He also had me sign stacks of documents so he could transfer stocks and bank accounts, the house title, and sundry other properties and businesses to my name.

My proximity to our old house made me long for my mother. When I dialed Grandma Iris's number, an automated operator still droned: "The number you dialed has been disconnected." If I'd known which sanitarium Mom had been sequestered in, I would have sent my own hatchet man to rescue her. I started dialing the rotary dozens of times to call Nonna or Betty, but I couldn't complete the calls. I didn't yet have any words to utter if they did answer, especially if the topic shifted to Ray-Ray.

I spent the rest of my time snooping into La Strega's many, many rooms, looking for secret dungeons and cauldrons, books of incantations, a closet full of Garnet voodoo dolls. I found none. What I did find was that my geography, which had been dormant for a decade, began rearranging itself with a vengeance. Every morning I awoke to discover countries split in two, whole islands submerged, borders incrementally shifted, as if ten years' worth of tricks were playing out in one week, which left me with the deeper mystery: If not La Strega, then who? Or what? Or could it be Sweetwater itself?

Outside, the rose garden had been put to bed for winter, the barbecue pit draped in plastic. I discovered the foundation of the whippet-tipped springhouse that had erupted a decade before. Instead of rebuilding it, La Strega had cemented over the spring. I heard burbling water, and after clearing away dead leaves, I found a pipe jutting from the side of the concrete slab. A right angle sent the pipe into a grate-covered trench that led from the springhouse to the chateau, providing the house's water supply. There was no supply for the Sweetwater villagers below or for the empty reflection pond, its cement sides crumbling, the scary elements of the heating system corroded.

When I wasn't snooping I began my penance anew, working through La Strega's library on Nicky's behalf but mostly sniffing as I looked at the chair my mother had sat in years before. I also set up a stool in the conservatory because the acoustics made my saw playing sound better than ever. As I coaxed strains from the blade, I imagined them swirling around the room carrying my unspoken proclamation, which I hoped would somehow reach my father beyond the grave.

My other pastime was looking out various windows at my old neighborhood, now quite bedraggled. Eventually local kids appeared at my gate, trios and quartets, perhaps offspring of the children Nicky and I had grown up with, pressing their faces against the iron bars like inmates. These were the homeliest children I had ever seen, covered in rashes and boils, hair falling out in clumps, skin tinged gray instead of a healthy pink. A few of their parents sauntered up. All of them looked unkempt, and I wondered what plague had descended on Sweetwater since I had moved away. Eventually a smattering of hill nonnas, looking older and bent, appeared, but not the four nonnas who had helped make those Saint Garnet necklaces, one of which was tangled at the bottom of a Charlottesville briar patch. The nonnas hovering at my gate made the sign of the cross when I accidentally ruffled the drapes and I thought, *Crap, that sainted bullshit still lingers.*

The Saturday I discovered the whippet room, the buzzer in the pillar by the front gate sounded throughout the house. I looked out and saw a nun standing there, or more likely a novice, judging by her in-training white veil. I was going to ignore her as my predecessor would have, but several of those mangy children ran to her, and at the sweet way she received them, Pharaoh's heart was softened. I bumbled downstairs, shrugged on one of Radisson's coats, and went outside.

The children squealed, not *Sister, what's wrong with* — but "It's her! It's Saint Garnet!"

"Yes, it is," the nun said.

By the time I reached into the little box and pressed open the gate to slip outside, I knew who the nun was: Dee Dee Evange- lista.

"Garnet," she said, eyes moist with nostalgia.

"Hi, Dee Dee." I looked to see if she was carrying a Betsy Wetsy doll, but she was holding the hand of a little girl who was smiling broadly, her gums as gray as the cloudy-snow sky. I was afraid Dee Dee was going to heft the child and place her in my arms for a healing, but she merely said, "I just wanted to welcome you home."

"Welcome home!" the children squealed, flocking over to hug my legs and squirm their fingers into my hands. At first, I mar- veled at the fact that they were not repulsed by my skin, but then, looking at them, I realized my stained flesh was no longer such an anomaly. Three of the old hill nonnas ambled up, their faces covered in sebaceous cysts and warts. "It's-a her!" They brazenly pushed the children aside, falling on their knees to kiss my hands. I pulled free and yanked the nonnas upright. "Stop that! Stop that right now!"

"Ladies." Dee Dee nudged them back a few paces and planted herself between them and me. "Don't crowd her."

The nonnas were insistent, trying to reach around her to grab my coat, my hair. "But it's-a Santa della Collina."

"She return just-a like I knew she would!"

"Help us, Santa Garnet. Please heal-a the bambinos."

"And us! Please heal-a the old nonnas first!"

Behind them, a black sedan pulled up; the back door popped open and out jumped a priest who wasn't even wearing a coat. He bolted toward me. "Miss Ferrari! I'm Father Shultz! The new par- ish priest!"

"What the hell?" I said, overcome by ordination.

"I'd like to talk to you about donating a new roof for the church!"

"Father!" Dee Dee scolded. "Now is not the time."

I didn't bother with farewells, just stepped inside my fence and slammed the gate on not only the priest but Dee Dee, the old nonnas, and the children, who were beginning to whimper.

I ran to my front door but before it closed behind me Father Shultz yelled, "We look forward to seeing you at Mass!"

Thus I started hiding again, not inside makeup, but inside another mansion, though this time it had nothing to do with shame. I couldn't fulfill the requests of those aggressive old women and children, and I refused to grant Father Shultz his.

Eventually I moved into the main house, and one afternoon as I unloaded groceries delivered from the A&P (formerly O'Grady's), the buzzer sounded. I thought it might be Dee Dee or those persistent nonnas, but when I looked out front I saw Nonna holding a shirt box of sweet bliss, Betty standing beside her. I ran outside to buzz open the gate, not put off by Nonna's dingy braid or Betty's acne-splattered face. Nonna enveloped me in her python's grip, an E note pouring from her mouth. Her warm embrace sent surges of electricity through us both.

"You feel-a that?" Nonna said.

When we pulled apart, her hair—and mine—was charged with static.

Betty planted kisses on my face. "How we've missed you! You've gotten so skinny and tall!" We wept until a swarm of nonnas and children raced my way. I pulled the women inside, closed the gate, and we hustled to the mansion, where they gawped at the luxury.

Nonna paced the upstairs kitchen trying not to touch those frightening appliances, but she found La Strega's coffeepot. She lifted the lid on that box of chocolate-dipped cannolis, and I sighed when she laid them on a platter. I built a fire in the parlor, where we sipped Nonna's strong brew, the two women smiling, exposing stained teeth.

"The coffee is delicious," Betty said, scratching a pimple.

"It's a-true," Nonna said. "Best coffee I make since a-before . . ."

She didn't have to finish.

Betty delicately recounted how she and Nonna had reunited just a day earlier. Everyone in Sweetwater knew that someone had moved into La Strega's mansion, and rumors abounded as to who it might be: Le Baron's love child claiming his birthright; Jackie Onassis; Hugh Heffner, who would turn it into a Playboy mansion. Though several ordained people confirmed that they had seen Garnet Ferrari, for most of the populace, that was harder to believe than Jackie O.

Betty was determined to see for herself and used the opportunity to reunite the fam-i-ly, a brave maneuver, and I adored her for it. She convinced Nonna that it was time for the iron curtain to come down for my sake, if it was indeed me on the hill. They kept their mission a secret from their husbands, and now Nonna was sitting in my parlor glaring at her daughter-in-law, though she relaxed somewhat when Betty relayed the news that Ray-Ray was MIA in Vietnam, that land sliver on my right hip that had also gone missing. I watched her eyes to see if it pained her that her stepson was possibly, quite probably, dead or a POW in some jungle hellhole. She held her cards closer to her chest than I would have thought possible. I was not wearing a poker face, and neither was Nonna, our scowls expressing that we hoped the bastard was a pile of rotting bones sunk beneath a rice paddy.

Nonna mercifully changed the subject. "You know, the Plant-a, she close. The whole town, she is in-a ruin."

"Dommy had to take a job selling shoes in Vandalia," Betty added.

Why did my heart feel like singing?

We gossiped and ate cannolis until the women had to sneak back to their husbands, but for five days straight, they slipped out and visited me to guzzle that delicious coffee.

Eventually my identity was confirmed in the newspaper: "Garnet Ferrari New Hilltop Monarch!" Thus, on Nonna's and Betty's sixth visit, they came bearing not gifts, but ogres. When the buzzer sounded I spied Uncle Dom and Grandpa, each holding a grocery sack as they stood beside their apologetic-looking wives. I was tempted to ignore them, but I understood that if I wanted Nonna and Betty in my life I would have to endure their mates.

As I walked to the fence, Dom checked his breath and Grandpa adjusted his number-one newsie cap. When I clanked open the gate, Dom dove forward and hugged me for much longer than was necessary, though he kept looking over my shoulder as if he thought someone else would be traipsing from the house. Grandpa didn't hug me, but he removed his hat, revealing a spectacularly liver-spotted pate.

"Garney." His eyes scoured my face. "You look-a so, so . . ."

"Yes, you do," Dom finished.

We approached the front door, Grandpa growling at the gargoyles his brother had sculpted and that I had once been so afraid of. Now I was delighted to have them protecting my stoop. I allowed the men inside, and naturally they tromped ahead of me and their wives. Betty leaned close to my ear. "We are so sorry."

The men crossed the hallway, picking up vases along the way to read markings, looking behind paintings for secret wall safes—something that had not occurred to me, but, boy, would I be flipping paintings that night.

We settled in the library in those clawfoot chairs, Grandpa claiming the one Nicky used to sit in, me in the one beside him, Uncle Dom on La Strega's settee. Betty and Nonna hovered by the door.

"So where's your mother?" Dom asked. "She upstairs?"

Mother. No one had asked about her, Betty and Nonna perhaps too afraid or angry.

"She's living with Grandma Iris." I didn't know what else to say.

Dom's shoulders slumped. "Oh. Well, I brought you a few gifts." He pulled out of his grocery sack a wedge of Fontina cheese and a bottle of sambuca, but no *Playboy*.

"Me too." Grandpa heaved a jug of homemade wine onto my lap. Grandpa looked at his wife. "Go get-a some glasses."

"And cut up this cheese," Dom ordered Betty.

Nonna and Betty left me alone with the men, Dom standing to scan bookshelves for first editions.

"So we hear you inherit quite the *fortuna*." Grandpa's eyes roved from treasure to treasure.

"Such-a big house. Bigger than Dommy's over in Grover Estates."

Uncle Dom sneered.

"With a lot of-a rooms. So many, many rooms."

I already knew where he was heading and wanted to spit out, *Guess the hill is good enough for you now.*

"You know, Nonna, she is-a getting so old she no clean-a the house so good. She no cook-a so good and the laundry, she comes out gray. Look. Look at my shirt!"

The shirt was indeed discolored.

"It would-a be so nice if she no had-a to clean no more. If she had more space to, uh, put up-a her feet." He paused, hoping that I would immediately invite him and Nonna—but mostly him—to move in. I didn't utter a peep.

Betty and Nonna returned with a teacart loaded with fruit and cheese and cordial glasses—not a single juice glass. Betty had filled Grandpa's wineglass with mini-cubes from the automatic icemaker, a contraption that both confounded and frightened Nonna. "That thing will bite off-a you hand!"

Betty rolled the cart in front of Grandpa and me. Dom sat back down, casually sliding one of my books into his jacket pocket. I was about to say something when Betty tucked a napkin into her husband's shirt and filled his plate with food. Nonna did likewise for Grandpa. I wanted to protest and make Yvette proud, but I didn't want the women to pay the consequences later for my outburst.

They stayed for an hour, the men blabbering about themselves. I was never more relieved in my life than when Grandpa untucked his napkin, threw it on his plate, and took his leave.

The next day all four showed up again, though this time Grandpa paraded to the sunniest expanse of lawn in the backyard, near where the springhouse had once sat. He walked heel-toe in a rectangular formation as if he were engineering a project. I finally ushered him inside, where he again sat in Nicky's chair and he and Dom ordered their wives around. That was the day the gold candlesticks went missing.

The pattern continued, them showing up to eat my food and be waited on by their women. Uncle Dom broadened his snooping to include every room on the main floor; he scribbled in a notebook and even snapped photos when he thought I wasn't looking. Little figurines and silver lighters disappeared, though when I questioned him, he always said, "What lighter? I don't know what you're talking about. I brought you more Fontina!" I began to wonder if the man actually did have a job selling footwear, as his afternoons were habitually free and his own shoes looked worn.

On the last Friday in March, though the hill had been hit with a hefty early-spring snow, I again opened my gate for the fam-i-ly. Grandpa and I went to the library, and he sat and tapped his fingers on his knees. As I built a fire I could hear Dom in the conservatory strumming the harp, tickling the ivories, taking pictures for whatever photo album he was assembling. Finally he strolled in holding something that made my blood shudder.

"This is Angelo's saw." He traced his fingers over my father's curlicues.

Grandpa grumbled at the Sicilian import, but I ran to Dom and yanked the saw from his grip. "Leave that alone. It's private. *Private!*"

"Sorry," Uncle Dom said. "That's a beautiful Steinway. Betty always wanted a piano. Of course, there's no way we could afford one now."

I ignored him, set the saw on the mantel, and rearranged logs with an iron poker.

"Real shame. She always, always wanted a piano."

I kept my lips tightly shut.

Grandpa took over. "And Nonna sure like-a your kitchen. All those fancy machines."

Pah. Just the day before Nonna had discovered the rustic kitchen beneath the main one, and she knelt down and kissed the floor. The old-timey refrigerator with the motor on top and the metal ice trays was a convenience she could understand.

"She said she could-a cook up a storm in a kitchen like-a that. If only she could somehow make-a use of it three or four times a day. But that's a lot of going back and a-forth, back and a-forth lugging food from her tiny, tiny house down on Via Dolorosa. Back in Italia, you know, the grandparents live with their children."

"You could always move in with Uncle Dom."

Dom choked on a hardened gumdrop he'd dug from a candy dish.

Grandpa pursed his lips. "Perhaps, but he no have-a the room you have here. So many, many, *many* rooms."

"Plus, I'm not your child."

Grandpa squinted at me. "That-a may be, but you are my only grandchild. And Nonna's. You know she want to move in here with-a you. Why you want to break-a her heart?"

I nearly laughed, since this man had been breaking her heart for decades. "Maybe I'm your granddaughter, maybe I'm not."

Grandpa's face drained of color as he tried to decipher all the four-tooth-chisel innuendoes gouged into that statement. His hands balled into fists and he opened his mouth just as unsuspecting Betty and Nonna wheeled in the teacart.

Nonna handed Grandpa his wineglass, ice cubes tinkling inside.

Grandpa looked at the glass. "What the hell is-a this?"

Nonna looked at him, puzzled.

"I tole you I wanted mini–ice-a cubes. Can't you ever get it right, *puttana*?" Grandpa flung his cubes on the floor, where they skittered across the parquet. "Go getta me the good ice cubes. Now!"

Nonna started to leave, but I pounded my iron poker against the hearth. "No! Get them your-goddamn-self!"

"What did-a you say?" Grandpa stood to face me.

I thought he was brave, considering I wielded fireplace tools. "I said get them your-goddamn-self."

Grandpa started to slap me, but I held up the poker. His eyes bored into mine. Instead of hitting me, he shoved Nonna's shoulder, knocking her backward so that she stumbled over the teacart and fell. I lunged toward her, but Grandpa blocked my way.

"Now go get-a my goddamn ice."

Nonna cupped her right elbow and moaned.

Dom squatted to help the woman who had birthed him, but Grandpa yelled, "Leave her!"

We all looked at Dominick, and like my father all those years ago, Uncle Dom suddenly began shrinking back into a quivering child. The thought of Dad fully ignited my fury at Grandpa, who had been bullying us all for too long.

"You son of a bitch. I want you out of my house!"

Grandpa looked at me with loathing and opened his mouth, so I clocked him in the head with the poker, not fatally, just enough to knock his newsie cap onto the floor and deliver a lovely welt.

"Get the hell out!" I seethed.

Grandpa harrumphed, scooped up his hat, and headed to the front door, followed by Dom.

I herded the men to the gate and pressed the button to bluster them out. They realized their wives were not with them, and Grandpa shouted over my head, "Diamante! Get-a you ass out here right now!"

Dom parroted him, his voice cracking like a pubescent boy's: "Betty! Get your ass in the car!"

The women appeared; Betty ushered Nonna through the door as Nonna clutched her arm to her bosom.

"Not you!" I called to them. "You live up here with me now!"

They looked at each other in disbelief. Betty pointed a finger to herself to see if she was included in this deliverance.

I nodded vigorously. "Both of you. Please stay."

It was as if the millstones tied around their necks had suddenly been cut loose: their shoulders straightened, their chins jutted out.

"The hell-a you will!" Grandpa tried to push back inside, but I used that strength of a mother protecting her young to muscle him out, and then I pressed the button to close the gate.

"I'll get-a you for this!" Grandpa pointed at the bump on his forehead. "I'll sue you for every penny you have! Then you'll-a see who lives in-a this fancy house. And I no make-a room for you either!"

Dom by then had lost all language skills, but he raised his tiny fist through the gate, babbling. Grandpa hefted Uncle Dom and shoved him into the car like a watermelon, got in himself, and off they sped, Grandpa rolling down his window to offer obscene hand gestures as he barreled away.

It sounded exactly as it should have. Metal and glass plunging into bricks and mortar. A screeching, crunching, grating roar that was thunderous enough to rouse even the deepest of sleepers on Dagowop Hill . . . You get the idea. If Grandpa had survived, he really should have sued the city planners who'd chiseled out a spiraling road where spring waters froze over a particularly treacherous bend and caused inexperienced, distracted, or irate drivers to meet tragic ends.

Nine months later, a widow with a matrilineal fortune left her daughter in a sanitarium in an undisclosed locale to return to Charlottesville for a monthlong stay. The matron was unpacking her jewels while imbibing her favorite potable when she ran out of pearl onions. Rather than sending her cook or maid, who were un-sheeting furniture, she ran the errand herself. As she returned home, her Cadillac skidded across an icy patch of road, crashed through the fence surrounding a sewage-treatment plant, and drove headfirst into the basin of churning feces. The widow was knocked unconscious and subsequently drowned, her lungs filled, according to the coroner, with poo sludge.

· · ·

Okay, okay. I know you're shaking your head at the implausibility of all these ice-related crashes, so I feel I should mention that it's quite possible Grandpa Ferrari did not die in a car wreck after speeding over No-Brakes Bend. Perhaps one day while ripping up a patch of Fiore Pergusa in his backyard, he stepped on a rake, fell backward, and fatally cracked his skull on a two-foot-square concrete slab intended for a statue of Mary of Lourdes. It's also more than reasonable to believe that rather than kicking the bucket, Uncle Dom left Aunt Betty for a big-bosomed waitress from Dino's Lounge. According to the *Sweetwater Herald* police blotter, a certain hilltop tycoon reported the theft from her home of a number of items; she suspected her uncle of the crime, as several of the items turned up in a pawnshop in Vandalia. Rumor had it that Uncle Dom and the waitress used the money to hightail it to Las Vegas, where she became a blackjack dealer and he got a job parking other people's fancy cars.

Grandma Iris died exactly as described.

Thoroughly Modern Miracle

Archie:

This afternoon Betty had a thirty-seat dining table delivered to the ballroom, which is an entire wing, so it's virtually a glasshouse, windows on three sides offering fabulous views of the spring-house and pond. After dinner Nonna and Betty shut themselves in there and taped a sign to the door: *Keep Out (That means you, Garnet!)*. They think they're pulling off some grand holiday scheme.

It's two in the morning, another sleepless night. I've had insomnia for days, Padre. An itch in my marrow because I can feel something coming, I just don't know what it is. While my roomies were snoozing I slipped downstairs to see what they're up to. The new table is covered in Christmas paper, Scotch tape, and hundreds of boxes filled with red socks and mittens, candy canes and globe pencil sharpeners, four-inch Saint Garnet statues—badly retooled Statue of Liberty souvenirs, but I was not consulted. Nonna bought the statues at Holy Treasures of Sicily in what used to be Paddy's Pub, the residual tater tots grinding their molars at the Dagowop encroachment.

Tucked in each mitten is a Saint Garnet holy card, though it's nothing like the cartoon ones I drew all those years ago at my Saint Brigid desk. The illustrator gave me pouty lips and bedroom eyes. My birthmarks are present, but the geography is all wrong. This Saint Garnet stands atop a volcano holding pumice stones in one hand and a bloody handkerchief in the other. I don't know where the artist got her information, since I have no idea what a bloody handkerchief has to do with me.

I bet Nonna is dreaming about the looks on the children's faces when she hands the gifts over. When she first moved in I granted her three wishes that made her grin like a little girl. The first was a vegetable garden, since she had always wanted her own plot not crowded with Grandpa's bitter radicchio. She and I dug up La Strega's rosebushes—though I secretly apologized to Radisson. Nonna's second wish was a trellis on that sunny spot Grandpa had marked off beside the springhouse, where she would plant, not his swill-producing Gaglioppo grapes, but his brother Angelo's much sweeter Orgoglio della Sicilia. We hired a carpenter who built a Japanese-influenced arbor. On the night of a full moon, Nonna led me outside with soupspoons and clippings of the grapevine she'd gotten from who-knows-where. I stuck in my spoon and out popped pumice stones. Nonna unearthed seashells. I opened my mouth, but Nonna blurted, "It's not-a me!"

The only drawback was that Nonna had to lug bucket after bucket of water from the spigot on the side of the house all the way to her garden and grapes, spilling much of it along the way. I bought her a hose, but she said the rubber made the squash blossoms taste like balloons. Finally she asked for wish number three, though she plied me with eggplant parmigiana first.

She centered the steaming dish on the casual dining table set with La Strega's second-best china. Nonna even wore a new jersey dress, and she did look pretty, her dingy braid once again silvery white. Betty looked lovely in a mink cape, her acne cleared up. We attributed these recoveries to posh living.

"My cooking she is so much-a better up-a here." Nonna dished out the eggplant. "I no understand why it went-a so bad after you left, but now you back and my food is-a *delizioso* once-a more."

Betty and I could only nod, our mouths crammed full.

"So now I ask for my last-a wish."

Nonna wanted to unplug the spring so that the water could

flow freely, not only to her vegetables and grapevine and the patch of Fiore Pergusa she'd cultivated, but to the heated reflection pond on the other side of the fence so she could soak her aching feet.

With eggplant like that, who could-a refuse, especially now that I was a woman of means.

We hired contractors with jackhammers to break up the concrete, the grating noise drawing the attention of not only the saint seekers but the Water Authority director, Rodney, who showed up at my fence with a basket of fruit. I was suspicious, but Nonna kept trying to wrestle a pineapple through the railings, so I let him in. He sprinted to the still-plugged spring as workers cleared chunks of cement from around the original pipes, which, according to Rodney, had once funneled spring water to both the pond and Le Baron's underground system that fed the village below. During the post–World War II boom, the city tapped into Le Baron's system so that all those cracker-box hill dwellers could also cook, bathe, and flush with the sweet water.

After the Great Explosion, when La Strega corked the headwaters, all of this dried up. Rodney tried countless times to coax her into letting the water flow, since the village had to tap into the water from where it now gushed, beside the Plant, and pump it back up into the hill houses at great expense. Plus, that water just tasted plain funky. La Strega had refused. Now, if Nicky had been alive to ask the witch—hmmm.

Rodney stared longingly at the spring and finally asked if I would pretty please let the naturally filtered water flow from atop the hill once more.

I asked myself what fifty-two-minute-fortune Radisson would have done, and I had my answer: "Of course."

Rodney tittered and said he'd send up engineers to oversee the project and make sure the water started flowing in its new direction at the same time the system below was shut off. "And for the unveiling, we could have a parade!"

"No parade," I said. "Please."

Engineers and contractors worked diligently over the next two months, as did the pool men hired to replace the corroded heating elements and restore the reflection pond. My surprise to Nonna was to have the bottom inlaid with a mosaic of a Nereid modeled after the statue Great-Uncle Angelo had sculpted years before. It was not easy keeping that secret from Nonna.

The official uncorking was set for a Saturday in August. Rodney asked if I'd like to be mistress of ceremonies. I declined.

On that propitious day, from my open parlor window, I used binoculars to scour the villagers gathered around the stone basin and pump where the original craftsmen used to rinse their necks. Father Shultz and Rodney flanked the pump, surrounded by hill folk and villagers, children tied to helium balloons, and two men holding up a giant banner for my benefit that read THANK YOU, SAINT GARNET, though the man on the left rolled his eyes. There was Sister Dee Dee and Pippa Fabrini, as well as Nonna and Betty.

At exactly noon, just as the Saint Brigid church bells pealed, Father lifted his arms to bless the endeavor. I scanned the top of Italia Imports for a row of tomatoes but found none. Father bellowed into a microphone: "God bless the people of Sweetwater and this water that is so sweet. May it flow for a thousand years!"

When the Padre concluded, Rodney raised a red handkerchief as a signal to whoever was at the controls. I heard glugging in the chateau's pipes, knocks and pings, toilets flushing on their own. Down below, Nonna had been granted the honor of turning on the new system, and she ambled to the pump, but before she worked the handle, she held up her arms and offered her own prayer: "Santa Garney send-a her healing upon this water and upon all of-a you, especially the bambinos with all of the bumps and a-splotches. May all-a you skin disorders be-a healed. So amen!"

"Amen!" cheered the crowd.

Thanks a lot, Nonna.

Nonna pumped the handle up and down, the townsfolk staring expectantly at the spigot, and then *whoosh!*—out poured that delicious sweet water they hadn't tasted in years. Children jumped into the filling basin, as did a handful of adults, even Sister Dee Dee, all of them splish-splashing.

They were too busy to notice that a few miles away at the end of Via Dolorosa another jet of water shot into the sky. I was startled, and even more so when something crashed through my parlor window, whizzed by my ear, shattered a Ming dynasty vase on a pedestal, and landed in the fireplace. I focused my binoculars on the plume of water that was losing pressure fast until it was reduced to a steady stream pouring from the lips of the Nereid statue. I ran to the fireplace, got on my knees, and rooted around in layers of ash until I found what had apparently been corking the nymph's throat for fifty years: a six-inch section of marble braid, no doubt snapped off and shoved down there by a mean-fisted tyrant who couldn't stopper his drifting wife's love.

Nonna returned at dusk, the sun a blood-orange ball hovering above the horizon. Because the hill folk and villagers were still feasting below, I led Nonna to the new globe-tipped springhouse that hid the engineers' mechanizations. We went through the back gate to the reflection pond, where for the first time Nonna saw the undulating Nereid below the water. Nonna gripped my hand and a lightning bolt shot up my arm as another spring flowed freely from her eyes. The tears dripped from her chin into the pond, sending out concentric rings. It looked as if the tears sliding from Nonna's eyes were glowing. She noted it too, capturing the wetness and holding it up like a palm full of lava. She let the liquid spill into the pond, where it spread across the surface like a sheet of colored glass.

"The red water of Lake Pergusa," Nonna said. She pointed below to the stone trough at the base of the hill: the water inside also glowed red, as did the stream pouring from the mouth of a sea nymph on the street where Nonna once lived.

When the sun slid behind the earth it took the colored water with it; Nonna's tears returned to saline. "It's a sign," Nonna said, but she didn't say a sign of-a what.

I don't know exactly what happened that night, Padre, if it was just the reflected sunlight or something else that made the pond change color and glow—fluorescent algae or calcite, perhaps. Red leakage from microscopic organisms like the ones in Lake Pergusa. What caused Nonna's tears to glow, I have no clue.

Regardless, within two weeks, even more hill and village children, old nonnas, and parents were pressing their faces against my fence, grateful for the sweet water plus the fact that their rashes and boils were clearing up. One afternoon I stood on my bedroom balcony looking down at the throng, marveling that their gums were no longer gray, their hair was growing back, their skin pink and smooth. That was the precise moment a little *ping!* sounded in my head. I felt like a dolt that it had taken me so long to figure it out: it was the water healing these people, and probably had been for years.

I wanted to share the news that would send them packing, so I shouted: "It's the water healing you, not me!"

One of the nonnas answered back: "*Sì.* Saint Garnet, she send the healing waters!"

"No! It's not me! It's the water! The water!"

Someone in the back of the crowd hollered: "What did she say?"

"She said she blessed the water so it would heal us!"

"Thank you, Saint Garnet!"

"It's not me!" I yelled. "It's whatever is in the water!"

"And may God bless-a you for it!"

"No!"

"We love you, Saint Garnet!"

No matter what I said, they just wouldn't listen. Admittedly, though I had an explanation for some of the Sweetwater magic, the water never cured me. And there was still the riddle of who had been rearranging my personal geography over the years. In fact, at breakfast this morning, I discovered that Quebec on my inner elbow had separated from its sister provinces, microscopic inhabitants waving au revoir. Perhaps not so coincidentally, Nonna was flipping an omelet at the stove singing "'Dominique, a-nique, a-nique.'" Still, at least now I had something concrete — or liquid — to point to that might siphon some attention away from me.

As summer slid into fall, word about me spilled into bordering states: Ohio, Kentucky, Pennsylvania, Maryland, even Virginia, our severed twin, whose inhabitants had to swallow their pride before crossing the state line to beg for a healing.

But there were other forces that had a vested interest in keeping the Saint Garnet industry alive, a point driven home to me when I sent a water sample to Rodney for analysis so that I could offer the pilgrims irrefutable proof. He claimed that the lab lost the first sample, so I sent a second. Which was apparently contaminated by faulty equipment, so I sent a third, which a technician supposedly dropped. After the sixth bungled vial, I was visited by not only Rodney but the head of the newly formed Sweetwater Tourism Board and Father Shultz, all of whom showed up together at my intercom box with gifts, not Fontina cheese and sambuca, but Saint Garnet refrigerator magnets and bumper stickers printed with *St. Garnet* ♥ *Sweetwater!*

I reluctantly opened the gate, and as I led Rodney, Ms. Abigail Stork, and Father Shultz to the springhouse, all three slathered me with appreciation for healing the people. They prattled on about how blessed Sweetwater was to have been gifted such a saint. The lines were well rehearsed and they couldn't have sounded more disingenuous.

"Please." I pointed to the water burbling into the pond. "You're college-educated people. You know it's not me doing the healing; it's whatever is in the water."

They rushed at me with hands ready to clamp over my mouth so the pilgrims wouldn't hear. *If only they would hear,* I thought.

"Don't say that! That's not true! Don't deny God's gift!" they sputtered all at once.

I pushed them back to arm's length. "For Pete's sake. I have nothing to do with healing these people, and the sooner we clear this up, the sooner they can go home to their families and leave me alone."

"But Garnet," Father Shultz said. "Would you deny these people their hearts' desires? Would you deny God's purpose for you?"

My face pulsed and I guess the Padre had been informed about my previous run-in with Father Luigi, because he stepped back several paces.

Ms. Stork bravely approached, hugging a clipboard. "Ms. Ferrari. I can see that you're a practical woman who wants what's best for the community she loves." She held up a bumper sticker as proof. "Before you returned, Sweetwater was nearly a ghost town. Now, after only eight months, the village businesses are seeing increased profits, new stores are opening every day, and home sales on the hill are up twelve percent, which of course means rising property values and thus more paid in taxes to support Sweetwater's infrastructure."

It's hard to argue with statistics, and the village did look livelier. Folks on the hill were mending roofs and resurfacing driveways. Overgrown shrubs were being pruned. Maybe I wasn't a healer, but somehow I had inspired civic pride.

"But it's not me," I pleaded.

"Whether you're healing them or not, Sweetwater is coming back to life *because* of you." She gripped my wrist. "As a citizen, you have a duty to the public."

At least she had taken God out of the equation.

"Then take the water! Bottle it and sell it, for all I care!"

That recommendation lit a spark in Ms. Stork's eyes and she madly scribbled notes on her clipboard.

"But please leave me out of it so I can live in peace!"

Father Shultz stepped closer. "It's about much more than the water, Garnet. Don't you see? The people need a figurehead. They need to believe in you."

"Father, you can't really believe in all this nonsense."

He studied a crepuscular sun ray shooting from a gap in the

clouds, then he looked directly at me. "I believe in the people's belief."

I said, "What you really believe in is more coins in the coffers."

Just then Nonna bustled outside. "Why you no tell-a me we have the important company?" She rushed forward to kiss Father's hand. "Please come in for the cuppa coff and a sand'!"

Father patted her shoulder. "We don't want to be a bother."

"It's-a no bother. Garney should have invited a-you herself." She clucked her tongue at my bad manners.

Father looped his arm through Nonna's and they walked toward the house, me close on their heels.

I marveled at Nonna's deference to this holy man since I'd thought, like me, she'd had enough of priests on the day Father Luigi swapped our loved ones' lives for my mother's soul. Apparently in the intervening years, Father Shultz had unplugged Nonna's heart so that a stream of forgiveness could spill out, a miracle confirmed when he leaned close to Nonna's ear and said, "Thank you for the cannolis."

"Thank-a you for blessing the grapes." They looked at the flourishing arbor, and I wondered how they had kept that ceremony a secret. I shook my head at this improbable pairing that offered no saint-dispelling escape route for me.

One December evening I sat in the whippet room beneath that painting of the boy in a Lord Fauntleroy suit. I was rifling through the postcards Yvette had sent me over the past year. Since college, she had become quite the world traveler, chasing her mother, who was always two countries ahead. Yvette was joined by a variety of companions, some male, some female. I wasn't a bit jealous, Padre. Truly. I hadn't been pining for her like a certain Nereid had pined for her lover, but I was pining for something.

Suddenly Aunt Betty appeared at the door, a man standing behind her wearing a hat and carrying a briefcase. Mr. Brodsky was Grandma Iris's Charlottesville attorney. He sat across from me, flipped open his briefcase, and delivered both good news and bad, the bad news being the loss of a perfectly good Cadillac in a sewage-treatment plant.

When he finished, the first thing I asked was "Where is my mother?"

"I'll get to that, but first, there's the matter of your grandmother's will."

Grandma Iris had left her estate to her daughter. However, several years before, she had declared said daughter of unsound mind. Thus, the estate went to the contingent beneficiary, moi, since I was now the only-child daughter of an only-child daughter of an only-child daughter, all the way back to the *Mayflower*. All I can say is who would have thought that on June twenty-fourth, 1950, the baby bursting from her mother's womb would be the default heir to not one fortune, but two? Ah, that duality once again. I looked up at my substitute brother in his velveteen knickers, understanding that this inheritance should have been his.

"That's nice, but where is my mother?"

Brodsky ignored me and instead handed over yet another ring of skeleton keys to a house with a three-tiered fountain, tennis courts, a bricked-up study window, remnants of slave quarters, and a Hall of Mirrors that I never, ever, ever wanted to step foot inside again.

The other good news was that I did not have to. Brodsky opened an accordion folder containing the contents of Grandma's safety-deposit box, which is when I discovered that I had a blood relative living on the premises, namely, one six-fingered, butt-chinned aunt.

I opened my mouth to ask again about Mom, but Brodsky held out his hand. "There is the matter of the house. Would you like to close it up until you decide what to do?"

Brodsky balked at it, but here is what I decreed: the Charlottesville mansion and its grounds and contents (except the reference books, globes, and two paintings whose subjects now wink at each other from inside my bedroom) would be given outright to

Aunt Cookie. Though Grandfather Postscript would have loved the irony, I delighted in imagining Grandma spinning on her fiery spit at the idea of the *colored* help now wearing her diamonds, driving her cars, and, worse, drinking her vodka. I could imagine Chompers and Bowler and Taffy and Skiff seething as they thought, *There goes the neighborhood!* But they would have said that if I had moved in too.

I also finally found out Grandma's unlisted phone number, and I called Cookie immediately from the phone beside me. Cookie and I blubbered at our forced separation, our shared gene pool, our astounding good fortunes. When she finally understood that the mansion was hers, she started singing as if she really believed it: "'There *is* a balm in Gilead!'"

Since then Cookie has turned Grandma's estate into Charlottesville's hottest discotel, part disco, part posh hotel that caters to the hip black set. Cookie had a lit-up dance floor installed in the Hall of Mirrors and replaced Fanny Brice's chandelier with a disco ball. It had tickled me to think of Aunt Cookie ordering Opal around (*Opal, bring me more tea!*), but in a tremendous act of grace, Cookie had made Opal the official mink-coated hostess. Muddy is now head of a maintenance staff of twenty. Cedrick packed up his silk scarves and sped the hell away in a Mercedes convertible painted aquamarine with pink interior.

But on that December night in the whippet room, the last thing I blubbered into the phone was "Cookie, where is my mother?"

"I don't know, sugar. I never, ever knew."

Emboldened by the power of two fat bank accounts, I hung up the receiver, stood, and leaned over Brodsky, hands on my hips. "Where the hell is my mother!"

Brodsky fiddled with his necktie. "Vermont. Your mother has been in a sanitarium in Vermont."

I nearly collapsed. All those years I had been in New Hampshire, my mother had been less than ninety miles away. Grandma Iris was a cruel woman.

Brodsky pulled out two forms. I was to sign the one in his left hand if I wanted to commit Mom permanently to the facility, the one in his right if I wanted her released into my care.

Thus, that year on Christmas Eve, delivered unto me was not a babe swaddled in a manger, but my mother swaddled in the back of an ambulance that had to honk to clear the pilgrims away from my gate.

As we hovered by the front door waiting, Nonna and I struggled with conflicting emotions. We were elated that Mother was returning, but Nonna grieved anew over the loss of her treasured son and grandson, her ire resurrecting as if she still blamed Mom. I ached for the mother I hadn't seen in ten years who had brought me joy, but also great pain.

The ambulance arrived, and Dr. Trogdon and an attendant hauled my mother out of the back on a gurney. My still-dozing mother looked like a skeleton beneath the sheet. Her ponytail now measured three feet and rested outside the covers.

Aunt Betty sobbed. "What did they do to you? What did they do to you?"

Even Nonna softened at the sight.

I practically crawled onto the gurney, bawling like a five-year-old, hoping Mother's eyes would pop open, that she would sit up, wrap her bony arms around me, and lavish me with maternal love.

But Mom remained inert.

We rolled her into the library by the window that faced Nonna's garden. Dr. Trogdon opened his medical bag and began unpacking amber bottles, placing them on the table beside Mom's bed.

"What are you doing?" I said.

"Setting out her prescriptions. I've also taken the liberty of contacting a physician in—" He looked at the attendant. "What's the name of that town?"

"Vandalia."

"Yes, Vandalia, where their pharmacies are much more, how shall I say it, relaxed."

Dr. Trogdon reached into his bag for a syringe filled with the brown liquid I remembered from the Night of the Cracked Mirrors. He pulled Mom's limp arm from beneath the covers and revealed what looked like a junkie's track marks.

"Until then." Dr. Trogdon held the needle to Mother's translucent flesh.

"Stop!" I grabbed the syringe. "No more injections!"

"But your grandmother decreed—"

"To hell with my grandmother." I swept my arm across the chess set of vials. "No more pills!"

"You can't just stop these medications cold turkey. The consequences could be dire."

I pointed at my virtually dead mother. "Are you out of your fucking mind?"

I angled myself between the doctor and Mom. Nonna and Betty stomped over to stand with me, and we puffed out our torsos, a regular fortress of mammaries. "I want you out of my house!"

Dr. Trogdon opened his mouth, but Nonna growled. The quack snapped his bag shut. "It matters not to me."

Once the doctor was gone, Nonna fetched her valise of counter-*malocchio* measures. She spread them around the library: amulets and rue branches, crucifixes and red afghans, even a certain four-tooth chisel. We sat by Mom's bedside for the next seventy-two hours monitoring her pulse, watching her chest rise and fall, Nonna muttering her prayers.

Mom did not convulse or froth at the mouth. Neither did she wake up.

Week after week we kept vigil, giving her sponge baths, combing her hair, though I hired a nurse to tackle Mom's private functions. Nonna continued praying aloud, mostly as she strolled her garden and grapevine or soaked her feet in the reflection pond surrounded by pilgrims. Children cuddled beside her and stroked her hair as she begged God to send a healing wave over us all.

Nonna's God didn't see fit to zap my mother back to life, but more and more pilgrims claimed that I was healing them. Word spread across the country, the continent, because ten-year-old burns were healing, chickenpox scars were unscarring, and ringworm and scabies patches were disappearing, all of which had nothing to do with the sweet water, or me, I assure you. The worst were the parents who brought their perfectly fine children, wanting only smaller pores or fairer complexions. I raised my fist and shouted: "Love your children! If you don't, you will rue the day!"

Nine months later I lay beside Mom on her hospital bed gazing out the open window at Nonna in the distance harvesting the last of the butternut squash. She looked so content with her gnarled hands covered in dirt. Occasionally one of the pilgrims would shout, "God bless you, Nonna Ferrari!" Nonna would smile and blow a kiss. It was quite lovely and I wanted to share it with Mom. I wanted to see the aquamarine spark in her eyes. I wanted to hear her laughter, or even her voice raised in anger or blame. I wanted, I wanted, I wanted. I began crying anew at my guilt, at my *portafortuna*-stealing hands that had robbed my mother of her husband and son, and at the improbability of my vast fortunes that could do nothing to alleviate her pain, or mine. "Why won't you wake up? I know it's my fault. It's all my fault. But why don't you please-please-please wake up?"

I heard sniffling and found Nonna standing outside the window resting her chin on a hoe, tears welling.

Later that night, there was a full moon, and I padded through the house in my bare feet looking at moon shadows trembling on the parquet floors.

A familiar droning of bees drew me out onto the patio, where I tilted my ear at the noise that was coming from beyond the springhouse. I was drawn to it and walked there, the cold wetness of the grass on my exposed soles. Soon I recognized the drone as the rosary, someone gently chanting, "Our Father, Who art in-a heaven," followed by the congregants, "Hail Mary, full of grace."

Just inside the fence, I hid behind a clump of pampas grass at the edge of the pond's concrete deck and spotted Nonna, her back to me, sitting on the lip of the reflection pond, mist rising up as warm vapors met chilled air. She was surrounded by pilgrims, though they did not crowd her. Some were kneeling in the pond, all with their heads bent, eyes closed. Mother was draped across Nonna's lap, her head cradled in Nonna's arms. As she prayed, Nonna dipped her hand down into the water time after time and poured the warm liquid over Mom's head, her drenched ponytail hanging in the pond and fanning out like gold kelp. Some of the water spilled onto the concrete deck, slid beneath the fence and through the pampas grass, and enveloped my feet.

When the rosary was finished Nonna traced her fingers over mother's lovely jaw and offered one final prayer. "I was the one who bring this curse on-a you, not Garney, so now I must-a remove it. God, please restore this mother to her daughter. Bring her back-a to life."

"Bring her back-a to life," prayed the pilgrims.

"So amen," said Nonna.

"So amen," sighed the crowd.

Suddenly the puddle I was standing in felt charged with electricity; a surge shot up my leg, torso, and neck and into my hair, which flared into a staticky cone. Nonna's bun wiggled until it sprang free, the end of it levitating like a magic trick. I jumped back onto dry ground, severing the current that connected Nonna and me, and raced to my room wondering if La Strega had somehow enchanted this land before she died.

The following morning, Nonna, Betty, and I were eating waffles in the upstairs kitchen. Betty was hogging the syrup, and I was about to wrestle it from her when Mom walked in in her nightgown, hair disheveled, and asked, "Is there any more coffee?"

I don't remember tipping out of my chair, but the next thing I knew I had my arms wrapped around her, dampening her nightgown with my tears. Nonna and Betty surrounded us, our twined arms hugging, prayers of thanksgiving squeaking out from Nonna and Betty until Mom asked, "Where the hell are we?"

Let me state for the record: It was Nonna's prayer that woke my mother up, not mine.

I won't delve too deeply into Mom's rehabilitation, into how we covered all the mirrors, hid all the pens and paper scraps, and judiciously doled out the news of where we were, of why we were living atop Dagowop Hill, of our vast fortunes, of her dead mother, of her half sister Cookie, of skull-cracked Grandpa Ferrari, of the resurrected Saint Garnet nonsense. I assured Mom time and again that all those probing eyes were not scrutinizing her. Aunt Betty carefully orchestrated their reunification, tempering it with the news that Ray-Ray was completely out of our lives, which meant we had to explain Vietnam. Though the TV was still abuzz with the news of Ford's stunning pardon of Nixon—so we had to explain Watergate—Mom could not pardon Ray-Ray, and neither could I.

Mom's physical strength improved daily, as did her mental stamina, so many hours in the library or reading the paper to see what political, cultural, and sexual revolutions she had missed, Gloria Steinem her new hero. I wondered what Dad would have thought about his wife's feminist leanings. Though Mom and I cried often about Nicky, she never brought up my father, and I was too afraid to bring it up myself lest she slip away from me again. Nor did we bring up the Night of the Cracked Mirrors.

One afternoon as I played torch songs in the conservatory I felt someone watching and found Mom at the door, but she swiftly walked away. Later that night when I passed Nonna's den, I heard whispers inside. I peeked in at Mom sitting on one arm of Nonna's Barcalounger, hands looped with red yarn, which Nonna was twining into a ball.

"How long has she been playing the saw?" Mom asked.

Nonna shook her head. "Since I move-a here."

"Why does she do it?"

"I no know for sure, but I think she miss-a her dad."

I watched Mom's eyes to see if they sought out a shiny something to dive into, but they did not.

The following Sunday, on the morning in July when Saint Brigid's was dedicating the new stained-glass windows, Mom and I lay head-to-head on the pews in the chapel eating Popsicles. It looked as if Gethsemane Jesus could have used one too. We were admiring the light patterns speckling the ceiling when a sudden swell of adoration roared up from the pilgrims. "We love you, Saint Garnet! Thank you for healing us!"

Mom had been apprised of my sainted status, of my belief that it was all so much bunk and that the real healing came from the water, or maybe from Nonna, but Mom had not divulged her opinion.

Maybe it was because we were in that holy place, but after the spontaneous praise, Mom said, "They certainly adore you."

I snorted.

"They do!" The top of her head bobbled against mine as she spoke. "And with good reason."

"Are you kidding?" I wondered if Rodney, Ms. Stork, or Father Shultz had gotten to her.

"I'm not. You give them something to hope for."

I guffawed but immediately regretted it, since I think Mom needed something to hope for too. Still, I couldn't help myself. "You don't really believe I can heal people."

I imagine she was rolling back two decades to the time when she not only abided my pillowcase veil, but defended it.

"I don't know, Garnet. I see how the pilgrims look at you. Their devotion is so pure. I suppose I believe in their belief."

"What?" This was not the first time I had heard that cryptic sentiment from someone.

"Garnet, it may be too late for me, but it's not too late for you to believe in — well, something."

I was stunned even more by what came next. "That's one thing I admired about your father, his faith."

Though I wanted to sit up and look at her, I resisted.

"I did love him," Mom said. "I know that wasn't always apparent."

I swear I heard the sound of sawing wood. I swallowed hard. "What did you love about him most?"

Mom sighed, as if in her mind she was unpacking the fifteen years they had lived together.

"His decency," she finally and graciously said, considering the infidelity of Annette Funicello. Over the years I had gathered enough clues to understand that they had, as Grandpa Ferrari would have said, consummated this. I'm sure Mom knew it too, but still she added, "He was the most decent man I ever knew."

Without any bidding, Mom related the story of how they'd met, that initial icy patch, their lopsided walk, his arm wrapped around her waist as he mumbled, "I've got you."

Then the stunning revelation that the date she most treasured was when he took her to Easter Mass: Latin, incense, and hallelujahs swirling around the rafters. I pictured the hundreds of times I'd watched Dad kneeling in Saint Brigid's, head bent over the pew in front of him, rosary laced through his fingers. His mouth moved as he silently chanted responsive prayer after prayer to God, millions of words all told. I was suddenly angry at my father, who spoke so few words to me. Maybe a thousand in all the years we'd overlapped on the planet, and only once did he offer those three words. Of course, I'd never said them either.

Mother confessed that she'd watched him during that Easter Mass too. She admired his faith, which she'd never had. Such an odd curiosity, which made his willingness to elope all the more stunning. He loved her that much.

"I always regretted that," Mom said.

"What?" I tried to act like a grown-up confidante and not a daughter sniveling over her lost daddy.

"Not getting married in the Catholic Church. It would have meant so much to him. And Nonna. I was a selfish girl."

"You sacrificed a lot too." I pictured the hundreds of times I'd seen Mom scrubbing the toilet, flushing her coddled Charlottesville life—and what that might have meant for all of us—into the sewer.

"I do wish he'd shown you more affection, Garnet."

I wasn't sure whether to laugh or cry. "When did he ever show me any?"

"I know, I know," Mom said, "but he did love you. That's one reason he bought you that bracelet."

I sat up and looked down at Mom, her eyes closed as she tapped a Popsicle stick against her temple.

"What bracelet?"

Mom's eyes popped open and she assessed my alarm. She also sat and pushed my hair out of my eyes. "You know, the charm bracelet you wanted from Flannigan's."

Sudden pressure behind my sternum as the heart-shaped box began shuddering. My throat tightened, but I sputtered, "He bought me the bracelet?"

"Well, yes, honey, don't you remember? With the locket on it. He gave it to you on—" Mom's hand flew to her mouth. "Oh God. He never had the chance."

I shook my head no. Mom wrapped her arms tightly around me as I cried for what that bracelet might have meant. A new charm for every birthday and Christmas, which he would pick out, or maybe we would pick them out together: a rue branch, an ankh, a globe.

When the sniffling subsided I wondered where that bracelet was now, if it was tucked under the insulation in the cracker-box attic or if Mrs. Walczak had found it and was now wearing my father's proclamation to me. At least I like to think he had had my heart's desire engraved there. Then I longed to hold the bracelet in my hand as concrete proof, since I wasn't sure how much I could trust Mom's drug-addled memory.

I was also working up the nerve to confess my own three-word omission, but Mom whispered the thing we had both been ignoring since she woke up.

"That night at Grandma's party, when I dragged you upstairs and—"

A boa constrictor squeezed my throat.

She tipped her forehead against mine. "I am so sorry."

All I could do was nod, but even in that small gesture, I felt something release inside of me, genuine forgiveness, an act of grace I didn't think I was capable of.

After several minutes we started to leave, but as we neared the chapel door Mom stopped me, as if we were in a confessional and now was her chance.

"You know what else I regret?"

I didn't open my mouth in case it had to do with bearing too many children.

"Not finishing college."

This was such a non sequitur I laughed in case she was kidding.

She wasn't.

"Really?"

She nodded.

I could have said something like *But you're here now with me and we'll be together forever!* Instead I said, "You could always go back."

Mom glanced at Jesus kneeling in the garden, and then she looked at me. "I couldn't," she said, but her eyes pleaded, *Could I?*

I wondered if she heard my thumping pulse. "You want to go back to Wellesley?"

By the speed of her answer I knew she'd been considering this awhile. "Yes. Well, no. I want to enroll at Smith."

Gloria Steinem's alma mater. I should have known.

I stood there, agog. The woman who'd slept through forty percent of my life was going to abandon me again. I suddenly had a craving for a vodka martini. "You know Vandalia University is less than an hour away. You could still live with me and commute." As soon as the words dripped from my tongue, I heard Grandma Iris adding: *We have plenty of excellent schools for Garnet too.*

Mother's eyes closed and I knew she was also hearing Grandma's voice.

"No. You should go to Smith," I said. "It's not that far away and you deserve this."

Mom looked at me to see if I meant it.

"You do. You really do."

Mom hugged me tighter than she ever had, which was a good thing, because a month later, just this past August, she drove off in a brand-new Volkswagen Beetle to begin her life as a forty-five-year-old coed.

Don't feel bad, Archie. She calls every night, her head swimming with philosophy and contemporary literature. In fact, to celebrate the completion of her first semester, at this moment she is enjoying a European adventure, which includes trips to not only the Sorbonne and Oxford, but the town of Tredegar in South Wales, Grandfather Postscript's birthplace. She's not alone on her quest to flesh out that side of her fam-i-ly tree. She's accompanied by Cookie, her sister, my aunt, a woman who was devoted to me even before she fully knew why.

La Vigilia

Buon Natale, Padre:

It's Christmas Eve and we're all waiting for something, keeping La Vigilia until midnight, less than an hour away, when the Christ Child will slip from His mother's womb for the 1976th time. I'm shivering on the widow's walk, not easy to get to (especially while one is tipsy, which I am, I confess, a state heightened by the insomnia I'm still suffering). I'm also out of breath from climbing into the attic and up a spiral staircase, then wedging through a hatch beneath the cupola. Still, it's beautiful up here. Worth the cobwebs and dust and bird shit on my hands (this has always been a favorite perch for the chimney swifts too).

The night sky is splattered with a million stars. The hill and village below are swaddled in snow; Christmas lights illuminate houses all the way to Grover Estates and beyond, to the Ohio River, where a barge draped in red and green lights is chugging downstream. The water behind it roils as if forty-nine Nereids are in search of a lost sibling who has been pining for too long. Someone has strung Madonna-blue lights around Nonna's statue so it looks as if she's spitting cerulean water. If only she would wave so her nymph sisters might spot her.

(Wave, Nereid, wave!)

Shit. Almost dropped the binoculars.

Father Shultz just trudged from the rectory to the church to prepare for Midnight Mass, the stained-glass windows looking glorious with the light pouring through, making psychedelic patterns on the snowdrifts outside—patterns that seem more swirly than usual, given my inebriation. The church has been packed daily, the many pilgrims plunking their coins into boxes, one under the sign that reads *The font where Saint Garnet was baptized!* and another one under the sign saying *The pew where Saint Garnet prayed!*

Betty is already down there fashioning two hundred poinsettias into a giant tree on the chancel. I'm sure Father has asked if I'll be in attendance. I will not. I did, however, give Betty a fat check to toss into the collection plate so Father will stop hounding me about new school desks to accommodate the swelling student population.

Betty is also there because she has been keeping her own *vigilia* concerning a certain lounge-owning widower—baseball-bat-wielding Dino—who has been making incremental advances for the past two months. First sitting three rows behind her during Mass, then two, then at the end of her pew, then moving five inches closer by the week until just last Sunday, he knelt so close their shoulders grazed. Betty hopes that tonight when they offer the sign of peace he'll keep hold of her hand. That's my wish for her too, since she deserves one decent man in her life.

I'm on the widow's walk for two reasons, Padre. The first is that Christmas Eve is the one night when most of the pilgrims go home to their families. This year there are two dozen or so stragglers, folks who have no family or no home. They are the lowest of the low, the Lowlies, Nonna calls them, an unwashed, raggedy lot who camp in shadows down by the Plant. They are also cursed with such severe lesions that other pilgrims shun them. I just found out about them last week. The news broke my heart and only added to my sleep deprivation. The Lowlies' plight breaks Nonna's heart too, which is why she's skipping Midnight Mass. It's also why she called Sister Dee Dee half an hour ago and asked her to round the Lowlies up and bring them to the hilltop so Nonna can feed them our leftovers. My aim is to get them a shot at the healing pond water.

Tonight we celebrated the Festa dei Sette Pesci, Feast of the Seven Fishes, an Italian tradition on this particular day. Grandpa never let Nonna prepare it before, probably because he was a carnivore who refused to give up bloody clumps of meat for anyone, not even his Savior.

But this year Nonna decided to inaugurate the tradition, and she cooked all week. So much baking, nut-cracking, fruit-peeling, pasta-cutting. I tried to help, but I annoyed her with questions about why seven dishes. She had a different answer every time:

They stand for the seven-a sacraments.

The seven days of-a creation.

The seven hills of-a Rome.

The seven deadly-a sins.

The number seven, she means-a perfetto.

Seven gifts of-a the Holy Spirit.

The seven utterances of Jesus on-a the cross.

If you ask me one-a more time I'm-a gonna clock you for sure!

The meal was spectacular, made even more so by the fact that we had to wait until eight thirty to eat. Nonna had nestled a Pergusa blossom into her pink ringlets, and the roasted-almond-and-nutmeg scent of it lingered as she led us to the antipasto in the parlor, where she uncorked wine number one. Then we migrated to the ballroom, that virtual glasshouse, where the moon bathed us in cool light. Nonna had set the most beautiful table, the one that seats thirty, and she had thirty place settings, though there were only us three. La Strega's best-best china and crystal and silver gleamed. At the center of the table sat a gigantic bowl of pasta *aglio e olio*, a simple pasta to mix and match with any of the surrounding seven platters of calamari, steamed mussels, scungilli, clams, shrimp, *baccalà*, snapper.

Nonna stressed the importance of sampling all seven, no gulping tonight, since endurance was key. She also had a different wine to go with each dish, which is why I'm blotto, but I couldn't insult our hostess. When we could eat no more she served brandy and sambuca in the library before the fireplace, she and I humming with content, until we had enough room for dessert: strong espresso with *panettone* and *struffoli*, over which I made a discovery: espresso has an amazing ability to clarify one's buzz without killing it.

Afterward we snuggled around our candlelit Christmas tree in the conservatory while Bing Crosby crooned carols from the Victrola. We swapped well-chosen gifts, though the real paper-tearing will be tomorrow. I gave Nonna season tickets to the Vandalia Bruisers, a girls' roller-derby team she cannot get enough of. To Betty I gave front-row tickets to see Elvis. I only hope Dino is a fan.

Betty gave me an antique snow globe from Sicily with Mount Etna inside. When you shake it, orange glitter pours out of the volcano and swirls a firestorm around the watery sky. She also gave me an herbal remedy that supposedly cures insomnia. I probably shouldn't have taken three — okay, five — since now everything that moves leaves the faintest tracer.

Nonna gifted me a basket of imports from her hometown: chestnuts, cork bark, and goat cheese. When she handed it over she pressed her warm hand on my forehead and uttered: *May God grant-a to you your heart's desire.*

How I wish someone could. I'm no longer yearning for my mother, but I am longing for something.

Yesterday, because I couldn't keep the secret bulging in my mouth, I presented Nonna her heart's desire: Angelo, the original, now eighty-six, my maybe-maybe-not grandpa. It took a year to track him down in Sicily, where he had acquired, not a wife, but a vineyard named Profezia di Diamante. Tonight Nonna is keeping La Vigilia not only for Jesus but for Angelo, who will arrive tomorrow by train, the second reason I'm on the widow's walk. I want to clean it up, since I know she'll be here in the morning scanning the horizon for her lost love. I have a feeling I should also ready the bridal chamber, though perhaps I'm being overly optimistic.

A jet is flying overhead and I bet a hundred Sweetwater children are pressing their faces to their bedroom windows because they are certain that's Santa whooshing across the sky.

The plane is heading northeast toward New England and any number of boarding schools where discarded children are crying themselves to sleep. But not me. Even farther east, across the iceberg-strewn Atlantic, Cookie and Mom are having a fabulous time. They called earlier, both drunk on Welsh beer, giggling over their supper of cockles and faggots. They sounded like schoolgirls instead of middle-aged sisters, which was a Christmas gift in and of itself.

After I hung up I went to my room to open the present I received today from Yvette: a pair of Chinese slippers. Seems she made it to the Far East, but this time her traveling companion is her mother.

Here come the Lowlies, Padre, led by Dee Dee, carrying candles as they trek up the last turn of the hill. Underweight mothers with children, old-old men and bent women relying on canes. I should have sent a fleet of cars. Dee Dee is leading them to the reflection pond. Earlier today, Nonna and Betty positioned half a dozen metal drums loaded with firewood around the deck. A few minutes ago Nonna marched from drum to drum squirting in lighter fluid and dropping in lit matches, flames erupting, heat pulsing so intensely I can feel it up here. Nonna has also scattered luminary candles around the rim of the pond, and it's unbelievably charming. The Nereid below the surface shimmers. It looks as if she's pulling water into her gills, her giant fishtail quivering as if she might push off at any moment.

Dee Dee is instructing the Lowlies to remove their shoes and socks or stockings, roll up their pant legs or lift the hems of their tattered dresses, and dip their feet into the warm water. She's handing out washcloths and bars of soap so they can slough off the grit behind their ears, around their necks, under their nails. I should yell down and tell them to soak for a while, let the healing water do its job, but I don't want to call attention to myself. The old women are at one end of the pool, the old men at the other, all of them flagrantly peeling down to nothing, easing their liver-spotted flesh into the liquid. Dee Dee doesn't seem perturbed by the skinny-dipping. In fact she's laughing, and so is everyone else, mothers stripping their children bare, lathering soapsuds to rub over filthy arms and legs, dipping their heads in the pool, scrub-bing their scalps, all of them giggling at the clean-clean feeling they likely haven't felt in months.

Here comes Nonna through the gate with a wheelbarrow full of red towels for the mothers to wrap their children in, for the old men and women to dry themselves with as they huddle around the barrels. Nonna is taking Dee Dee by the hand into the spring-house and now here they come pushing more wheelbarrows filled with a mishmash of La Strega's old clothes: dresses and shoes, underwear and minks, and an assortment of hats, which the old women are tittering over. Dee Dee's barrow contains arm-fuls from Le Baron's closet, and the men are sifting through the finery, modeling the vests and spats and ascots. These clothes have never been put to better use.

Nonna is making yet another trip to the springhouse and now she's hauling out shopping bags full of new clothes for the chil-dren. Mothers are sobbing as they rifle through coats and boots. "Take-a more," Nonna is saying. "She need-a more undies. Take-a the six-pack. No! Take it-a for sure!"

Listen! Can you hear the Saint Brigid choir warming up? Organ pipes luring in the congregants who are funneling into church. I keep waiting for Nonna to roll out teacarts filled with food, and she's heading to the back gate that's been meager protection be-tween me and the pilgrims, whose devotion might lead them to gouge out my eyes. But Nonna is opening the gate and motioning for Dee Dee and the Lowlies to come through.

(No, Nonna! No!)

Oh crap. Now they're all looking up here.

(It's her!)

(It's Saint Garnet!)

(Saint Garnet! Come down and heal us, we beg you!)

Thankfully, Nonna is drawing their attention away from me, but I can't believe she's leading them past the springhouse, her garden, the grape arbor, and through the French doors into the ballroom and that thirty-seat table. So the Lowlies have been the primary guests all along.

They're behaving themselves quite well, Padre. Not slipping the silverware into their coats, their posture immediately improving as they sit and drape napkins across their laps. Dee Dee and Nonna are wheeling food out and centering dishes on the table. Again I am amazed that the Lowlies aren't diving right in, since they all look as if they could use a good meal, or seven. But they are waiting for Nonna to sit at one end of the table, Dee Dee at the other, and now they're holding hands, a linked chain as they bow their heads. Nonna's mouth is moving as she prays and I can read her lips to make out the last words: *Now dig-a in!*

It's off to the races as hands reach for platters and bowls, mothers doling out fish and pasta for the old folks first, then the children, and finally themselves. I imagine La Strega is seething in her tomb, but if bliss has a face, I've seen it on these beggars who for once have a seat at the queen's table.

I could stay here all night, but the church bells are pealing so it must be midnight. Nonna hears the bells too, her head perking up, and now she's standing and slipping quietly out through the French doors. She looks absolutely angelic fingering that flower in her hair, her face tipped to the heavens as "Ave Maria" pours into her ears. She's going back in now. No, wait. She's heading to the springhouse, through the gate to the pond ringed with luminaries and piles of dingy clothes. I hope Nonna isn't planning on collecting them.

No, she's—what is she doing? Padre, Nonna is slipping off her shoes, reaching up her legs to roll down the support hose with the elastic tops. Now she's—what the hell is she—unbuttoning her jersey dress and letting it fall to her feet. And there goes the slip, the bra, the parachute panties. I can't believe I'm watching my roly-poly nonna with her drooping breasts and ripply belly baring it all. But what the hell; it's Christmas and stranger things have happened on this night. She's easing into the heated pond and I wonder how many other nights she's been indulging in an au naturel swim. She's walking to the center of the pond, directly over the Nereid, and lying down over it, her body mimicking the maiden's beneath the surface, Nonna's face the only thing exposed. There it goes beneath the water, once, twice, thrice, in the name of the Father, Son, and Holy Spirit. Each time she comes up she shoots a playful spray of water to imitate her sister statue below. Now she's completely underwater and I'm counting for her: one-thousand-one, one-thousand-two, one-thousand-three . . . one-thousand-eight. She has remarkable lung power, but it's making me nervous, and the red Pergusa just bobbed to the surface. One-thousand-twenty-four. Come on up, Nonna. Nonna?

(Nonna! Come out now!)

One-thousand-thirty-two.

Fuck. She's not coming out. I have to get down there. Goddamn trapdoor and—shit. I just slipped on the stairs. Wait. I have to run. Running. Running. Through the foyer, the hall, the solarium, now out the back. Passing the springhouse, through the gate and I still see Nonna hovering beneath the water though I have to get at her. Forget the shoes. I'm going in.

(There you are! Thank God.)

Nonna just lifted her head from the water.

(You scared the hell out of me! What are you laughing at?)

You should see her, Padre.

(Nonna. Say hello to Padre.)

(Buon Natale, Padre!)

(What are you doing? You're getting me wet!)

She's kicking her legs, flapping her arms, working up a swirling froth of water, more commotion than I thought she could churn up at her age. And there she goes again, sliding beneath the surface, still roiling the water, which bubbles like mad. I wonder if one of the heating elements has gone kablooey.

(Nonna? Are you all right in there? Nonna?)

What the— Oh my God, Archie. I . . . I'm seeing it, but I'm not seeing it. It's . . . what the hell is this? It's not Nonna coming out of the water. It's a giant fishtail flapping up. I swear to God. A silver tail fin splashing the water's surface. It's gone and now there's Nonna sitting up, standing, with her long braid restored and fish scales from the waist down.

(Oh, come on. Nonna! Is this some costume Betty mail-ordered? Is this some trick?)

(It's-a no trick, Garney!)

She's laughing, Padre. Can you hear her?

(I almost-a forget!)

(Forget what? Nonna! Don't go!)

She's diving back in, rooting around the bottom as if she's looking for a dropped coin. Here she comes back up, something in her hand.

(I find it! I find it!)

(Found what, Nonna!)

(Your father wanted me to give this-a to you.)

(What?)

(The charm bracelet from-a you dad!)

Now I know I'm tripping.

(No! Look-a! Look and you see the words carved on-a the back. See? Right here.)

This isn't real.

(It's a-real, Garney. See for yourself. You catch.)

(Shit! You threw it over the fence! Let me just go—)

(I have-a to go now, Garney!)

(Wait, Nonna. I just need to find—)

(I have to go hug-a my son.)

(Wait! Will you give him a message?)

(Sure thing.)

(Would you tell him that . . . he needs to know that . . . I love him too.)

(I will, Garney. You rest-a for sure. I go tell him right now.)

There she goes, diving back in with that giant tail fluke, the liquid swirling in her wake and then . . . nothing. Not a ripple, not a concentric ring, the water calm and smooth, and below the surface, nobody. Just a mosaic sea nymph wearing a beautiful smile and a red Pergusa tucked in her hair.

Archie, my head feels woozy and I'm going to think I've been hallucinating unless I find that bracelet. I'm moving through the fence to the pampas grass where it landed. It's so dark back here. I can't see a thing, and my shoes are wet, and this grass is pricklier than it looks. It's no use. I'll come back in the morning, or maybe I won't, because you know something? I don't need tangible proof anymore. I believe what Nonna said. For the first time in my life, I believe my father loved me, and now he'll know that I loved him too.

(Garnet!)

(Who's that?)

(Garnet! Come in! It's cold out there!)

Oh no, Padre. It's Dee Dee leaning through the French doors. How can I get out of here? Those pilgrims, those crazy—but they don't look crazed right now. In fact, they're standing calmly behind Dee Dee; they don't seem ready to yank out my hair.

(Did you see the Nereid? Did you see Nonna?)

(What?)

(Did you see Nonna?)

(Nonna's in the kitchen!)

(Nonna's not in the kitchen!)

(She is! Garnet, come inside now.)

It does look inviting, that room made of windows, the candlelit table. Against my better judgment, I'm actually considering going in, Father. What have I got to lose? It's Christmas and I'm so tired of hiding. But wait. The Lowlies are coming out to me. There's nowhere to run. But they're smiling so sweetly, especially the children, who are, frankly, beautiful. They're still covered in lesions and boils, but they are exquisite.

(Garney! You have to come in now. It's-a time!)

Father, there's Nonna! She *is* in the house with her dripping pink ringlets and wet jersey dress.

(Saint Garnet. Come inside. Please!)

The children are coming out and I wish you could see them darting up to me like minnows, gently holding my hand, wrapping their arms around my legs, my waist —

(I love you, Saint Garnet.)

(I love you too, sweetie.)

Oh, Father, these children are beautiful, lavishing me with tears and kisses, and they might as well be twenty-four fat-bellied cherubs ladling dippers of love over me.

(Come on in, now. Please come inside with us now. You belong here with us.)

I have to obey. Finally. I just have to, as they pull me inside where it is warm and they are all looking at me so hopefully, so expectantly, as if I might perform a miracle right before their eyes, and you know what? With Nonna beside me, maybe I will.

But first I have to put the recorder down, Father. I have to stop taping. I have to stop all of this now.

Dear Committee:

I'm back at the Vatican after spending three days in Sicily tracking down the origins of the Saint Garnet lore. It was fascinating to visit locales Garnet mentioned in her tapes, including Nonna's hometown of Sughero and the Strait of Messina. I also met three elderly sisters who not only knew Diamante but remember very well the legend of Saint Garnet. However, they shared with me a version that had been buried in the papers of their great-great-great-etcetera-uncle, which I'll type up and include with this correspondence. The version was unearthed after Diamante left Sicily, so it's unlikely she was privy to it.

I apologize for not sending an account of my visit to Sweetwater last month, but I'll do so now. Garnet's estate was quite changed from my initial meeting with her seven months prior. No longer were the pilgrims surrounding her fence, clamoring for just a glimpse of their healer. Now the gates are wide open, and visitors are free to wander about the grounds and even enter the mansion. I spotted Nonna sitting on the edge of the reflection pond, a dozen children snuggled beside her, all of them splashing their bare feet in the water. There was commotion on the widow's walk, and when I got closer I saw a swarm of children leaning over the railing holding kites. In the midst of them was Garnet, her distinctive hair billowing, dangling the biggest kite of all. It wasn't the improbable sight of her kite-flying that most startled me, but the sound of her laughter—it was not the cynical snickering I had grown accustomed to on her tapes but genuine guffaws, which lightened my heart.

Since that visit, the mole on my cheek has shrunk and faded even more than it had the last time we measured, which is something I planned to include in my final report regarding Garnet, but today I received rather alarming news.

The Vatican is closing this investigation for now and

reassigning us to what they feel is a more pressing concern. It involves a recently murdered Romanian girl who claimed to have been visited daily by the Blessed Virgin. The girl was an outcast because of her arms, which were red and scarred from an accident involving a vat of lye. Fortunately the girl kept a diary of her conversations with Our Lady, listing places and dates of future disasters, the last one on June 24, 2025.

We are to begin our task immediately, so next week, if my traveling papers are in order, I shall slip behind the iron curtain, where I'll correspond as I am able.

Kissing the Sacred Purple,
Dolan

THE LEGEND OF THE NEBRODI TWINS

I spent the afternoon of March 21, 1976, in the kitchen of the three Agresta sisters, octogenarians all. As we sipped espresso and ate *cuccidati* they shared with me a version of the fascinating tale of Saint Garnet.

Like the first version of the legend, this story begins with a poor couple from Sughero in the Nebrodi Mountains. However, this pair was blessed with not just one daughter but two, red-haired twins named Garnet and Diamante. The children were devoted to their parents, to each other, and to God. Other than praying, their favorite pastime was trying to mimic the sound they heard issuing from Mount Etna, which they insisted hummed them to sleep every night, though no one else heard it.

Once the girls came of age, they drew the unwelcome attention of the region's marquis. (Here the Agresta sisters admitted that they were descendants of that original Marquis Agresta, a name that means "sour grapes.") Marquis did not intend to marry either of the comely sisters with hair that hung to their knees; he planned to move them to his hilltop estate to "work" in his service. Everyone knew what carnal service he had in store for them. Though Marquis tried countless times to bribe the girls' parents to turn over their daughters, they would not relent, and the girls would not be persuaded.

As the original legend describes, both parents were imprisoned, and Marquis had Garnet tied to a stake atop erupting Mount Etna. This new version, however, critically includes the mention of volcanic lightning, a common phenomenon, apparently, that occurs within the ash plume when negatively and positively charged ash particles collide. The bolts struck around Garnet, making her hair jut up like a tongue of fire. As pumice stones and lava balls pelted her, she prayed ceaselessly to the Blessed Virgin, who sent twenty-four fat-bellied cherubs to ladle cool spring water over her throughout the night. In the morning Garnet pranced down the volcano totally nude and now mapped with the world. No one was healed in her presence, but the townsfolk still exalted her, since surviving the furnace of Etna and being tattooed like a globe were apparently miracles enough.

For Diamante, Marquis chose a different torture. At the same moment her sister was being dragged up Mount Etna, Diamante was yanked by Marquis's minions down to the Strait of Messina. There, they bound her hands and feet with braided rope and tossed her into a gigantic wine vat that had once held Marquis's swill. They left the top end open, and Diamante screamed as the minions heaved the barrel into the water and tied an anchor around it so that it would not budge as the tide crept toward the barrel's lip. Unless Diamante relented, the water would fill up both the barrel and her lungs. Like her sister, Diamante prayed ceaselessly to the Virgin, who sent twenty-four fat-bellied cherubs to ladle seawater out of the barrel as fast as the tide rushed in. Unfortunately, their chubby arms couldn't work quickly enough and soon the barrel filled.

Early in the morning, half the townsfolk ran up the hill to discover the fate of Garnet; the other half raced down to the strait to discover the fate of Diamante. As the tide receded, the still-upright barrel became exposed inch by inch; they rushed into the surf, tipped the vat over, and out spilled seawater as blood-red as Lake Pergusa—but no girl.

The old women wailed until a gaggle of children pointed into the sea at a giant silvery fishtail emerging from the surf. Everyone stared at the receding tail, and then their mouths fell open when in its place Diamante surfaced, first her head, then neck, then shoulders. Her hair was no longer red, but silver, as if bleached by the salt water. In addition, her tresses were now fashioned into a braid, the same length and thickness as the rope that had so recently bound her.

The crowd was mystified since as she neared the shallows she did not stand to walk out but instead used her arms to pull herself toward them, exposing her breasts, then the fish scales that began at her waist and covered her lower half, which was now, most decidedly, a fish's.

"The Pining Nereid," one of the sailors muttered.

The onlookers fell to their knees and gave thanks to the Virgin who had saved Diamante by turning her into a sea nymph. Though there were no miraculous healings, the crowd venerated her anyway because learning to breathe water and becoming half fish were apparently miracles enough.

The jubilation drifted up to the hilltop revelers, who looked down at the other miracle unfolding. Garnet screamed and rushed, still nude, to her sister, gathering speed and spectators as she made her descent. When she reached the shore, Garnet lifted her twin upright and gave her an embrace that shot volts of energy through both their bodies, since water and electricity do not mix. Garnet's hair sprang even higher, and the whip of Diamante's braid curled up like a fiddlehead fern. Even more spectacular, everyone in proximity could feel the power emanating from the sisters, coating them in a supercharged ethereal net. That's when the suddenly healed town harlot began dancing the jig, the broom maker's mole shriveled to the size of a chickpea and fell off, the blacksmith's burn disappeared, and the mangy town mutt lost his mange.

When Marquis came upon the scene, he was, as in the other tale, repulsed by the now-changed girls and was overtaken by all manner of oozing pus. Instead of losing his sight, he lost his mind, but rather than holing up in the Cyclops's cave, he swam out into the Strait of Messina and dove headfirst into whirlpooling Charybdis, which swallowed him whole.

The townsfolk cheered, threw cloaks over the twins, hoisted them onto their shoulders, and carried them up the hill to Marquis's estate. They deposited Diamante in the cypress-lined reflection pond, where she flipped her tail in the water with glee. They deposited Garnet in the highest tower, where she acted as the first-ever lightning rod, happily protecting the area from Etna's volcanic lightning for the rest of her days.

Every sunset, Garnet descended from her tower and sat beside her Nereid sibling at the edge of the pond. People from near and far gathered around them with hopes of healings nestled in their chests, because when the twins held hands, their weird circuitry colluded in such a way that all who were in proximity, including the sisters themselves, received their hearts' desires.

THE NEW YORK TIMES

Mt. Etna and Mt. Saint Garnet Erupt

By MARIE MANILLA

June 25, 2025

SICILY, Italy—In a strange geologic coincidence, volcanoes on two continents simultaneously erupted yesterday. Though Sicilians are blasé about the frequent belches from Mt. Etna, residents of Sweetwater, West Virginia, were abruptly awakened when the once-dormant volcano that had begun smoldering in 1980 came to life on June 24, the seventy-fifth birthday of their most famous resident, Garnet Ferrari. Oddly, when scientists recently measured the spectral density of the Mt. Garnet Hum, a low-frequency sound inaudible to most, they found it to be in the same range as the Mt. Etna Hum recorded decades ago.

The eruption destroyed the 1880s mansion built atop the volcano where Ferrari lived from 1973 until 1980, when heirs of the original owner successfully contested a will that had bequeathed the estate to Ferrari. Most of the structures in the vicinity were also destroyed, including Ferrari's childhood home, the Nicky Ferrari Library, and the bulk of Sweetwater, a once-thriving community largely abandoned at the turn of the twenty-first century.

The local Catholic church sustained heavy damage, although, according to Sr. Desiderata Evangelista, certain items remained unscathed: a statue of St. Brigid of Tuscany and the steeple bells.

Garnet Ferrari rose to international fame in the 1970s when reports of her healing powers drew the Vatican's attention. An investigation ensued, with inconclusive results. At the height of Ferrari's renown, Sweetwater hosted five hundred pilgrims a day; they infused life into the village, which had been in decline since the 1968 closing of its primary industry, a metal-processing plant. Sweetwater was briefly rejuvenated by the influx of pilgrims but deteriorated again after Ferrari was ousted from her hilltop manor, which is also when the long-forgotten volcano, dubbed Mt. Saint Garnet, began smoldering.

Heirs of the original owner soon discovered high amounts of zeolites in the natural spring, which are useful for removing heavy metals from the human body and can be used to treat various cancers, mental illnesses, and skin disorders. The family immediately began bot-

tling the now-famous Acqua Dolce, popular in high-end markets in North America, Europe, and Asia, according to retired CEO Abigail Stork.

It is rumored that Ferrari, now a recluse, relocated to a villa in Sicily's Nebrodi Mountains with other relatives, but locals here will neither confirm nor deny this. However, a Ferrari crypt in the local cemetery holds the interred remains of Dia-mante Lapelle Ferrari, Ferrari's grandmother. Artifacts resting on the tomb include a Whitman's Sampler box, a bottle of Marsala wine, and pictures of Pope Pius XII and Diamante's second husband, Angelo Ferrari. Also present is a statue of Mary of Lourdes in a grotto; the figure sports a white braid of human hair that, according to the grounds-keeper, grows 1/32 to 1/16 of an inch per year.

Acknowledgments

With deep gratitude I offer the following:

A boxcar of biscotti to Kate Garrick, my agent, who believed in *The Patron Saint of Ugly* when I was still quivering in my boots over the audacity of it all.

A case of Marsala to my editor, Lauren Wein, whose unerring eye helped me rein in the beast whenever it threatened to run wild.

A set of Pliny's *Naturalis Historia* to my copyeditor, Tracy Roe, knower of all things. I'll also offer one Hail Mary as penance for each dangling participle.

A chunk of the Sistine Chapel ceiling for Ellen Weinstein, who illustrated the book's spectacular cover.

A round of limoncello for the Houghton Mifflin Harcourt team who polished *Patron Saint* to a high gloss and launched her into the world.

Italian cream cake and sambuca for my writer pals who endured those early drafts: Zoë Ferraris, Paul Martin, Mary Sansom, Laura Treacy Bentley, and John Van Kirk.

A row of votive candles for Pier Paolo Claudio, who helped with the Italian translations.

Rosaries and novenas of thanksgiving to my holy trinity of cheerleaders: my mother, Elaine Manilla; my sister, Chris Palmer; and my husband, Don Primerano.

Mille grazie!